Kellie McCourt has worked as a national and international television anchor, scriptwriter, producer and reporter. Kellie is also an experienced print journalist and magazine editor.

She has a double BA in Journalism and Creative Writing from Curtin University, studied journalism in SE Asia and completed a postgrad scholarship program at UNSW. Alas, her mother is still waiting for her to 'get a real job', like a lawyer. Or an accountant.

Kellie had a misspent youth as a wayward socialite, and loves shoes, friends, reading, shoes and baked goods.

Kellie is passionate about creating entertaining, gender empowering stories. She lives in Sydney with her two incredible children and two scruffy toy poodles.

Also by Kellie McCourt

Heiress on Fire

MURDER MOST FANCY

KELLIE McCOURT

FICTION

First Published 2022
First Australian Paperback Edition 2022
ISBN 9781867204305

MURDER MOST FANCY
© 2022 by Kellie McCourt
Australian Copyright 2022
New Zealand Copyright 2022

Published by
HQ Fiction
An imprint of Harlequin Enterprises (Australia) Pty Limited (ABN 47 001 180 918), a subsidiary of HarperCollins Publishers Australia Pty Limited (ABN 36 009 913 517)
Level 13, 201 Elizabeth St
SYDNEY NSW 2000
AUSTRALIA

® and TM (apart from those relating to FSC®) are trademarks of Harlequin Enterprises (Australia) Pty Limited or its corporate affiliates. Trademarks indicated with ® are registered in Australia, New Zealand and in other countries.

A catalogue record for this book is available from the National Library of Australia
www.librariesaustralia.nla.gov.au

Printed and bound in Australia by McPherson's Printing Group

MIX
Paper from
responsible sources
FSC
www.fsc.org   FSC® C001695

To my girlfriends, I dedicate this book to you. Your support is so appreciated.
I hope that writing funny, twisty, diverse murder mysteries without commodifying sexual violence against women or children makes your lives safer and more secure, as well as the lives of your children, and their children.

CHAPTER 1

THE GARDEN MISER

I was sitting quietly in the morning sun, sipping freshly squeezed juice, having popped around the corner from Mother's Barbie Life in the Dream House Vaucluse mansion to Grandmother's Downton Abbey Vaucluse mansion to borrow a cup of sugar and to admire her spring bulbs.

'I CANNOT BELIEVE YOU EXPECT US TO PAY THAT KIND OF MONEY FOR *THIS!*'

Well, I might have known Grandmother was away in London this week. And by sugar, I mean a tiny Vermeer oil painting. And a minuscule Monet. Both simply *borrowed*, you understand.

I might not actually have been in direct sunlight per se; rather, I was laid out inside Grandmother's enormous glass orchid palace, with hundreds of handcrafted hanging baskets lined with dazzling green sphagnum moss suspended from the transparent ceiling by copper rods, brimming with white Cattleya orchids. The vast polished concrete floor thick with giant ceramic pots of vibrant blue Vandas, pink Cymbidiums and purple-blooming Phalaenopsis. Impossible to pronounce, but very pretty to look at.

And by juice, I mean a caipiroska. Which *is* full of lime juice.

'IT CANNOT POSSIBLY TAKE A TEAM OF YOU THREE MONTHS TO GROW A FEW BULBS!'

Spring in Sydney is usually a happy time. Bulbs planted in the winter work their way up through the rich dirt, blooming into a rainbow of tulips, fragrant oriental lilies and bright daffodils. The more spectacular the spring garden, the more adulation the proud estate owner receives, and the larger the garden staff's Christmas bonuses. The Gorgeous Garden Game is a kind of win-win spring sport that doesn't involve horses, shooting or a roulette table.

'AM I SUPPOSED TO BE IMPRESSED BY THESE PALTRY TULIPS, CLAIRE?'

The obnoxious voice belonged to Bettina Holly, a classic Garden Miser. The Garden Miser is a child or grandchild who thinks all estate expenses, from garden staff wages to life-support bills, should be cut to the bone or, better yet, switched off and the resulting surplus diverted directly into their trust fund.

Having Christian and surnames hyphenated four times (my name is Indigo-Daisy-Violet-Amber Royce-Hasluck-Jones-Bombberg) means I have multiple trust funds. I don't want any additional funds diverted into any of them. This doesn't mean I want less—I have a certain lifestyle to maintain. My point is I am in no rush to turn off anyone's hoses.

I didn't usually give much thought to the Gorgeous Garden Game. After all, my primary residence was the three-storey penthouse of a recently exploded Double Bay apartment building. Not much ongoing gardening there. However, the louder Bettina the Garden Miser shrieked, the more I felt the borrowed paintings, wrapped carefully in silk scarves and sitting safely in the bottom of my black leather Bottega Veneta Cabat, glow with not-quite-yet-bequeathed, could-possibly-technically-be-considered larceny.

In my defence, Grandmother has so many and I needed the art to freshen up Mother's pool house, where I was residing until the insurance company and the local council deigned to cooperate long enough to rebuild said three exploded storeys. While it's true that my living arrangements had changed because my penthouse had been set on fire by me, it was a *complete accident*. I was not responsible for the exploding part either. Okay, maybe I was *technically* responsible for some of the little explosions, but not the giant fatal ones.

'YOU THINK *THIS* IS A GOOD RESULT?'

I may have also set my husband, Dr Richard Bombberg MBBS FRACS, a shortish, endearingly plump, thinning blond-haired, uber-conservative, ultra-reliable, reconstructive plastic surgeon and a very loyal sex worker named Crystal Devine, on fire. Another terrible accident. I should clarify that their deaths were *not* my doing, even though I had been the prime suspect.

A video of me escaping said fire while *on* fire was watched by two billion people. A torrent of Heiress on Fire tabloid and social media gossip followed. Overnight I went from mysterious, elusive billionairess to black widow, social circus freak. Mortifying.

According to the best PR women in New York, London, Singapore and Sydney, a scandal of this magnitude would take two to three years to fade from the minds of polite society. And that's assuming Extremely Good Behaviour and Zero Publicity on my part. On the upside, being a disgraced billionaire social pariah has saved me from having to attend dozens of dull parties, at least six weddings and innumerable fundraisers for charities no one has ever heard of.

As tempting as it was to hide out on a host of incredible tropical islands forever (I'd spent many, many months island hopping, so believe me, two to three years on *any* island *is forever*), I realised I needed to come home to Australia. I was not exactly sure what I was coming back to *do*, but whatever it was, I was going to do it extremely quietly.

'IF GRANDFATHER WERE ALIVE, HE WOULD NEVER HAVE ALLOWED SUCH WASTE!'

Bettina is the granddaughter of Grandmother's neighbour and, despite all odds, best friend (not that Grandmother would admit to having a best friend), Dame Elizabeth Holly. Bettina is a petite, mousey brunette who has fewer muscles than a banana and, if my childhood memory served—I attended St Ignatius Ladies College (SILC) with Bettina and her sister Gilly—ate nothing from the fun food groups.

Unlike Bettina, Gilly or Grandmother, Dame Elizabeth is a lovely woman: kind, generous and gentle. She donates a shocking amount to the liberal arts and although her granddaughters are neither liberal nor artistic, she donates a shocking amount to them too.

'WELL?! SPEAK, CLAIRE! SPEAK! SAY SOMETHING!'

Through the gaps in the orchid-clad glass wall, I could see Bettina standing at the edge of Dame Elizabeth's garden, shrieking at a shell-shocked, khaki-clad middle-aged woman desperately clutching a couple of gardening tools. That had to be Claire. Poor, unfortunate Claire. Claire who was now desperately looking around for something—perhaps Dame Elizabeth to use as a human shield, or a seed bag with which to suffocate Bettina.

'PRIZE-WINNING?! I DOUBT IT!' Bettina yelled, pointing to a row of metre-high tulips with heads the size of teacups.

Tulips are to Dame Elizabeth's enormous garden what orchids are to Grandmother's glass palace. Her garden is a sea of flowers. If she chose to turn commercial, Dame Elizabeth could give the Netherlands a run for its money in the tulip exportation game.

With immaculate timing, Esmerelda exited Grandmother's scullery and sauntered down the garden path into the orchid palace while snacking on a sandwich inconceivably wide with filling.

'Dude,' she managed between bites, 'that chick next door's pissed about them flowers.'

'Where is my caipiroska?' I asked, inspecting my now-empty glass.

She shrugged. 'I dunno. Who the hell's John Quills?'

Bettina had stopped yelling about tulips and had moved on to the jonquils.

'Jon*quils*,' I explained, joining the flower back into one piece.

'Huh?' she asked, shaking her head, pointing her half-eaten sandwich at me.

'It's a flower. A type of daffodil.'

'I get it.' She nodded, taking another bite. 'Like River.'

It was my turn to deliver a blank look.

'You know, Jonquil, and like, River.'

Working the lanky surfer out was like trying to escape from mental quicksand. The more you resisted, the more trapped you became.

'Rain,' she said loudly between chomps, raising her voice to be heard over Bettina's yelling. 'Summer!'

I tried not to struggle. It was almost always best to breathe deeply, assume the prayer position and wait for the sand to stop moving.

'Phoenix,' she said once she'd finished her sandwich. 'You know, River Phoenix. Jonquil Phoenix. The actor dudes. They've all got them nature names. Rain and Summer Phoenix.'

See?

Esmerelda is a five foot ten Asian–Australian with a rap sheet of *suspected* crimes almost as long as she is. She has impossible cheekbones, naturally flawless skin and long silky shampoo ad hair. Her beach-browned body is too toned for someone who has never seen the inside of a gym and too thin to be fair. Esmerelda is like a Limited Edition crocodile Birkin bag—with the teeth left in.

I am not remotely exotic. I come from all British and western European stock, am at least an inch shorter, bounce between size 10 and 12 (okay, mainly 12), have bright green eyes, skin that is only flawless thanks to high-priced pharmacological adherence, and too-thick long brown hair that requires highlights and daily professional maintenance.

When Esmerelda's luck at dodging convictions finally ran out, she found herself in Silverwater Women's Correctional Centre. Which is where my mother found her, up for parole, and the perfect candidate for Mother's latest pet project—the absurd, but very real *and* state-sanctioned Model Mentor Prison Program.

My mother is Catherine 'The Cat' Jones. Yes, *that* Cat Jones. The flawless, semi-retired, six-foot, super slim, supremely gorgeous blonde supermodel, super mogul, semi-Buddhist woke guru.

If you think that sounds wonderful then *you* stand next to her in a bikini.

While modelling *loved* Esmerelda—she walked for Dior and Gucci in her first few weeks of freedom—*she* did not love *it*. She did not like being touched by strangers. Or being told what to do. Or wearing anything except spray-on jeans and T-shirts. Esmerelda would rather skirt the law than wear an actual skirt. Even if the skirt is Chanel. And the designers at Chanel are willing to pay her to wear it. This was problematic.

Being gainfully (ahem, *legally*) employed was and remains one of Esmerelda's parole conditions. Given her limited legitimate employment history and her dislike of modelling, she ended up with me. Richard's death devastated me, and I had needed someone unconventional to assist me in addressing the many issues that arose from being a mourning widow *and* a double homicide suspect. Esmerelda was uniquely qualified.

Technically speaking, Esmerelda is my personal shopper, although I would die before I let her shop for me. For anything. And that includes basics like bread and water. Her role lands closest to Extremely Unique Personal Assistant (EUPA).

Shockingly, we work well together and were able to find Richard and Crystal's killer. Then again, not finding the killer could have landed us both in jail, so we were highly motivated. Regardless, it was an enormous relief—for a while there, even *I* thought I was guilty.

I always thought Esmerelda would be an improper influence on me, and she is, but to be fair, I may also be a tiny, ever so slightly, not completely law-abiding influence on her. Only when absolutely required though. Such as when one needs a Monet.

After the real murderer was arrested, I went into hiding in the Phi Phi islands, dragging Esmerelda with me. I needed time to grieve, time to think. Some people fake their deaths; Richard, my perfect, nutritious, Bran Muffin husband had, as it turned out, faked his life. Which meant that the life I'd thought I had with him was an illusion.

Esmerelda was walking along the inside edge of the glasshouse, tapping at the polished concrete floor with her sneaker-clad foot.

God, the sneakers. I cannot discuss it.

Bettina continued to berate the poor gardener. She seemed determined, through sheer volume, to trip someone's security alarm or awaken one of the ancient security guards.

'For goodness sake, Bettina!' I shouted through the glass wall. 'Be quiet!'

Bettina's voice paused momentarily, as if she had heard me, then started up again.

'LOOK AT THESE, CLAIRE! THERE ARE CRAWLY BUGS ALL OVER THEM!'

She was not going to stop. Ever. And I had my eye on a sweet little Ming vase that would look fabulous in the pool house kitchen. Its addition to my tote would be difficult if Grandmother's security guard woke up.

I found myself involuntarily up and out of my intensely padded *Titanic*-style deckchair. I stalked out of the orchid palace and down the path towards the perfectly trimmed chest-high boxwood hedge that separated the two properties.

'They're ladybugs, Ms Bettina,' Claire said. 'Ladybugs eat aphids. That's a *good* thing.'

'Excuses, Claire, excuses! And I've told you before, address me as *Lady* Bettina.'

Many modern Australians are embarrassed by their inherited English titles and either never mention them or actively hide them. Not Bettina. She attempted to have all her SILC teachers call her Lady Bettina. It was not a popular move.

The stone pathway was annoyingly uneven and was wreaking havoc on my balance and my heels, so I broke a cardinal etiquette rule by gluing my eyes to my feet. I'd had some bad experiences with heels and tripping. It can lead to surprisingly flammable catastrophes.

I was wearing ankle-length grey Dior Homme pants, so I had a clear view of my feet (which were encased in a pair of perfectly manageable Jimmy Choo stilettos), and a pale tailored silk shirt, buttoned bra-line low in rebellion. Which was fine because Grandmother was 17,000 kilometres away. Even so, I could hear her voice in my head. *Indigo! For goodness sake, look up, child! Your feet cannot possibly be that interesting. Why is your shirt like that? Have you lost half of your buttons?*

I slowed my stalk to a walk and peeled my eyes off the ground.

'Bettina!' I growled venomously. 'Be. Quiet!'

Even from a distance I could see Bettina's head swivel towards me and her eyes narrow. It had been years since I had seen her in person. I was astonished to discover her nose had changed shape yet again.

'Look what the cat dragged in, Claire,' Bettina said, not looking at Claire. 'It's Cat's Little Kitten, Indi-slow.'

Bettina had been using the same witty taunt since the third grade.

Claire was sharp enough to know a diversion when she saw one. She began backing away from the briefly distracted Bettina. 'I'm going to find Dame Lizzy. She can explain the jonquils better than me.'

'You mean Dame *Elizabeth*,' Bettina snarled, her head snapping back to see Claire's swift retreat.

'Right you are, Ms Bettina,' Claire said, her head nodding as she ran. 'I'll go get Dame Lizzy Holly.'

'But she's not home,' Bettina yelled after her.

Too late. Claire was gone. I didn't expect her back. Wise.

Bettina made an exasperated face and turned her attention to me. 'Shouldn't you be in jail or something for killing your dead husband?'

We weren't eight anymore; I was going to rise above the insults.

'Bettina, please, just be quiet,' I said, desperately trying to channel some serenity. 'We don't *all* need to know what you think about your grandmother's gardener.'

With my eyes confidently fixed on Bettina, I navigated my way down the last section of the garden path, twisting between hedges and beds of fresh spring flowers. I peered more closely at her. 'What on earth are you wearing? Did you steal that poor woman's clothes as well as her dignity?'

It just popped out. In fairness, they didn't teach serenity at SILC. And Bettina was sporting an *awful* lot of khaki and there were pockets in everything. I could not see her feet, but my money was on Birkenstocks.

'Shut up, Indigo!' she spat, dusting dirt off her cargo pants. 'Shouldn't you have your hooks in another dull pudgy accountant by now?'

I was busy ignoring the fact that Richard was a reconstructive plastic surgeon, not a bookkeeper, as I attempted to correct my footing and stay upright on the rocky garden path. Perhaps manageable was not the best word to describe my shoes. I was more falling than walking towards the hedge line.

'What's the matter, Kitten?' prodded Bettina, lurking her way towards the hedge. 'Cat got your tongue?'

Just as I rounded a particularly curvy bend, my arm whipped up to point at her. 'Bettina, you absolute f—'

My violent arm action threw me even further off balance. My feet twisted beneath me, taking me off the rocky path and onto the soft lawn. One spiky satin heel sank suddenly into the damp green grass while my other foot tripped over something.

I looked down, ready to brace my fall, and there, lying almost directly below me, dressed like a severely underpaid gardener, his head and shoulders partially hidden in a bed of gorgeous pink oriental lilies, was a man. An old man. A dead man. An old dead man. Stiff as a board. And I fell on him, like a tree being felled to the forest floor.

I woke up face-to-face with death. It felt a lot like lying on an ironing board. Most unpleasant. Not that I had ever touched an ironing board, but what I imagined it might feel like—hard and covered in unflatteringly coloured, coarse, ill-fitting cotton. I was completely horrified and immediately passed out again.

We Hasluck-Royces do *not* do well with mortification. It tends to make us throw up and then pass out. Although the reflex has stopped many drunk ancestors from choking to death, it has, in my opinion, outlived its usefulness. I was, to the best of my knowledge, the only Hasluck-Royce who, with hard work, determination and the resolve to not be completely ridiculous, had kicked the vomiting part. I was still working on the fainting.

I woke up annoyed that I had passed out again and wondering if it was at all possible to avoid the police if one found a dead body.

'Dude.' I heard Esmerelda's voice from above me. 'He's like, dead.'

'No kidding!' I screeched at her. 'Help me get up!'

'You're conscious? I thought you'd be like *totally* passed out.'

'I've passed out and come to twice already. Where the hell have you been?' I said, straining to see her.

'I dunno. I was checking out the floor in there,' she said, gesturing to the orchid palace. 'It's funky.'

How interesting could a concrete floor possibly be?

'I don't care about the floor!' I yelled. 'Get me off this body before I faint again.'

I prayed Bettina was not witnessing this humiliating spectacle. Given my luck, she was probably livestreaming it.

Esmerelda attempted to lift me off the corpse by grabbing both my shoulders and pulling me directly upward. Perhaps, having spent so much time watching YouTube or memes on her endlessly updated smartphone, she was endeavouring to simply hit rewind on the fall. I would have had to have been as stiff as the corpse and significantly lighter to make that a possibility, and I was dropped twice before she gave up on that method and switched to trying to heft me over her shoulder like a sack of potatoes. This was more successful, but not a complete success and, again, I found myself face-to-face with the dead man.

Eventually, I shooed Esmerelda away and, seeing no other options, placed my hands variously on his stiff shoulders, chest, left hip, right thigh and eventually foot until I was in a standing position.

'Jesus, Indigo,' I heard Bettina holler from what sounded like much closer quarters. 'I've seen newborn foals get up faster and with more grace. Why's that guy passed out in your grandmother's yard? She's going to be livid.'

Bettina was drawn no doubt by the heady smell of humiliation in the spring air. She wedged her sharp, tiny frame between two of the boxwood hedges that separated our grandmothers' gardens and forced her way through.

She strode towards me, phone held upright in both hands at chest height. I heard the distinctive *woosh* of a something being digitally transmitted. I prayed it was a text to her dentist, but I doubted it. Bettina's social media network would be primordial and vast. It would be Heiress on Fire all over again. Only this time I would be Heiress of Horror. This did *not* constitute Zero Publicity or Extremely Good Behaviour. There was *no way* I was going to pass out on top of that body again. I stomped my ruined Jimmy Choo stiletto deep into the lawn and anchored my swaying form.

Esmerelda moved quickly towards Bettina. 'Is that the new iPhone—' There was a blur of arms, a *whomp* and Bettina was suddenly, inexplicably, seated on the lawn on her khaki-clad derrière and her phone neatly pitched into a nearby fountain. *Plop.*

'Dude,' Esmerelda said, dusting Bettina down and helping her up all at once. 'That lawn's like, pretty friggin' slippery.'

It all happened so quickly that Bettina was briefly stunned into silence. Esmerelda turned her focus to me.

'It's not like dead dudes are totally gross or anything,' she said quietly, eyeing the corpse apologetically, 'but I'd like, prefer not to hang with them. They tend to attract cops. And I prefer not to hang with them either.'

I could feel her mind racing through the likely upcoming scenarios. Police are called. Names are taken. Names are run. Names pop up in the system. Parole officers are called. People are searched. Bags are searched. Uncomfortable explanations are required. Grandmother's two borrowed oil masters were a good example of things which might require an explanation.

'I'm gonna head,' she said, stepping away.

'Yes. Good idea. Perhaps you would be so kind as to take my *luggage* home.' And I jerked my head towards the orchid palace where my tote lay.

'Yep.' She nodded in agreement. 'Totally.'

'Hello?' Bettina piped up, coming out of her Esmerelda shock. 'You may *not* leave! You took my phone! I'm pressing charges.'

'I was never here,' Esmerelda said convincingly.

Getting to her feet, Bettina shot Esmerelda a sour look. She was clearly unimpressed by Esmerelda's blatant attempt at gaslighting.

'You might have thrown my phone into the fountain, but I've already posted the video to Insta.'

I willed myself to stay focused. Passing out would *not* help.

'Bullshit,' Esmerelda responded.

'Really?' I asked Esmerelda in surprise. 'Bettina is a bit of a, you know … Posting the video on Instagram does seem like something she would do. I heard the swish.'

'Totally not her posting sound,' Esmerelda replied confidently. 'Totally her texting sound.'

'You don't know that!' Bettina raged, her face turning the same shade as the pink oriental lilies. She peered at Esmerelda, assessing her thoroughly for the first time. 'Who the hell are you?'

'Dude,' Esmerelda said as if explaining something to a toddler. 'I'm. Not. Here.'

Bettina gritted her teeth. 'Fine. Be like that.' She turned her attention to me. 'And I thought your taste in weirdo BFs couldn't sink any lower.'

A quick swipe at my long-time best friend, Anna Del Rico. Anna was a serial lover. After her recent annulment (nineteen really was *too* young) Anna was living in the US, being pursued by a besotted ball sports player of some kind. He was undoubtably gorgeous and between the ages of twenty (Anna's new minimum age requirement for matrimony) and twenty-five (several years older than her previous maximum age). If Anna were a man, they would give her an award and write songs about her. But she was not. Hence the dig.

Bettina stepped towards me, almost standing on the body between us. 'Your psycho friend is right though. I did text it. To *Dylan Moss*.'

Dylan Moss. My stomach flipped and my feet felt slippery under me. In the dessert bar of men, Dylan Moss was an oven-warm blondie with hot caramel fudge and bright candy sprinkles. He was my first love and had scorched my sixteen-year-old heart so badly that I swore off delicious males forever, opting for safe, reliable Bran Muffins like Richard. Except Richard had *not* been a Bran Muffin.

Do not *pass out! Maybe Bettina did send a video of you falling over a dead body to the man who broke your heart and humiliated you, maybe she didn't. There will be a way to find out, there will be a way to get the video back. Think.*

Bettina roughly poked the poor man with her foot. I was horrified … and then it dawned on me. Bettina did not realise he was dead. She was attempting to wake a corpse.

CHAPTER 2

TWO ODD FEET

If I were to be kind in my assessment, I would observe that his head and face *were* hidden in the oriental lilies. If I were not so generous, I would point out that Bettina had never been the most observant person and was plainly toeing a corpse.

Esmerelda gave Bettina a small tap on the back of the shoulder. 'Dude, like don't do that to him. It's totally not cool.'

Because Bettina is tiny and Esmerelda is not, the small tap caused Bettina to stumble forward, trip on the man's stiff, outstretched arm and fall over him. Bettina managed to brace her fall and effectively found herself in plank pose over the top of the body.

'What's wrong with you?' Bettina growled at the corpse, attempting to get up without touching him. 'Say something! Hello?'

Esmerelda and I looked down at her.

'Oh,' Esmerelda said in realisation. Then to Bettina, 'Lady, he's like, totally dead.'

Bettina eyed the man sceptically through the lily foliage and poked him. Nothing. She knitted her eyebrows and put her palm flat on his arm. I knew from recent personal experience he was a little too cold and a little too hard. It was *not* a pleasant sensation.

'Oh my God!' Bettina screamed. 'He's dead! HE'S DEAD!'

It was difficult to hear anything after Bettina's screaming kicked in, but I think Esmerelda said, 'And I'm *not* psycho. They test you for all that stuff, you know,' she winked at me, 'at finishing school.' By finishing school, she meant prison.

I couldn't wait for Bettina's phone to dry out to check whether she'd really sent a video of me tripping over an elderly, dirt-covered dead man to Dylan Moss. Although I had no idea where Dylan was, Google did. It led us straight to his PR agency website, which provided us with his office phone number. Dylan's assistant was more than happy to tell a (fictional) prospective new client (Esmerelda, in the greenhouse, using a background noise-cancelling app) that his boss was currently coming in from LA but could see her tomorrow.

I knew from personal experience that no matter which airline you used, all the commercial LA to Sydney flights landed between 3 pm and 4 pm. All Esmerelda had to do was sit at the international arrivals gate and wait. Oh, and perhaps do some light pickpocketing.

Just in case Bettina *had* saved a video on her phone, Esmerelda suggested several methods to extract the password from her, but she needn't have bothered. Bettina was not the tech security savvy type, and I knew her birthday: April Fools' Day. Very unfortunate.

During our SILC days Bettina and her birthday parties had fallen prey to a bonanza of juvenile joke-store tricks like whoopee cushions, exploding gifts and slime-filled lunch boxes. Eventually, Bettina had skipped her birthday week at school and hired security for her parties. Esmerelda eyed Bettina sympathetically, mumbled something about bad birthday juju and disappeared with her sodden phone and my weighty tote.

Bettina was so hysterical that I hoped she might have no memory of Esmerelda at all. Could amnesia be considered good luck? I hoped so.

The last thing I wanted to do on a fine spring day was sit by a dead body I had absolutely no information about and be repeatedly asked questions about it. Sadly, what I wanted and what I got had, in recent times, become quite different things.

*

Bettina's screaming eventually attracted both Grandmother's and Dame Elizabeth's staff.

I spent the afternoon being interviewed by a Detective Rope. Rope was five nine with dark hair and eyes and dressed in a suit made of fabrics that were at least two decades old. His shirt was a low cotton thread count and his tie was thin and frayed. That said, his hair was neat and tidy and he was clean, even if he wore enough after-shave for himself, his partner Detective Winters, and the rest of his department.

Rope asked me, once again, if I knew the deceased man half-hidden in Grandmother's oriental lilies.

'No,' I exhaled in exhaustion. It had been hours. 'I do not know him.'

That was the truth. I had no idea who the man was. There was, however, *something* about him that prickled some small memory deep in the recesses of my mind. But I could not put my finger on it, let alone articulate it.

'And your grandmother's not home?'

God help me, how many times had we been over all of this?

'No, Detective Dop—I mean, Detective Rope.' Absolutely accidental.

'And you don't recognise him?'

Shoot me. 'No.'

'And what were you doing here?'

Isn't there some kind of IQ standard in the police force?

'Visiting my grandmother.'

How could some detectives be so fast and bright and gorgeous, and others so slow and dull and unattractive?

'But she's not here; she's in London?'

'Correct.'

'You came over when you knew she wasn't going to be home. When you knew the house was going to be empty,' he said in what I can only assume was an attempt to be tricky.

I stared at Detective Rope in exasperation and swept my arm across the garden. Gathered at the periphery of the blue and white chequered crime-scene tape were Grandmother's housekeeper Mary Moore, a soft, gorgeous woman who had been more grandmotherly than my own grandmother when it came to feeding me and listening to me whine about boys, Grandmother's driver Mr David, a hulking Samoan man, as kindly as he was wide, the maid, the cleaner, the chef, Grandmother's two gardeners, her groundskeeper and a pool maintenance person. And that was just on my side of the tape. Gathered on the other side, just over the hedge, were Dame Elizabeth's staff: cook, maid, pool person, cleaner. Everyone except Dame Elizabeth's driver and her PA, both of whom I assumed were with her, wherever she was, and Claire the gardener, who had been wise enough to run away from Bettina and never come back.

Bettina had been given a sedative by the ambulance paramedics upon arrival and was making cow eyes at one of them (who *was* rather handsome) while Rope's partner, Detective Winters, attempted to get some coherent answers from her.

While Detective Winters was too old to be a hipster, he was just the right age to be a mature-age hippy. He was five foot eight with well-groomed grey hair (too long to be considered conservatively groomed, but too short to be tied in a man bun), sharp blue eyes and a beard (which was two inches all over and white everywhere but the chin). His suit would have been a pricey purchase, albeit thirty years ago, and his shoes were shiny and new. He pulled the whole look off. I wanted to trade detectives.

Bettina was not as tolerant as I about being asked the same questions over and over. And she did *not* appreciate being interrupted to answer said questions during her sedative-induced, addlebrained paramedic wooing.

'Oh. My. God!' she spat impatiently. 'I've told you a hundred times. I don't know any dirty old people. How would

I? I don't do soup kitchens.' She smiled at the paramedic. 'Gilly and I, we do charity events. Lots.' Then back to Winters. 'No, I haven't seen anyone weird hanging around. I've been working in Italy for two months; I only got back last week.'

'Gilly is Giuliana Holly, your sister?' Winters asked, pronouncing Giuliana as Jill-E-Are-Nah instead of JOO-lee-ah-nah.

Everyone had called Giuliana Gilly since Year Three. Responsibility for this nickname can be laid squarely at the feet of then nine-year-old know-it-all Bethany Kilmer. During a biology lesson about frogs and tadpoles, Bethany pronounced the two almost imperceptible pin-prick holes in front of Giuliana's ears to be gills. Bethany claimed they were left over from the time Gilly's ancestors were fish, the underlying insult being that Bettina and Gilly's family were not only unevolved, but that Gilly was a frog. Or a tadpole. Or a fish. Bethany is now a senior partner divorce lawyer.

Bettina gave him a death stare. 'My sister's name is *Lady* Giuliana Holly. And, as I have also told you a billion times, you may address me as *Lady* Bettina Holly.'

'We don't do titles, Ms Holly,' Winters said flatly. 'You got back from Italy two weeks ago?'

'*One* week ago. Una.'

'And you don't recognise this man?'

I felt a little sorry for Bettina. Then again, it was probably karma for being such a raging b—*lady* to everyone all the time.

Rope asked me again where I lived and what my movements in the last forty-eight hours had been. As if he didn't remember the first five times: I lived 800 metres away, in the pool house on my mother's estate. Cat Jones. Yes, *the* Cat Jones. Yes, the supermodel. Yes, I am quite sure she is really my mother.

Mother had recently come out of almost a decade of celibacy to date Jed the giant fireman, after he'd pulled me from a burning building (albeit from the ground floor). I had been with the genetically blessed pair from Friday afternoon until they'd left for Bora Bora at 8 am. No, I was not expecting them home anytime soon.

I left my felonious assistant out of my alibi. Surely a supermodel and a heroic fireman were good enough?

Rope's head was turned by the arrival of a young woman with a white pixie cut. Her outfit somewhat resembled Esmerelda's: black jeans and a short-sleeve cotton T-shirt. But the T-shirt was plain, the jeans unripped and she wore it with a cotton hoody and no-nonsense sneakers. And instead of being built like an overgrown surfboard, she was a normal person shape and height.

She was carrying what looked like a large metal make-up case, the kind that folds out to reveal layered shelves with little compartments. A clear plastic bag containing something white and vaguely fabric-ish was tucked under her arm.

'Bugger,' Rope said, unhappily assessing the woman. 'They sent Bailly.'

Bailly had a slightly annoyed expression on her resting face, or perhaps she had just met Detective Rope before and knew what she was in for. She nodded self-consciously to the female police officer standing guard at the crime-scene tape, carefully handing her the metal case. She then unpacked the contents of the clear bag to reveal a one-piece

Tyvek suit. She gently unfolded it, stepped in and zipped it up. She then covered her sneakers with blue surgical booties, retrieved her metal case with a short, unsure smile to the officer, and ducked under the tape.

'Dr Bailly? Where's Dr Oldham?' Rope wanted to know as she approached.

'Dead,' she said flatly, pulling on a pair of surgical gloves. 'Myocardial infarction last Tuesday.'

Dr Bailly opened her case. I saw an array of brushes, powders and small containers, but no false eyelashes, Dior lipsticks or Chanel eyeshadow palettes. I was disappointed. The joy of shiny blue, black and gold cosmetic cases and their happy, coloured contents never failed to delight me.

'What?' Detective Rope asked in shock. 'He's dead? You're kidding?'

'No,' Dr Bailly said in a tone that did not invite further rhetorical questions.

'I didn't know that,' Rope grumbled, unimpressed at being swindled out of Dr Oldham, whoever he was. 'No one told me that,' he persisted.

'You are a detective,' she said without malice or sarcasm, surveying the body, which was still half covered by Grandmother's oriental lilies with his bottom half protruding onto the lawn. 'You should have known that.'

The police officer on guard by the body stifled a laugh. Rope shot the Tyvek-covered woman a dirty look, which she didn't notice, then gathered himself and began barking.

'What took you so long?'

'You called me out here on a Sunday afternoon. I don't work Sundays. I was at the pet show buying a Symphysodon discus,' she said, eyeing the general area in which Rope stood but not Rope directly. 'You interrupted me.'

Rope obviously had no idea what a Symphysodon discus was (neither did I), but her annoyance clearly brought him joy. He continued with a distinctly more pleasing demeanour. 'Can you give me time of death?'

'If I puncture the liver to take body temperature, I might damage it. What if he was stabbed in the liver? I could compromise evidence.'

'He was homeless. I don't think he was stabbed in the liver,' Rope retorted.

'You—'

'I'm willing to chance it,' Rope said, cutting her off. 'Body temp?'

'You don't think homeless people have liver damage?' she persisted.

Good point. Not to generalise, but I'm going to generalise and say the words *homeless guy*, *alcohol* and *liver damage* go together like the words *socialite*, *cocktails* and *rehab*.

'Well then, Dr Bailly, do it the other way,' he said and jerked his head to the left, pointing his pointer finger upwards. 'You know.'

'You want me to insert a thermometer into this man's rectum? Here? In the open?' And although she did not make eye contact with him, she folded her arms in a gesture that made it clear she had zero intention of doing as he asked.

I glanced around at the array of spectating staff members.

'He's dead,' Rope said with a shrug.

'He's a person,' she said evenly.

'He was a vagrant, for Chrissake!' he shot back. 'I don't think his family will object.'

Dr Bailly looked like she wanted to take Rope's temperature *the other way*, but said nothing.

'You might want to avoid interfering with the body like
that in front of Bettina,' I put in, although why I was speaking at all was a mystery to me. *Do not speak, Indigo. Get
away as quickly as possible and do* not *get involved.* 'She can
be rather sensitive.'

Yes, what he was proposing to do to that poor dead man
in front of a dozen onlookers was awful, but was it my
problem?

'She actually *is* a Lady,' I persisted. 'Her grandmother is
Dame Elizabeth Holly.'

Mental head thump.

A wave of recognition passed over Detective Rope's face.
He and I glanced over at Bettina who, sedated or not, was
clearly using every gram of socialised strength she possessed
to not kill Detective Winters. The paramedics were packing up. The moment that gorgeous paramedic stepped into
his ambulance and drove away, all hell was going to break
loose. Nice, polite Bettina would be gone along with him.
I wondered if they even knew they had been *getting* nice,
polite Bettina.

Oh dear. They were in for a surprise.

'Jesus! Don't do it then!' Rope exclaimed. 'But if we can't
get a decent time of death because you're too precious to
take a temperature, it's on you. Just go and collect some
trace. Hands, nails, you know.'

'Now?'

'No, at Christmas. Yes, now,' he growled.

'It's best if we bag this man's hands, feet and head, and
do swabs and run trace back at the FM triple C. We run the

risk of cross-contamination if we cut or scrape or swab out here in the open,' Dr Bailly said.

'You wanna wait to get him back to the lab 'cause you're worried about contamination? It's a bit late for that; both these girls have already fallen over this guy.' He nodded towards me, as if I had not been standing next to him for the past few hours, and then towards Bettina as she said goodbye to Mr Ambulance.

Girls? Rope held none of the social or biological qualifications that would allow him to use that designation when referring to Bettina or myself.

Dr Bailly acknowledged my presence with a nod of the head. She then eyed my hands. 'Has someone processed you?' she asked.

Although I didn't know what she meant by 'processed', I was sure I would have known if it had been done to me and that I would *not* enjoy it. I considered my brand-new manicure. 'Maybe,' I said. 'Maybe I have. Yes, I think I have.'

'Has this woman been processed?'

'Nope, that's your job. And then do the body.' With that, Rope walked off towards Winters and a simmering Bettina.

'He's not a wise man,' Dr Bailly said to herself when Rope hit the hedge.

Unlike Bettina, Rope was nowhere near slim enough to squeeze between two hedges. When, after several aggressive, hippo like attempts, he failed to wedge his substantial girth through them, he heaved himself onto the poor shaped shrub and leaned into the next garden. I waited for the sound of snapping branches. Nothing. Claire was an excellent gardener.

'Jem Bailly,' Dr Bailly said to me by way of introduction while squatting by her metal box. 'I'm from the FM triple C.'

FMCCC? That didn't sound like a laboratory, it sounded like a radio station.

'I don't know specifically what the FMCCC is,' I said, feeling somewhat simple.

'The Forensic Medicine and Coroners Court Complex,' she said plainly. 'FM triple C. I'm a forensic pathologist. I'm going to take swabs and nail cuttings, okay.'

Although the word 'okay' was included in her sentence, it was clearly *not* a question.

'A pleasure to meet you, Jem Bailly,' I said, even though discovering a body and meeting a forensic pathologist on a sunny Sunday while trying to borrow a master painting or two was not my idea of pleasure. 'I'm Indigo Hasluck-Royce-Jones-Bombberg. Indigo.' Out of habit, I offered her my hand.

She stood with a plastic vial in one hand and nail clippers in the other, peering at my outstretched hand. Right. Had I learned nothing in the past few hours? No one shakes the hand of the woman who finds the body. Or touches the body. Or falls over the body.

'Doctor,' she said to the clippers. 'I am Doctor Jem Bailly. You can call me Bailly.'

'Me too,' I said, before clarifying. 'Not doctor. My first name is actually Indigo-Daisy-Violet-Amber.'

A microsecond micro smile nipped across her face and she briefly looked me in the eye. 'Your name is *Indigo-Daisy-Violet-Amber Hasluck-Royce-Jones-Bombberg*? There's no way Detective Rope is going to be able to remember that. Or spell it correctly in his report.'

Searing remembered it. Then again, Rope was clearly no Searing. I had been spoilt by the quality of the homicide detective I'd had investigating me.

Bailly's eyes went down to the plastic vial in her hand. She expertly flipped the lid off with her gloved thumb and turned it sideways, assessing the blank label. 'I don't think the name Indigo-Daisy-Violet-Amber Hasluck-Royce-Jones-Bombberg will fit onto the evidence container labels. Your name is a problem.'

Preaching to the choir.

She efficiently swabbed my hands and cut my nails. I was in the midst of bemoaning the unexpected and rather brutal death of my manicure when I had an unexpected flashback. I recalled being in the back of an ambulance, racing to the hospital after the fire. My mother was there. And someone, I suddenly realised, just like Dr Bailly was swabbing my hands and clipping my nails. *Swish, swish. Pat, pat. Clip, clip.*

'Can you smell smoke?' I asked her.

She sniffed, her nose in the air like a rabbit, carefully analysing its contents.

'No.'

'It must be me.'

'We're done,' she said. She closed her case, bagged the minutely labelled vials, then binned her gloves, booties and suit and put on new ones.

My nails were cut to the quick and a complete mess. I could have done a better job if I had gnawed them off. Or had a beaver do it.

I watched her walk to the body and open her case again. I had no idea how she was going to get a substantial nail sample.

'He's had a very recent manicure,' I said to her, again speaking before I intended. 'The manicurist did an excellent job. His nails look exactly two point five millimetres long. Not a lot left for clipping.'

I was, unfortunately, in possession of this intimate nail knowledge due to the sheer number of times I had fallen on him.

Without raising her head, Bailly said, 'Yes. You're correct. Very observant, Indigo-Daisy-Violet-Amber. Why do you think the manicure was recent?'

There was no note of sarcasm in her voice. Her memory was impressive.

'The nail is buffed to a shine. That only lasts a few days,' I answered.

Who was I, Nancy Drew?

She examined his hands. 'Huh.' She then leaned into the oriental lilies and examined his face.

'He's had a very neat shave quite recently,' she said.

I didn't know if she was speaking to me or not, but I had nothing else to do and it was more pleasant than dealing with Detective Rope.

'He has had regular cutthroat shaves. I would say he had one yesterday,' I said to her. 'Not many people do that themselves.'

This is mainly because giving oneself a cutthroat shave is ridiculously difficult and perilously dangerous. Richard was one of the best reconstructive plastic surgeons in the country, possibly the world, and when he attempted to use a cutthroat razor, he looked like he'd had a run-in with Sweeney Todd.

Bailly turned slightly towards me. 'Why do you say that?'

'A shave that close is definitely a cutthroat razor and it has hardly grown back. The skin on his lower face is in perfect condition. No tears, no rash, no ingrown hairs. So, not his first time. I would say he, or his barber, uses a hot towel.' I had no idea why the poor deceased man was so endlessly fascinating to me. I tried not to look while I was *down there*.

'And he smells of Atkinsons California Poppy Hair Oil,' I continued. My grandfather's barber used to use the same product on him. I felt surprisingly satisfied to be so helpful before wondering *why* I felt the urge to be so helpful. Was I even being helpful? And was the familiar scent of Grandfather's California Poppy Oil the thing that had prickled something in my memory earlier?

'Huh,' she said, quietly crab-walking from her squatting position near the head down to the end of the body. She examined his feet. 'No chronic wounds,' she said to herself. 'Peripheral debris only.' She stayed in that position for a long time. From where I was standing, his feet did not seem that interesting. They were covered in lawn, dirt and tiny pebbles, which seemed about right for a homeless person.

I rapidly lost interest—I was literally watching someone stare at the dirt on the feet of a dead vagrant. Ten seconds later, Bailly had my attention again. She was sniffing the body. I was about to ask her what she was doing when Bettina began actively yelling, demanding a lawyer and threatening to sue. Rope had managed to tip her over the edge, and without her emergency service man in attendance, Bettina had no reason to be reasonable.

Although I could not condone Bettina's behaviour, I was two minutes from pulling the lawyer card myself. It had been a long afternoon.

As if on cue, Dame Elizabeth appeared in the melee, her PA Andrew Saxton and her driver whose name I didn't know trailing close behind. The onlooking staff parted like the Red Sea, allowing her immediate access to Bettina, Rope and Winters.

To the unaccustomed, meeting Dame Elizabeth Holly was a bit like meeting a younger version of the Queen. Educated in the days of governesses and finishing schools, when five different forks were used at dinner (salad, fish, dinner, dessert and oyster) and polite women married when and where they were told, Dame Elizabeth had an air of stoicism mixed with genuine grace and highly bred patience that was rare and refined.

Dame Elizabeth went immediately to her granddaughter, gathering Bettina in her arms, cooing and kissing the top of her head. Bettina, for all her huff and puff, broke down in her grandmother's embrace. Once Bettina was breathing at a normal rate, without asking for permission, Dame Elizabeth silently handed her off to a household staff member, who promptly escorted her away.

Detective Winters immediately comprehended he was dealing with someone well above his political pay grade. Was he impressed by her staff's deference? Did he recognise her from one of her many philanthropical endeavours? From her portrait in the National Gallery? Her sculpture in the foyer of the Opera House? Whatever the motivation, he did not object to Dame Elizabeth excusing Bettina. Detective Rope, witnessing this, was silent. If he was not fully aware of Bettina's grandmother's high power and potency before, he was now.

Meanwhile, Bailly had been methodically occupied, gently paper-bagging the man's extremities and carefully sealing them with police evidence tape. This sounds a lot less traumatic than it looks. Unless it sounds extremely disturbing and traumatic, in which case, it's accurate.

I turned away as the man in the lilies was placed, presealed, into a navy blue body bag. The crinkle of the body bag's tent-like material, the swoosh of the zip and the crack of the plastic tie tag sealing his fate were like auditory daggers.

I was astonished to be at all affected. I didn't even know this person! Rope said he was homeless. Well, a homeless person with an excellent, longstanding barber and a fabulous manicurist. Was that even possible? While I was not up to date on the current costs of barbering, I was extremely well acquainted with the costs of personal maintenance, and they were high. If you could not afford a home, what were the chances you could afford daily personal grooming? Not wonderful, I would have thought. And why did Bailly smell him? And what on earth was he doing in Grandmother's backyard? Admittedly, there was a battalion of homeless people in Kings Cross, but it was *Kings Cross*, the home of seedy nightclubs, neon signs, teenage intoxication and twenty-four-hour eating establishments. Geographically close, yes, but worlds away. There was not a high homeless population in any of Sydney's other elite Eastern Suburbs, and especially not here in the closed community of Vaucluse. Lachlan and Sarah Murdoch lived on this street. What was a meticulously groomed hobo doing here?

I was awoken from my reverie by a voice so clear and strong, so refined in its tone, it tinkered on the edge of British royalty. 'What a tragic way for us to have met, Detective Winters. It is kind of you to say though. I am humbled it has brought you and your family such joy. It has been my great privilege to—is that Indigo Hasluck-Royce-Jones-Bombberg *standing* in *full sun?* Surely she has not been there all this time? Detective Winters?'

'Detective Rope?' asked Detective Winters, simultaneously passing the buck and throwing his partner under the bus.

'Well … err,' Rope said.

Dame Elizabeth looked embarrassed for them. 'Dear, oh dear, oh dear.'

CHAPTER 3

GRAND REQUESTS

Ignoring all policing etiquette, Dame Elizabeth patted Winters kindly on the arm and, in a biblical move, she seemingly walked *through* the immaculate boxwood hedge separating the two gardens and strolled up the stone pathway to me. I, along with the detectives, stared in astonishment. Then I heard a small rustle and caught the movement of greenery swinging closed behind her. *Click.* There was a false section of boxwood hedge in the boxwood hedge. Dame Elizabeth had unlocked it and swung it open, like a solid, leafy-green farmgate, giving her immediate access to Grandmother's garden.

'My dear girl!' she exclaimed.

'Dame Elizabeth,' I said, smiling.

'Pish!' she said, rolling her eyes. 'Your grandmother's not here to chide us. Please do call me Aunt Lizzy as you did when you were a child.'

'Yes, Aunt Lizzy,' I said, too polite to point out that while Grandmother did discourage me from using less formal forms of address, it was Bettina and Gilly's fierce objections to my using familiar terms with *their* grandmother that caused me to habitually call her Dame Elizabeth.

The physical resemblance between Dame Elizabeth and Bettina was striking, although Dame Elizabeth was slightly taller, with Helen Mirren-white hair, a naturally straighter nose and she smiled more frequently.

She gathered me in her arms, just as she had done with her granddaughter minutes earlier. 'What a terrible thing! You must be in shock.'

I could recall only two occasions when my own grandmother had hugged me. When her son, my father, had died and when the police tried to arrest me for a double homicide. By contrast, Dame Elizabeth hugged me almost every time she saw me. Well, every time she saw me in private. Still, she was hundreds of hugs up on Grandmother.

While Grandmother's taste in orchids and fine art was impeccable, she possessed almost no maternal instincts. Since Grandfather's death, the Hasluck-Royce corporation had thrived under her ferocious stewardship. She enjoyed psychological warfare and technical wizardry and disliked misogynists and post-postmodernism.

'Which one of Florence's staff found the poor soul?' she asked, pulling me away and checking me, as if I might have been harmed bodily somewhere. 'They're all fairly stoic having worked for her I suppose.' She smiled. 'Still, awful.'

'I found him,' I told her. 'Bettina and I were, uh, chatting over the hedge, and I accidentally ... I found him.'

'That must have been hours ago! Andrew said the alarm in Florence's main salon went off before lunch,' she said, gently patting my hair.

My vision blurred and I swallowed hard. 'The alarm?'

'Yes, your grandmother and her absurd electronics. The sensor in the main salon has a silent alarm. Loraine and Andrew are each other's emergency contacts for the security company when one or the other is away on business.'

Loraine was Loraine Bitsmark, Grandmother's long-time PA. Loraine was flawlessly organised, immaculately groomed and disturbingly stealthy. She had the sharpest, dead-straight, angled blonde bob I had ever seen. It had sat silky and smooth, parted in the same spot above her left eye, for decades.

'Florence is in London buying something or other,' Dame Elizabeth continued, giving me one last inspection and, satisfied I had not been injured by finding the body or tripping the alarm in Grandmother's salon, stepped back.

I knew the answer but hoped against hope and asked anyway. 'The alarm doesn't trigger the cameras, does it?'

'I assume so,' she said with little interest in the subject. 'Oh dear,' she said, stopping suddenly. 'Is that?'

Bailly was directing the removal of the navy blue body bag which unfortunately involved it being moved in our direction.

I nodded. 'Yes. The police think it was a homeless person.'

'Homeless,' she said, shaking her head sadly. 'How tragic.'

The detectives had finally managed to find the secret latch that opened the hedge door and made their way towards Bailly and the blue bag.

'Any chance we can call it natural causes, Dr Bailly?' Rope said, attempting to sound like the man in charge. 'I'd like to let the men on the doors and by the tape go.'

I looked around; at least half the police standing guard were female.

Bailly directed two people also covered in Tyvek to continue removing the body while she paused to answer Rope.

'That's not something I can tell you until an autopsy is performed, Detective Rope. Have you found his family? I would prefer to get their consent before I begin.'

'No, sorry,' Winters responded for Rope, 'no ID on him. No hits on the prints you pulled. We'll check the missing person's database, ask around the usual spots, soup kitchens, shelters. Try to ID him. Try to find relatives.' He shrugged. 'Never know. Might get lucky.'

'Might not get lucky too,' Rope chipped in. 'Might never find next of kin. Sometimes they don't ID them on purpose. Don't wanna own them. Funerals aren't cheap. You know how it is.'

'I'll begin as soon as possible then. Fresh is best.'

'What if you cannot find any family?' Dame Elizabeth asked. 'What will happen to him?'

'We'll keep him,' Bailly said flatly. 'In the deep freeze.'

'Permanently?' Dame Elizabeth asked in astonishment. 'In the freezer?'

Bailly paused to consider her answer. 'Yes. He will stay permanently in the deep freezer.'

Dame Elizabeth's eyes widened in shock. She was clearly taken aback that this man could be frozen for life. Or afterlife. 'Surely we can do better than that? I am more than happy to pay for his funeral if that is acceptable.' She squeezed my arm. 'We shall give him a full burial. Something lovely. Something dignified.'

'No,' Bailly said. 'It is not acceptable.'

As modest and kind as Dame Elizabeth was, she was not accustomed to hearing 'no'.

'Pardon?' she said, as if Bailly had genuinely made a mistake.

'No, it is not acceptable because you cannot pay for a funeral or give him a funeral because I cannot release the body to you.'

'I do not understand,' Dame Elizabeth said. 'Surely if he has no family, there can be no objection to our taking care of him.'

'I have no personal objection to your providing him with a funeral,' Bailly said. 'It seems like a civilised act of kindness. However, it would be against the law for me to release an unidentified body.'

Dame Elizabeth looked to me. I shrugged. How on earth would I know?

Detective Rope appeared very much like a man who was about to be asked a legal question to which he should have known the answer but was a little fuzzy on. He immediately set off to speak to the policewoman on guard at the cordon tape before the inevitable happened.

'Is that correct?' Dame Elizabeth asked Winters.

He nodded sadly. 'I'm afraid so. No ID, no release. I'll do my best to find out who he was, if he had family, but I can't make any promises. As my partner said to Dr Bailly, it does happen that we're sometimes unable to ID people. The homeless can be tough. I'm sorry.'

Dame Elizabeth rearranged her face from displeased and disappointed into placated.

'That is sad news. I appreciate your efforts, Detective Winters. Can I assume you will release Indigo to me? I am sure it has been a difficult morning for her.'

'Sure, that's fine.' And to me he said, 'We'll be in touch if we have any more questions. We have your contact details.'

'You haven't asked me about cause of death,' Bailly said to Winters. 'Detective Rope always asks me to tell him cause of death at the scene.'

'Do you have cause of death?' Winters asked, surprised.

'No. I won't have a definitive cause of death until I've completed a full autopsy,' she said. There was no inflection of sarcasm in her tone.

'Then why'd you bring it up?'

'Because you didn't ask,' Bailly explained. 'And Detective Rope always asks.'

Winters gave her a gentle smile. 'Duly noted, Dr Bailly.'

'He does have a laceration on the back of the head,' she added, as what seemed like a less pertinent thought.

'Size and location?' prompted Winters.

'It's the size of a turtle egg, and above the hat line,' she said tellingly.

I glanced around. I didn't see a hat. Had he been wearing a hat?

Winters raised an eyebrow. 'Above the hat line?'

'Yes. The blunt force injury has caused the skin to split. It feels like a stellate on the scalp. I would say the impact was broad.'

'What's a stellate?' I asked, refraining from asking about the missing hat, which I had a premonition was not an *actual* hat.

'A stellate is a star-shaped bone fracture in which fracture lines radiate from the central point of impact,' she explained.

'Okay,' Winters said, quickly shutting the conversation down. 'Dame Elizabeth, a real honour to meet you. Why don't you take Ms Hasluck-Royce-Jones-Bombberg inside?'

Dame Elizabeth wasted no time in accepting his suggestion, ushering me up the garden path towards the orchid palace.

I put my head down, ignored my nagging inner-Grandmother and glued my eyes to the path. I was not going to trip over anything else. My feet and I followed Dame Elizabeth past the orchids, into the scullery Esmerelda had so casually strolled out of just hours before and towards the butler's pantry. I guessed Dame Elizabeth avoided the formal back entry because of the police tape. There was no such tape on the servants' entrance.

We entered the butler's pantry, its vast walls lined with glass-fronted, whitewashed Tasmanian oak cupboards containing all the magical ingredients and shiny appliances that made Mary Moore's baking so legendary. The benches below the cabinets were topped with Nero Marquina marble, as was the vast centre island Mary used as a worktable: all were polished to a hypnotically flawless sable. There was not a single stain or speck of dust, flour or sugar in sight.

The door between the scullery and the butler's pantry closed firmly behind me. I was faintly aware of the sound of the double swinging doors between the butler's pantry and the main kitchen in front of me opening. A waft of caramelising brown sugar hit me and beneath it, the smell of something else, something familiar. Something warm and melt-in-your-mouth delicious. There was only one treat in the world that smelt that good. I was suddenly hungry.

'Dame Elizabeth Holly,' I heard him say. 'My condolences on this tragedy occurring so close to home. I'm Detective Sergeant David *Sea*ring.'

'Oh well, of course you are,' Dame Elizabeth said with a tint of girlish delight in her refined voice. Seeing all six foot two of Detective Sergeant Searing did tend to bring out one's delight. 'Mrs Hasluck-Royce senior has told me not *nearly* enough about you.'

Searing and his perpetually peeved partner Detective Sergeant Nicole Burns had tried quite hard to arrest me for Richard's and Crystal's murders.

Searing was a problem, and not because he had thought I was a murderer. The problem was Searing was hot—which was undoubtedly why he pronounced his last name *Sea-ring* instead of Searing. He was built like an Olympic swimmer two weeks after the Olympics: firm but supple in all the right places. His dark, thick, wavy hair sat artfully on the top, and just past his ears on the sides. His eyes in contrast were the lightest golden brown. On more than one occasion, I had lost my train of thought looking into them. It felt like falling somewhere lovely. And he smelt good too.

Yes, yes, I was undoubtably a shoddy widow. But my Bran Muffin husband *had* been more fibber than fibre. For a start, Richard had a secret Irish family of origin, the Smiths (he'd told me he was an English orphan with no siblings). James Smith, Richard's mysterious brother, was also a problem. He was a physically, socially and charismatically advanced model of Richard: five foot ten, built like 007, dark blond hair and a perfectly toasted tan. His eyes were royal blue and they held an intensity that frightened me. He was almost certainly *not* the humble Irish train driver he claimed to be, and he gave me feelings that were *not* okay for one's brother-in-law.

Yes, yes, again, inappropriate widow. But again, uber-fibbing dead husband.

As well as being plastic surgeon to the stars, I was ninety-five per cent sure Richard was also giving extreme full body reconstructive and plastic surgery makeovers to international fugitives and criminals. He'd left me a secret USB containing a folder labelled *Mediterranean Men's Club*. The folder was chock-full of before and after photographs and dossiers of said criminals.

In an unauthorised misstep, Esmerelda gave the Mediterranean Men's Club USB to Searing, who promptly ran it through the Australian Federal Police (AFP) and INTERPOL's databases, creating an inerasable electronic trail.

I was not pleased.

I did not want to be connected to any police investigation, federal, international or otherwise. I did, however, want to know what Richard had been up to, so, Searing and I struck a deal—I would be a *mute* (the USB speaking for me), unnamed, confidential informant (CI) and in return he would ensure I received regular updates on the investigation. However, apart from one brief phone call in which Searing said he was about to go to work on a joint NSW Police and AFP taskforce, presumably to chase down all the Mediterranean Men's Club criminals, I had heard nothing. I was not sure what was more offensive: that Searing had only called once after we'd kissed or that he lied about keeping me in the loop.

Yes, I kissed Searing. To be fair to both of us, the kissing only happened after I had been *completely* cleared of both murders. And only once.

I looked up at Searing. He was wearing a tailored dark blue suit with a crisp white shirt, no tie. The suit could easily have passed as Dior. Searing could easily have been cast in the Dior ad as the gorgeous guy who sells the suit. His hair was immaculately tousled and his golden eyes were weary, but still full of sparkle.

'Thank you,' he said to Dame Elizabeth, although I was unsure if his response was a question or a statement. 'I wonder if I could speak with Ms Hasluck-Royce-Jones-Bombberg,' he caught my eye and held it, 'just briefly? Alone.'

Dame Elizabeth appraised me, unsure. 'Now might not be the most opportune moment.'

It was one thing to have an unexpected encounter with the gorgeous man who had undoubtably been the subject of much gossip in spas and at galas. It was clearly another matter to hand a single, unchaperoned young woman over to him. Especially when that young woman was your best friend's granddaughter. And especially when that granddaughter had just spent the afternoon with a corpse.

The sad truth was the body didn't bother me as much as the boredom of spending the afternoon with Detective Rope. And the boredom was low rent compared with the pain of being ignored by a man you had exposed yourself to. Emotionally speaking.

How much *did* Grandmother know? How much had she shared with Dame Elizabeth? Evidently, Grandmother had said *something* about Searing.

'I'm fine, thank you,' I assured her.

She shook her head, not convinced, and said to Searing, 'Perhaps another time.'

'Really, Aunt Lizzy,' I said, somewhat manoeuvring her. 'I'm sure Detective Searing will be *very* brief.'

She paused, assessing. 'Perhaps just a few minutes then,' she said.

Dame Elizabeth moved with slow, deliberate steps to the swinging doors that separated the butler's pantry from the main kitchen. She stopped, turned, assessed Searing again and said to me, 'I shall find Mary and have her bring something to revive you.' She delivered one last furtive glance, gave a sigh tinted with a tiny smile and said under her breath as she walked through the door, 'Young love.'

I got in first before he could speak. I wanted to say, 'How dare you ambush me like this! You promised to keep me in the loop about the Mediterranean Men's Club investigation! You fibbed! You only called once! Once! You devious scrumptious men, you're all the same!'

But I did not do that.

Instead, I closed the space between us in a few quick paces and grabbed him by his perfectly pressed suit lapels. I put my elbows into his firm, but not overly sculpted abdomen and walked him backwards, his rear end landing on the protruding Spanish marble benchtop, seating him. I dragged his face down to mine and kissed him with months of compounded, unspoken anger and frustration. He kissed me back without hesitation, stroking my face and hair with a tenderness that was as gentle and joyful as my grip on him was fierce and angry.

I was only able to pull back when I found I had climbed up him, my right knee bumping into the recessed glass-fronted cabinets. I feared I might smash a pane. Kissing

Searing was truly excellent but destroying the sacred place Mary Moore's baking originated from was an affront to the deity of a different kind of deliciousness. I was not willing to risk it. I still had good eating years ahead of me.

I had lost all track of time. It might have been sixty seconds. It might have been an hour. Searing did that to me.

I unpeeled myself and slid off the bench. My head was spinning. I turned and grabbed a hold of the island to catch my breath and stop myself from falling.

And *then* I said, 'How dare you ambush me like this! You promised to keep me in the loop about the Mediterranean Men's Club investigation! You fibbed! You only called once! Once!'

I left the part about devious scrumptious men out. I didn't think I could say it out loud.

He was attempting to tuck his shirt in and straighten his tie and seemed dumbfounded to have been groped *then* yelled at.

'Hang on, Indigo, just give me a minute,' he said, buttoning the wrong button into his shirt buttonhole. 'I need to talk to you, but my brain needs a second to start functioning again. There's absolutely no blood circulating in the top half of my body.' He unbuttoned it and then, yet again, buttoned it into the wrong buttonhole.

I was certain that my soft curls so deliberately crafted by Franny, my loyal and ever-patient stylist/hair and make-up guru, who was coincidentally Anna Del Rico's cousin, were in complete disarray. I was making a vague attempt to pat them down when the door from the main kitchen swung open and Dame Elizabeth strode in with Mary Moore following close behind.

Dame Elizabeth smiled at Searing and said kindly, 'You are finished with your brief word here, Detective?'

'I haven't had the opportunity to get too many words out, Dame Elizabeth,' he said, finally matching his buttons with his holes.

'Yes,' I said, briskly smiling at her. 'We're done.'

'No,' he said sternly. 'We aren't.'

'Wonderful,' Dame Elizabeth said, stepping over to me, looping her arm kindly around my waist and walking me back towards the main kitchen. 'Mary has a lovely pot of tea and a fresh batch of cinnamon scrolls set up for you in Florence's drawing room. I must get back to my darling Bettina. Poor dove, she's not like you, my love. She must be completely distraught.'

Dame Elizabeth walked me out of the room, leaving Searing in her wake. Mary Moore used her gorgeous roundness and the pretence of reaching for ingredients that happened to be in the cupboards closest to the door to prevent his attempt to follow us.

Dame Elizabeth fluffed my cushions and fussed over me while I seated myself on a carved mahogany baroque armchair with creamy velvet upholstery and buttoned tufts in Grandmother's private drawing room. After reassuring her several times that I was quite alright, she glanced about, clearly in a hurry to get back to Bettina.

She sat quickly. 'Are you really fine?' she asked, seemly more curious than concerned.

'Yes,' I said honestly.

I had vented my frustrations on Searing and that felt rather good. He seemed flustered, so that was satisfying. Esmerelda had escaped unnoticed with my borrowed artwork and I was confident she could easily relieve Dylan of his phone at the airport, deleting the video Bettina claimed to have sent him. Providing she could find him. Bettina was far, far away from me and I was unlikely to see or hear from her for years to come. The man in the lilies was unfortunate, but he was old and the forensic pathologist seemed, well, she seemed odd, but capable of taking excellent care of him. And Grandmother would be cantankerous with or without my having borrowed a Monet. Overall, these were good outcomes for me.

'You *are* remarkable,' she said, looking at me with what I can only describe as a type of admiration. Given my choice of profession, namely that I did not *have* a profession and lived off my trust funds, this was not a look I received often. 'I wonder, dear, if I could ask a small favour of you?'

'Of course,' I said. 'Anything.'

'I feel just awful about that poor man in the garden,' she began.

'Yes, awful.' I nodded in agreement, pouring two cups of tea. I felt a little awful about it too, obviously nowhere near as awful as the kind-hearted, uber-liberal Dame Elizabeth, but still, it was sad.

'I cannot abide the idea of an elderly man simply sitting in a deep freezer in some dreadful morgue for time immemorial. It is worse than a pauper's grave,' she said earnestly. 'It will *not* do. I know you and your young friend, the personal shopper, did such a wonderful job finding out who your mystery guest was in last summer's tragedy. I wondered if I might ask you to look into the identity of the homeless man? If you can discover his name, they will allow me to bury the unfortunate soul. Give him a headstone. A service. He would not be lost … forgotten.'

This could *not* be happening. I was *not* an Heiress *for Hire*. I was *not* the Heiress *on Fire*. I was *an* Heiress. Full stop. The end. No additional qualifiers. Just Heiress. Like Monet. Or Madonna. Or Moët.

Without waiting for a response, Dame Elizabeth patted my hand and stood to leave. 'I greatly appreciate this, Indigo dear. Any assistance I can give you two goes without saying. Any cooperation you might need from various quarters, please do ask. I have a few friends.'

That was an understatement. Dame Elizabeth was almost as powerful as Grandmother, although in a different way. Her work with large art institutions, from premier fashion and design universities to acting schools, galleries, opera companies, orchestras and museums, meant that she had heavy social sway and deep-rooted genuine connections. Not to mention her considerable financial and political heft. Plus, she was lovely. People liked her. She had it all over Grandmother in that department.

Wait. You two? God, was she suggesting I involve *Esmerelda*?

'As much as I would love to help you, Dame, pardon me, Aunt Lizzy,' I said, desperately trying to sound calm, 'I'm not—we're not qualified to conduct that type of research. Surely the police would be better placed to find the man's name and family?'

'Oh yes, thank you for reminding me,' she said, heading for the door. 'His family. We must also try to find his family. That sounded quite important.'

'But the police?' I insisted, attempting to put my teacup down while standing up.

'Oh yes, Indigo dear. The police. Rope, was it? Winters? They will do their best, won't they? But,' she paused, collecting her thoughts, 'they did not seem very ... hopeful. I am concerned that this poor man's social status may impact the resources dedicated to the task.'

Translation: no one will care if a homeless man is identified or not.

Dame Elizabeth was continuing to speak as she journeyed to the door. '—and that is why I would never interfere with a police investigation. But there is no law saying a quiet, parallel investigation could not take place.'

'Pardon?' I said, finally getting to my feet. *What did she just say?*

'Someone with more developed.' She paused and I could see her searching her internal political correctness thesaurus. 'More acute sensitivities. After last summer, you two are certainly qualified. Use your unique methods. You understand.'

And she was gone.

It was unlikely that she would be able to find someone less qualified to investigate the man's identity than I. The exception being, as she had inferred, that Esmerelda and I investigate together. That exponentially increased the possibility of the whole operation becoming deeply and more profoundly disastrous.

The only things I had ever done with any real methodology were the organisation of social schedules and shopping expeditions, and the study of fine arts. The only thing I could think Esmerelda had ever done studiously was to avoid arrest and any sense of fashion.

Our investigation last summer was born of desperation, and its success was a mashup of insane acts propelled by acute fear, and sheer dumb luck.

I made a mental note to come back to Dame Elizabeth in a day or two and explain in more explicit and firmer tones that this was not a task I was qualified to perform. Nor was it a task I *wanted* to perform. And if that failed, I would ask Esmerelda to explain we needed to be excused on the grounds that we were lacking in emotional development and general, practical sensitivity.

CHAPTER 4

HITCHHIKERS

Three cinnamon scrolls—Mary Moore's famed cinnamon scrolls were not only fluffy but coated in a thick layer of candied lime and orange glaze, with rings of cinnamon a centimetre wide, stuffed with caramelised crushed brown sugar and walnuts—and two cups of Orange Pekoe later and I was pleasantly numb.

I drifted into a sleep that featured Searing and orange glaze. Then Searing suddenly turned into Jed, which ended all romance, before Jed disappeared and I was left back in the foyer of my burning penthouse, the smell of smoke filling my head.

'Hello, gorgeous,' said the smoke.

I responded in a less than ladylike way, but I was dreaming and the fire *was* threatening to consume me.

'That's no way to greet an old friend,' said the grey voice.

Wait. Was I no longer dreaming?

I opened my eyes and found Dylan Moss standing less than two metres from me, his mischievous eyes dancing around the room.

He was exactly as I remembered, a teenaged Hugh Grant. Floppy hair, angelic grin, flawless English rose skin. He had aged a little but, as was the universally unfair truth, the lines around *his* eyes, mouth and forehead just worked to make him more masculine and therefore more attractive.

'Back in the private drawing room, eh? No cameras, no trick furniture. This *is* a full circle moment,' he said, tapping the back of the lounge like a trucker kicking tyres. 'Still as sturdy as ever I see. They really built things to last back in the seventeenth century.'

I tried to speak, but nothing came out. While not ideal, it was a vast improvement on what would have come out several months prior. Mortified at being caught napping, wrinkled and covered in cinnamon scroll crumbs by the man who irreparably fractured my ability to believe in romantic love, I would have lost my lunch and promptly passed out. Not anymore. I was going to be coherent, conscious and communicative. At least for the next thirty seconds.

'What on earth are you doing here?' I asked, although I had a few ideas and they all involved Esmerelda.

'Your leggy *Pazzia* cover model friend out there hitched a ride with me from the airport,' Dylan said, sitting down opposite me.

I attempted to pull myself upright on my chair. 'My *Pazzia* cover model friend? Mother? That's not possible. She's in Bora Bora.' *And,* I thought silently to myself, *she would never get in a car with you.*

'No, not Cat,' he said as if no time had passed, as if we were old friends simply catching up. 'No, her protégé. The odd one. She did the cover of *Pazzia Australia* last summer. She was a bit of an enigma, no name, no details. I'm sure it's her.'

I was completely lost. Last summer had not been a good time for me. But I was not *so* distraught that I had missed an edition of *Pazzia*. Surely no one was ever *that* distraught?

Esmerelda sauntered into the room, looking, if I did not know better, admonished, but still holding onto a fresh cinnamon scroll.

'That's her!' Dylan exclaimed, turning to Esmerelda. 'I could have sworn it was you on that *Pazzia* cover.'

'Dude, like I told you, totally not me,' she said evenly.

'Were you really on the cover of *Pazzia*?' I asked her, astonished.

'Nope and I'm not gonna be again. It's embarrassing. But it definitely wasn't me, so it totally won't be me again.'

Dylan's eyes went wide and his head bobbed along as he tried to understand each word she was saying in its grammatically massacred context. In the end, he seemed to have some level of comprehension, if not a complete understanding.

'Um, anyway, we bumped into each other at the airport, I was just coming in from a short trip to LA, a few things on the boil there.' He smiled his dazzling smile at me. 'And I just couldn't refuse her.'

Esmerelda eyed him. 'Dude, *you* asked *me*.'

He ploughed on. 'Imagine my surprise when she gave your grandmother's place as her address!'

'Nuh-uh,' Esmerelda said, chomping down on her rising irritation with Dylan. 'I totally told you a different address. Like ten doors up.'

'Models,' Dylan said, rolling his eyes playfully. 'So secretive.'

'I'm *not* a model,' Esmerelda growled, taking an angry bite of her scroll.

'I put two and two together: the protégé, the address so close to the mother-in-law's house, and bingo, I found you.'

'Why would you be trying to find me?' I asked, pushing down my rising panic. Had he seen Bettina's video?

'It's just been so long. You know, Indie, you always were the one who got away,' he said, making piercing eye contact.

In the years after the cheating scandal, I had steadfastly managed to avoid almost all contact with Dylan Moss. Being a widower and a social shut-in had not changed my policy on avoidance.

'I was young and stupid,' he said earnestly.

'Eh,' Esmerelda grunted.

Dylan ignored her. 'I don't care about this Heiress on Fire stuff. About the gossip. I'm in PR, you know. I could make the whole flambéed-husband-clueless-bungling-heiress thing go away.'

It was as if he thought his words were in some way helpful or useful or wanted. And who said anything about clueless? Or bungling? *I* was hoping for trusting and slightly clumsy.

He continued. 'You're still my—'

'Would you excuse us for a moment?' I said.

Dylan regarded Esmerelda expectantly. 'If you wouldn't mind.'

'Not you,' I said to Esmerelda. I turned to him. 'You, Dylan. Can you excuse us for a moment?'

And before he had a chance to offer a response, I gestured to the door and thanked him for his patience.

He smiled. 'Of course, Indie, of course. I'll be waiting.'

The second he exited, I pointed to the door and swirled my finger in a motion to close it. Esmerelda trudged to the door and flicked it closed. I then motioned her to come to the opposite side of the room.

'Dude. You're like a mine.'

A mine? A *mime*.

'What happened?' I hissed as she sat down.

'I went to delete the video off the phone, like you said, but the dude was taking selfies the *whole* time. The only way I was getting my hands on his device was to get in the car with him,' she said, irritated. 'He's very touchy about who touches his thing.'

That had not been my experience in high school, but people change.

'Did you delete it?'

'Nope,' she said and picked up her second scroll.

'No?' I exclaimed.

'Nup,' she said, shaking her head.

'You brought him to *me*, to Grandmother's home, into her *private drawing room* no less, but you didn't manage to get rid of the video Bettina sent him? What were you thinking?'

'Dude, chill. First, he's a total tool. Second, I checked it out in the limo,' she said and bit into the scroll. 'He never got no video from the yelly chick.'

'Are you sure?'

'Yeah, totally. I hadda lock him out of his ride to check, so I was thorough.' She touched the teapot, frowning in dismay at its tepid temperature.

'You searched his phone?'

'Totally.' She eyed me. 'Do you wanna know what kinda stuff he had on there? Dude had loads of shots on his roll.'

No, I didn't. Unless … Unless he was still carrying around snaps of me as a sixteen-year-old, which would have done my ego wonders. Especially after the hopeless comment.

'Do I want to know?' I asked her half-heartedly, hedging my bets.

'Nup,' she said, shaking her head with distinct disinterest. She laid herself out on a downy caramel lounge and finished her scroll.

The subject seemed closed.

It had been a close call from the get-go between asking Esmerelda about the success of the mission to erase the humiliating video Bettina had *claimed* she'd sent to Dylan *or* digging into the allegation Dylan had made that Esmerelda was a *Pazzia Australia* cover model.

There was no longer a contest. It was easy for me to accept the idea that Bettina was a liar. That she had never sent the video, if indeed there even *was* a video of me accidentally disrespecting a corpse. I readily believed that she had tricked me. However, the notion Esmerelda had been the summer darling of *Pazzia Australia* editor-in-chief Laurie Heinsmann was a fish of a different colour. Or a dog of a different stripe. Or something very, very different.

'Is Dylan right? Were you on the cover of *Pazzia*?' I asked.

'No way,' she lied. 'That'd be totally humiliating.'

Oh. I see.

When Esmerelda had brought me my fashion magazines last summer, she had told me the front cover of February *Pazzia* was a colour photocopy (which had been sticky-taped on) because the original cover had been ripped off in a car door accident. She had told me I had been blocked from the *Pazzia* website because it had a virus. God, maybe I *was* clueless. Then again, in what universe would I have suspected she had torn the cover off and hacked my devices because she *was* the cover? I mentally added publication fraud, Photoshop and cover model to the list of Esmerelda's special skills. Hacking was already on the list.

I could understand why Esmerelda did not enjoy modelling. Having a mother who was the world's most supreme supermodel for several decades has endowed me with many not-so-glamorous behind-the-scenes experiences. There are things I know.

Modelling casting calls are commonly referred to in the industry as cattle calls. Forty or fifty astonishingly beautiful women are herded in a tiny, decidedly unglamorous room (all of which seem to have the same unpleasant smell of something dry and airless, are painted in the same shade of plaster white or hospital blue, and possess smudged mirrors, one of which is inevitably cracked somewhere) only to be called out one by one into a larger, more glamorous room to see a single powerful client—almost all of whom are male—like a king holding court, evaluating prospective concubines one at a time. Here, the women are judged. Is her hair lustrous enough? Her body mass low enough? It is not unheard of for a model to have her teeth examined, like a horse up for auction. Or to be rejected because she lacks the mythical—ahem, *fictional*—It factor. Sometimes there is the added bonus of all this occurring while almost naked.

Catwalks are not fun; they are terrifying. Heels are high, surfaces are often shiny and slippery, and outfits are complicated and difficult to wear, especially the couture.

Then there are swimsuit shoots. Most models live with rigorous diet and exercise regimes for weeks beforehand, many forgoing even fluids for the final twenty-four hours, all for the privilege of standing in freezing water for hours on end, sand wedged in all the wrong places, wind in their face, salt and sun in their eyes, being told to look sexually aroused. What's not glamorous about that?

But landing the cover of a stalwart fashion behemoth like *Pazzia*, *Vogue*, *Elle*, *Harper's BAZAAR*, *Marie Claire* or *Vanity Fair*, waning readerships or no, has long been and remains a coveted honour. It is not just the prestige of being chosen for a cover, being shot for a cover and being recognised as one of the elite, the few, the anointed; it's the leverage the cover gives you. From covers can come insanely lucrative cosmetic and fashion house contracts. Contracts in the five, six, seven and even eight figures.

And power. Do enough high fashion covers and there are no more cattle calls, just meets in cafés or restaurants or resorts, where your value is carefully and respectfully negotiated by your agent *and* your manager.

Although Esmerelda had never taken to modelling, I was sure she liked money. Truthfully, I didn't *specifically* know if she did or didn't. One just assumes everyone does. Especially those who have been in prison, are willing to accept slightly tainted diamonds as bonuses and know how to pick a lock with a ring pull from a No-Sugar Vanilla Coke can.

'Far be it from me to outright call you a fibber, Esmerelda,' I said innocently, 'but if I called Laurie Heinsmann at *Pazzia* and asked him if he knew you, what would he say?'

'He's a total asshole,' she said quickly. 'You don't wanna talk to him.'

'So it *is* true!' I gasped. 'You made the cover of *Pazzia*? And the summer edition?'

'Like, that's not what I said,' she defended.

'Oh, so if I google the *Pazzia* February cover, what will I find?' I enquired.

Silence. And a deathly stare.

The irony was that the poutier and more petulant she became, the more she looked like a supermodel. I went back to my original question.

'How about I just call Heinsmann?'

Normally, I asked Esmerelda to look up numbers and then dial them for me. That would not work in this instance. Fortunately, Grandmother was old-school and there were landline phones all over the mansion, including one in the drawing room (which had a cord and a rotary dial face). Were there still operators at the end of dial tones? How did one dial Google on a rotary phone?

'Dude's a frigging psycho,' she said resentfully. 'A full-blown psycho.'

She had me there. It was an open secret in the industry that Heinsmann was unhinged.

'He's also a genius. The two things do sometimes go together,' I said truthfully.

Come to think of it, turning 'unhinged' into 'genius' was masterful PR on Heinsmann's behalf. Perhaps I could turn my 'bungling' label into 'artistic' or 'original', my 'clueless' status into 'non-judgemental'? And when I say 'I' I do mean someone else. Someone professional. Someone *not* Dylan Moss.

Esmerelda shot me a look of revolt and disgust.

'*Pazzia* is now the only fashion magazine that has run a profit in hard copy and digital for the past three quarters straight,' I said. I really had to stop listening to so many podcasts poolside; they were too chock-full of accidental learning. 'The only other magazines making a profit in hard copy these days are gossip mags,' I said with a nose wrinkle.

'Dude's a psycho,' she repeated.

'Mental health is no joke,' I said.

She stared at me in a unique blend of frustration and earnestness. 'I'm totally not joking. He's *legit* psycho. Won't leave me alone. Calls friggin' constantly. Sends me stuff.'

'Heinsmann?'

'Yes, Heinsmann!'

'Calls you? Esmerelda?'

I was having difficulty wrapping my head around the concept.

'He like totally wants me to do this thing. Dude won't go away,' she said seriously. 'He's, like, a little ... scary.'

In the short time we had known each other, Esmerelda and I had faced some uniquely terrifying and intimidating characters, none of whom had seized her attention. But Laurie Heinsmann, an effeminate middle-aged magazine editor, apparently troubled her.

'What does he send you?' I asked.

Horses' heads? Dead fish wrapped in newspaper? Roses with their heads snipped off?

She leaned in conspiratorially. '*Gucci* sneakers,' she said with disgust. 'Chanel sneakers. Like, hello? What the fuc— frig, right?'

'Heinsmann sent you Gucci and Chanel and from that you got psychotic?'

Personally, I questioned the mental health of someone who thought turning down free Gucci and Chanel was problematic.

'*Sneakers!*' she said earnestly and leaned back, as if that answered the question.

Honestly, some puzzles are more complicated than others, and some puzzles are just, well, puzzling.

'But you love sneakers,' I said, walking straight into the trap.

'Dude, I love *real* kicks. They're not real. Do you know what would happen if I went around in Gucci sneakers? My rep would be trashed.'

You can't die on every hill. What I really wanted to say was, 'Are they Ace? Or Rhyton platform? If so, I can dispose of them.' But I didn't. I let it go. Getting to the end of this conversation was worth more to me. I could buy the sneakers, not that I would; sneakers were not really my 'thing', unless they were select Jimmy Choos and were free, and then I would be willing to try them on. But time spent scurrying down the rabbit hole with Esmerelda? I could not buy that back.

'Okay,' I said, pressing forward. 'Apart from the shoes, what seems to be the problem? Why is he scary?'

It could not be sexual harassment. Esmerelda was over twenty-one and not a nubile young man fresh off the cover of *GQ* or *Men's Health* with abs and skin like a baby's tooshie, if a baby's tooshie was tanned to perfection, as was Heinsmann's preference.

Silence.

This was going to be good.

'Esmerelda?'

She touched the teapot again, as if it may have magically warmed up in the past ten minutes. I picked up the rotary dial phone from the Burr Walnut Queen Anne coffee table and ordered more tea.

We waited in silence for two minutes until the tea arrived.

The tea was poured.

I sipped the tea.

At this stage in my spiritual growth, three minutes was my Zen maximum.

'So?' I prompted, stretching out the word to leave no room for interpretation that I would be requiring a definitive answer.

'He like *totally* suckered me. When I signed the deal for the cover last summer, I didn't realise it was a two-cover deal.'

I am sure she *used* to be better at flat-out lying to me. Perhaps I can just see it with greater clarity these days. I raised my eyebrows in a rhetorical, *I don't believe you* manner and pressed my lips together to convey the same sentiment.

She exhaled heavily in exasperation. 'Fine. Like, I knew a tiny bit it was a contract for two covers. But, like, I didn't think he'd wanna go again.'

And then it hit me. 'You mean he's sending you designer shoes—'

'And flowers. And clothes. And booze. And bags, and—' she paused in disbelief, '—make-up!'

I started over. 'The editor-in-chief of *Pazzia* is sending you all manner of free designer swag because he wants to put you on the cover? Again? For the second time in less than a year? Essentially cementing you as Australia's most desirable model.'

I tried to hide my astonishment while making a mental note to circle back to the exact whereabouts of the Heinsmann gifted clothes, handbags, cosmetics and designer goodies.

'Yep. This totally sucks. I only did the first cover 'cause I was desperate. Without the modelling stuff, I would've been unemployed and like, broke my parole. This was before I became your personal shopper, before you set Richard and Crystal on fire—'

'—accidentally,' we chorused together.

She nodded. 'Yeah, totally. Anyway, Eddy said it was a good gig.'

Eddy was mother's long-time manager. And after a string of managers who were thieves and incompetents early in her career, a godsend.

'Eddy was absolutely correct. A *Pazzia* cover is an incredible step in anyone's career.'

I explained to her about the power of the cover model. No cattle calls. Big contracts. Big opportunities. Big money. Lots of people being nice to you.

'Still totally not worth it. I'm just, like, not into it.'

'But—' I said, attempting, against my better judgement and biases *against* modelling, to explain the many advantages of being an uber model.

'Indigo, dude,' she implored. 'I don't *wanna*.'

It was simple really. Someone was offering to make her a princess. But she didn't *want* to be a princess. I was pretty sure she would have been happy to have the financial resources, the palaces, the chefs, the jets, the holidays, all the luxuries that came with being a royal, but she did not want the fine print. She didn't want to be tied up by the many anti-freedom strings, conditions and expectations that came with the role.

For not the first time, I thought Esmerelda might have been a genius.

Or a spiritual guru.

Or maybe she just didn't like the work.

'I'd rather do this,' she said, leaning forward on the lounge, pointing her finger enthusiastically backwards and forwards between herself and I. After a few moments, she caught herself and stopped her hand gesturing. Her cheeks warmed slightly under her flawless tan.

I didn't know what to say so I didn't say anything. But somewhere, something hidden deep, *deep* inside me became exponentially happy.

Esmerelda rolled off the lounge and sauntered towards the door. The second she turned the handle, Dylan slid back in through the crack. He missed touching her by mere inches.

His charming smile was lost on her.

'Like, you're a total douche,' she said matter-of-factly, and left.

I noticed all the cinnamon scrolls were gone and the fun felt like it had departed the room too.

'She's a feisty one,' Dylan said, ignoring the insult and strolling, uninvited, back in.

He had no idea.

'Tough too,' he said, checking the door had closed completely. 'She almost got taken out by an enormous row of renegade luggage trolleys at the airport. It was like a runaway train. I managed to move her out of the way just in time. I don't mind saying it scared me a little. But she didn't bat an eye!'

I didn't know if he was telling the truth or not; either way, I had little interest in his story. 'I'm tired,' I said, and I was. 'It's been an eventful day.'

'I heard,' Dylan said, switching gears and pulling a single chair, leg to leg close to my lounge. 'The staff told me you found a body in the garden this morning! A homeless guy who'd wandered in from the Cross, they said. I can only imagine how horrible that was.'

He sat down and leaned towards me. He was very close. He smelt the same as he had in high school, of Kouros by YSL. By today's standards (and possibly by standards in my teens), it was not a sophisticated scent; however, it remained for me, against all common sense, highly charged and bluntly alluring.

The last time he was this close to me ...

I found myself in a mental time machine that involved the kind of intense and wonderous kissing, stroking, touching and ... well, other things that happen in that magical time between your first teen kiss and your first time. I was so enamoured with that particular transition period, I managed to stretch it out for many, many years.

For me, one of the great benefits of pre-sex romance was that while there were substantial amounts of hope, there was no precedent. That left plenty of space for ambition and creativity.

Dylan was creative *and* ambitious. We played almost every note in every symphony a youth orchestra can play. Repeatedly. With movement variations. But we didn't play the *final* symphony. Dylan chose to have his rollicking finale with Tiffany Goldstein—while we were still dating. Yes, he was a horrible cheater, but he was magical in other areas.

He set the bar high for every man who came after. Searing was one of the few who had sailed easily over. I suspected James Smith could clear that bar without even touching a woman.

You never forget the first few notes and I could see from his expression that Dylan was about to kiss me. A picture formed in my mind of Dylan's hands roaming up a thigh clad in a SILC school skirt, but it wasn't my skirt. Or my thigh.

I was transported back to the moment I found them together. The horror smacked me in the face like the first cold wave of an ocean swim, mortification washing over me. My stomach dropped and my face burned with humiliation. I knew what was coming and I embraced it. I passed out, falling gracefully backwards into my baroque lounge like a seventeenth-century heroine.

'Still?' I heard Dylan splutter in astonishment.

I knew I would wake up somewhere lovely and Dylan Moss would be gone. I was right. It was a good day after all.

CHAPTER 5

NOTHING DOING

A week later, I had managed to avoid Dylan and Searing and do absolutely nothing whatsoever to identify the dead homeless man in the lilies. That job belonged to Rope and Winters.

I had every intention of telling Dame Elizabeth I could not possibly be of any assistance, but the time just never seemed right. There were three unprecedented thirty-degree spring days that required swimming and sunbaking. Dior, Hermès *and* Alex Perry had sales—two days' work. And it took Esmerelda and I the best part of a day to figure out how to hang the new paintings in the pool house. I did not feel it terribly wise to bring in professional help to hang art so recently *repurposed*.

I tried to find an Esmerelda-free device to google her *Pazzia* cover. But devices untouched by Esmerelda were thin on the ground. Eventually I had to ask her to find me one, at which point she used a word so shocking, so unprecedented, that I agreed to stop searching for the cover photo. That word was *please*. I was speechless for at least thirty seconds.

Mother remained overseas with Jed and although I had the run of the estate, I stayed in the pool house. It was cosy and her staff were on call but not living with me. Esmerelda, for reasons unknown, chose not to divulge the location of her permanent residence, but was, for the time being, and with Mother's blessing, living in the main house.

There simply was no time to investigate the identity of the dead man. Plus, I didn't want to. While it was true I didn't have a job, it was also true that I didn't *want* a job, and if I *did* want a job, it would *not* be identifying dead people for Australian royalty. I still had many months of entitled widow mourning ahead of me before there was even a hint of expectation that I 'do something' with my life. Besides, I *was* doing something: shopping. I was patriotically supporting the Australian economy. And the Italian economy. And the French economy.

I was sitting on my bed, buying shoes online, when I heard it. The dreaded knock. Anyone knocking on a pool house door had already made it through security in the main house (that is, mother's maid, Patricia), through the somewhat giant and meandering house proper, down the garden path, past the gardens, courts, pool and outdoor staff and, most frighteningly, past Esmerelda.

In my advanced state of vigilance, the opening of my bedroom window mere metres away made me jump.

'Like, your nanna's here,' Esmerelda said, leaning into the room through the hip-high window she had surreptitiously opened. From the outside.

There was no way my grandmother was hand-to-wood knocking on a door. I had never seen it done. I pointed towards the front door. 'My grandmother is actually knocking?'

Esmerelda withdrew her head from inside the room to check the status of the door.

'Nup, some other chick's doing the knocking,' she reported.

There was a second knock, small and polite. If a knock was refined, this was it. I was filled with a sense of dread. 'An older lady? Looks like she supports the arts? And gardening?'

'Dude?' Esmerelda said, shooting me a look.

'Okay, looks like a slightly cooler, younger version of the Queen?'

She popped her head out again. 'Oh yeah! Totally. She's super cute.'

God help me.

'Could you take care of it?' I asked hopefully.

'I like, don't work for you. Answer your own door.'

'You *do* work for me,' I reminded her.

'I think I might still like, technically be your personal shopper. This is totally not shopping.'

She had me there.

Only Esmerelda could describe one of the world's richest women and the country's biggest philanthropist as 'your nanna' and 'some other chick' who was 'super cute'.

'For goodness sake, Elizabeth!' I heard Grandmother's impatient voice chastise before the handle turned and the unlocked front door opened. 'Just walk in!' I could picture her rolling her eyes at poor Dame Elizabeth.

'You are such an impatient old bull,' Dame Elizabeth said in a voice I felt certain she reserved for use on Grandmother alone. 'What if she has company?'

'With the fleetingly friendly felon hanging out of her bedroom window?' Grandmother said. I could imagine her glaring at Dame Elizabeth while pointing at Esmerelda half-in, half-out of my bedroom window.

'Your nanna totally remembers me!' Esmerelda beamed proudly.

The sound of footsteps in the hall was closely followed by the two matriarchal women entering my bedroom.

'Dudes. I mean chicks. I mean ladies,' she said by way of greeting.

Esmerelda's road to self-improvement was paved with rocky road.

'Grandmother! Dame Elizabeth!' I exclaimed in false delight. 'What are you two doing here?'

'The better question is, what are *you* doing here?' Grandmother demanded, removing several crisp Dior shopping bags from a cream satin club chair and offering it to Dame Elizabeth. Dame Elizabeth accepted, plucking a wet bikini from a green silk tufted shell chair opposite her and, after pressing the damp patch with a hanky from her purse, offered it to Grandmother.

It was an unfortunate turn of interior design events that the only table in my bedroom, a lovely German-designed one-piece sandalwood affair with the smoothest polish, sat almost directly underneath the very window that, at least temporarily, housed Esmerelda.

The dame, the dragon and the degenerate.

'Well? Why are you here?' Grandmother repeated.

I was lost. Where was I supposed to be? I opened my mouth to speak but Dame Elizabeth beat me.

Putting her hand on Grandmother's, she said, 'Don't be so hard on her, Florence! Perhaps there is a reason they are recreating?'

I had never noticed it before, but the two of them had a patter going. They played off one another with such ease, it was clear this was a rhythm they had honed over many years. And, quite possibly, many cognacs.

'After all, it has barely been a week. Perhaps they are having a break?'

'Dude!' Esmerelda snorted to Dame Elizabeth. 'Like, her whole life is a break.'

'You will notice Dame Elizabeth used the plural, not the singular,' Grandmother said to Esmerelda.

Esmerelda may not have been a grammatical whizz but she instinctively knew when she was being insulted. She narrowed her eyes at Grandmother and stood straight in the window frame. Flat-footed or not, she was intimidating at her full height, and surf-slack Esmerelda disappeared, replaced with street hustler, gut-you-with-a-rusty-butter-knife Esmerelda. The tension in the room accelerated.

I had a horrible sinking feeling I knew what the passive-aggressive duo were implying.

'You think we should be out hunting down the identity of the man who died in your garden?' I asked, desperately hoping I was wrong.

'Is there another task requiring your urgent attention?' Grandmother lobbied, eyeing the glossy shopping bags lining the bedroom walls.

'But Grandmother—' I began, getting to my feet.

'Don't give me that widow-in-mourning spiel,' she growled. 'That only works on your hapless mother. God knows it would have worked on my son.'

Dame Elizabeth silently crossed herself at the mention of my dead father.

Grandmother pulled herself straight in the shell chair. 'I may have coddled you for too long when he passed.' She paused to structure the next sentence, probably to include a plausible deniability clause. Wise. She had essentially run my life from the time my father died until I married Richard. Then I may have let Richard do it.

The point was, *I* was running things now.

'Indigo, dear,' Dame Elizabeth said, taking over. 'I think what your grandmother is trying to say is that too much pity is not good for one's soul.'

'Definitely,' Esmerelda said, accidentally releasing some of her intensity. She immediately crossed her arms at Grandmother in compensation for the lapse.

'I'm not sure I understand the direct correlation between an end in my mourning period and my ...' I thought about it and, taking into consideration the intense look on Grandmother's face and the look of—what was that? Concern?—on Dame Elizabeth's face, rephrased from the singular to the plural, '... *our* finding the identity of the man in your garden. With all due respect, again, I really do think the police are the best people for that job.'

'I'm sure Detective Winters is a very capable officer,' Dame Elizabeth said, failing to mention his less astute partner, Rope. 'However, I believe you, you *two*,' she said, looking up at Esmerelda in the window, 'are uniquely qualified.'

I had assumed when she'd asked me to investigate the dead man's identity the week before, it was more of an off-the-cuff request, an emotional appeal in the moment, soon forgotten. Why was she so determined to identify him?

'Like, you seem like a sweet old lady,' Esmerelda said, sensing my scepticism, 'and I'm not saying I'm *not* awesome at investigating stuff, but, like I feel like there's some shady bullsh—'

'Oh, uh,' I interrupted. 'I wonder—we wonder, Dame Elizabeth, *why* you think we are so uh, uniquely qualified? Why you feel we would have any more luck than the police. *Professionals*.' I thought back to Detective Rope. Maybe professional was a stretch. 'Professionally trained police.'

'She doesn't need to give you a reason, Indigo,' Grandmother snapped. 'Dame Elizabeth made a request of you; you accepted. You're obligated to follow through.'

I sometimes wondered how being overseas on business so often had impacted my relationship with my grandmother. Did she know me at all?

'Like, I totally didn't agree to working with the cops,' Esmerelda put in, shaking her head, leaning back, arms still crossed.

'Oh, no, you would not need to work *with* the police, dear,' Dame Elizabeth said with her patient doe eyes and soft smile. 'They needn't even know you're having a quiet look around.'

'Oh,' Esmerelda said, relaxing her arms. 'I could totally be into it then. Wait,' she backtracked. 'I'm getting paid, right?'

'Is she paying you?' Grandmother gestured to me.

'Yeah,' Esmerelda said, insulted.

'Then yes, you will be paid.'

So, Esmerelda *did* like money.

'Thrilled you two were able to come to an agreement,' I chimed. 'I'm so sorry, but I'm busy.'

'Doing what, may I enquire?' Grandmother asked, casting a lazy eye around the dishevelled room. My bedroom was strewn with half-unboxed shopping packages, shopping bags, wet towels, a half-eaten fruit platter, a tea tray, two sets of wet bathers (to avoid tan lines without the embarrassment of going topless, one needed swimmers with a variety of strap lines), a recently closed laptop, a mostly eaten box of Maltesers and a stack of magazines. The magazines may not have been stacked so much as scattered. At least the bed was made. Okay, so Patricia made the bed.

'I am assisting Esmerelda with a legal matter,' I said, eating one of the remaining Maltesers.

'What?' spurted Esmerelda who, once alerted to the presence of chocolate, had managed to lean in through the window, scoop up a fistful of the candy and half consume it. She had the reflexes of a hummingbird and the metabolism to match.

'Yes,' I said, trying to telepathically signal her to go along. 'She has a rather sticky situation with Laurie Heinsmann.'

'*Pazzia*'s Laurie Heinsmann?' Dame Elizabeth asked, surprised.

Grandmother glanced at Dame Elizabeth for verification of the name.

Unlike artistically inclined Dame Elizabeth, Grandmother held little genuine interest or heartfelt regard for fashion beyond it being an expensive annoyance. She had a stylist who shopped and chose her outfits, outfits she wore because it was expected that the head of a billion-dollar company dress a certain way, and because wearing a $10,000 Jil Sander jacket and matching $8,000 pants intimidated people. Moreover, *not* wearing a $20,000 outfit might give some in the business community the impression you were suffering financial restrictions. One misplaced rumour about fiscal vulnerability and sharks started circling. Cauterising that kind of rumour inevitably costs substantially more than a designer wardrobe.

'He's after me,' Esmerelda said between malty bites, crumbs falling from her perfect mouth onto the table.

Dame Elizabeth appeared charmed by this. Wide-eyed recognition crossed her face. 'You're the mystery cover girl, aren't you? How delightful!'

Esmerelda's eyes narrowed, the happy-go-lucky crunching disappearing. I thought she might attempt to bite Dame Elizabeth.

'No, no,' I quickly corrected, sitting down opposite the pair. 'Not delightful. We are not delighted. Esmerelda would very much like to be discharged from her contractual obligations to Heinsmann.'

'I don't understand. Promotional obligations for the summer issue must have finished many months ago. What further commitments could she have?'

I rolled my eyes. 'She accidentally signed a two-cover deal.'

'The pen just slipped out of her hand and onto the contract, did it?' Grandmother said.

Esmerelda gave Grandmother a single, sharply arched, never-seen-tweezers-in-its-life eyebrow in addition to her death stare. 'Yeah. It slipped.'

'You seem like a sweet young lady,' Dame Elizabeth said, quick as an old fox, 'and I'm not saying you're not *awesome*, but I too know a line of BS when I hear one.'

This got a wry chuckle out of Grandmother.

I was speechless. I had never heard Dame Elizabeth utter anything remotely resembling profanity before. Not a crap or a damn or even a darn.

Esmerelda swallowed whatever was left of her Maltesers and said, 'You've got a kind of petrifying pink sugar vibe going on. Like, you're totally on-the-down-low scary.'

I agreed. It was most disconcerting.

'Esmerelda didn't think Heinsmann would want a second cover,' I blurted, slightly throwing Esmerelda under the bus.

'*That* I believe,' Grandmother grunted.

Esmerelda side-eyed me. 'You're totally crap at this game.'

'I can see it,' Dame Elizabeth said, assessing Esmerelda. 'Esmerelda has something.'

Esmerelda had something? That was an insult opening too wide for Grandmother to resist walking through and if Dame Elizabeth was a nine out of ten on the down-low-scary scale, Esmerelda was a twelve. Despite appearances, my bedroom had been cleaned that morning. Blood would leave a terrible mess.

I quickly interjected. 'I'm busy trying to get her out of the contract. I would otherwise have loved to help you. Sorry.'

'I can have a word with Laurie Heinsmann. I'm sure he can be persuaded to nullify the contract,' Dame Elizabeth said. 'That would free you two up, wouldn't it?'

'Deal!' Esmerelda said, poking her long, tanned arm through the window at Dame Elizabeth. Dame Elizabeth had her hand pumped by Esmerelda. My fate had been sealed without my consent. Again.

'You're not so hot at this game yourself,' I muttered to Esmerelda.

Grandmother stood to leave. 'We're all in agreement then.'

'No!' I squealed, bolting up off the chair. 'Not in agreement. I … I have … I am …'

'I simply do not have time for this,' Grandmother said, briskly walking to the door. 'I have a twelve o'clock.'

'It's already one thirty,' Esmerelda said, peering at the sun. She was like a surfing mystic, divining the time.

'It *is* one thirty!' Dame Elizabeth said in delight, looking at her watch. 'Esmerelda, you *are* special!'

Esmerelda attempted to fist-bump Dame Elizabeth in response.

Grandmother narrowed her eyes and said flatly, 'My twelve o'clock is midnight in New York.' To me she said, 'You borrowed two important paintings from the main salon in my Sydney home last week. I can either view that— and I do mean "view that" literally—event as grand larceny, or I can view it as granddaughter loan-ery. What's it to be?'

As out-of-character as her flagrant blackmail and almost playful grammatical aside was, it was not enough to suppress the spike of panic that ran through me. She *could* be serious. She was my grandmother, but she was also seriously controlling and a complete barracoota.

Grand larceny. There was video. There could be memes. This was neither Good Behaviour nor Zero Publicity. My legs grew instantly weak.

'No! No, you don't!' she barked. 'No fainting! It was bad enough I had to put up with it from your grandfather. You could be twice the man he was if you just put your back into it, Indigo!' She leaned towards me, one hand on the door. 'You need a purpose. A drive. As sad as Richard's passing was, it pumped some jazz back into you.'

'Back?'

'You were an extraordinary child, Indigo,' Dame Elizabeth said with a smile. She patted me on the arm as she stood. 'So curious!'

'That's not true,' I said weakly. I had no recollection of ever having 'jazz' or being 'extraordinary' or 'curious'. Had I been?

'I'm not here to chat with you or cuddle you. I am your grandmother.'

Dame Elizabeth regarded Grandmother with an ironic gaze. Perhaps those were indeed the qualities of a grand-mother? It was lost on her.

'Grand larceny or granddaughter loan-ery?'

'Loan-ery,' I said, deflated.

'Excellent,' she said, all business. 'Elizabeth, you have your undercover investigators.'

'I am ever so pleased!' Dame Elizabeth squeezed me with a hug in clear view of Grandmother. Nothing like a little blackmail to embolden the hidden intimacies in one's relationships.

I was flabbergasted. How on earth was I going to find the identity of the homeless man from the oriental lilies? And what did she mean by 'undercover investigators'? Perhaps I could appeal to Dame Elizabeth's reasonable side.

'Dame, I mean, Aunt Lizzy,' I said, desperately clinging to her arm. 'While I appreciate your incredible generosity of spirit in attempting to give that man a resting place, this all seems a little ... extreme.'

'Tell her, Elizabeth,' Grandmother said, holding onto the door handle, the expression on her face saying she was actively resisting the urge to tap her foot with impatience.

Dame Elizabeth made a flapping motion past the front of her face with her left hand. 'Oh, it's nothing. I'm sure it's completely unrelated.'

'Her boyfriend stood her up the night before the body was found and he's been missing ever since.'

Boyfriend? Dame Elizabeth?

'Knew it!' Esmerelda exclaimed to everyone. 'What'd I say? BS shady!'

'No, no, that is not it at all,' Dame Elizabeth defended. 'I do *not* have a boyfriend. Max is a friend. Max and the man you found—' she stumbled.

'In the lilies,' I helped.

'Yes,' she said, recovering her footing, 'are different people. The man you found in the lilies is *not* Max. Max spends almost as much on his wardrobe as your grandmother. Unlike your grandmother, he makes *some* attempt to wear our wonderful Australian designers as well as those *European* ones.' And with that, she gave Grandmother's not-remotely-locally-designed-or-made ensemble a satirical scan. 'Max is unlikely to be mistaken for a homeless person while dressed head to toe in Armani. No, I wanted you to find that poor lily man's name and family so he could be buried, *not* frozen, just as I said to you on the day. No, Max cancelled our dinner at the last moment because he had an urgent family matter to attend to at home, in Western Australia.' She eyed Grandmother. 'He said he would be away for a few days, and so he has been. It's a coincidence, that is all.'

I could see Esmerelda doing maths. Mainly because her fingers were moving.

'Eight days,' I said, articulating for her.

'Yeah,' Esmerelda said, nodding in agreement. 'It's been like eight days since we, I mean she, found the dead dude.'

'Eight is a few,' Dame Elizabeth said, not noticing Esmerelda's slip. She unpeeled my fingers from around her wrist and walked towards Grandmother.

'Like more like a few few,' Esmerelda whispered, leaning into the window frame.

'Besides, we have only been … friends for a short while. He is not obliged to call me every day,' Dame Elizabeth said, joining Grandmother at the open bedroom door.

'Two months,' Grandmother piped. 'For over two months, you two have been attached at the hip. The man was clearly gaga.'

Esmerelda looked quizzically at Grandmother, then at me.

'No,' I said before she could ask. 'Nothing to do with Lady Gaga.'

'You *are* being dramatic, Florence,' Dame Elizabeth said, following Grandmother into the hallway. 'Max will call when he is ready.' She turned back to address us through the doorway. 'Just find out who the man in the lilies was.'

A moment later, the front door closed and they were gone.

Esmerelda gave a guarded smile and a nod in the direction of the departing duo. 'I dunno how he got homeless so quick, but her boyfriend is totally toast.'

'Max is *not* the man in the lilies,' I said optimistically, wondering how many bottles of wine were currently chilling in the pool house fridge. 'It's just a coincidence.'

'Dude,' she said in mild exasperation. 'Seriously?'

I had a sinking feeling she might be right. The manicure. The cutthroat shave. The hair oil. Although, theoretically, a homeless man *could* have shaved and manicured himself. He might have been an extremely hygienic, well-groomed homeless man.

'How much is a bottle of Atkinsons California Poppy Hair Oil?' I asked.

'Can't find the oil, but the aftershave is two hundred and twelve bucks,' Esmerelda said five seconds later, staring at *her* one true love, the latest smartphone.

God help us. Was Dame Elizabeth dating a dead man?

CHAPTER 6

THE NO-FLY LIST

There was no wine left in the pool house fridge. I spent the afternoon drinking gin and tonics, pondering how Dame Elizabeth's dashing new boyfriend could have wound up dirty, dishevelled and dead in her neighbour's garden. I could not think of any.

Esmerelda was unable to make Bettina's drowned phone function again. This was a surprise because Esmerelda's ability to make smartphones bend to her will was freakishly impressive. Although the newer models were water resistant Bettina's 'totally ancient' handset was unable to resist Grandmother's fountain, which was apparently more chlorine than water.

Definitively deleting the possible footage of me tripping over the dead man, who was conceivably Dame Elizabeth's missing suitor Max, was not possible without a working handset. To ensure the footage was either non-existent or contained within the defunct phone and not sitting on a cloud somewhere, we were going to have to go to the source. It seemed that no matter where I turned, I could not avoid the Holly clan.

Dame Elizabeth Holly's family of origin, the Hansons, had somewhat humble beginnings. Their fortune of origin story was that they'd sailed from England with nineteen dairy cows in tow (three bulls and fourteen cows survived the journey), hoping the grass was greener on the other side. The grass was not greener in Australia; however, millennia of fastidious agricultural care by the First Australians meant the land *was* ripe for the grazing. Within fifty years, the Hansons had the largest dairy farm on the east coast. Twenty years after that, they had the largest group of dairy farms on the east coast. The Hanson family had a lot of new money, but no social reputation or standing. To rectify this, Dame Elizabeth, then plain old Elizabeth Hanson, the only child and heir to the somewhat distasteful Hanson dairy cow fortune, was married off to Earl Alexander Holly.

Earl Holly didn't have two farthings to rub together, but he was in possession of respectable lineage, a title and high social connections. While Earl Holly was, by all accounts, much like his father-in-law Dashiell Hanson—extremely proficient in organising female company—he was unlike his father-in-law—*not* proficient in business.

Dashiell Hanson's wild financial success and his eventual monopolisation of the dairy industry, along with his and his son-in-law's flagrant philandering, meant that rumours about the Hanson-Holly family were rife. Mrs Hanson was, apparently, lost between her domineering husband, Dashiell, and her bombastic son-in-law, Earl Holly. She spent most of her time in town, buying furnishings for a country home she steadfastly avoided visiting.

Luckily for young Dame Elizabeth Holly, who was then known as Lady Elizabeth Holly, her husband, Earl Holly, spent most of *his* time in Turkey, investing in technology to mass-produce women's shoes. His endeavours were unsuccessful and he died of malaria in Istanbul a month before his forty-seventh birthday. Her father died soon after in a bull stampede. Her mother never visited any of the farms ever again.

Ironically, once *Lady* Elizabeth Holly was given a damehood—for her years of philanthropic work—and became *Dame* Elizabeth Holly, she outranked her husband, Earl Holly, dead or alive.

Dame Elizabeth's eldest son Astor, who had barely survived after being born premature, defied the odds and grew to be a business powerhouse. He took the reins of the dairy farms before he was even out of university. Astor was quite a lot like Mother: tall, blond, very attractive and insanely eco-friendly. Unlike Mother, Astor came from a very wealthy family, had an amazing nose for business at a young age, never married and had thus far produced no heirs (good news for his next-of-kin nieces, Bettina and Gilly, and their father, Astor's only sibling, Gregory).

Astor was well ahead of the ideological curve in his understanding of cows, methane and global warming. He diversified the family's interests, first adding real estate, then digital technology stocks. Being a man of environmental consciousness and action, he eventually sold the family's dairy assets and bought a successful chain of eco-friendly hotels, branding them Holly Oak. He then used the financial resources of their technology stocks to develop the real estate holdings he had accumulated into luxury Holly Park resorts, quickly building a hotel and resort empire. For most people, the dairy farms are a distant memory. For the younger generations, not even that. Born just eleven months after Astor, Gregory was, like his father and grandfather, a serial womaniser.

When Astor declined his father's title, Gregory eagerly snatched it up. He had no moral qualms about living off 'family money' (made by Astor), no qualms about asking for more than allotted, and no desire to produce any money himself. Gregory's short-suffering wife, Sue-Anne, died when Bettina and Gilly were young. Rumours once again swished around the Hollys, this time postulating Sue-Anne had left Gregory for a more loyal, useful human. However, I distinctly recall Grandmother flying in to attend Sue-Anne's funeral. After a bad experience in the 1980s, Grandmother only attended funerals once her lawyers had checked death certificates and, where possible, corpses. Sue-Anne was most certainly dead.

Theoretically, Astor, Gregory, Bettina and Gilly all work in the family business headquartered at the flagship Holly Park Sydney. As well as being the award-winning, hands-on General Manager of the Holly Park Sydney, Astor is also the CEO of Holly Family Holdings, the parent company that owns all the Holly family holdings and companies.

From what I had heard, Bettina was the manager of internal organic fabric acquisitions. This meant she bossed around a team of unfortunate hotel employees under the pretence of finding eco-friendly bamboo napkins, tablecloths, sheets and towels for the Holly Park hotels. This gave Bettina an excellent excuse to spend many months of the year travelling around the world, staying at various family-owned six-star resorts, buying organically certified linens on the company's Visa Infinite.

Gilly apparently described herself as head of organic food paradigms. This sounded like heiress-speak for eating out on the company card and posting photographs of meals on Facebook and Instagram. She was undoubtably often out-of-office.

Gregory was, if I recalled correctly, technically one of the managers at the Holly Park Sydney. However, his 'allergies' meant that he could only work in Sydney for three months of the year. It was with some incongruity that those three months were always spring. While *Lord* Gregory Holly's title found no purchase in Australia, he had greater luck overseas. Perhaps his desire to be called Lord, along with his desire not to work, was what kept him out of the country so often.

Dame Elizabeth, being the matriarch, outranked all of them, fiscally and socially. She worked exclusively at giving the family fortune away to the less fortunate, and the artistically inclined.

Although I steadfastly avoided Bettina and Gilly (and, truth be told, their father Gregory too), I only seemed to manage to avoid Bettina. This led me to believe that Bettina did *actually* work consistently at the hotel. Or she put as much effort into avoiding me. If I assumed both things were true, then it stood to reason that the best place to find her would be the Holly Park Sydney.

After consuming a comfortable level of beverages, opening my unopened shopping packages, patting my newest pair of heels and having my hair and make-up redone by Franny, I was still not ready to go.

I had made it as far as the main house and was in the kitchen re-checking Mother's vast walk-in pantry for signs of pre-made carbohydrate life. Apart from Patricia's home-made jam, there were none.

'Dude,' Esmerelda said, sticking her head into the pantry. 'It's like dark out.'

That was a statement and not a question. Therefore, it didn't require an answer.

'If you wanna check there's no video of you stacking it, we've gotta go find this chick. Then we've gotta figure out how to figure out if dead homeless dude is actually dead boyfriend dude.'

'Do you really think the dead man was Max?' I asked, backing out of the pantry.

'Yep. The dead dude is totally Max.'

'If that's true then there is no work to do. We have successfully identified the man in the lilies. It's Max. Max … what did she say his last name was?' I asked, hoping she had heard more than me.

'No clue,' she said, walking across the kitchen.

'Well,' I said, seating myself at the giant Karri breakfast bar that was the centrepiece of Mother's kitchen, 'if we find Max's last name, his family, we can give that information to the police. Mystery solved.'

'Like, your nanna said *undercover*. I don't think *undercover* includes the cops,' she said, pulling both French doors of the refrigerator open. A disappointed, resigned expression crossed her face and she shook her head as she mumbled, 'Bloody fruit. Nothin' but bloody fruit.'

I gave the undercover comment some thought. 'Well, we could tell Dr Bailly then.'

Esmerelda's head popped out from behind the fridge door. 'Dr who?'

'Dr Bailly. She examined the body.' Albeit briefly.

I could hear tech searching noises, *click, click, click.* Esmerelda had her phone out while her head was in the fridge. 'Dr Jemima Bailly?' she wanted to know.

Jemima could be Jem. 'Yes?'

'She's a forensic pathologist,' Esmerelda said, reading from the screen and emerging with a banana and an apple. 'She works at the ah, the Forensic Medicine and Coroners Court Complex. So, she like, works *with* the cops. But she's *not* a cop.'

'She didn't seem very fond of Detective Rope,' I said.

'She totally sounds like our chick then,' Esmerelda said, biting into the apple. 'We find out about this Max dude, then she can check and see if he's the dead dude.'

Was it possible that Bettina knew her grandmother's boyfriend's last name? Maybe if I asked her *very* nicely? I could kill two annoying birds with one incredibly awkward stone. I immediately began racking my brain for things I could give Bettina to bribe her and if that failed, things that might be used to blackmail her.

Five minutes later, we were in Mother's garage arguing over whose car was more appropriate. Or inappropriate.

My Bentley was abhorrent to Esmerelda for the same reasons Gucci sneakers were abhorrent to her. That is, no good reason. For a renegade who took laws and speed limits as loose suggestions rather than legislative requirements, she seemed overly concerned about her 'rep on the street getting trashed' by being seen driving my Bentley.

Also, she refused to get in the car while I was behind the wheel. True, my driving skills were a little shaky, but they were a lot less shaky than Esmerelda's car, which was held together by rust, various shades of blue paint, sheer force of will and more visible duct tape than a nightclub when the lights come up.

At least I was relatively transparent about my self-worth being tied to luxury items and the opinions of complete strangers. No, I was not deep. No, it was not good for my mental health. But I was aware of it and I was considering working on it.

We landed on a compromise. We'd 'borrow' Patricia's car. Since I had lost the argument to choose the type of car *and* the argument to drive, Esmerelda was stuck with writing Patricia a note explaining the 'borrowing'.

Less than ten minutes later, we pulled into the driveway of one of the largest and most prestigious hotels in Sydney: Holly Park. It was glamorous understated elegance wrapped in an environmentally friendly bow. Its entire front entrance was spotless glass embedded with some type of microchip that reduced the need for heating and cooling, and changed colour with the seasons. It was currently a calming turquoise. Its desks, floors, art and furniture were immaculate and made from recycled banana peels and bottle tops. Okay, maybe not all of it was made from banana peels, but it was equal parts cutting-edge technology, beauty and environmental consciousness.

Its circular stone porte-cochère looked original, but given it was ten metres wide and sealed with organic bitumen, I surmised it was built long after the days horses and coaches delivered guests to hotels.

Esmerelda pulled into the back of the valet parking queue and said, 'You can't go in there.'

I had already unbuckled my seatbelt before her words registered. 'Pardon?'

'Like, you totally can't go in there.'

Yes, that was much clearer.

'You just spent the last hour telling me I *had* to go to the Holly Park,' I said, bewildered.

'Oh, like you totally do,' she said, furrowing her brow and nodding enthusiastically.

'Then we're going in?' I asked, pointing to the massive glass doors, which currently resembled a cool ocean, opening to the lobby entrance.

'Nah.'

I know that screaming is never the answer, but surely, sometimes, it *is* the answer.

'Um, you're like on the no-fly list,' said Esmerelda with a shrug.

'The no-fly list?' I said incredulously. 'This is a hotel.'

She rolled her eyes. 'Well yeah, but like, you're still on the no-fly list.'

I motioned her for more information.

'At. This. Hotel,' she said slowly, as if I were a toddler. 'No. Fly. List.'

Honestly.

'That's ridiculous,' I said, getting out of the car. I marched up the perfect driveway and walkway, towards the massive glass doors, talking to myself. 'Hotels don't have no-fly lists. And if they did, I would *not* be on one. I would be on the yes-fly list.'

'Ms Hasluck-Royce-Jones?' asked a smiling young concierge the moment I walked through the doors.

'Yes!' I said and turned to give Esmerelda a smug look over my shoulder. But she and Patricia's car were gone.

'What a delight to have you visit us at the Holly Park!' he said, guiding me towards a rather statuesque bellman on the other side of the foyer. *Two* rather statuesque bellmen.

'We're sorry to report there are no rooms available,' he said, giving me a sad smile. 'And all of our restaurants are fully booked.'

'What?'

'However, in compensation we'd like to offer you the premier suite at the Holly Oaks Resort in Palm Beach. And dinner at any one of the Holly Oaks five incredible Palm Beach restaurants,' he said, neatly parking me in front of the two bellmen who, upon closer inspection, were not bellmen but security guards.

'I didn't ask for a room. Or a restaurant reservation,' I said in my best Entitled Heiress tone.

'Complimentary!' he chipped in. 'On the house. You're so special to us!'

I tried annoyed. 'I don't understand, that is not what I—'

'I know!' he piped cheerily, cutting me off. 'We do like to anticipate our guests' needs here at the Holly Park Sydney! A car is available to take you now.'

If I wanted to spend an hour travelling up the coast to Palm Beach, I would stay in my own damn beach house.

'I'm not in the mood to travel to Palm Beach,' I retorted.

He glanced up at the two gentlemen I was parked in front of.

'A car is available to take you now,' he said, smiling again. He was the concierge version of a Stepford Wife.

'I see,' I said. 'I might take a walk around the harbour first.'

'Excellent!' he beamed. 'Tom and Ron will be waiting for you. Outside.' And he pointed to a black Mercedes idling at the far, *far* right-hand end of the circular driveway.

Ron and Tom followed me through the front doors and then stood like sentries on either side of the calming turquoise glass.

I looked back to the concierge and made a mental note to find out who he was and put *him* on a no-fly list. Even if I had to buy an airline and create a no-fly list to put him on. Maybe I could find out where he lived, buy the building and have him evicted. When it came to revenge, I had no interest in achieving personal growth.

I had made it almost completely out of the yawning driveway, no longer under the protection of the porte-cochère, when Esmerelda pulled up beside me in Patricia's sad little car. There was no fear of me passing out; I was only ten per cent mortified. The other ninety per cent of me was furious.

'Told ya,' she said the second my hand was on the car door. 'No-fly list.'

I yanked hard on the door and fumed at her. 'How did you know that was going to happen?'

'I got a guy on the inside.' And she winked at Tom. Or Ron.

'If you knew I was going to be ejected, why on earth did you talk me into coming here in the first place, you strange, infuriating woman?!'

''Cause we gotta go in!' she barked back.

I hit my head on the side roof of the car. On purpose.

'We can't go in the *front*. But—' She jerked her head towards a cavernous tunnel that led under the hotel, presumably to an underground car park. I had never noticed it before. The last time I went into an underground car park with Esmerelda, I had exited the building by being dropped unconscious from a fire escape. It was both better and worse than it sounded.

'We're goin' in the back door,' she grinned.

How bad would it be, really, if Bettina had footage of me falling over? Her view *was* obscured by the boxwood hedges. Most likely she hadn't even captured my falling over the *actual* body. Likewise, Grandmother's footage of me borrowing a Monet. We were family. I was the Heiress. People wouldn't judge me, right?

'Like, get in, Indigo, before our buddies on the front door notice you loitering.'

It was one thing to be escorted to the front door by a security guard, it was another thing to be escorted to the kerb. That would be bad. I got in the car.

Esmerelda turned a hard left and we plunged into steep darkness. Well, dimly lit-ness. We drove around and around in a circular tunnel until I was completely dazed. It was like driving down a corkscrew. It was what I'd always imagined being kidnapped would feel like.

We emerged into an enormous underground garage that was abuzz with activity. There were people emptying food scraps into giant composters. There were delivery trucks offloading everything from green crates of fruit and vegetables to white oblong foam containers stamped *FRESH SEAFOOD*.

Esmerelda pulled into the last free space on the far left, where a number of electric cars were being charged at docking stations. She got out and picked up the cord for the electric car charger.

'Does Patricia drive a Tesla?' I asked, examining the darkened console for clues.

'Nah,' she said and shoved the cord through the back seat window, powering the window up until the power cord was wedged tight. 'Only rich people drive Teslas.'

Elon Musk would *not* be happy to hear that.

A second later, we were covered in light as a minibus emerged from the tunnel.

'That's our ride,' she said, nodding towards the minibus and yanking me out of the car's passenger seat.

A multicultural train of young, middle-aged and some older women and men piled out of the minibus, chatting in familiar terms to one another. They all wore black sneakers and white socks with their shorts, jeans and T-shirt ensembles. Except one lady. She had pink hair and wore a pink tutu over her shorts. Her black shoes were ballet slippers.

These were not guests. These were workers. They formed a line and perused a large open cabinet of flat-packed linens, quickly choosing one bundle each. They then moved in through the untinted utilitarian glass doorways into what I assumed was the Holly Park's service entry.

Esmerelda pulled me across the cavernous but busy space and into the back of the line. I looked down at my feet. Black and pink Jimmy Choo strappy stilettos paired with a knee-length, pink and gold floral princess cut Zimmermann dress. I looked at Esmerelda. Navy blue high-top Converse sneakers paired with faded jeans and a printed T-shirt. At least my shoes were black. Mainly black.

'Grab a bundle,' she said to me as the line snaked towards the entry. I was so shocked to be sneaking in the service entry of a hotel I had just been both thrown out of *and* offered a free premier suite by that I picked up the closest bundle to me—a work uniform—and plodded in with the rest. Except I made more of a clicking sound than a plodding sound. Half the line wound left into the women's dressing room, the rest peeled off to the men's changeroom on the right.

I examined my uniform. It was a perfectly pressed, white short-sleeved dress with a pointed turn-down collar and emerald green trim. It had an invisible zip running from navel to sternum. It was a size 22. In essence, it was a stiff, giant, triangular paper napkin. Esmerelda had chosen a size 8. She casually rolled up her jeans and the dress floated gently around her sleek frame. With the rolled-up jeans peeping out and the worn Converse, she made it look somehow designer. Maybe that was what Heinsmann saw.

I, on the other hand, appeared as if I'd just stolen washing from the line of a bleach-and-starch-happy stranger. I unzipped the dress, stepped into it like a cardboard tent and zipped it up. It was so long I didn't even need to tuck my dress up. The saving grace was a matching baseball cap. I pulled it down low and hid.

We strolled out of the change area and into the corridor.

'Now what?' I asked, grabbing Esmerelda by the arm before we hit a more public area.

She peered deliberately at my clutching hand. 'Dude.'

I refused to let go. 'What if somebody sees me? I'm dressed as a maid!'

'Exactly.'

'Exactly no one will see me? Or exactly I'm dressed as a maid?'

'Uh-huh.'

Kill me.

'I. Look. Like. A. Maid!' I hissed as two actual maids walked by, exiting through a blue door that led to a set of stairs. I smiled apologetically at them.

'Yep,' she said, following the pair through the door.

I froze, not wanting to go any further but not wanting to be left to my own devices in the service bowels of the Holly Park.

'I don't have the patience for your riddles today!' I snapped.

She turned, hand on hip, exasperated, looking like a gorgeous maid, but still a maid. 'Like no one's gonna see you *'cause* you're a maid.'

Was that true?

'We don't even know if Bettina is here!' I shot back.

'Dude,' Esmerelda said, pulling her phone out of a pocket in her uniform. 'She's having dinner with her family in the—' she read, 'Holly Tree Terrace. Whatever that is.'

I moved closer to examine her screen. 'Are you tracking Bettina?'

'Course. I wouldn't've come down here otherwise.'

I was astonished. How had Esmerelda managed to get a tracker on Bettina Holly? It had been over a week since our unfortunate encounter. Surely Bettina had changed out of those sad cargo pants by now?

'Did you break into her house?' I asked, following Esmerelda through the rabbit hole and up the stairs to the main floor of the hotel.

'Dude, no. I'm on parole.'

I rolled my eyes at her back as she climbed the stairs. I climbed after her, albeit slowly in my stilettos. We made it to the landing of the stairs. There were arrows and locations stencilled in black spray paint on the walls: left for main kitchen, right for reception, and up two flights to the Holly Tree Terrace Private Dining Room.

'You slipped something into her handbag?'

'*Into* a handbag?' she asked incredulously, easily making her way up the next flight of white-painted bumpy metal tread stairs. 'That'd be a first.'

I scurried after her, hefting my tent of a dress off my calves. 'How do you know she's in there?'

'She's like a total social wannabe,' she said over her shoulder.

At the second-floor door, I stopped to rest my head on the whitewashed cinderblock wall. It was probably made of compressed apple cores and corn husks.

'I have no idea what you are saying, Esmerelda. This dress is chafing me. My shoes were not meant to be worn while climbing endless flights of stairs. I am dressed as a maid in the same hotel I was just thrown out of. Give me an answer that I understand or I shall make sure your beloved excuse for a car is replaced by *the* most ostentatious Rolls-Royce I can find and I will have the Louis Vuitton symbol sewn into every pair of sneakers and jeans you own.'

She said something about logging into a search bar, locations, results, hashtags, usernames, map marker icon IDs, open pages, copy something, URL, digits, paste and plug-in.

She showed me her phone. 'Instagram?' I asked, flicking through various screens until I got to a recently posted photo of Bettina's dinner. Carefully inscribed on the side of her floral dinner plate were the letters *HTT.* Holly Tree Terrace, the private dining room where Bettina was apparently eating dinner.

'Why didn't you just say Bettina posted her location on social media?' I asked, irritated, fanning my legs with my uniform. These stairwells were not airconditioned.

'What? Nah, she didn't post *where* she was. I hacked her location.'

'Her dinner plate is embossed.'

Crickets.

'HTT,' I said, tapping a butchered fingernail on her phone's screen. 'Holly Tree Terrace.'

'Oh,' she said, tilting her head in to read the inscription, somewhat disappointed. Ever the optimist, she soon bounced back. 'Sweet! Let's crash this party.'

CHAPTER 7

GATECRASHERS

While my mind continued to ponder the wisdom of this visit, my feet followed her. I found myself in a wide hallway with plush eggshell-weave pear green carpet. The walls were covered in a pale hand-drawn wallpaper featuring yellow holly. The perfectly contrasting architraves, skirtings and ornate cornices were probably made of actual eggshells. The hallway had a peaceful eco-garden feel.

We reached a set of double doors. A panel beside the door said *Holly Tree Terrace – Private Dining Room*. I was certain I had attended either a wedding or a divorce party in this room. Although a private dining room sounds like an intimate room you might have at home, it is not. Unless you live in a castle, then it is. This room was not for a single table of guests or a couple on a romantic night out, although undoubtably it was sometimes employed that way.

From memory, this room could seat a hundred people, two hundred if your guests were prepared to stand cocktail style.

The far end featured a lectern for speeches and a wet bar. Hidden behind those was a dressing room and a private galley kitchen for guests who preferred to bring their own culinary staff. This was a surprising number of people, from pop princesses to presidents to actual princesses to fussy eaters with money to spare.

Esmerelda peeled the door on the right back a fraction and peered inside. 'Dining room? What the crap? You could play hoops in there.' She shook her head. 'Rich people.'

I peeked in too. The Holly family—Bettina, Gilly, Gregory and Astor—were seated at a round table on the opposite side of the room, to our right, between the lectern and the wall. Their table was covered in a gold tablecloth that ran like a river of silk, falling gracefully over the rounded edges and skirting the floorboards by a whisper. The tablecloth was probably made from biodegradable jam jar lids and the floorboards from recycled organic wine corks.

The table, which could accommodate ten, was set for four. Dame Elizabeth was obviously not expected.

There were nine identical tables lined up, edge to edge, in a row along the wall to our left, the first one quite close, the farthest left of the lectern. They also had golden tablecloths except for a few which had been rudely stacked upside down on top of the base tables, so that the silver legs of the top tables were laid bare for all the world to see.

'Okay, like, in you go,' said Esmerelda.

'Me?' I said, pointlessly pointing at myself. 'Surely *you* have a plan.'

'Yeah,' she snorted, insulted. 'Like *this* is my plan.' She motioned around the empty hallway. I waited for more information. None was forthcoming. I had a dreadful feeling her plan had ended the moment I was escorted out of the hotel and she had been winging it ever since.

'Did you know about the service entry?'

'Yeah. Totally.'

'So you planned for us to sneak in with that shift of workers?'

'Um, yeah, sure,' she said, nodding. 'I totally planned all that crap. Now it's your turn.'

The table was being cleared by a couple of waiters who had come from the galley kitchen behind the lectern which, upon further examination, was more like a miniature stage.

When *had* I been here before? A fundraiser? A silent auction? A fashion show? One of Anna Del Rico's weddings? Or was it one of her engagement parties? Anna didn't have divorce parties. She was one of those people who seemed to innately know how to extricate herself from a relationship, seemingly with no hurt feelings. Very Gwyneth. Even with her no-children policy and generous fiscal spirit and resources, it was still a feat of emotional and relationship magic.

I could feel cogs turning. Something was sparking. I felt a tug on my cardboard dress and blindly followed. What was it about Anna, this room and getting information out of Bettina? Bettina hated Anna. No surprises there. Anna disliked gossips. As did Dame Elizabeth. No one likes being gossiped about. Bettina loved gossip. Anna loved marriage. Did Max love Dame Elizabeth? Bettina loved Dame Elizabeth. Bettina would *not* have liked her grandmother having a boyfriend. Grandmother wanted us to work 'undercover' to find Max. Why? So Dame Elizabeth could avoid gossip? Or scandal? Or her family?

Wait.

'Gossip,' I said to Esmerelda. I looked around. I had been dragged through the door and into the dining room by Esmerelda who was pulling on my uniform's apron-like skirt. I appeared to be sneaking along the edge of the dining room wall towards the row of skirted tables. What was supposed to happen when we got to the tables was anyone's guess.

Esmerelda suddenly dropped behind me and shoved me under one of the tables. I crashed through the tablecloth like a Mack truck through a waterfall. I skidded along the floorboards on my hands and knees, my head connecting with the metal table leg in the centre of the second table. *Clank.* The tables pushed together, along with their silky gold tablecloths, created a giant fort. It was a canopy of gold, with metal table legs and feet everywhere.

'There,' Esmerelda said with satisfaction. 'I totally planned that.'

I rubbed my head and ferociously scrutinised her. 'I seriously doubt that.' I held out my hand. 'Phone.'

'Nuh-uh,' she said, turning her back to me, instinctively clutching her empty phone hand to her chest.

The last time I'd borrowed her firstborn, I may have cracked its screen somewhat. However, I was good to my word and immediately purchased her a new one.

We were both crouched under the table. The stiffness of her dress, although not a patch on mine, was firm enough to keep the front of her uniform in place when she turned her back to me. And there, poking out of the front pocket of her maid's uniform, like a joey in its mother's pouch, was her phone.

'Dude,' she whispered in warning tones, eyeing me. 'Don't do it.'

'Trust me,' I said in a tiny encouraging voice. It was pistols at dawn, or hands in pouches under tables at dinner. I was the quicker draw.

The handset was locked.

'Unlock.'

She narrowed her eyes at me.

'Please.'

Nothing.

'Heinsmann,' I said simply.

She unlocked the phone and I dialled.

'Anna? It's Indigo,' I whispered into the handset.

'Darling!' came her booming voice from the other side of the world.

'Anna,' I hissed. 'You have to be quiet. I'm hiding under a table in the Holly Tree Terrace dining room.'

'How wonderful! I think I got engaged there once!' she squealed—that solved that mystery. 'Who're you under there with?'

'Esmerelda,' I said reluctantly.

'Kinky,' she purred. 'I didn't see that coming, Indie. What happened to the two hot guys? The cop and the brother-in-law?'

'Nothing. I mean, there was, but—'

'Ooh, details please!' she roared.

'Anna! Lower your voice and focus!' I scolded.

Esmerelda *shh*-ed me. I pressed *mute*. Had they heard? I sat silently, trying to concentrate on the chatter coming from the other side of the room. Astor seemed to be having a conversation with Bettina about seesaws. Wait, no, sea cells. Lice cells?

'Vegan stuff,' Esmerelda explained. She spent way too much time with Mother.

Gregory was telling Gilly about the spa he'd just returned from. I blocked out the details regarding his ablutions.

I unmuted the phone. 'Anna, be serious,' I whispered. 'I need a favour.'

'Anything for my favourite maid of honour. Or matron of honour. Do you become a maid again when you're a widow?' she asked.

I could hear cheering in the background. I was tempted to ask where, specifically, she was, but I didn't have time for the explanation. She could be almost anywhere, as long as anywhere featured her latest gorgeous young love. I turned the volume down.

'Anna, how quickly could you start a rumour about Dame Elizabeth getting married?' I wanted to know. 'To a man called Max, ah, last name unknown. Money. From WA.'

'Is Lizzy getting married to some mining magnate?' she asked, suddenly attentive.

'No,' I said. 'She is not.'

'You want me to start a baseless rumour?'

'Yes, please,' I whispered back.

'I don't like gossip, Indie, and I like old Lizzy. She got me into the Whitehouse Institute of Design, you know.' I could hear a siren and the pop of a Champagne cork.

'You went to fashion design school?' I asked, wondering how I had missed that.

'No, darling, but I absolutely could have. You see? She's a sweetheart,' she said patiently. 'Yes, Iggy, darling, love another.'

'Pardon?' I asked.

'I'm at a game, Indie. You really should fly over for one. Bring your new friend. She sounds like a blast.'

'The rumour, Anna. Can you do it?' I persisted.

'Well, of course I could, but I won't. It goes against my good conscience.'

While all manner of things floated right past the good conscience of Anna Del Rico, the right things, the important things, did not. Mostly.

'What if you could do it so that only Bettina and Gilly heard about it?'

This got me a few seconds of silence.

'How would I do that?' she asked, more cheering in the background. 'Well done, darling!' Presumably, that was not directed at me.

'I don't know, Anna, be creative,' I said in a rushed whisper, one ear listening for signs the Holly family were on the move.

'Why would I do that?' she asked cautiously.

'Dame Elizabeth might be in a tiny bit of trouble. She might be about to have her heart broken,' I said, ashamed I had used Anna's Achilles heel—love.

'By this fiancé?' she asked. The sound of her drinking stopped. I had her attention.

'Possibly,' I said, unsure. The truth was I didn't really know one way or the other.

'Bettina and Gilly would go wild if they thought old Lizzy was finally getting married again. That would drain the trust-fund pool. Oh my God!' she yelped so loudly I pulled my ear away from the phone.

'Be quiet, Anna!' I hissed.

'Gregory Holly would lose his shit if his mother married! He could get cut out! Imagine that. He's a horrible old sleaze; can't count the number of times I've had to slap that hand down. Lord my ass,' she said, ignoring my pleas for quiet. She paused. 'Old Lizzy wouldn't get hurt, would she? Are you sure, Indie? I mean what ...'

Esmerelda parted the golden tablecloths and we peeped out. Gilly and Bettina were both pushing away untouched desserts. They might slip out before the meal was over. Esmerelda was shaking her head. 'Dude, get on with it. And gimme my phone back.'

'It would absolutely kill Gilly and Bettina and it would help Dame Elizabeth get closure,' I blurted. 'She might even find love.'

Most likely the man in the lilies was *not* Max and who knows, maybe Max would turn up and they would live happily ever after. Still, I felt like I was going to go to Cupid Hell, via Best Friend Purgatory. I silently promised myself I would make it up to her.

'Anna?'

'Done and done,' she said and resumed drinking.

'Thank you!' I said, giving Esmerelda the thumbs up (quite possibly the only time I have given a thumbs up signal while not underwater). 'Anna, how long do you think—'

'Oh! My! God!' Gilly screamed from the other side of the room. 'That trucking bitch! Bettina, did you see this?'

'Never mind.'

Anna's family had made their money in something just slightly more glamorous than dairy cows—trucking transportation. The Del Rico clan were a one hundred per cent Sicilian blood line, so what specifically was transported in those trucks, especially in the early days of the business, was the subject of some speculation. I didn't care. As a child, and as an adult, I found Anna's family delightful. Compared to my family, they were practically traditional. They were my port-in-a-storm family.

'You're welcome, darling!' Anna said, signing off.

I returned the phone to Esmerelda and motioned her forward under the cover of our bizarre tablecloth tent city. We had only crawled halfway down the row of unused tables but it was far enough to give us front-row seats to a double-header Gilly and Bettina meltdown. I was hoping they would *download* while melting down.

Gilly grabbed Bettina's phone, clicking onto something. 'Here!' she said as she shoved it back under her nose. 'She's sent you one too!'

'Classy,' Esmerelda said, grinning at me under the table.

'Daddy!' shouted Gilly. 'I thought we'd decided this loser wasn't good enough for Granny! Now he's marrying her?'

'What?' Gregory said, dropping his fork onto his embossed plate, giving his lemon meringue pie a well-earned break. 'We did. He's as good as gone.'

'Anna Del Rico just messaged me asking if it was true that Granny was marrying some magnate from the ass-end-of-the-earth Perth,' Gilly demanded. 'Perth! God, she can't even gossip right.'

Gilly looked nothing like Bettina. One of Bettina's more irritating features was that she seemed to be in perpetual motion. She was dark and slight and her hair had never seen a straightening iron it didn't like. Gilly, on the other hand, was a bigger woman, both horizontally and vertically, with fairer hair, usually worn in loose curls around her face to cover her tiny gill holes. Gilly moved at a more regular human pace, if not slower. Which was not to say she was slow. She was a plotter, a planner. Like a boa constrictor.

Gilly, much like her father, spent vast amounts of time and money at health, beauty and wellness spas. Gilly got more value for money than Gregory.

Astor was, without doubt, the genetic jackpot of the family. He was quick like Bettina, clever like Gilly, and graceful and generous like Dame Elizabeth. A pristine model.

Gregory's thoughts, as limited as they were, revolved around Gregory. He was like a factory second, an overstuffed, tuna mornay pie with filling spilling over its wonky pastry seams. Astor was symmetrical—all his seams lined up.

'Granny's dating?' Bettina asked, looking at her sister and then her father.

'Yes, you idiot!' Gilly snapped. 'While you were off scrutinising some ridiculous vegan napkins, we've been taking care of Granny. Fending off some gold-digging geriatric from Adelaide.'

'They weren't napkins, they were ecologically sustainable inhouse hygiene wipes. And at least I *do* my job, Gilly. You spent the first two months of winter trialling food in the south of France. We all know what the food in the south of France tastes like, Gilly. It tastes the same as it did last year and the year before that. It tastes like an all-expenses-paid eight-week vacation.'

'It was not eight weeks! It was seven and a half, not including flights, and I've been sweating it out in the kitchens every day for a month!' She slammed her fist on the table, making the tea and coffee cups jump.

Bettina eyed Astor. 'Is that true, Uncle Astor? Has she been in every day?'

Astor gave her a semi-hearty nod. 'Giuliana's trying very hard. She's been in almost every day ... well, every weekday, for weeks, except when she's been under the weather. One can't help being unwell. Great work, Giuliana!' he encouraged.

'I had a migraine,' Gilly explained.

Gilly had so many migraines in primary school, the principal recommended she visit a neurologist. In high school, her migraines were miraculously replaced by stomach aches. It seemed migraines were making a comeback.

'Dude,' Esmerelda murmured. 'Sisterly love.'

'What do you mean Max Weller is "as good as gone"?' Astor said to Gregory, doubling back to the earlier comment.

Yes! I had a name: Max *Weller*.

'Well, you wouldn't do anything about him, Mr PC,' Gregory said, starting back in on his lemon meringue pie.

'Max Weller is a guest at this hotel. I'm not about to let you into his room to snoop through his things. I know you're unfamiliar with the finer aspects of hotel management, Gregory, but that's generally frowned upon. And illegal.'

'Oh God, Astor, everything's bloody illegal with you!' Gregory said, forking the last piece of his pie.

'What did you do, Gregory?' Astor said seriously.

All eyes at the table turned to Gregory.

'Nothing! Nothing. I just had a little talk to him,' Gregory said, looking around defensively, hands in the air. 'Told him to leave Mother alone and bugger back off to Adelaide. *Man* to *man.*'

'This better not have happened at the hotel,' Astor warned.

'So what if it did?' Gregory shot back. 'Rules, rules, rules.'

'Wouldn't, like, both the dudes in that conversation hafta be a man to make that work?' Esmerelda whispered.

'And he left,' Gregory said. 'Haven't heard from him since.' He slid Bettina's uneaten pie over.

'He agreed to leave Mother?' Astor asked, astonished.

'Well, no,' Gregory blustered. 'But he walked away. Didn't come back at me, not like a *real* man.'

Esmerelda shook her head at me and mouthed the words *dude* and *tool*.

'But he hasn't checked out of the hotel. Has he?' Astor queried.

'I don't know, Astor,' Gregory said, shrugging in irritation. 'I've been at the Diamond Goat Health Spa cleansing for the last week.'

'Yes,' Astor said, watching the first bite of Bettina's lemon meringue pie disappear into Gregory's mouth. 'I can tell.' Astor studied Gilly and Bettina. 'Do you two know anything about this?'

Bettina was incensed. 'I've been away sourcing fabrics. I've been home less than a fortnight. I didn't even know Granny was dating. *Somebody*—' she glared at Gilly, '—should've told me. When did it even start?'

'A few months ago,' Gilly said matter-of-factly. 'They met at the opera in Byron Bay. He wormed his way in, pretending to like opera. I mean, really, who likes opera?'

Gregory snorted.

'Uh, hello?' Bettina said. 'Granny likes opera.'

Gilly rolled her eyes at her sister. 'Well, duh, Bettina. Not just opera. All of it. They've been to every sculpting studio and orchestral performance from here to Brisbane. Every play ever written the two of them have snuck into once the curtain was up, thinking no one knew. As if he's into all that.'

'Did it occur to you, Giuliana, sweetheart, that perhaps they do have common interests? That maybe they just wanted some privacy?' Astor said in a tone that was close to reprimanding but not quite there.

'Granny's *old*, Uncle Astor! He was trying to take advantage,' Gilly said, pouting.

'I don't know that he is,' Astor said, meaningfully. 'Max has retained the Forrest Suite here for many weeks. While I think the Holly Park Sydney represents excellent value for a six-star hotel—'

Esmerelda snorted at this remark and I shushed her.

'—that's not something one can do on a pension. He's always immaculately dressed. Uses the inhouse barber almost daily—'

I shoved Esmerelda in the ribs at the mention of a barber.

'—the inhouse laundry service, has manicures and pedicures at the spa. These are not things a man on a budget does. And I think his prayer bracelet is Tahitian black—'

'Spas? Pedicures? Bracelets?' Gregory piped. 'Pfft! What a gigolo,' said the man who almost single-handedly supported the survival of exclusive spa resorts on the east coast.

Gilly snorted and nodded in agreement with her father, before adding, 'Well, it's all mood now, because according to *this*—' she tapped a nail on her phone screen, '—he's back, and he's proposed and she's said yes.'

A wave of financial fear went around the Holly family table, crashing hard over everyone but Astor. Unsurprising. He was the only one who knew how to earn a living.

Esmerelda shot me a questioning look and mouthed *mood?*

'Moot. I think she meant moot.'

Esmerelda's expression did not change.

'I'll explain later,' I hushed.

'Not for long, he's not,' Gregory blustered. 'I'm going to go and have another talk to him. He can bugger off back to Asia.'

'I thought you said he was from Adelaide?' Bettina queried.

'That's what I heard, but he told one of the bus boys he worked most of his life in Asia. Who knows with these gigolos?'

Astor laid a hand on his brother's arm. 'I think Max is a bit long in the tooth to be a gigolo. Mother's been trying to get to know this man quietly. Perhaps we should let her.' This was not posed as a question.

'But Father's—' Gregory started.

Astor removed his hand from Gregory's arm. 'Father has been gone for a good many years now. I think you and I both know he had his own *interests*,' he said purposefully.

'Why wouldn't she tell me?' Bettina uttered, more to herself than anyone else.

I felt some genuine sympathy for her for the first time since the fourth grade, when she'd had her school bag, lunchbox, drink bottle and pencil case all superglued shut as an April Fools'/tenth-birthday prank.

Then I recalled her interaction with Claire the gardener and her Garden Miser status. I understood why Dame Elizabeth might not want to introduce Bettina to a man Bettina might perceive as a threat.

It was Bettina's turn to be soothed by her uncle.

'I'm sure she'll tell you. In time. Besides, you've been away, hard at work for months. You'd barely landed when you spotted that poor homeless man who'd wandered into Florence Hasluck-Royce's back garden. Laid out in the lilies. So sad.'

'What?' I squeaked in objection.

'I still can't believe you scaled that boxwood hedge and broke into the old cow's garden to try to rescue him,' Gilly said, retrieving her untouched lemon meringue pie from the centre of the table, where it had, *not* of its own volition, but assisted by Gregory, migrated.

'Yeah,' Esmerelda muttered. 'Totally hard to believe.'

'Giuliana!' snapped Astor. 'Mrs Hasluck-Royce has been an excellent customer for many years. She's also a dear friend of your grandmother.'

'Come on!' Gilly exclaimed. 'We all know she's a—'

'She's a bit prickly, yes, but she's also an incredible feminist. A trailblazer.'

Gilly, Bettina and Gregory all rolled their eyes. In truth, Grandmother was both prickly *and* a trailblazer. She would, however, be furious to be called a feminist. They were far too left-leaning in her opinion. But what was important here was that Bettina was claiming to have found the man in the lilies. I wondered if I figured in her version of the story at all. I hoped not.

Astor switched subjects. 'You were extremely level-headed to have secured the scene and called the police, Bettina.'

'Well, of course, I would have taken care of it had I been there,' Gregory said, eyeing Gilly's dessert. 'But I was working.'

'Working? At the Diamond Goat Health Spa?' Gilly scoffed, her eyes moving from her father to her dessert, which had once again begun moving across the table towards him.

'Research, dearest. I'm always researching ways to improve the Holly Oak resorts.' His hand reached across the centre of the table and took her pie.

'I think you've heroically done quite enough research for us, Gregory,' Astor said. A sentence I am guessing he had said to his brother many, many times before.

Astor moved the spotlight back to Bettina, the real hero. 'You were very brave, Bettina. And to have calmed poor Indigo-Daisy ... Violet.' He paused. 'I always forget the last one. Some kind of crystal, isn't it? Amethyst?' He looked around the table for help. Shockingly, the rest of the Holly clan had no interest in contributing to a conversation about me or my names.

'Yes, Indigo was terribly distressed. And a little drunk I think,' Bettina added in a conspiratorial tone.

'Well, the apple doesn't fall far from the tree, does it?' Gilly sniped.

I felt like I had been punched in the chest. I was *not* drunk. I hadn't even had my second caipiroska for the day! And *I* found the body. Well, I tripped over the body, but still. Plus,

I was not the one who had been hysterical. The nerve of that woman! I looked to Esmerelda for moral support, but she was gone, crawling under the table like a demented paratrooper, towards the final tablecloth. I had forgotten about her undying loyalty to Mother, and to Mother's impressive sobriety. If someone had plucked me out of prison and placed me in a harbourside mansion, I would probably be quite loyal too.

It was likely that Esmerelda was about to try to beat Bettina and Gilly about the face with those lemon meringue pie plates. It did not pay to think about what she would do with the tiny dessert forks.

I lunged after her and grabbed her by a sneakered foot. 'No! Stop!' I very almost yelled.

I pulled her lanky brown legs towards me, grabbing hold of the rolled cuff of her jeans now not-so-hidden under her maid's uniform. 'She's a horrible gossip!' I hissed. 'Ignore her.'

Esmerelda may never have seen the inside of a gym, but she *had* seen the inside of a prison cell. It was like playing tug of war with a body part. I'd pull her legs towards me only to have her grip the floor like Spiderman and pull herself back towards the thin gold cloth that separated us from the Holly family.

With a wave of panic, I realised the family were moving about. They'd heard us! At any second, Bettina was going to pull back the silky tablecloth and my humiliation would be complete. I would be the drunken Heiress who had set fire to her husband and then groped a maid under a table.

The voices grew louder as the family walked towards us. My world blurred at the expectation of discovery and humiliation. I knocked myself on the side of the head with my right palm to clear the fuzz that had gripped it, while my left hand and arm struggled to pull Esmerelda's squirming leg up to my chest into a bear hug.

'I think she likes a bit of strange,' came Gregory's voice as his legs walked past the tablecloth. He was so close the cloth waved in the wake of his motion.

'*I* think she likes a bit of rough trade,' Gilly said, following behind. 'Big poles.' I saw Gilly's shoe skim the bottom edge of the cloth. Blue satin Manolo Blahniks with a crystal embedded buckle. She was not worthy.

Both Gregory and Gilly were, at least momentarily, out of Esmerelda's reach. But not mine. *No one* slut-shames my mother. I lunged. I was going to rip that shoe right off her foot and plant its heel in her eye socket like a spring bulb.

Thin, scrappy arms wrapped around my upper thighs, pulling me back. I scratched at the floor and scrambled to grab hold of one of the metal table legs for leverage. I was so wild with rage I could not speak. Small guttural noises came out of the back of my throat, risen up through my heart and my chest.

'Dude,' Esmerelda huffed as she pulled at my arms and legs, trying to wrestle me back from the edge.

I heard the door clop closed at the end of the room and the voices stopped.

They were gone.

'I'm like, *so* totally proud of you,' Esmerelda said earnestly.

CHAPTER 8

UNDER THE TABLE

Almost. They were *almost* gone.

I don't know who was more astonished to see whom: Astor Holly, head tipped almost upside down, floppy hair hanging, his hand holding back the tablecloth, bright blue eyes taking in the view, or me, both my billowing uniform skirt and my own dress skirt up over my waist (my underwear was mercifully new and well-fitting), one foot (no shoe—it had fallen off in the struggle) clutched tightly under Esmerelda's arm, the other wedged on her shoulder (I was trying to use her as leverage to launch myself at Gilly). At least my cap was still on.

I pulled my skirts down and blocked the humiliating, dizzying image of Astor Holly seeing me this way. As I retrieved my shoe, I reassured myself that while Astor did seem to adore beautiful women (he sent Mother a large basket of Chanel on her birthday every year), he had only ever been publicly linked to male partners. The realisation that he would probably have less than zero interest in my underwear comforted me and my head cleared.

'Aren't you … ?' he said, pointing at me.

'No,' I said smartly.

'Oh, so you must be …' he said, peering at Esmerelda.

'Nope,' Esmerelda said, shaking her head, outfit akimbo, trying to appear casual. Our reputation preceded us. To his credit, Astor did not run away or call me out. 'I see. Well, then, ah … social visit?'

I shook my head.

He smiled mischievously. He was probably in his early sixties, but he wore it well. The work he'd had done was exceptional. 'Job interview?'

I recoiled. Esmerelda snorted in laughter.

'Well, ladies, I'm out of ideas.'

'Like,' Esmerelda started, 'I was thinking of getting one of these tables.' And she thumped the thick centre leg of the table.

'I see. Just checking on their sturdiness?'

'Yep, exactly,' she said. And for all the world I believed her.

He tapped the top of the table and grinned. 'We like them. Perhaps you'd like to see them from the outside?' He offered Esmerelda a hand to help her out. She declined.

'I'm good here,' she said, examining the table's underside.

The expression on his face was a mix of intrigue and bafflement. As he studied us, a thought crossed his face. 'I do apologise for my niece and brother.'

'Which niece?' Esmerelda wanted to know.

'The rude one,' he said.

Esmerelda eyed me. I shrugged. They were both rude in my book. I still felt I had the moral high ground on both sisters, even while spying on them from under a table.

'The rud*er* one, then,' Astor said, trying to avoid repeating the insults. 'Giuliana.'

Esmerelda looked at me, still confused.

'Gilly,' I said to her.

'Yeah, thought so. The other one's just got a few karma problems. Bad juju from that birth date. Can't pick ya birthday.'

I was about to tell her that yes, in fact, you could choose your birthday, well, your parents certainly could. No one civilised gave birth to a child through, you know, the pre-historic way. And if you were having it done on an allocated day, then you might as well choose a day that is convenient to you. Or fits with your astrological chart. A day that is *not* April first, Friday the thirteenth or the twenty-ninth of February. I digress.

'Is there anything I can get you ladies? A cushion? A glass of Champagne?' he said, his face beginning to darken slightly as all the blood ran into it.

'That is kind of you to offer,' I said, shaking my captured foot free from Esmeralda, untwisting my body parts from her body parts and generally trying to elegantly extricate myself from under the table. 'I would just love a manicure.'

His eyebrows jumped, and once I had crawled from beneath the golden canopy, he held out a gentlemanly hand to assist me into standing position.

'That wouldn't have been my first guess. Then again, who doesn't like a manicure with their nightcap? You always were a trendsetter, Indigo,' he said with a smile.

That was a big lie. I bought my outfits straight off the catwalk. The only things I changed, on occasion, were the shoes. And the handbags. And the jewellery. Perhaps accessories didn't count. They were, after all, so personal.

'What about me?' Esmerelda wanted to know, emerging like a butterfly, stretching out to her full five foot ten.

'Oh, yes, of course,' Astor said, thoroughly amused. 'What can I get you, miss?'

'Esmer—' She stopped. 'I mean, Jane.'

'Don't bother, Esmerelda,' I said to her. 'We live in a small world. He already knows your name.'

'Not your last name,' Astor said helpfully.

'I'd like an ice cream sundae. And some of that lemon meringue pie,' Esmerelda chimed, not missing a beat.

'But first,' I interrupted, 'what you *really* want is to see the inhouse laundry, and then you would just *love* a haircut from the salon.'

'Frig off,' she reproached. 'I totally don't wanna do that.'

'Yes, you do,' I said with all the dignity I could muster, unzipping my now wrinkled uniform and shaking my shoulders out of it. It fell in a pointy starchy heap at my feet. 'Remember? You said you wanted to see the *laundry* because it's where they shot that movie.'

Astor and Esmerelda both stared at me, confused.

'The movie *shoot*,' I prompted.

'Oh, right!' Astor said, clicking his fingers in recognition. 'It wasn't a movie shoot, it was a photo shoot. For *Pazzia Australia*. And they shot in the—'

'Yep, totally wanna see that laundry,' Esmerelda said, changing her attitude so quickly she had ideological whiplash. 'I'm a movie location buff. Big, big buff.'

'But—' Astor tried.

'Buff!' Esmerelda insisted. She wrenched my stolen uniform out from under my feet so quickly, I tripped on it. In stark contrast, she unzipped her uniform and gracefully shed it like a catwalk pro slipping out of a Valentino jacket as she stalked towards the exit.

'I can have someone escort you to the laundry,' Astor called out to her back. 'To give you a … a tour.'

'No need,' she said, marching on.

'Oh. But the hair salon is closed. The only salon open is the barber,' he said, palms open, trying to negotiate.

'Totally fine, dude,' she said as she neared the door. 'I'll meet you there after my uber exciting trip to the laundry.'

'Perfect!' I smiled brightly.

Although she was halfway through the door, her right arm cradling two slightly used stolen hotel uniforms, I swear she gave me the finger.

I don't know if it was the shame of being related to Gilly, Bettina and Gregory or the dignity inherited from Dame Elizabeth, but as we walked down the hall to the elevator, Astor neither asked me why I had been, nor admonished me for, spying on his family dinner. His only concession to the idea that this might be an odd situation was him fidgeting with his hair, pulling it down past his ears to cover the tiny holes he shared in common with his niece. She did the same thing to cover hers when feeling unsettled.

'Is your mother well?' he asked, tugging his hair before pressing the elevator's down button.

'Quite, yes, thank you,' I said politely. I was not going to make small talk about her vacation with Jed. She was happy. She deserved to be with whoever made her happy. I was unsure if my father had ever made her happy. I liked to think he had, at least for a while. Before it had all unravelled.

'And your grandmother?' he said, grinning. 'She's got spirit.'

'Yes,' I replied, recalling Grandmother's recent visit with Dame Elizabeth. 'Your mother is fairly spirited herself.'

He laughed, delighted. 'She certainly can be. She's a sweetheart, but sometimes you have to watch the quiet ones.'

No kidding.

'I saw her just yesterday. She seemed very well,' I said as the elevator doors pinged open.

'Is she?' he asked, not moving. 'She's been *very* happy of late.'

We exchanged looks. What could I say? He probably knew more about her relationship with Max than I.

'You've met him?' I asked, discarding the pretence that heiresses simply hang out under tables in private rooms as a recreational activity. Perhaps he thought I was Grandmother's spy, come to check up on her best friend's mysterious new beau?

'Yes, many times,' he said, allowing me to board the elevator first then following. 'Max is a lovely man. Solid. Polite. Kind. An excellent tipper.' He grinned. 'The staff like that.'

I smiled back. 'Always a positive sign. I'm sure he and your mother will be blissfully happy together.'

He smiled radiantly. 'I think so too. The others will get used to him.'

A silence sat between us as we stood in the elevator.

'I appreciate trust, loyalty *and* protectiveness in a relationship,' he said finally. 'Between new partners and between *old* friends.'

So, he *did* think we were spying for Grandmother. Who was I to correct him? 'Me too.'

He stepped out of the elevator. 'I have just the manicurist for you.'

According to Astor, Shale was the best manicurist at the inhouse spa. Shale was five foot zero, early twenties, blonde and had freckles in her tan. She was traditionally good-looking, but also had that unique confidence that some petite women have. She seemed very certain of her place and space in the world. This made her even more attractive.

After introducing me to Shale, Astor made a quiet exit, leaving us to chat. Shale was happy to talk Max. She'd done his nails on many occasions and he was, just as Astor had reported, kind, polite and a fantastic tipper. She added he was always punctual, never sleazy (which must have been a relief to her) and was actively interested in the comings and goings at the hotel. She had given him the lay of the land.

Who was dating who: everyone was dating everyone, including Bettina, who was allegedly dating the concierge who had shown me to the door (that explained that).

Who was whose boss: as predicted, Gregory Holly spent very little time actually being a manager except when it suited him, which was mainly when celebrities were staying.

Who worked hard and who was a slacker: surprisingly, Bettina was considered a hard worker, although no one wanted to work *for* her. She was a nightmare boss. Gilly's dedication to her job was, however, sporadic at best.

Which were the best rooms: least noise, best view, optimal layout, the perfect distance to the elevators.

Which were the best times to use the gym and pool: either when no one else was using them, or when everyone else was using them (Max preferred to use the pool when no one was around).

And, of course, how to score hotel 'freebies' like free valet parking, drinks, meals and massages.

I carefully, but shamelessly, pumped Shale for additional information about Max. He was five foot seven-ish, somewhere between seventy and eighty, 'most days he got out and about', had longish white hair, no wedding ring, dressed in expensive clothes but never wore a belt, carried a bundle of cash—fifties and hundreds—never took change (hence the tipping), never used a credit card or hotel credit, swam in the hotel pool (at the times suggested by Shale, between 9 and 10 pm, receiving maximum privacy), didn't drive, had an older model smartphone but never used it and, on *no* occasion, had he *ever* come into the hotel with a woman.

Everybody loved Max. And Astor.

If this manicurist had known Max was dating Dame Elizabeth, she would have told me about it three seconds into our conversation. The woman had a memory like a steel trap and missed nothing.

'Jesus, that's an improvement,' she said, admiring her work. She had performed miracles with the nails butchered the week before by Dr Bailly. I wanted to tell her that forensic pathologists made rotten manicurists, but since I didn't want Jimmy the valet parker, who was dating Cindy from the front desk, to know before I exited the spa, I kept it to myself.

The good news was that Max seemed like a great guy. The bad news was that his physical description was similar to the man in the lilies.

'Oh,' Shale said as I was leaving. 'Some days he has an amazing appetite. Steak and all.'

That seemed like a strange observation. Then again, she was a young, urban Gen Z. Maybe anyone with a diet that wasn't keto, raw food or vegan was odd. Or was she implying he was overweight?

'You said he's very trim. He swims,' I said, trying to be casual.

'Oh yeah, he's super trim and he does swim, but, you know, old people, they're not great eaters,' she said in a tone that implied I knew what she was talking about.

I did not.

'My nana, she never eats apples anymore. You know. And my grandpa's always going on about how he misses steak,' she added with a lopsided grin.

I did not know. I was not more enlightened. Less, in fact. My grandfather ate anything and everything until the day he expired. My grandmother was no slouch in the eating department either.

'Oh crap!' she suddenly gasped. 'Your grandparents are dead, huh? I'm sorry, babe.' She gave me a soothing pat and explained patiently. 'You see when they get really old their teeth go, they get dentures. You can't eat a steak with dentures. It's hard to swallow some stuff too. Slows them down, eating wise.'

'Max eats steak?' I pondered, mainly to myself.

'Oh yeah!' she answered, wide-eyed. 'On his eating days, he goes steak, corn on the cob, pizza, apples, burgers.'

'His eating days?'

'Yeah, you know oldies, some days they don't eat much. Then other days it's just savoury, other days just sweet stuff.'

I did not know, but I encouraged her to finish.

'He gets free snacks and meals from the restaurants *all* the time. Salads, desserts, coffees, soup, you name it. Sometimes they deliver them here. I heard he even got free lobster once! Never seen that before. Then again, he's a *crazy* good customer. And super cool. And a hella tipper.'

High value customers did often get free extras. I certainly did. When I was able to get into a hotel, that is. None of this was really news.

'But I haven't seen him in a while.'

'He's probably popped up to Byron or out to Lord Howe,' I reassured her, standing to leave.

'Yeah, probably,' Shale said, packing her equipment away. 'I know he's just a guest and all, but I kinda miss him.'

I thanked her and slid into the barber's shop next door to find Esmerelda about to have her elbow-length, sun-streaked locks shaved off into a buzz cut, a la Britney. I reminded her that Britney became more conspicuous than ever with her sparkling bald head, and the paparazzi doubled down on their efforts to stalk her to death. She made a comment about me ruining her buzz cut buzz, which got a chuckle out of the somewhat bemused barber.

As it turned out the barber, Mayson, was a master at trimming split ends, not that *I* had any. Mayson was six foot, built like a man who saw a gym often, his hairless brown arms covered in a careful choreography of intricate bright green, pink, yellow and turquoise tattoos. His hair was nothing but stubble on the back and sides, with longer hair on top that was moussed into submission and combed into shiny rows. It suited him.

Mayson was not quite as well informed about hotel goings-on as Shale, but he happily volunteered some similar information about Max: five foot seven, good guy, excellent customer, amazing tipper, no cards, no change, cash only, staff loved him.

He released a section of Esmerelda's hair from a metal clip and combed it through, saying, 'The guy comes in at eight every morning. *Boom*. Like clockwork. Cutthroat shave, hot towel, the whole deal. Real old-school. Except …'

'Yes?'

'Except not for the last week,' he said, hesitating, not wanting to speak out of turn.

'Oh,' I said. 'Perhaps he's off doing a wine tour in the Hunter or walking the beaches down south.'

'Yeah,' he smiled. 'Prob'ly.' But then a shadow crossed his face and he shook his head 'no' despite not having been asked a question, and talking to himself, gave a reprimand.

'Something else?' I asked nicely.

'Nah.'

'Cross my heart, I won't tell a soul. I hate gossip. I would never start a rumour.'

Esmerelda coughed violently and I threw a dog-eared *Pazzia* in her lap.

'It's not even a negative. It's amazing really,' he said, flicking his razor in and out in a trance.

'He sounds like an amazing guy,' I encouraged.

'Totally,' Esmerelda added from under a blanket of damp hair that had been combed over the front of her face.

Mayson expertly flicked his razor open and sliced the scrappy ends off another section of Esmerelda's hair. 'He wears his hair long. Not like hipster long, but beachy. Still-cool-in-a-tux long. And he was grey, you know, salt and pepper,' he said. Comb, razor, slice, comb, razor, slice. 'Not a criticism.'

He had my attention. The man in the lilies had snowy white hair. No grey.

'Grey is very distinguished,' I said happily. Max sounded lovely. I hoped he and Dame Elizabeth would be très happy together and spend all their money on abstract art and opera productions.

'Yeah, it is, right?' he said, pointing both comb and razor at me in enthusiastic agreement. 'I think so too. It's wild that anyone who's salt and pepper would dye their hair, right?'

'Not really,' I said, feeling defensive. I single-handedly put my colourist's son through medical school. According to my mother, going grey early was a genetic trait passed through on her father's side. A genetic trait that, of course, skipped her and came straight to me.

'I think it is perfectly fine to cover a few greys. Even if you're a man.'

'No, no,' he said, gesturing apologetically, 'it's not that. It's that he dyes it white. Bleaches it. It's salt and pepper at the roots but he whitens it. You'd never know he was salt and pepper. I mean, I noticed but, you know, I'm a professional. I've just never seen an old guy do that. Make it look white on purpose. Most of 'em are keen to hang on to the dark ones, mix 'em up with the whites. Go George Clooney.'

I felt a distinct drop in the bottom of my stomach.

'So, Max *looks* like he has white hair, but he's really salt and pepper?' I clarified.

'Yeah, a hundred per cent.' Comb, razor, slice. 'Fully odd.' Comb, razor, slice.

'Do you use Atkinsons California Poppy Hair Oil?' I asked Mayson.

'Not yet,' he said, not objecting to the conversation's change in direction. He combed out another section of hair. Slice.

'But you intend to?'

'Yeah, I've ordered a couple bottles,' he said, examining both sides of Esmerelda's hair to see if they were even.

'Really?' I feigned surprise. 'It seems a little, well, old.'

He laughed. 'I'll say! I had to order it off eBay. It's fully vintage. But, you know, lots of old-school stuff is making a comeback. Look at whisky.'

I dreaded the answer but I asked anyway. 'What gave you the idea?'

'Oh,' he said, making a final, tiny slice on Esmerelda's now perfect hair. 'Max uses it. It's great on him. He rocks it, you know?'

Slice, comb, slice.

'Yes,' I said quietly. I knew.

'There!' Mayson said, spinning Esmerelda in the chair. Her newly razored hair looked amazing. She was more beautiful than ever.

She ran a hand through it. 'Cool,' she said to Mayson by way of thanks. Then, turning to me, she said, 'Bummer.'

CHAPTER 9

THE MORNING AFTER

I decided I had earned a sleep-in and so refused to budge from bed until 11 am. Not only had last night been emotionally exhausting and socially awkward, but Esmerelda decided to use a streetlamp instead of the brake pedal at an intersection on the way home.

Patricia would not be pleased. Her car had a massive scrape down its left side and a substantial gap where its left headlight used to be. Actually, there was a substantial gap where most things on the front left side used to be.

Esmerelda swore the brakes 'weren't sticking' but I suspect her laces came loose and wrapped themselves around the accelerator pedal. Either way, it was an excellent reason for me to win the right to drive, and to drive my own car, the next time we required private, *non-driver driven* transportation. I had thus far lost that argument. It didn't help that my somewhat spotted driving history had been so thoroughly documented by the paparazzi.

Esmerelda ordered a tow truck and an Uber. The tow truck beat the Uber to the scene and we were left standing by the side of the road for several unacceptable minutes. I did *not* enjoy my first Uber experience. The car was older than I was, the driver was younger and there was nothing five-star about it. Unless it was five out of ten. There would not be a repeat experience.

'Where's my car?' Patricia wanted to know as she bustled in with my breakfast tray.

'Getting cleaned,' Esmerelda lied, walking in her wake, eyeing my waffles. 'But like, if you won Lotto, what kinda car would you buy?'

Patricia glared suspiciously over her shoulder at Esmerelda. 'I just had it cleaned. You'd better not have left it somewhere shady.'

'You have your car cleaned?' It seemed odd that a housekeeper or a maid would have her car cleaned.

'What?' she said, dropping the tray on the table by the window. 'I have to clean in my downtime too?' Her hands moved to her hips and her head cocked to the right.

'No, I just thought that—'

'Yes?' She leaned towards me, as if trying to prompt the rest of my sentence.

'Why're you so crabby?' Esmerelda said, deftly snagging half a waffle. If I didn't make it to the table soon, my tea would disappear as well. I slid out of bed and wrapped myself in a peach silk robe, making it to the breakfast tray just in time to remove Esmerelda's hand from my teapot.

'It's that Dylan Moss boy. He's been calling for you all week. He's annoying the crap out of me.' Patricia scowled.

'Dylan called the house?' A long-forgotten butterfly floated in my stomach.

'Called? Yes, he's called! He's also been coming 'round! Sending flowers. The hide,' she said, her voice rising several octaves.

I sat in the shell chair and peered at her in what I hoped was a poignant way. She remained silent. 'And you did not tell me because …?' I finally prompted.

'Your mother said if he ever came 'round here, I was to say nothing to you and to tell him you weren't home,' she said matter-of-factly. 'And to bugger off.'

'When did she say that?' I queried, pouring my *own* tea.

'You know,' she said, pulling up the sheets on my bed and fluffing my pillows.

I did not know. I started on my waffles.

'When he …' She paused, searching for the right words. '*Hoodwinked* you. Cad of a kid.'

'When he …' I too searched for a way to say what we were all thinking—when he'd cheated on me and broken my heart.

'Dude, just say it. When he got it on with that other chick,' Esmerelda said, ever helpful.

I looked to Patricia for confirmation. She nodded.

'When I was sixteen?' I asked, my fork, loaded with waffle topped with banana and strawberries … okay, and clotted cream and Canadian maple syrup, stopping halfway to my mouth.

She nodded while banging a pillow. 'Uh-huh.'

I gazed at her, eyebrows raised. 'In year eleven?'

'What?' she said defensively. 'Cat's given me no reason to think she'd changed her mind. No update in the *Bugger Off Dylan Moss* policy.'

Esmerelda made a face, indicating she conceded the point.
I let out an exasperated sigh.

'What?' Patricia cajoled, eyeing me. 'You wanna see that
little troll?'

'No!' I yelped, shocked at the very notion. My gut and my
nose might have had a school-girl reaction to him but
my brain had no such issues. *Clueless. Bungling.* 'Most definitely not.'

'Then eat your waffles and let me be annoyed with him,'
she said, hanging clothes up in the walk-in robe.

'I could take care of it for you,' Esmerelda offered.

'Are you prepared to work for free?' Patricia asked from
inside the wardrobe.

'I'm prepared to work for waffles,' Esmerelda countered.

'Deal,' Patricia said happily, and popped out of the wardrobe to give Esmerelda a hearty handshake.

What was it about this bedroom that made it so condu-
cive to deal-making lately?

'He's such a pain in the ass I would've paid you to get rid
of him,' Patricia said, heading back into the wardrobe.

'He's such a douche, I would've done it for free,' Esmerelda
responded, taking one of my waffles.

Get rid of him? Take care of it? Those phrases gave me
pause. After all, Esmerelda *was* still on parole. Perhaps if I
spoke with him instead, he might revert to the relationship
we'd had since our teen break-up: none.

Why was Dylan the first person Bettina had threatened
to send the video to? It had been years since high school.
Perhaps it was because the last I saw either of them for
more than sixty seconds was *in* high school. Perhaps it was
just low-hanging fruit. Perhaps she felt my Heiress on Fire

scandal combined with a falling-over-a-dead-body scandal *added* on to my historical being-cheated-on scandal would be the most humiliating possible combination? I bet Bettina didn't even have Dylan's number. It was all just a fake-out and I fell for it.

Given Bettina's heroic claims of having found the man in the lilies herself, it was unlikely she would now release a video of me stumbling over him. It would make her look like a liar. I would have liked to check her phone to be sure, but after last night I was no longer actively concerned.

I shuffled the teapot and the platter of waffles around the tray as I thought. There was a cream envelope made of thick cardstock wedged under the platter. I pulled it out. It was addressed to me. Sort of. It was typed by an actual typewriter and addressed to Indigo Jones-Bombberg.

Patricia emerged from the closet with an armful of garments needing to be dry cleaned. I waved the envelope. 'Is this for me?'

'Uh-huh,' she said, heading for the door. 'Came this morning.'

'Old-school,' Esmerelda said, eyeing the stamped envelope while forking bananas onto a pink flowered Royal Doulton side plate.

Patricia returned and unloaded the remaining contents of the tray: milk, cream, two napkins and one unused knife onto a Versace Le Jardin placemat on the shiny sandalwood table. 'I'll be back for the dishes in a bit.' And she was gone.

'Do you think Bettina will show anyone that video?' I asked Esmerelda, turning the envelope over.

'And out herself as a bullsh—liar? Nup. Nuh-uh.' She shook her head and rested on the windowsill to drink her tea. This time from the inside leaning out. 'It's done.'

'Do you think she ever had it?' I mused, examining the back of the envelope. No return address.

She shrugged. 'Dunno.'

That was a productive conversation.

'Probably not,' I said to myself. I used the clean breakfast knife to slit the envelope open. There was a stiff white card inside, also hand-typed. It read:

> The dead body you found had:
> * manicure
> * pedicure
> * aftershave
> * hair lotion
> * bleached hair shaft

Esmerelda was reading over my shoulder. 'Dude,' she scoffed. 'Like that's hardly news.'

'*That's* what you're taking from this?' I asked, flapping the sheet of card at her. 'You don't think it's odd I just received a random typed note containing confidential police-type information about the man in the lilies?'

She shrugged. 'Oh yeah, that's totally weird. But maybe … maybe we got a street rep now. For like, solving crimes.'

Her gleeful face filled me with terror. It passed quickly. I seriously doubted anyone, street or otherwise, thought Esmerelda and I were a crime-fighting duo.

'But getting old-school mail is super weird.'

That was way too many weirds for a Tuesday morning.

'Who else would have this information?' I wondered. 'And why are they sending it to me?'

I mentally willed Esmerelda not to say anything about crime-fighting duos. Surprisingly, I won.

Instead, she shrugged again. 'There're loads of different people at crime scenes. Any one of 'em could've overheard. And, I mean, like, you worked out about his funky hair oil and nails at the scene. Plus, stuff gets 'round.' She paused. 'Not that I know about crime scenes.'

I was not going to touch that one.

'What about this?' I pointed to the line that read: *pedicure*.

'What?' she shot back. 'You said the doctor lady said he had clean feet.'

What Bailly had actually said was that his feet had 'no chronic wounds' and 'peripheral debris only'. After several Google searches, Esmerelda and I discovered this probably meant his feet had no old cuts or scrapes and were relatively clean. That the dirt, pebbles and grass I saw were, most likely, newly acquired light-wearing accessories rather than long-term wardrobe staples. Once I had given it some thought, I understood why Dr Bailly had commented. A homeless person with no shoes is likely to get all sorts of cuts and scrapes on their feet, possibly on a daily basis. Their feet are also likely to have some seriously ingrained long-term grime and filth, rather than just a smattering of freshly cut lawn, and store-bought pebbles and soil that were probably straight from a bag infused with garden nutrients. And maybe she was smelling him for the same reason. Maybe he didn't smell homeless.

The point was, who else would know about the pedicure? I tried again. 'What about this then?' I pointed to the second last line that read: *bleached hair shaft.*

'Yeah, that's totally weird. Who says "shaft"?'

I inhaled and exhaled to gather patience. 'But we didn't know anything about his hair being bleached until last night,' I pointed out. 'When Mayson the barber told us.'

His hair appeared snow white to me at the scene. Not that I was checking for re-growth. I was sure Bailly would have said something if she'd noticed he'd had bleached hair.

'It's fully freaky,' Esmerelda conceded, peering suspiciously around the room. 'Do you think we're being followed?'

'Followed? You mean someone is watching us?'

She nodded.

I thought about it. It would have been virtually impossible to follow us into the hotel garage, sneak in behind us, trail us to the dining room, wait for us to come out, split into two, one person following Esmerelda and one following me, and then somehow eavesdrop on our conversation with Mayson the barber.

'No,' I concluded. 'More likely we were bugged.'

Wait, where did that idea come from? Had we been bugged?

'Seriously?' Esmerelda said, patting herself down.

I surveyed the room, got up and walked to the closet. I motioned for Esmerelda to follow me. She shook her head. 'Nuh-uh.'

I jerked my head towards the open closet door. She began assessing the dimensions of the windowsill. Was she going to jump? I gave her a look I hoped said *Don't do it!* Then I heard myself say, 'Don't do it!'

Oh yes, I would make a master spy.

She huffed, shot off a hasty text message and slouched across the room.

'Dude,' she said, joining me in the wardrobe. 'Like if I was gonna bug someone, I'd put it in their handbag.'

We looked across the wardrobe in unison at the row of handbags on our left, including the floral green Dior saddle bag with a cute pink tassel I'd had with me last night.

'I left my handbag in the car when I went inside the hotel. The second time,' I said.

'Or their shoes,' she said, pointing right, to the black and pink Jimmy Choo stilettos. They sat among a rack of over two dozen shoes. They could all be bugged for all I knew. But why? Why would anyone bug us? We had only just begun looking into Max slash the man in the lilies. And if someone had bugged or followed us, why would they then repeat that information *back* to us? On an antique type-writer and by post, no less. They wouldn't.

Regardless, for the next half hour I checked every hand-bag, and Esmerelda every shoe, for a listening device. We found nothing. Another thought occurred to me. I had only just finished telling Esmerelda about Shale the manicurist when we were interrupted by Esmerelda smashing Patricia's car into a lamppost last night. We didn't get a chance to discuss what she had found in the laundry.

'What did you find out in the hotel laundry?' I asked, picking up a pair of silver Stuart Weitzman stilettos and double-checking them for listening devices.

She gave me a blank stare. 'I was supposed to find out something?'

'Yes!' I squeaked. 'You were supposed to search through Max's dry-cleaning, his clothes. For clues.'

'Huh,' she said, eyeing my handbag rack. 'I totally didn't get that.'

God help me, I was going to kill her. Or myself. Or both of us. Or Grandmother. Someone. I thoroughly disliked being in this situation. There had to be a way out.

'What if I hired Earl Stevenson or Nigel Barker to get you out of your contract with Heinsmann?' I asked, taking a pink Balenciaga Hello Kitty bag out of her hands and placing it back on the shelf.

Earl was the long-time Hasluck-Royce family lawyer. Pure Sydney Grammar, Savile Row. Nigel 'Barking' Barker was an east coast lawyer famed for getting his celebrity clients out of crimes they quite obviously committed, often on flimsy or absurd excuses.

'You ever gonna use that?' she asked, pointing to the Hello Kitty bag.

'No. But it could become a collectible,' I said, adjusting the red bow. 'What about Earl?'

'Heinsmann would eat Mr Bowtie for breakfast.'

'Barker then.'

'Your mum and Eddy already got onto him. He says Heinsmann's not into it. Won't let me outta the contract. Last I heard Barking was like trying to swap me out for one of his clients. Alice someone.'

'Alice Gold?'

'Yeah, that's the chick.' More handbag touching. Alice Gold was the hottest actress in the country. She had Oscar and Golden Globe buzz. I wondered what she'd done to attract Barker's services. Whatever it was, Barker had kept it quiet. He was good.

'Heinsmann won't budge?' I asked, following Esmerelda as she walked along the row of handbags, removing her hands as she casually touched pristine pieces I had not even used yet.

'Nope. Told you. Psycho. But I reckon old Lizzy's totally got the goods,' she said, clipping and unclipping the brass hook and clip on a straw Valentino tote.

It was difficult to argue with her. Dame Elizabeth had many friends in many high fashion places. Besides, even if I could fix Esmerelda's problem with Heinsmann, I still had the small matter of my blackmailing grandmother. I could not currently think of a workaround for that.

I brushed her hand from a Chanel clutch. It was classic Chanel. She would have hated it. 'What is with all the handbag touching?'

She withdrew her hand immediately. 'Nothing. I was just like double checkin' for bugs.'

Lie.

'No, you weren't,' I said, narrowing my eyes and straightening the clutch. 'You miss the old days?'

In a previous life Esmerelda had worked in 'pre-retail fashion'. That is, she sold and distributed fake, high-quality designer shoes, handbags, clothes and God knows what else, for a professional counterfeiting outfit. They were manufactured at a sweatshop in the western Sydney suburb of Bankstown. Esmerelda had dubbed it the Bankstown Boutique. No, you will not find it in a Google search. I tried.

Esmerelda had probably had her hands on just as much Dior, Chanel, Valentino, Gucci, Prada, Mu Mui, Dolce & Gabbana, Louis Vuitton et al as me. The difference being that none of mine were stolen or imitation. That I knew of.

'Yeah, I was, and nup, I don't,' Esmerelda said in another obvious lie. It was incredible to me that sometimes I could tell immediately when she was lying and other times I could not have been sure if my life depended on it.

'It's okay. We all like beautiful things. I love playing with them,' I said, being more vulnerable than I felt comfortable. It was not often Esmerelda and I had common ground. Not in shopping anyway.

There was a small tap on the outside of the wardrobe door.

'Geez,' said a familiar voice, 'I didn't mean to interrupt. I mean, if you're in the middle of something, I can wait outside.'

How on earth did Searing get into my bedroom? How did he get onto the estate? How did he get through Patricia? Wait, I knew that part. Patricia was all kinds of fond of Searing. Truth be told, once you worked out the Patricia part, the rest fell into place.

'Handbags!' I shouted at him in an unnecessarily loud and high voice through the wardrobe doors. 'We were talking about handbags.'

'Like, no we weren't,' Esmerelda casually retorted, putting a square, clip-close, ivory base with solid gold filigree overlay Dolce & Gabbana purse back on the shelf.

I held my palms out in exasperation and stared at her in disbelief. 'What do you think he is implying we're doing in here?' I hissed. It took her a few moments and then understanding settled in.

'Dude, I'd totally rather be a lesbian than a sybarite,' she retorted. 'Gay chicks have the best sneakers.'

What on earth is a sybarite?

'I do not know what that is,' I whispered, 'but if I'm insulted when I look it up, I will expect an apology.'

'You're gonna be disappointed,' she said over her shoulder as she walked to the doors.

Do. Not. Struggle. By the time I talked myself out of being distracted by Esmerelda, I had already been distracted by Esmerelda and the closet doors were open.

I was soon out of the closet and face to chest with Searing. Was he always this tall? Was he always this shape? So movie-set godlike? Who was in charge of hiring at the police academy anyway, William Morris? Kenneth Branagh?

He latched onto me with those golden eyes and I immediately felt my mouth water. This was ridiculous.

'How did you get in here?' I demanded.

'Well,' he started, 'I spoke to Patricia and she—'

I held my hands up to silence him. 'No need. I can imagine how it went from there.'

I attempted to back him out of the room by walking towards him as I spoke; however, he took only a tiny quarter step for every one of my full steps, the result being I ended up even closer to him. He was once again in a perfectly fitting suit which, for a man of his height, had to be custom.

'What are you doing here?' I demanded.

'The caped crusader here,' he said, gesturing to Esmerelda, who had wasted no time in eating the remainder of my sliced bananas, 'sent an SOS on the bat phone.'

'Must you two always speak in riddles?' I asked, looking up at him in exasperation.

'Like, I texted him we're being bugged. Or followed. Or like bugged and followed,' she said between bites.

'Since when are you two so tight?' Esmerelda had no love for the police. Or parking inspectors. Or magistrates. There was a list.

Esmerelda pointed a banana-and-strawberry-laden gold fork past me to Searing. 'Dude's been busted down to cold cases. He's basically a mini cop again. Who's he gonna tell?'

I surveyed Searing for confirmation.

'Cold cases are important work,' he said. 'Everyone deserves justice. Even if it takes a while.'

Esmerelda chuckled. 'That line's straight outta the dead job manual.'

She was doing it again. Derailing me. Redirecting my brain. It was hard enough to concentrate around Searing. I'd come back to the awkward career move from AFP liaison to cold case detective, *after* the being followed or bugged conversation.

I leaned into Esmerelda, who was seated in my tufted shell chair, and said quietly, 'You told him Dame Elizabeth asked us to track down the identity of the man in the lilies? Who is probably her super-perfect new boyfriend Max?'

'No,' she said, eating a banana slice. 'But like he's right there, so he probably knows now.'

I glanced at Searing. He was looking at the slightly borrowed Vermeer hanging on the wall near my bed.

'Were you listening?' I demanded.

'No,' he fibbed. 'Is that a real Vermeer?'

'No,' I fibbed back.

'I really like the honesty we have in our relationship,' he smiled. 'Tell me why you think you're being followed. Or bugged.'

CHAPTER 10

SECRETS, FAITH AND DENTURES

I reluctantly filled in the blanks, leaving out the lack of permission around Grandmother's oil paintings, hiding under a table at the Holly Park and faltering all over the body. Instead, I just said I had noticed a few things about the man in the lilies that day, Dame Elizabeth didn't want him left in the deep freeze, Grandmother had casually noted Max was possibly missing and we'd had an impromptu chat to some of the Holly Park Hotel Sydney staff about him.

'Dead dude is totally boyfriend Max dude,' Esmerelda said, ever helpful in delicate conversations.

'We received this in the post this morning,' I said, handing him the typed card and envelope.

He took the envelope and peered inside. There was nothing. I had already done that. He examined the stamp and the post mark on the envelope. 'SWPF.'

'Dude, English.'

'Oh, SWPF, the Sydney West Postage Facility. It was processed in the city,' he said. 'That narrows it down to a few million people. Thousands of post boxes. Typed? Huh,' he remarked, examining the card.

'I know,' I said. 'It's a little dated.'

He nodded. 'Yeah. It's old-school,' he said, echoing Esmerelda's earlier comment. 'Or trying to appear old-school.'

I exchanged glances with Esmerelda. That was a good point. Why didn't we think of that? A seventeen-year-old pretending to be a boomer could have written it with an ancient typewriter bought at a thrift shop for five dollars on purpose, to throw us off.

Searing examined the typed card, front and back. He ran his finger gently across the surface of the typed word 'shaft' and then the word 'bleached'.

'You didn't know about the deceased's hair being coloured until you spoke with the barber?' he checked.

'No. Who dyes their hair white? I mean, apart from people who want to go blonde. Or platinum. Or ...' there were so many shades of blonde you could dye your hair. I started over. 'What kind of man dyes his hair white when he is lucky enough to still be Clooney salt and pepper?'

'A man who wants to change his appearance. Be less recognisable,' Searing said.

Oh. Why hadn't I thought of that?

'The bigger question,' he went on, 'is who uses the words "shaft" and "bleached" when expressing that? I'm not that familiar with the whole hair dyeing thing but wouldn't you just say, "dyed hair white"?'

He was right. It was an odd way of expressing it.

'From what you've told me about last night—' he raised an eyebrow, as if he suspected this might have been an edited version of the truth, '—I don't think you're being followed. It would've been virtually impossible to follow you into the hotel and then into the barber *and* the manicurist unseen. Plus, you two were alone with the barber, right?'

Esmerelda sat silently, eating waffles and playing on her phone. She probably tuned out somewhere around Clooney.

'Yes,' I agreed.

'If someone was following you, they'd likely be trying to get information *from* you. Or to intimidate you,' he said matter-of-factly.

He made good points. I could see how he passed muster as a real-life detective despite his ridiculous good looks and stature.

He handed the card and envelope back to me. 'Could someone from inside the investigation be trying to help you?'

That would mean that someone from inside the investigation knew about our investigation. Only Dame Elizabeth and Grandmother knew about our poking around and neither of them would want the police knowing. If the man in the lilies was Max, Dame Elizabeth would not want it publicised that he was found dead, with a hat line head wound, whatever that was, in her tyrannical tycoon neighbour and friend's backyard. That would be bad. The rich did *not* enjoy scandals. And even if Dame Elizabeth had asked someone inside the investigation to help us, which was unlikely, the police were not exactly on the former-double-homicide-and-arsonist-suspect-Indigo cheer squad. I doubted they would oblige. That brought me back full circle.

'I don't think so,' I said, pouring myself tea and sitting in the cream club chair.

'I think it's unlikely too,' Searing said, pulling up a chair. He paused and breathed deeply. There was more to say. 'You might be bugged though.'

'Excuse me?' I faltered, sloshing tea all over my saucer.

Esmerelda stopped eating. 'What now?'

Searing exhaled again. 'I don't think you're being followed. But ... you might be bugged.'

'You think Rope and Winters know we're snooping around?'

'No.'

'What the hell then?' Esmerelda demanded.

'Yes,' I said, pointing at Esmerelda. 'What she said.'

He exhaled again and put his hands flat on the table. 'Okay. Here goes.' He pulled out his phone, switched on some classical music and placed it by the closet. He walked back to us and began.

'What I *tried* to tell you last week at your grandmother's,' he said as he slid me a private look, his sculpted golden-brown cheeks colouring slightly, 'was that ...' He paused. 'It's just that ...' He paused again. And then exhaled.

'Dude!' Esmerelda barked. She looked like she might punch him.

'Okay, okay. I'll have to start at the beginning. When I ran the faces from the Mediterranean Men's Club USB last summer, I had to use a contact at the AFP to access INTERPOL's facial recognition database. To ID them.'

Esmerelda and I nodded. This we knew.

'Then you and I,' he pointed to me, 'had our conversation about the USB, the night you left for Phi Phi. You said you wanted to be a *confidential* confidential informant.'

'What?' Esmerelda quizzed.

'Indigo didn't want to be named as the CI who provided the USB,' he explained.

'You're a *CI*?' Esmerelda asked in a tone that was as close to surprise as I had ever heard from her. Well, at least equal to the time we accidentally found a yeti. Long story.

'Yes. No. I mean, I am sort of an unnamed confidential informant.'

A small detail I had evidently forgotten to share with her.

Esmerelda dropped her waffle and stood from the table, her eyes narrowing. 'But, like, aren't you guys,' she said, pointing at Searing, 'supposed to register the names of your CIs with like the intelligence division?'

Searing eyed Esmerelda. 'How on earth did you know—I mean—I can't answer that question, specifically, but fundamentally, essentially, that could be construed as somewhat accurate.'

Esmerelda look to me for a translation. 'That's a yes,' I said.

'But you didn't?' Esmerelda pressed.

'No.'

'Like, dude, I'm kinda proud of you and all, but you can totally get into deep shit for that,' she said, striding towards the door. 'So,' she said, increasing the volume of her voice, 'I wanna say I didn't do anything. I didn't deliver anything. I don't know nothing. I'm gonna split. Catch ya.'

And she walked out. *Whip, crack.* Doors, bedroom and front, closed.

It was my turn. 'Is Esmerelda right? Have you broken some rule? Are you in trouble with your boss?'

'Yes. No. A little, but it's all under control.'

'Really?'

'Really.'

'Okay,' I said slowly. Searing was a terrible liar, but when he said he had it under control, it felt like he was telling the truth. 'Go on.'

'Because I wouldn't provide the AFP with the name of my CI, they said the source of the USB was unverified and that the Mediterranean Men's Club wasn't a "real thing".'

'*Is* it a real thing?' I asked, amazed.

'Yes, of course it is.'

I clattered my cup in frustration. 'What the hell then?'

'Indigo, please let me finish. Then you can be angry at me.'

'Fine,' I huffed, drinking my rapidly cooling tea.

'The AFP theory is that the Mediterranean Men's Club are just a group of men ...'

I interrupted him. 'A group of men who are *all* serious criminals.'

'Yes, they acknowledged that. But they said the criminals were strangers. Strangers who just happened to have been operated on by one common person. That there is no organised club. That the surgeon or dentist or operator just nicknamed a random group of clients the Mediterranean Men's Club.'

'Is that likely?'

'No. Not at all,' he said wryly. 'Well, very, *very* unlikely.' He rubbed his eyes. 'Most plastic surgeons don't do dental work *and* hair implants *and* play stylist, and vice versa; dentists and hair implant clinics don't perform extensive reconstructive surgery.'

No kidding. Plus, I doubted it was dumb luck that *one* surgeon just happened to attract *so many* wanted criminals. 'So the AFP dropped the whole thing?'

'They said that without verification of the source of the USB, there was no proof the Mediterranean Men's Club was an organised group.'

I was aghast. 'Surely there were other crimes at play?'

He shrugged. 'No. The actual surgeries weren't illegal. What plastic or reconstructive surgery a patient decides to have done is entirely up to them. If, theoretically, the surgeon doesn't know the patient is a wanted criminal, then they haven't done anything wrong in operating on them. It's not like Medicare pays for tummy tucks or nose jobs. It's all privately funded. And it's not illegal to pay for surgical work in cash.

'They argued that most of the people on the USB were obscure, high-ranking, international criminals. That the average citizen wouldn't have a clue who they were. Even if their surgeon *did* suspect, they can't provide confidential patient records to the police without the patient's consent. To access confidential medical records, the police would have to serve the surgeon with a warrant or a subpoena. And they'd need cause outside the doctor's suspicions to do that.'

He was right on too many counts. The security I'd felt in the investigation into my dead husband's illicit surgical activities fell away. I felt naked. Exposed. A tiny grain of panic sat at the edge of my throat.

'What if you *had* told the AFP where you got the USB from? That it came from me and belonged to Richard?' I asked.

'I couldn't tell them.' He slid his hand across the surface of the table to mine, our pinkies touching. 'I promised you I wouldn't.'

'What if you did? What if you told them now? Today?' I pressed.

'I honestly don't know. Probably not a great idea. I might be charged. I might be promoted. I might be demoted or moved sideways. Maybe nothing at all would happen. The inner workings and politics of the justice system are a bit of a crapshoot.'

It hit me. 'That *is* why you lost your position. Why you're working cold cases instead of being on that AFP joint task-force thing.'

'No, no.' He shook his head emphatically. 'Cold case is solid. It could be considered a promotion.'

Now he was lying.

'Are you and Burns still investigating the Mediterranean Men's Club?'

'No, not really. Not officially,' he said solemnly. 'Maybe just a little. On the side. Just the couple of people who might have operated locally. A few questions. Running a few leads down. Known associates. No rules broken. Just a little stretching.'

'Anything you would like to share with me?'

'Oh, uh, no, not really. Nothing solid at the moment.'

'Are you two working cold cases together too?' I asked, letting his obviously shaky answer go and dreading his next answer.

'Oh, yeah, of course. Burns and I are partners. She's a cop's cop.'

That was the truth. She was going to kill me for imploding her career. I wondered how she felt about their side hustle of hunting down the local Mediterranean Men's Club criminals.

I left my pinkie with Searing but spread the fingers of my other hand out and rubbed my head just above my hairline. I tried to process.

'Why do you think this place,' I swept my hand around the room, 'is bugged?'

'Well, this *room* is not bugged,' he said confidently.

'How could you possibly know that?'

He patted a black-grained leather briefcase with loop handles that bulged suspiciously on both sides. It looked like YSL.

'I swept it with a non-linear junction detector while you two were having a little closet talk … I had to look it up too.'

'A non-linear junction detector?'

'No. That's a bug detector.'

'A sybarite?' I guessed again.

'Yep,' he grinned, amused.

'Should I be insulted?'

'Not really. You're a kickass sybarite.' And he lifted his hands off the table and onto the sides of my face.

I was sure there was a way to resist him, but I didn't know what it was. The kiss was not the hard-bitten encounter of the butler's pantry. It was gentle, but also teasing and fraught with suppression. The tenderness simply added to the intensity. Like a tightly wound spring, growing tighter and tighter, pressing down, holding back. Resisting Searing was like trying to hold lust jelly in a sieve. Impossible. I once again found myself on his lap. God, he felt good. I straddled him. This was dangerous. There was a bed in this room. *My* bed was in this room. If I didn't move off him soon, I might never separate from him.

My mind had gone over this moment a thousand times in a thousand different ways while I was away. While stretched out in a cabana on the beach. While in a deck chair poolside. While swinging in a white cotton hammock in the private resort gardens. While swimming. While alone.

His hands pulled up at my waist just as I tried to stand up to extricate myself from him, the combined result being I was virtually launched off him.

'I can't,' he said breathlessly.

'I can't either,' I panted back.

I stumbled into the bathroom and clasped the marble countertop. I recklessly threw cold water on my face then patted myself down with a plush towel. I was going to look like the bride of Frankenstein. Perhaps that might help?

It took me a few more minutes to return to normal colour and to cover the kissing marks and splashing streaks with foundation.

'Right. Okay,' I heard him say, to me or to himself I wasn't sure. I walked out of the bathroom. He was standing. He'd reorganised his shirt and pants and re-tied his tie.

'I need to finish. I need to tell you. I don't think the AFP believe any of that stuff they told me. They know the Mediterranean Men's Club is real. They know my CI is real.'

'Do they know it's me?'

'I was the lead detective on Richard and Crystal's murder investigation. Richard was a highly skilled reconstructive plastic surgeon with an international network of clinics, clients *and* contacts. The USB turned up during that investigation. I think they *strongly* suspect it's you. That's why ... that's why I was concerned they'd tapped my phones. To find you.'

My eyes and jaw went wide with amazement. 'Is that why you ghosted me?! You thought the AFP were listening? Waiting to confirm some connection between us?'

He nodded. 'I'm sorry. I can't be *absolutely* sure they are, or were, but I'm pretty certain.'

That was the best excuse I had ever heard for being ghosted. Either this was the most honest and honourable man in the world, or he was such a great actor that he had me convinced he was a terrible actor when he was really a full-blown mastermind liar.

We stood staring at each other. Thinking.

He broke the tension by pulling his briefcase onto the table. He unzipped it and took out a large suction cup-looking device. He attached it, *snap*, to the end of a black pole coated in heavy plastic. He then locked a black rectangle keypad thing into place in the pole's midsection. Each component lit up once attached.

'Do you mind?' he asked. 'I didn't get a chance to scan the closet while the two of you were in there.'

'Sure,' I said. What was I supposed to say?

It's quite difficult to make small talk with a man scanning your closet for listening devices which may or may not have been planted by the federal police. Especially when you're simultaneously rifling through his briefcase, searching for any information or clues he might have discovered about the secret club of international criminals your dead plastic surgeon husband may or may not have created, but was undoubtably heavily involved with.

'So, Searing, how, how is your, uh, pet? Do you have a pet?' I said, pulling my hands out of his bag just long enough to pocket one of his business cards.

I jumped as he stuck his head out of the closet and smiled broadly at me. 'No, Indigo, I don't have a pet. Thank you for asking though.'

He strolled back into the closet and began scanning my hanging section. *Click-click.* 'I'd like a dog, but I work long hours. It'd be a bit unfair.'

'But you work cold cases now,' I said, a pang of guilt spiking up my throat as I dove back into the bag. 'Those must be shorter hours.'

What the heck did I know? Cold case could have meant investigating the whereabouts of missing pallets of banana Paddle Pops for all I knew.

I stopped foraging when I found a bulging manila folder labelled *UP GREENACRE 0101 WEST*. Was *West* one of the Mediterranean Men's Club people? Was *Greenacre*? Maybe 0101 meant this was the first Mediterranean Men's Club person they were investigating. I didn't recall anyone called West or Greenacre, but I didn't spend a lot of time examining the USB's contents.

The fat cream folder was bound with a yawning black and silver bull clip and tied with horizontal and vertical elastics. I could never get it undone without making a complete mess. So I stole a pen and another business card and jotted *UP GREENACRE 0101 WEST* on the back.

'Not really,' he continued, oblivious. 'Cold cases have all the same elements as homicide, but with mounds of old paperwork. The original leads, plus any new ones, or any that might have been overlooked, all need to be run down. Everyone has to be re-interviewed. Places need to be re-canvassed. Evidence reassessed. DNA tests need to be pushed along. Sometimes cold case forensic evidence sits in a backlog queue, waiting. I've asked for a new autopsy on our case, but I seriously doubt I'll get one approved. I'm not sure how, uh, *thorough* my cold case victim's autopsy was, back in the day.'

Wait. I knew an autopsy person. Didn't I? What exactly does the forensic pathologist do?

'Who does the autopsy?' I asked, trying to casually see into the closet to check on him while replacing the over-stuffed file into the centre of the briefcase. 'What's their title?' I asked, sticking my hands into the briefcase's side pocket.

A half a second after my hand had left the pocket (it was empty, save a pen and a blank pad of Post-it notes), Searing suddenly turned around and smiled at me through the open closet door. That was enough foraging. Any more and I might have a stroke.

'The forensic pathologist,' he said, moving from my shoes to my beloved handbags.

Bingo. I did know someone. I'd bet a Louis Vuitton steamer case Dr Bailly was exceedingly thorough. I didn't have a lot of swabbing experience, but I'm guessing not everyone did a full inventory of their equipment at the scene before swabbing began. She used almost as many pieces of equipment from that case as Hung Vanngo did from his make-up box. And while Hung never knew what he was going to do when he walked into a room, Dr Bailly seemed like the exact opposite. She was a woman with a detailed plan. They did have one commonality—they both seemed to assess each body according to its needs.

I felt guilty for having rifled through Searing's bag. I would try to make it up to him. I walked over to the window. Esmerelda was on an outdoor lounge by the pool, about ten metres away, bathing her face in the almost midday sun. She had her feet up on the end of the lounge, sneakers still on, dark T-shirt rolled up to reveal lean biceps, black torn jeans not rolled up. I assumed this was how skateboarders and possibly even snowboarders baked. I had no idea how surfers baked. Perhaps they were already so overexposed to the sun and the elements, they didn't need to.

I checked Searing was still in the closet then leaned out over the window frame and waved at her. Nothing.

'Psst!' I whispered, flailing my arms about. 'Esmerelda!'

Of the pile of waffles Patricia had brought, there was only one left. It was a cold, sad little waffle and a sacrifice had to be made. I threw it at her. It landed nine metres short, in the loamy, black dirt of a garden bed. With some sense of culinary karmic justice, it landed in a strawberry patch.

Esmerelda turned her head and eyed me like a warm, lazy crocodile. 'You wanna talk to that Dr Jem Bailly chick, don't you?'

Had she been listening? I was feeling slightly paranoid. Which seemed fair, since my Manolo Blahnik sandals were currently being checked for bugs. I narrowed my eyes at her until I could barely see.

She turned her face to the sun and closed her eyes. 'She'll see you tomorrow afternoon.'

'How did you know I wanted to see Dr Bailly?' I demanded.

'Dude,' she sighed, like a teacher tolerating a slow-moving child, 'where else were we gonna go next?'

She had a point. If we were going to find out if the man in the lilies was Max Weller or, better yet, not, we were going to have to compare what we knew about Max with what Dr Bailly had found out about the man in the lilies. It was a happy coincidence that I could ask her to re-autopsy Searing's cold case at the same time.

'How did you get her to agree to see us?'

'I told her you thought maybe the dead dude was like a long-lost great-uncle. That like you hadn't seen in ages. Maybe he wandered into your nana's yard and carked it. You'd forgotten about him, 'cause you hadn't seen him since you were little. But you just remembered,' Esmerelda explained, eyes still closed.

'Is my estranged great-uncle's name Max Weller?' I asked her, catching on.

'Yup,' she said, pulling a black baseball cap down over her eyes. 'Uncle Max.'

CHAPTER 11

THIS BITES

Searing cleared the pool house. I was bug-free. He packed up the equipment he had officially *not* borrowed from the police squad's tech room, having officially said *nothing*, done *nothing* and heard *nothing*. It was slightly possible that I was a bad influence on the straitlaced Searing. Unless he was a master double agent. Unlikely. Surely the police department tested its detectives for these things?

He left without either one of us making firm plans about any future contact.

I was too afraid to venture into Sydney's elite spas, where I was sure I was still a punchline. So, I had Esmerelda call Franny to ask her if she could give me a laser hair removal session, an antioxidant light therapy vitamin facial and a quick Swedish massage. Franny apparently laughed. I consoled myself by buying half a dozen sets of highly impractical bras and knickers from Galleria Intima online. Firm plans with Searing were not made, but I didn't want to get caught out. I wondered what was worse: being gossiped about or getting intimate with imperfect skin and hairy legs?

I was happy I had wrestled the right to drive from Esmerelda until I realised that the forensic pathologist, and FMCCC where she worked, were located in the faraway suburb of Lidcombe. I had been to Paris twenty-six times, had homes in Palm Beach, New York, London and Tuscany, and had visited more tropical resorts than I could count. But I had never been to Lidcombe. My Bentley's odometer was only in the four figures. The airport was as far as I had managed to venture while driving.

I was not ready to drive to Lidcombe on large, complicated freeways with many confusing lanes and exits.

Esmerelda refused to drive my 'old dude' car.

Mother had taken her keys, and Jed's keys, to Bora Bora. Her lack of trust was not completely unwarranted.

Patricia's car was in a coma at the panelbeater.

A debate ensued as to what constituted a 'real car'. *My* real car had leather seats, seat warmers, exemplary climate control, many reassuring lights, buttons and light-up technological looking things. Their shine put me at ease. For Esmerelda, it was a Toyota. I had no idea why this would be, and after half an hour in the garage, I didn't care. Once we'd agreed a Lexus was a middle ground car, it took less than half an hour to call a local dealership, buy a Lexus RX (it had the best picture) hybrid (this would win me points with Mother) and have it delivered.

The FMCCC was surprisingly lovely. I reassessed my genetically built-in Heiress reservations about paying taxation. The government seemed to have spent well. The building was a three-storey architectural blend of modern white lines, sparkling glass, soft wooden curves and a circle-of-life theme so abundantly apparent that even Esmerelda recognised it. The building was surrounded by giant trees and featured comforting plant-related art like hanging tree sculptures and tree murals. It felt professional, but not clinical, spacious and calm, but not cold.

Dr Bailly met us in the lobby. She wore a white lab coat with a large square pocket in the top right corner, blue jeans and immaculate white Adidas sneakers. We silently followed her past a giant white and grey marble reception desk, which probably cost more than the Lexus (and I was back in the government overspending camp) through to a pale wood and natural tone meeting room.

'Indigo-Daisy-Violet-Amber Hasluck-Royce-Jones-Bombberg,' Dr Bailly said without a hint of sarcasm before we were even seated. 'You have recalled something?'

'Yes. Please, Dr Bailly, call me Indigo.'

I sat down in a soft but utilitarian cream chair. Esmerelda followed suit.

'Indigo-Daisy-Violet-Amber, you may call me Bailly. Have you recalled something?'

Well, it was four names less than the last time, so I was going to call it a win.

'Yes. My Great-Uncle Max. He was estranged from the family. It just occurred to me that it might have been him. He might have wandered into Grandmother's garden.'

'Good,' she said. 'I will need some proof of identity. Your personal assistant didn't want to share his surname over the phone. Why was that?'

Because I have no great-uncle, Weller isn't any one of my four surnames and I just wanted to see if I could get in a room

with you so I could try to figure out if this poor man is indeed
Max Weller, my grandmother's neighbour and friend's new
boyfriend.

'I wanted to be sure it was him first,' I lied a little too flawlessly.

'I am supposed to verify your relationship with the deceased before discussing the deceased,' she said, not quite looking me in the eye.

'Like, I'm working on that,' Esmerelda piped.

'You're the personal assistant?' Bailly wanted to know.

'Yeah, I help out.'

'That seems unlikely,' Bailly said. 'You don't appear at all like a personal assistant.'

'I could so totally be a personal assistant!' she barked.

I suppressed a laugh at Esmerelda's outrage. Most people were too polite to point out she looked like a street urchin.

Bailly made a small humming sound. She pursed her lips at an angle and assessed Esmerelda again. She shook her head. 'Nuh-uh.'

Esmerelda's hackles went up. Her body tensed, like a cobra ready to strike.

Bailly was not impressed. I, however, still found it incredibly scary.

'You're right, Dr Bailly, Bailly,' I faltered, attempting to bring some calm. 'Esmerelda isn't my PA. She's my support person. I didn't want to come alone.'

That part was completely true.

'Support people are allowed. Personal assistants are not,' Bailly said matter-of-factly.

Esmerelda eyeballed Bailly, only moderately placated. 'Fine. I'm a support person.'

'Good,' Bailly said, placing her hands flat on the table. 'What can you tell me about your great-uncle? Last name first, please.'

Esmerelda and I stared down at her flat hands. The table was clear. No coffee cup. No pen. No folder.

'Shouldn't you be taking notes or something?' Esmerelda asked.

'Why, would it make you feel more comfortable if I took notes?'

'No,' Esmerelda shot back. 'I don't care.'

'Good.' Bailly looked to me. 'Name please.'

'Yeah but like, why aren't you taking notes?' Esmerelda asked, anger losing the fight to inquisitiveness.

'I have an echoic memory,' Bailly said impassively.

Esmerelda side-eyed me, fishing for an answer. I guessed. 'You can remember everything you hear?'

'I can recall it, yes,' Bailly said.

'Cool!'

'I will use a notebook,' she said, taking a small yellow spiral notebook out of her topcoat pocket. 'Many people feel more comfortable when I'm taking notes. It appears more caring. I can take notes.'

'No, Bailly, it's fine, really. We trust you,' I said, giving her a reassuring smile. 'My great-uncle's name is Max Weller. He is five foot seven inches tall. He would be in his late seventies, early eighties. He was not, the last time I saw him, quite some years ago, homeless. He was a keen swimmer. As you may know, my family is quite comfortable. He would have been well taken care of medically and cosmetically.'

'Was your great-uncle a criminal?' she asked blandly.

'No!' I shot back, defending the reputation of my non-existent great-uncle.

'That description could match UP Rose Bay 0909 Winters then,' she said, ending our argument before it began. 'His fingerprints were not in the system. He had no criminal record.' She put her doleful notebook back in her pocket.

UP Rose Bay 0909 Winters? That must have been the file number or reference name for the man in the lilies. The format was the same as the one on Searing's manila folder. I guessed that 0909 was the date the man in the lilies had been found, 9 September. But what did UP stand for?

'UP is Unknown Person, right?' Esmerelda asked, leaning into the desk like an enthusiastic game show contestant.

'And 0909, it's the date the person was found?' I said involuntarily. 'And Winters is the name of the detective?'

'The lead detective, yes.'

Esmerelda gave an excited wave of the hand. 'No, no, don't help me, I can get it. Rose Bay is the cop shop? The local police command area, right?'

'Correct. UP stands for unknown person. Rose Bay is the local police command area. 0909 is the date the body was discovered, September ninth, and Winters is the name of the lead detective, Detective Winters.'

Esmerelda leaned back, satisfied, as if she had won something. I was not sure what.

Cogs turned as I pondered Searing's bulky manila folder. I leaned in close to Esmerelda and whispered, 'Is Greenacre a suburb in Sydney?'

Esmerelda eyed me in disbelief. 'Uh, yeah.'

'It sounds quite rural. Somewhere one might find acreage, horses and fruit stands. Is it?'

'Dude, it's like next door to Bankstown. You'll find bookies, migration agents and chain jewellery stores. No fruit stands.'

Honestly, marketing people had so much to answer for. I had rifled through Searing's bag only to find the file number of his cold case. Great.

Bailly ploughed on. 'It's unusual for a homeless person to be in such good condition and to have no record with the police. Vagrancy is illegal. As is begging and being publicly intoxicated.' She turned to me. 'You noted he'd had a recent manicure, a cutthroat shave and smelt of Atkinsons California Poppy Hair Oil.'

Her auditory memory was indeed spotless.

'Yes,' I said.

'That's also unusual for a homeless person. Did the smell of the hair oil trigger an olfactory memory, perhaps relating to your great-uncle or another male relative?' she probed.

'Yes, my grandfather,' I said, impressed.

'And then later that triggered memories of your missing great-uncle, Max Weller?'

'Sure,' I fibbed.

'You were confident in your detection of a specific scent on the body. I believed you. I sent a hair sample for chemical analysis to see if the compounds in it were the same as the compounds found in Atkinsons California Poppy Hair Oil.' She gave a slight smile. 'They matched. You were correct.'

I felt sick. 'Does the height match?' I suspected it would, but I hoped my memories of the man in the lilies were incorrect. Perhaps he was taller than I thought. It is hard to tell when the person is lying down.

'Yes,' she nodded.

'Oh,' was all I could manage.

'We CT scan all bodies. UP Rose Bay 0909 Winters has many dental implants. They're expensive. If your great-uncle was rich, he could afford those. Did your great-uncle have dental implants?'

How on earth would I know that?

I inhaled deeply, closed my eyes for dramatic effect and slowly exhaled, desperately trying to buy myself time while I thought. Would a great-niece normally know if her eighty-year-old uncle had dental implants? Getting implants of any kind seemed like a very private thing to do.

Wait.

Dental implants.

'Would a person be able to eat steak and corn with those?' I asked, recalling the manicurist's odd comments about Max's diet.

'Yes. Most elderly people have dentures. This man did not. He had dental implants, either grafted or screwed into the jawbone. They are much better than dentures. But they're expensive. About $10,000 each. He had twenty-four.'

'Dude had quarter of a mill in fake teeth?'

'Dental implants,' Bailly corrected. 'Yes, at least. There was also bone grafting. That would cost more.'

Gilly and Gregory need not have worried. Max was a wealthy man.

'Okay, I remember now. He had dental implants,' I outright fibbed.

I was ninety-nine per cent sure Max Weller *was* the man in the lilies, who was sadly now known as UP Rose Bay 0909 Winters. How horrible for Dame Elizabeth; her lovely new boyfriend was almost certainly dead. For reasons unknown, he had been dressed like a homeless man and dumped in her best friend's garden.

How awful for her—God, how awful for me! She was going to ask me to find out who killed him! Wait. Maybe he wasn't killed. Maybe he just died of natural causes. Maybe he was dressed as a homeless person for a fancy dress party, got lost, wandered onto Grandmother's estate by mistake, had a heart attack (steak and corn will do that to you) and died among the lilies.

It could happen. Except for the head injury part. Maybe he fell over. Accidentally. He *was* eighty. I fell over with frightening regularity and I was nowhere near that age.

'When we were in Grandmother's garden together, just before you left, you said something about a hat and a star and a turtle egg?' I said, swinging the conversation. 'What was that?'

'Can you provide me with any unique details about UP Rose Bay 0909 Winters to verify he was indeed your great-uncle?' Dr Bailly said. 'I cannot discuss injury details without confirmation of a relationship.'

'He liked opera?' I said, grabbing onto the first thing about Max that came to mind. 'He was a stylish dresser? He— he—' I clapped my hands together. 'He dyed his hair! White! He had salt and pepper hair and he dyed it white!'

Bam! I was on Esmerelda's game show too.

'Yes, correct. His hair shaft was bleached. It was not naturally white, not all of it.'

Bleached shaft.

'If your Great-Uncle Max Weller is UP Rose Bay 0909 Winters, I should now be able to verify it through his dental records.'

'Wonderful,' I enthused. 'Please do that.'

This *was* going well.

'Please tell me the name of his dentist.'

'Pardon?'

'The name of his dentist,' she repeated.

I really had to be more careful with my rhetorical questions around Bailly.

'Why do you need the name?'

'I need to contact them so I can compare your uncle's dental x-rays to UP Rose Bay 0909 Winters. Would you feel better if I wrote it down?' she said, reaching for her pocket.

'No, no, that's not it. I haven't seen Uncle Max in many years. I don't know the name of his dentist. Isn't there a dental database or something? Don't you just run all the dental x-rays through a digital dental database?'

It seemed like a basic forensic tool.

'No. There is no dental database. Records are kept individually by each dentist. I need to retrieve your uncle's x-rays from his dentist to compare them to UP Rose Bay 0909 Winters.'

'Dude. How's that not a thing?' Esmerelda said, dumbfounded.

'A dental database is not a thing,' Bailly said simply. 'I need a name.'

We had nothing. I shook my head. 'Is there another way?'

'Yes. Some implants have individual serial numbers.'

'Great! Do that. Trace the serial numbers.'

'I can't,' Bailly said. 'There were no serial numbers. Only a batch number.'

I wished there was a shorter way to have this conversation.

'Can you trace the batch number?'

'Yes. There can be up to 2400 implants in each batch.'

It was as if Esmerelda had spawned in a parallel universe as a shorter, whiter, but equally exasperating academic doctor clone.

'It would take a great deal of time to investigate 2400 possibilities.'

I put my forehead in my hands and looked up at her. 'Is there another way?'

'Yes. There are many other ways. I may be able to verify identity through the driver's licence database. Do you know your uncle's date of birth?'

It was reasonable for a niece not to know her imaginary great-uncle's dentist, it was less reasonable for a niece not to know her imaginary great-uncle's birthday. I mentally tried to count back eighty years. Maths not being my strong suit and a fictional DOB weren't my only concerns. Shale from the Holly Park Hotel Sydney said Max didn't drive. I was flailing. So I did what any good psychopathic liar would do. I pointed at something else.

'The hat hit? Can you tell me about that now?'

'UP Rose Bay 0909 Winters,' she paused, 'feasibly Max Weller, has a blunt force, stellate injury, a laceration near the crown of his head. It's four centimetres end to end. It's the result of a broad impact.'

'He fell over and hit his head?' I asked.

'Unlikely. The laceration is above the hat line.' She illustrated on herself the area where a hat might sit on top of the head. She drew an index finger from above her left ear across to her forehead to her right ear, then around the back of her head.

'When people fall, they usually fall on their face or on the lower back of their head.' She demonstrated, leaning over to one side of her chair until her head was almost horizontal.

I had never thought about it before, but she was right. As a woman who had passed out on multiple occasions, I could attest to this being true. I had often woken up with a grazed chin, a bump on the lower back or side of the head, but never above my hat line.

'He was hit over the head?' I asked as I processed.

'Yes.'

'With?' I prompted.

'Unknown. Something flat. And heavy. I need to find an object to match the laceration. I'm also waiting for trace results. There was a substance in the wound.'

'Max died because he was hit over the head?' I was still a little stunned.

She shook her head. 'I cannot say that is definitively the cause of death. But he was hit with something. There are other tests I need to run to find definitive COD. Investigations I need to do. But I cannot.'

'Why not?' Esmerelda and I asked in unison.

'The chemical analysis test was expensive,' she said unhappily.

She had lost me.

'Like, for the hair oil?'

Bailly nodded. 'I also bought a bottle of the hair oil so I could compare the compounds. It was expensive too. I needed to purchase several cutthroat razors and several pigs to conduct testing. Shaving testing. They were expensive.'

'You shaved a pig?' Esmerelda asked, clearly impressed. I was betting Esmerelda thought those pigs were alive and well somewhere. I was betting she was wrong.

'Yes. Pigs are excellent. Very similar skin to humans, but—'

I guessed. 'Expensive.'

'Yes, pigs are expensive. Tests are expensive. UP Rose Bay 0909 Winters is an unknown homeless man,' she said, her hands beginning to flutter. 'I'm not the coroner. Or the deputy coroner. I work for them. The deputy coroner, Mr Kevin Pasty, says I request too many tests. Tests are expensive.' Her hand fluttering increased in speed. 'I don't like Mr Pasty. I think he's wrong. UP Rose Bay 0909 Winters isn't a priority case.'

Perhaps they could trade the marble reception desk in for some test money?

'Even with the manicures and pedicures? And the—'

'Pig shaving,' Esmerelda added, grinning.

'Yes,' Bailly said. 'He's still officially a homeless UP. I don't think he is a homeless person. Mr Pasty says he is. Our public policy says all cases are equal. That's not true. High-profile cases come first. Wealthy people come first. Well-known people come first. Homeless people, unknown people, quiet people, they come last.'

I felt like I should feel bad about the wealthy people part. But I struggled to work up the guilt. I was however surprised to find that I felt offended on Max Weller's behalf. Okay, maybe I felt a tiny bit horrible when she said quiet people come last too. Feelings were dreadful things.

'I think all cases are equal,' she went on. 'Why are the homeless or unknown less important?'

'Are cold case unknown persons a priority?' I asked before I could stop myself.

'No,' Bailly said. 'UP cold cases are not a priority. Unless someone does a podcast about them.'

She would have been entitled to say these things with a cynical or sarcastic tone. But there was no tone. She was stating facts. Facts that irritated her. Relatively speaking.

I tried to absorb this information while mentally holding onto several schemes with moving parts.

'We could pay for the tests,' I said, trying to ease my guilt and achieve one of my goals: definitively identifying Max. 'As many tests as you like. It would not be an issue.'

'Yes. It is an issue. You cannot pay for tests and you cannot order a private autopsy until you are a fully verified family member.'

She stood up. Was she leaving? Was that it?

'Let me check the driver's licence database for Max Weller. Although,' she said, leaning in closely to examine me, pointing at my face, then touching her own cheeks, 'you don't look remotely related to UP Rose Bay 0909 Winters. You've got none of his genetic facial markers.'

I pushed a flush of panic deep down into my Chanel clutch.

'Uncle by marriage,' I said quickly. 'They had no children. And, um, he was an only child. And an orphan.'

No DNA tests for me or any fictional second cousins.

I was getting way too good at lying.

Bailly exited without another word.

'She's totally weird,' Esmerelda said. 'Uber-science-nerd-woke. Like a pissed-off, super-smart muesli bar. I like, dig her whole vibe.'

I agreed with Esmerelda, which was deeply concerning.

Bailly returned two minutes later. 'Two Max Wellers with current driver's licences. One is twenty-three years of age and lives in Broome, Western Australia. The other is fifty-eight from Cairns, Queensland. She's a female.'

This was a problem.

I had no idea what to do next. Not wanting the day to be a total write-off, I changed gear and took out Searing's stolen business card with *UP GREENACRE 0101 WEST* written on the back. I slid it across the table to Bailly. She read the front, flipped it over and read the back.

'This unknown person may be related to my great-uncle Max,' I lied. 'The investigation is now with the cold case unit. Perhaps you could do a new autopsy? It might help. I'm sure science has improved since the first one was done.'

'The deputy coroner would not allow that,' she said, picking up the card, a hint of a smile flickering across her face. 'Cold case re-autopsies divert resources. Too many tests divert resources.' Her tone indicated she was quoting Mr Pasty, deputy coroner.

'Everybody's got a boss,' Esmerelda said, reading my mind.

'What if I spoke with my mother or grandmother? They could speak to the NSW premier, who could speak to the attorney-general, who could speak with Mr Pasty's boss, the coroner, to ensure you get the resources you need.'

Bailly shook her head. 'That would make UP Rose Bay 0909 Winters a priority.'

'Yes,' I said slowly, not following her shaking head. 'That would be ... good?'

'Good. Yes,' she said, shaking her head more vigorously. 'A high-profile priority.'

'Dude,' Esmerelda said. 'You know your head's movin' the wrong way, right?'

'I'm not allocated high-profile cases. I'm not good with people. They would move the case to Dr Eric Blackstone. Dr Blackstone's good with people. He's also much better at following protocol. He'd be authorised to order more tests than me, but he wouldn't order all of them. The autopsy would be acceptable. The coroner likes him. The deputy coroner likes him. Maybe UP Rose Bay 0909 Winters wouldn't be a homeless man if Dr Blackstone had him.'

Esmerelda and I both recoiled. A pathologist who followed protocol? That would be bad. Bailly was an unusual woman, but her interest in finding answers rather than following bureaucratic rules seemed helpful. My inside information about Max's dyed hair had bought me some authenticity. It might not work on Dr Blackstone. Dr Blackstone might think to google me and find out I had no Great-Uncle Max.

'Have you ever heard of the phrase, "Better to ask for forgiveness than permission"?'

Bailly furrowed her brow. 'No. Would you like Dr Blackstone?'

'God, no!' I said a little too enthusiastically. 'I mean, I would prefer you, Bailly.'

It was true.

'I think you will be more thorough.'

Also true.

'I trust you. I think you will do an exemplary job, with both cases.'

It was a relief to tell the truth after so many lies. An Heiress in her natural habitat tells very few outright fibs. There is a fair amount of air kissing and 'What a fascinating exhibition!' and 'You look wonderful!' type of social white lies. But outright, completely-made-that-up lies? No. There really is no need when you already get what you want all the time.

'Can we check in with you in a few days?' I asked, testing the waters.

She hesitated, looking at the card still in her hand. She read the case number quietly to herself and handed the card back to me. 'Yes, you can check,' she said.

No doubt about it, Bailly was a rebel in a lab coat.

CHAPTER 12

TRICKS

On the way home from the FMCCC, Esmerelda did a Google and social media search for Max Weller, M Weller and, just for fun, Maxine Weller. She found seven worldwide. Two in Australia. One was the twenty-three-year-old man in Broome. The other was a fourteen-year-old girl living in St Kilda, Melbourne. The fifty-eight-year-old from Cairns was invisible on Google and social media. None in country or out were men over sixty-five.

We were going to have to go back to Dame Elizabeth and surreptitiously get more information. I was not prepared to tell her Max Weller was dead. Nor was I prepared to tell her he didn't seem to exist. It was *possible* he was just a *very* private reclusive millionaire. A rare breed, but a breed none the less. That gave me an idea.

'Can you check to see if there is a Max Weller registered as a company director?' I said, turning my head very slightly towards her as I drove. I had decided to brave the freeway on the way home. Esmerelda was, along with the GPS, navigating. She clicked away at her phone. Five minutes later, I received a 'Nup'.

I managed to turn my face to her a little further without driving us into a concrete barrier at high speed. 'Can you check LinkedIn?'

More clicking.

'Nope.'

'Can you check if he is listed as a "C" on any of the ASX 100 companies?'

'You had me until the C bit,' she said, once again attempting to put her feet on the dashboard. I had never been car proud, but this one was only a few hours old. I pushed her feet off, narrowly avoiding ramming the car into a royal blue Mini in the next lane.

'C as in *CEO*, *CFO*, *COO*, *CMO*.'

Crickets.

'Are you playing *Candy Crush*?'

'Nup,' she said as the phone shouted about *Candy Crush*.

'Chief executive officer. Chief financial officer. Chief operating officer. Chief marketing officer.'

It took Esmerelda the rest of the trip home and a little while after, but eventually she strolled into Mother's home theatre with the same answer: 'Nup.'

I sighed in frustration. Max Weller was a millionaire ghost.

'What's on?' she wanted to know, plunking herself in the enormous reclining chair beside me. She placed her calves, not her feet, on an identical chair in front of her. It was hard to chastise her since the theatre seated twenty-four, was never used and was, except for us, empty. It was a legacy item from the previous homeowner, Lord Merton.

'The fall show from Gucci,' I said without much enthusiasm.

'Waste of a big screen. You could watch an epic car chase.'

'I would rather poke myself in the eye with an oyster fork,' I grumbled. And then I huffed.

'Spit it out,' she said, producing an enormous bucket of buttery popcorn from nowhere.

I turned to her. 'When we spoke to Dame Elizabeth, she said Max was from Western Australia. That he had worked in Europe. But Gilly and Gregory said he was from South Australia and that he had worked in Asia. I checked with Shale from the spa; she agreed he was from Adelaide and had worked in Asia.'

'Barber dude said the same thing,' Esmerelda crunched. 'Asia. South Australia.'

'Max was a liar,' I said unhappily. 'What if he *was* a con man of some sort? What if the awful Gregory and Gilly are right?'

Esmerelda squinted and wrinkled her nose. 'Why but?'

'Because Dame Elizabeth is a *very* wealthy woman,' I said, dipping into her popcorn.

'Nah,' she shook her head. 'I looked it up. That Holly Park Hotel suite they talked about he had? The Forrest Suite. It's like, $17k a night. He was there for two months, minimum. Say sixty-two nights. That's over a mill. No con man spends a million dollars on a hotel room. That's crazy town. And he never even took her there, to like, try to impress her? Nah,' she reiterated. 'Nup.'

She had a point. The hotel staff said Max never once brought a woman into the hotel. If you were a con man, why would you rent a luxury suite to impress someone and then never take them to see it?

I was lost.

Patricia walked into the theatre with a silver cordless phone. 'Dame Elizabeth for you two,' she said, handing it over. I shrank my hands away as if the phone was a hot potato. What was I going to say to her? Esmerelda stuffed her mouth with popcorn and then held her hands up in faux defeat.

'Well?' Patricia demanded. Patricia had too much power. She provided the food. Even when we ordered food, she was still the gatekeeper. Without her, I would starve. Or worse: I would have to cook.

I gingerly took the phone and put a white lie smile on my face and in my tone. I could only stall Dame Elizabeth with pleasantries for so long. Too quickly, she got to the point.

'Indigo, dear, what have you found out about the man in the lilies?'

I gave her the crib notes version. Well, a slightly altered crib notes version. We thought the man was from South Australia originally. Ahem. He had excellent dental work. He dyed his hair. I did not elaborate that he bleached his hair whit*er*. He enjoyed manicures, pedicures and razor shaves. I paused to let that information settle in. There was silence for a beat or two.

'It doesn't sound like this man was very homeless,' she summarised astutely.

I exhaled deeply, then realised she could hear me exhale. Esmerelda saved me.

'Like, hi, Lizzy,' Esmerelda said into the phone, which was on speaker resting on the tray table between our chairs. 'So, have you like gotten Heinsmann the Horrible to back off yet?'

It was Dame Elizabeth's turn to be uncomfortable. 'Not quite yet, dear. But he will relent. I am older than he is and I have more favours owed to me. Leave it with me, dear Essie.'

I stifled a childish laugh. Essie? *Dear* Essie. I expected fury from Esmerelda.

'Okay,' she said, shrugging and settling back into her recliner.

I tried to catch her eye to remind her to be indignant but she was focused on the Gucci fall show. Which is to say she was faking focus, leaving me on the line, so to speak.

'Have you had any more outings with your new beau?' I asked, fishing for more information about Max.

Another small silence.

'Not yet, but we have tickets to *Swan Lake* on Saturday night. He won't miss it. He loves Odette,' she said bravely.

'What's Max going to wear? Which Australian designers does he wear, specifically? Is he having something tailored?' I asked, attempting to extract specific, searchable information.

'Dude. They're rich people. Ask what jewels he's gonna wear.'

This got a laugh from Dame Elizabeth.

'Actually, Max *does* know a lot about jewellery.'

Esmerelda mouthed the words *jewel thief* at me. I shook my head and silently swatted at her.

'Did he, does he,' I autocorrected, 'wear a lot of jewellery?'

'No, not really. He wears one of those Buddhist prayer bracelets, just like your mother. Except Max's is a grey-black colour and the beads are quite like large pearls. It is rather beautiful.'

Buddhist prayer bracelets were beyond common. You could buy them everywhere from discount shopping centre jewellery stores to market stalls in Bali and Bondi.

'A watch?' I asked hopefully, glancing at my Patek Philippe, bequeathed to me by my late father. Watches could be very identifiable.

'A diving watch of some sorts. A black affair. No idea which brand. He's a swimmer.'

'Ahh-kow,' Esmerelda mumbled with a mouth full of popcorn.

'Ahh, ahh,' I stumbled, trying to cover up Esmerelda's knowledge of Max's swimming habits. 'Ahh, art! Art. Yes. Some wonderful exhibitions coming up you two could see.'

Oh yes, I was impressive. Indigo the master detective.

'You're quite right, Indigo. There is a Nyapanyapa Yunupingu exhibition on next week. Max is a bit of an expert on First Australian art. He has an extensive collection.'

'Really? Have you seen it? His collection?'

'No, dear,' she laughed. 'Max and I are not quite at the stage where I attend *his* home!'

'No sleepovers, huh?' Esmerelda interjected.

I just about choked on my own tongue.

Dame Elizabeth laughed. 'I didn't say he doesn't visit *my* home,' she replied cheekily.

I tried to scrub the visual from my mind.

Esmerelda gave a popcorn-ladened smile then fist-bumped the air over the top of the phone.

I rolled my eyes in disapproval. 'On that note, let's say goodnight.'

'Keep up the good work, ladies. I shall check in again later in the week.'

I pressed the 'end' button on the phone.

'So, like, he's a crazy rich dude who knows about jewels and art. Shocker.'

She was right. They were practically recreational sports in 'crazy rich' circles. And anyone who spent a million dollars on an eight-week stay in a hotel was crazy rich. Both the barber and the manicurist said Max paid in cash. Max was crazy like a fox rich.

*

I woke up the next morning still not knowing how I was going to identify Max Weller. The *real* Max Weller. Patricia brought my breakfast tray at 11.10 am. Oven-fresh, crispy on the outside, soft in the middle, imported French crois-sants with a trio of homemade jams and a trifecta of creams (clotted, whipped and pouring). The French press coffee brought a lovely balance.

The moment the coffee hit the bottom of the smooth tur-quoise Shanghai Tang cup, Esmerelda strolled through the door. No doubt, she had exceptional sensory gifts.

By the time I had crunched my way into my first crois-sant with raspberry jam and whipped cream, Patricia had made the bed, fluffed the pillows and collected the dry-cleaning.

Esmerelda plopped herself into the shell armchair and poured herself a coffee.

'You do know this is my private bedroom,' I said.

'This your jam, Patricia?' Esmerelda asked Patricia, ignoring me.

'Of course,' Patricia said, pausing on her way out of the bedroom.

'Did you put *Steel Magnolias* on in mother's home theatre last night?' I quizzed Esmerelda.

'Totally. It's a classic.'

I was deeply tempted to ask why, specifically, she felt that way but I was distracted when Patricia produced an envelope from her pocket.

'I almost forgot. This came for you this morning,' she said.

My stomach sank. I immediately recognised the typeface.

'Duuude,' Esmerelda warned after glancing at it.

I took the envelope and thanked Patricia. She almost fell out of the room in shock.

I examined the front of the envelope carefully. It was addressed to Indigo Jones-Bombberg. It had the same postage stamp, a golfing Santa. That was something Searing had failed to mention in his professional assessment. It also had the same post mark, *SWPF*. Only five million people living in Sydney. Easy.

I opened it. It was typed on the same card: a good base stock, nothing too fancy.

> The dead body you found had:
> - 24 dental implants - batch number 1331550011
> - a row of four identical 5 mm stab wounds, exactly 30 mm apart, in right upper thigh

'Did you know he had stab wounds?'

'No. I didn't see any blood. But five millimetres.' I pinched my thumb and forefinger closely together and squinted as I peered through what I estimated to be a five-millimetre gap. 'That's tiny. And his pants were a dark colour and pretty grubby.'

'Why would they be identical?'

'Maybe they were all made by the same weapon.'

'Yeah, but why would they be the exact same distance apart?'

I shrugged. 'A very neat attacker?'

This got me a deadpan look.

My eyes roamed the room searching for OCD weapons. There were a surprising number that fit the bill: my fork, a row of hooks, the wooden spindles that formed the back of a vintage chair in the corner.

'Cutlery? Furniture?' I mused out loud.

'Well,' Esmerelda said, clearly giving up on me, 'at least we got a batch number on the dental implants. That's more than we had before.'

'Bailly said there could be thousands of implants in each batch,' I said, placing the card on the table.

'Yeah, but that's like *up to*. And like, she doesn't have our contacts,' she said, dunking her croissant in her coffee. Which is the Parisian way to breakfast, but she didn't know that. Could Heinsmann and Dame Elizabeth be right? Did Esmerelda have something? I examined her outfit. No. Not possible.

'What contacts?' I queried, pulling my mind back.

'Dude, you like *own* a plastic surgery empire thing. They do loads of implants. They can track implants, right?'

My late husband had built and then bequeathed Sydney Plastics, a boutique, but still very substantial, international plastic surgery empire to me. Well, 67.5 per cent of it. The bulk of the rest he'd left to his not-so-dead family, whose quarterly dividend cheques were posted to them in Ireland.

'There is a large difference between a breast implant or a cheek implant or a whatever implant and a dental implant,' I said.

'Why? What's the diff?'

I thought about it. I drank my coffee. I ate a croissant. I hated to admit it, but she was right. Maybe there was no difference.

If anyone could trace Max's implant batch number, it was the new general manager of Sydney Plastics, Harvard MBA and all-round organisational genius, Rachael White. The brains behind plastic surgeon to the stars, Dr Bradley White.

'Do you think Rachael could do that?' I pondered, looking up from peeling the warm, crispy skin off my third croissant.

'She says she'll try,' Esmerelda said, pocketing her phone. 'Give her a couple days.'

'You've already contacted her?' Sometimes Esmerelda was frightening in her speed and efficiency. I didn't even get a response from this question. I had insulted her. 'You do know you work for me,' I prodded.

'I know,' she said, sipping St. Helena coffee out of a $200 china cup while eating an imported $17 pastry. 'Like, work, work, work.'

Do not go there. Let it go. It's a trap.

I picked up the card and pondered. *Bleached hair shaft.*

I heard Searing's voice in my head: *who uses the words shaft and bleached.* Bailly had used exactly the same words: *His hair shaft was bleached.* It was an unusual, very *specific* way of expressing it.

By the time I came to from my second reverie for the day, I had eaten two more croissants.

'How hard would it be to find out where a department of justice employee lives? Specifically, their home address,' I asked Esmerelda.

'Not too hard,' she said, rearranging her chair to get more sunlight through the window.

'Really?' I was surprised. I would have thought the home addresses of justice department employees like judges and prison wardens would have been highly protected and elusive.

She eyeballed me. 'Like, you totally don't know how to spend your money properly.'

'You would,' I lowered my voice, 'bribe someone?'

'You think your family got rich by following the rules? Your nanna's a freight train, man. Anyone she doesn't take out, she buys out.'

Her tone did not indicate derision. Surfer spy girl had strange heroes. Which is not to say I had any issue with buying my information. Or anything else. I just did not want to get caught.

'I already got it anyway,' she said, pulling the phone from her pocket. 'You want me to write it down? I can like totally do it in code.'

I had no intention of asking her about the code.

'You already have Bailly's home address?'

If Esmerelda and I kept thinking the same thoughts, I was going to have to fire my therapist and replace her with a trained seal. I could not live in a world where Esmerelda and I lived in the same headspace.

'What? Dude, no,' she said, shaking her head. 'Searing. I got Searing's home address.'

After the enormous relief of not being at one with Esmerelda passed, a deafening reality dawned on me. I had the power to find Searing at home. Alone. At home alone. My mind wandered Phi Phi far away. It was bad enough when Searing had been in *my* bedroom. A bedroom birth-control uncomfortably close to Mother's house. Having the location of his bedroom, far from any prying eyes or ears, was mind-bending. It was too much information. Too much power. It was like having Ryan Gosling's home address. Or being able to drop in on Chris Hemsworth … except … I knew where both of those men lived. So it was obviously much worse than that.

Esmerelda had been talking but I had no idea what she had said.

'… gotta get that fixed.'

'Pardon?'

She examined my face. 'You really gonna drop in on Bailly? I mean, if you got a plan and you're not gonna get busted, I could find her, but, like, you know.'

Did I know? Esmerelda sounded somewhat serious. How bad was it to confront a forensic pathologist working on the murder investigation of your fictional great-uncle in her home?

I wrinkled my nose. 'Is it *that* bad?'

She shrugged. 'It's not, like, *not* bad. It's not *as* bad as a judge, but it's like *worse* than a prison guard.' Her hand moved up and down in measurement, closer to the ground being a lowly social worker and closer to the ceiling being a High Court judge or the police commissioner.

We were running out of croissants.

'Why would you?' she wanted to know. 'Bailly said we could check in with her in a couple days. Like, what's the rush?'

'What if Bailly is the leak? What if she's sending the cards?'

'Well, yay for us then, 'cause she's helping out,' she said, choosing one of the last croissants.

'You don't feel like that would be utterly deceptive? She gives us information via these typed cards and then tests us on it when we meet her? That seems a little sick and twisted.'

'I totally don't think bullshitting's her style. But,' she shrugged, 'who knows what goes on with super-smart people? They're almost as freaky as rich people.'

I felt unreasonably angry with Jem Bailly. What if she *wasn't* just a quirky, super-smart scientist? What if she was a diabolical, manipulative mastermind? A fierce anger rose at the notion.

I'd had enough of being lied to. Enough of machinations going on in the deep background and being the last to know. Enough of being deceived by someone I trusted. Someone I respected. Someone I ...

It itched at me.

What if it was someone from within the investigation? Rope or Winters? Was Rope sophisticated or creative enough to hand-type a card? Would Winters jeopardise his career to help us? Not likely. Besides, how would they even know we were investigating? As far as they knew, I was just a fire-happy Heiress who happened to stumble across a body.

I had come full circle with no answers.

'Find the address,' I said finally.

'Geez, that took you a while. I thought I was gonna have to get a Happy Meal to snap you out of it.'

I said nothing. I was sulking.

'You look pissed,' she said, grinning. 'I'd betta drive.'

CHAPTER 13

BAKE OUT

Bailly lived surprisingly close, in a beachside suburb called Maroubra. The drive out of Vaucluse through Rose Bay, Bondi, Bronte and Coogee to Maroubra was soothing. I sat in the passenger seat (I was not in a driving mood) watching the hypnotic coastal landscape. It inoculated me to the fact that we had slipped silently out of the golden triangle and into the zone of middle-class beach dwellers. Maroubra had a flash-in-the-pan history of race riots accompanied by a more systemic side of violent surf gangs. It currently showed no signs of turmoil. Gentrification, skyrocketing real estate prices, social evolution and a limit on the number of houses and apartments you could physically build along the Sydney coastline had chased out all but the most vigilant bigots and bullies. This left a raft of middle- to upper middle-class Sydneysiders. These varied from forensic pathologists (Bailly), to school teachers (my high school English teacher), to share homes (my Pilates instructor) and blended families (just a guess, it seemed like a blended family kind of place) to deal with the many real estate brokers, British and Swedish backpackers and the eternally present cohort of sunbathing and surfing devotees.

We pulled up across the road from Bailly's address. Her white, five-storey, twin apartment block seemed to have been designed by a moderately sophisticated Ronald McDonald. Judging by the identical rectangular red front doors, the two blocks were each three apartments wide. The buildings were conjoined by a pair of walkable golden arches which had been haphazardly stuck on their fronts. The gap between the two blocks under the arches would have made a fine drive-through. Thinking about golden arches and drive-throughs made me hungry.

The problem was hunger was all I had. I didn't know what to do next. The calming drive down the coast had taken some of the sting out of my anger. I suspected Esmerelda was right. Jem Bailly was probably just a smart eccentric doctor. But then there was the itch. The *what if.*

It was possible I had trust issues.

'You got that look again,' Esmerelda said. 'If you're gonna be a while I could …' And she pointed to the ocean.

If I let Esmerelda loose on a beach, I might not get her back for days.

'No,' I said definitively. 'I have decided. I'm going to ask her flat out if she has been sending me letters.'

'Cards,' Esmerelda corrected.

'Whatever,' I huffed. 'I'm going to ask.'

'Three A. Third floor, first door on the left,' she said, pointing to a door near the left arch.

'Okay.' I nodded. 'Great. Terrific.'

Then I sat very still in my seat. Esmerelda lasted under twenty seconds.

'Like, today you're gonna ask? Or like telescopically you're gonna ask?'

Telescopically?

'Telepathically?'

'Yeah, you know,' she said, eyes wide with inflection. 'With your mind.'

'In person. I'm just waiting for her to come home.'

'How'd you know she's out?'

'Or to go out,' I volleyed. 'I'm just waiting for her to appear at her front door. Or in the drive-through, I mean garage. When she's *outside*, I will ask her.'

'You're not going in?' she asked, pointing to the building.

'There aren't any laws against running into a forensic pathologist or a judge or a parole officer *on the street*,' I said, improvising (lying) through my teeth. 'If we just accidentally, coincidentally run into her out here and ask a question or two, that would be completely innocent. You could not prove that we illegally acquired her home address. We would be blameless.'

Esmerelda eyed me suspiciously then nodded in appreciation. 'Smart,' she said, tapping the side of her head. 'Crazy like a cat in a box.'

Stakeouts on television always appear in thirty-second montages. In reality, stakeouts are long hours spent sitting in a new-car-smelling Lexus, listening to the sound of the ocean, drinking one-dollar coffee and eating whatever fresh Krispy Kreme doughnuts remain at the 7-Eleven across the road. This is topped only by the indignity of having to relieve oneself in a nearby 'self-cleaning' public toilet block. I don't know how much stakeout police get paid, but whatever it is, it should be more.

Esmerelda on the other hand seemed happy, content to lie back on the buttery leather of the reclined driver's seat and rest.

The sun literally set on our stakeout. Rays of red, orange, yellow and pink lit the whole building, bringing the golden arches to life. Perhaps it was not *as* bad as staking out a drug den in a ghetto, but still.

I'd been sitting in the darkness forever, we were out of doughnuts and my bottom ached.

'How long do these things usually take?' I asked, not for the first time.

'Dude, like I said, I don't know. She should've been home ages ago if she was at work, or come home if she was out. It'd be so much easier if we just needed to snoop around inside. Snooping's easy. Waiting sucks.'

It is a universal certainty that Esmerelda continued to talk, but I had no idea what she said. My day had been filled with croissants, doughnuts and uncertainty. Plus, I was parked in front of a building that reminded me of a restaurant that produced Happy Meals, but did not itself produce Happy Meals, which made me both unreasonably hungry and resentful—hungful. I fell asleep, dreaming of cheeseburgers with extra pickles and perfectly cooked fries covered in a salt that was so highly addictive, it could have been a neurotoxin and I would probably still have craved it.

The blinding rays of the rising sun woke me. Magnified by the reflective pale blues of the ocean, they were dazzling. I had slept in a car. This was a new social and personal low.

At that stage, Jem Bailly could have been selling algorithms to manipulate the US and British elections to the Chinese *and* the Russians and I would not have stayed another minute sitting in that seat. I was done.

I was too afraid to look in the mirror. My hair and make-up required strenuous upkeep and were attended to almost daily by Franny. My thick mane must have been a poufy, lion-like terror, and my face was bare of any helpful products, save for the remnants of yesterday's mascara.

I groped in my Dior tote for my sunglasses, wedged them onto my face and fell out the door. My dazed legs buckled underneath me, unaccustomed to sleeping rough, and I hit the pavement with a thud. Esmerelda stretched like a Bengal cat, ran a hand through her newly razored hair and looked photoshoot ready. Some days I really hated her.

'I'm done,' I said, crawling across the concrete path.

'Thank fuck for that,' she said. 'I gotta get a coffee.'

It had finally happened. One of *my* bad habits— caffeine—had rubbed off on Esmerelda. I also felt somewhat relieved that she too was in such poor mental condition after a night in the car that she forgot not to swear. She looked incredible but she felt lousy, so there was some justice.

'There's a bakery 'round the corner,' she said, offering me a hand.

'Is it bad?' I asked, touching my hair and face.

'What? Nah, but like, you gotta get up. If you're on the footpath at the beach at sunrise, you can get done for vagrancy. That'd be bad. I'm still technically on parole,' she said, hefting me up off the kerb.

Esmerelda saving me from vagrancy. My Heiress life had taken a sharp left turn into hell. This was tempered by the smell of the bakery—fresh yeast, hot dough, sugar glaze and roasting Jamaican coffee—mixed in with the salty-crisp-and-clean of the ocean breeze.

We trudged down the footpath, took a single right turn and crossed the street to the appropriately named The Cranky Baker. I collapsed onto the least salt-rusted chair at the cleanest rickety wooden table in front of the shop and handed Esmerelda my entire handbag. I was not willing to wait for table service.

'Buy everything.'

'Totally way ahead of you,' she responded, fishing out my purse and removing a gold credit card.

I cradled my head in my hands, inhaling the scents of carbs, coffee and seawater. I was in the early stages of an epiphany about purchasing more beachfront property when I heard a woman, who had apparently seated herself across from me, ordering.

'Would you like that as a latte or a flat white?' the waiter was asking.

'Either. I've had both beverages and they're identical.'

'Not really,' said the waiter, unfamiliar with his audience. 'You see, with the latte we have a small layer of foam, but with the—'

'No,' she replied without malice. 'I took samples from both beverages and tested them. They're empirically identical.'

I peeled my forehead off my hands and found myself face-to-face with Dr Bailly. I opened and closed my eyes repeatedly. Being locked in a car overnight with the frightening chemicals used on new upholstery could have caused some type of hallucinogenic reaction.

She was still there.

'Do you own a typewriter?' I abruptly asked her.

'No.'

She did not seem to think the question was odd, left of centre, or in any way out of place, even delivered at 6 am, by a virtual stranger in a café just thirty metres from her home.

'Do you need a menu, Indigo-Daisy-Violet-Amber?' she asked, offering me a well-worn piece of A3 paper folded in three. 'I don't need it. I know it off by heart. I always order raisin toast. The raisin toast is very good.'

'No, thank you, Bailly,' I said, smiling weakly.

I was torn. The resentment and fear of being duped again sat heavily in my chest. I wanted to grill her. I needed someone to be angry with. The problem was, I believed her. She was quite possibly a genius, but she was no criminal genius. She was without guile and sincerely kind. She was also missing seven out of ten social skills. She really grew on you.

Like an online shopper reluctant to click the pay button at a new store, I searched for Esmerelda for reassurance. With timing as immaculate as ever, she plonked herself down on the chair between Bailly and I.

'Hey, look!' she said excitedly, pointing back to the counter with its vast plexiglass front, innards filled with perfectly tanned baked goods. 'They got fresh croissants!'

'The croissants are also good,' Bailly agreed. 'Not as good as the raisin toast, but good.'

Esmerelda gave Bailly a wide grin, her stalking crocodile persona nowhere to be seen. She was all happy, cute koala, Bill & Ted's Excellent Esmerelda. It could have been that she was overwhelmed by fatigue and hunger, but I decided to trust my instincts, ignore my paranoia and go with

Esmerelda's gut. Plus, I was tired, and they had freshly deep fried vanilla-glazed bear claws stuffed with cinnamon apple and crème pâtissière.

Besides, no one who lived so close to a bakery this good could be rotten. That left one alternative: my penpal had to be someone from within the police.

'What do you know about Detectives Rope and Winters?' I asked Bailly as her somewhat terrified waiter appeared to deliver her coffee.

'They're police detectives,' she said, examining the sugar shaker, deciding against it and reaching for the packets.

'And?' I prompted.

'They're partners,' she said, selecting a packet of plant steroid brown sugar.

'And?'

'They're police detective partners,' she said, ripping the top off the tiny sachet and emptying it into her latte/flat white.

I could see that saying 'and' again would cause her to answer in a similar fashion, which would cause me to shriek violently. I tried another strategy.

'Are they *good* detectives?' I asked, hoping my emphasis on the word 'good' would connote some meaning regarding their ethical standards.

'Rope is *not* a good detective,' Bailly said, shaking her head and bobbing her body forward to emphasise 'not'. 'Winters is a *very* good detective. Between them, they make one *median* good detective. That's probably sufficient,' she said.

'Sufficient?'

'Yes. Sufficient. Adequate for the purpose. Enough.'

Okay. Sufficient. I didn't think she was referring to their moral compass. I would circle back to that. Might as well dive down the rabbit hole in front of me while the going was good. I straightened my spine and inhaled.

'Do you think that Detectives Rope and Winters will successfully investigate and solve the mystery of UP Rose Bay 0909 Winters?' I tried, very precisely.

'No.'

'No?' I quizzed. The moment the word came out of my mouth, I regretted it. I beat her to the response. 'No, okay, I get it. No means no.'

She nodded. 'Yes. No.'

Sadly, I knew what she meant.

'Why not?' I said, getting the hang of the gentle interrogation. Be calm. Be specific.

'Detective Winters had his arm broken by a farmyard animal. He's now restricted to desk duties, meaning he's unable to perform at full function. As a combined team, they now fall below the median of good into sub-par. The UP Rose Bay 0909 Winters investigation is difficult. UP Rose Bay 0909 Winters has not been listed as a missing person. You're the only person to come forward claiming knowledge and relation to him. His fingerprints aren't in the system. His DNA isn't in the system. Because he is elderly, his age is hard to gauge. He could be sixty-eight, he could be eighty-six. There are many indications he wasn't homeless—on the contrary, he presented as a very wealthy man—yet he was dressed as a vagrant and covered in detritus and organic matter. His injuries are varied and curious. Tests are expensive. He is not a priority. I would estimate that it is unlikely they will find his identity or his killer.'

'Like, that's a lotta words,' Esmerelda said.

Bailly's last word struck me.

'You think there was a killer?'

'Yes. I can almost certainly state that he was murdered. I have run many tests. I am waiting for results,' she said.

'You ran more tests?' I pressed her.

'Yes. I extended the autopsy to its full capacity,' she said, sipping her latte. It was definitely a latte.

'Are you going to get into trouble for that?' I asked, motioning for Esmerelda to take a note to remind me when this was all over, I'd need to have a word to the NSW premier about having Bailly's slate wiped clean with her boss's boss, the NSW coroner.

'Yes,' Bailly said, accepting her raisin toast from a new waitress. 'I didn't become a forensic pathologist so that I could be told not to be a forensic pathologist. There are more financially lucrative medical specialities. But none that communicate with the dead. I needed the tests to complete the autopsy.'

'Come back to the farm animal part,' Esmerelda said, as always focusing on the most important issue. 'What kinda farm animal?'

'A lamb.'

'Like, Detective Winter got his ass handed to him by a lamb?'

Bailly peered at Esmerelda. 'There was no donkey. It was a lamb. Lamb.'

She said the last word slowly. *Laaamb*.

I thought Esmerelda was going to punch Bailly. She was instantly inflamed, looking to me in indignant frustration, gesturing at Bailly with her right palm outstretched.

What I really wanted to say was, 'Kettle, meet Pot.' But I didn't. I was strong.

'Where might a homicide detective encounter a farmyard animal like a lamb?' I asked on Esmerelda's furious-curious behalf.

'In a farmyard,' Bailly said, sipping.

Esmerelda glared at me like the wounded party in a sibling fight. I understood why Bailly might have been tapped as the forensic pathologist with lower-end people skills. On the upside, if I needed to find out what an exploded Esmerelda head looked like, I knew where to come.

'Why was Detective Winters at a farmyard?' I asked calmly, not willing to risk any Esmerelda brain contamination on my bear claw.

'He has a hobby farm in the Blue Mountains,' she said, turning her attention to the raisin toast. Lightly toasted, butter on the side.

'I see. So he was at his hobby farm and he was kicked in the arm by a lamb?' I was getting good at being calm.

'No,' she said, spreading the butter generously. She was going to run out of butter.

Think.

'He was at someone else's farm and was kicked in the arm by a lamb?' I tried serenely.

'Yes.'

I was getting *excellent* at this.

'Dude!' Esmerelda said, finally getting a rush of some kind from Bailly's answers. 'It wasn't even his lamb? Someone else's lamb broke Winters's arm? Awesome. Like, I hope it was super fluffy and super cute. And like had a little bell 'round its neck.'

'Why?' I stupidly wanted to know.

Esmerelda glared at me like I was the investor who had turned down the opportunity to give the people at Google their seed money.

'It's totally way much more better that way.'

Of course it was.

I stopped a waitress. 'Could we have more butter please?'

Bailly eyed her nearly empty butter dish and then me. 'Thank you. You're very observant, Indigo-Daisy-Violet-Amber.'

I didn't know what to say. It was the second time she had given me the compliment. Bailly didn't seem like the most bountiful compliment-giver.

'Was it his left arm or his right arm?' I asked, sensing an opportunity to have my original enquiry answered.

'Right,' Bailly said, biting into her raisin toast.

'Is Detective Winters right-handed?'

Bailly watched the waitress place a small ceramic butter dish filled with curled globes of grooved butter in front of her and then nodded.

Winters was right-handed and had a broken right arm. There was no way he was the typewriter bandit. Rope was just not creative enough for stock card, posted envelopes and manual typewriters. Plus, according to a conversation I'd had with Bailly on the day we first met, Rope was a horrible speller. There were no spelling mistakes on the anonymous cards. Even the grammar was correct.

I was back to being frustrated and clueless. Which triggered my hungry button for sugar-filled foods.

Esmerelda was still on the lamb.

'So, like, did it kick him? Did he fall over it? Did it attack him? Was he running away from it?'

'Yes. He fell over the lamb, which had unexpectedly run in front of him. As he was falling over the lamb, the lamb's hind leg kicked out and hit the detective in the forearm. His ulna was broken. I do not know whether it was broken by the fall or by the kicking. Both are feasible.'

Bailly carefully examined Esmerelda's riveted expression as Esmerelda nodded her head in encouragement. 'And? It was fluffy, right?'

Bailly stared at Esmerelda for a long moment. 'Spring lambs are generally considered endearing. At that stage of development, a lamb would almost certainly have enough new wool to be considered fluffy,' she said finally. 'Therefore, I have no reason to believe that the lamb that injured Detective Winters was not "super fluffy and super cute".'

This made Esmerelda extremely happy. I was also happy because large volumes of baked goods began to arrive: pain aux raisins, chocolate cake, blueberry muffin, orange cake, brownie, caramel slice, raspberry white chocolate muffin, lemon poppyseed cake, croissant, pain au chocolat, apricot Danish, apple turnover, brioche, raisin toast and one vanilla-glazed bear claw. This was followed by a variety of teas and coffees. One of everything, as requested. We took up all the room on our table and the one next to us. I was not concerned. While Esmerelda and I were professional in very few ways, eating was an exception.

'Don't even think about touching that bear claw,' I said to Esmerelda with a mouth full of blueberry muffin while pouring my tea. Although I was primarily a pacifist, I worked out semi-regularly with an angry female kickboxing champion and I knew a few bear claw-worthy moves.

'You're not going to eat all that, are you, Mrs Hasluck-Royce-Jones-Bombberg?' said a voice behind me.

It was moments like these that restored my faith in God. That is, that God was very real, and really didn't like me.

I desperately tried to choke down my muffin, which was a tremendous shame because it had a perfectly browned crispy crust, was heavily scattered with fresh blueberries, and was soft, airy and delightfully warm in the middle. I hated to waste it on choking.

Esmerelda, who had a mouth full of pain aux raisins, frowned suspiciously at me. The expression of shock on my stuffed face evidently convinced her that I had no part to play in Searing's appearance.

'Dude,' she managed, twisting sideways to glare up at him. 'Like what the hell? You don't live near here.'

'And how would you know?' Searing asked, pulling out the fourth and final seat at the table. 'Do you mind, Jem?'

Jem?

'No,' she replied.

'You two know each other?' I said, trying to remain calm while simultaneously hoping I didn't have blueberry in my teeth.

'Oh yeah,' Searing said, flashing me his ludicrously gorgeous smile. 'Jem and I go way back.'

Searing seated himself. Unsurprisingly, every female member of waitstaff, and two of the males, were instantly at our table to take Searing's order. As if he wasn't attractive enough, he ordered a bear claw. Be still my heart.

'Seriously?' Esmerelda said, with no qualms about speaking while starting in on the raspberry muffin. 'You've been homicide for five minutes.'

'Detective Searing has been a detective for six years. Homicide for over two,' Bailly corrected. 'There are an average of sixty-one homicides per year in Sydney. There are currently six forensic pathologists at the FM triple C. Statistically speaking, it would be unlikely that the detective and I would not be professionally acquainted.'

Searing's bear claw arrived in a land-speed record, along with a chai latte I am almost certain he had not ordered.

I was so shocked that I had unconsciously begun to eat my own sugar-covered claw and only had two bites remaining. My latte glass was empty.

'Also,' Searing said, sipping his chai, 'we did a few units of criminology together at uni.'

'No,' she challenged calmly. 'Five. Five is more than a few. Two is a couple. Three is a few.'

The caffeine and sugar rushed to my brain and I realised I had asked Bailly to re-autopsy a case belonging to a detective she knew. Undoubtedly quite well. They were probably friends. 'So, you're friends?'

Bailly sipped her coffee. 'We're not friends.'

Or not.

'We're not?' Searing questioned.

Bailly shook her head. 'No. Cassie Roebuck, who sat next to me in Year Three, said friends speak every day. We don't speak daily. Fiona Carlson, who sat next to me in "Criminological Perspectives: Understanding Crime" at university, said adult friends speak at least three times a week. We don't speak three times a week.'

Esmerelda stopped eating just long enough to impart some sage advice about people named Cassie Roebuck and Fiona Carlson being, well, several colourful and unappealing adjectives, not all of which one would find in a dictionary. Her point being they weren't to be trusted. She added that even if Ali Wong, Sally Fitzgibbons and the Dalai Lama were her three best friends, she would still be unlikely to find the time to make contact with each of them three times a week. I wondered if the trio also made up her 'celebrities you would invite to dinner' list.

Bailly didn't look convinced.

'I don't speak to my best friend three times a week. Not even three times a month,' I confessed. 'And I've known her since kindergarten. Friendship is more about trust. Reliability. Looking out for each other. Otherwise you would technically be friends with the person who brings your post or your takeaway food, but not a person you've known and cared for since childhood.'

Bailly considered this new information. 'I may have more friends than I thought.'

'Great!' I said to her. 'So, we're all friends.'

'No.' She pointed between the two of us. 'We're not friends.'

Okay, then.

'We're, ah … professional acquaintances … who have, just now, coincidentally bumped into each other at a local café.'

'Agreed,' Bailly said.

It was partially true. What was Searing's excuse?

'David, I did not ask you here as a friend. Although it is possible we may be friends. I asked you here as Detective Searing.' She paused, adjusting herself on the café chair. 'I have begun a new autopsy on your cold case UP Greenacre 0101 West.'

Searing blinked slowly, shaping his mouth into an unintentional and yet flawless 'o'. If I were prone to falling off chairs, I would have done so. Instead, I forked a chunk of lemon poppyseed cake smothered in orange cream into my mouth. I was hoping this would stop me from speaking.

'Jesus! That's great, Jem, really.' He positively beamed across the table at her. He further digested the news. 'Did you say you've begun? You've already started on UP Greenacre?'

'Yes. A preliminary examination of the remains has unearthed some serious inaccuracies. The first one being UP Greenacre 0101 West was not Caucasian. He was almost certainly of south-east Asian descent. Also, he was not in his sixties. More likely he was only in his mid-forties.'

We all gaped at her in astonishment. No wonder Searing had been keen to have a second autopsy.

'Dude,' Esmerelda said, shaking her head and choosing between a chocolate cake and a brownie before settling on the latter.

I leaned into Searing. 'It's not just me; that is pretty bad, right?'

'Yes, princess,' a cranky female voice above and beside me said. 'Not that it's any of your business, but that's pretty fucking bad.'

CHAPTER 14

DUCKING OUT

Esmerelda inadvertently inhaled some of the loose cocoa powder sitting on top of her brownie, causing her to cough chocolate dust all over Detective Nicole Burns, the diminutive redheaded detective who had spearheaded the campaign to round me up, charge me with Richard's murder and throw away the key.

I was too frightened to turn and confirm her presence. This problem was quickly resolved when she pulled up a stool from a nearby table and sat down next to me. Burns's already frizzy red hair was alive and escaping its braids in the humid sea air. It was hairdryer-in-an-electric-socket frazzled. Burns was dressed in a pair of too faded, wrinkled jeans, a wrinkled denim shirt and, if I had to guess, I would say her socks were wrinkled too. I was yet to see her in anything ironed. Sadly, she had a penchant for linen and cotton. Whatever Burns lacked in coiffure, stature, poise and polish, she made up for in sheer frighteningness.

Luckily, Burns had more interest in Bailly than she did in me.

'You doing a second autopsy, Bailly?'

'Yes.'

'And what in hell are you two doing here?' Burns challenged. Luck was such a fickle thing. I noticed the waitstaff did not come running to serve *her*.

'We were just out getting breakfast and we ran into Dr Bailly,' I said, tearing the end off a brioche twist stuffed with raspberry jam and topped with a honeyed glaze, and using it to plug my verbal flood.

'Uh-huh,' Esmerelda agreed, making blatantly false eye contact with Burns. 'Like a total accident.'

'Where oh where have I heard that excuse before?' Burns sarcastically pondered, catching a fleeing waitress. 'Long black. No milk. No sugar. Strong.'

'Shocker,' the waitress said under her breath.

'What are *you* doing here?' I brazenly shot back. *OMG! Mouth, stop talking!*

Burns eyeballed me. 'Bailly tagged Searing. Searing tagged me. Happy, princess?'

'Uh-huh,' I nodded, vigorously shovelling brioche and praying I had an off button.

'There's little more to say at this stage,' Dr Bailly said, getting to her feet. 'UP Greenacre 0101 West was middle-aged and south-east Asian. There is still much to do in the new autopsy. I have ordered tests. Many more tests.' Her hands began to flutter.

I needed to shove Bailly out before she said something about Max Weller aka UP Rose Bay 0909 Winters.

'We really appreciate the coroner approving our new autopsy request,' Searing said, standing to shake hands with Bailly. 'You're for sure the best forensic path for the job.'

'Hmm,' Bailly said, her hand fluttering going up a notch. 'Yes, the coroner.'

'So, should I call him in a few days for an update?' Searing asked.

'Hmm,' Bailly said, adding some rapid blinking to her fluttering.

I *really* needed to confirm I could bail Bailly out after all of this. I looked to Esmerelda.

'Yeah, yeah, all good,' Esmerelda said, patting her phone and eyeing off the remaining baked goods. 'Don't stress.'

I pushed the plate with the croissant on it over to her.

'You don't need to call! Friends don't always have to call, remember?' I chirped to Searing, accidentally purposely patting him on the arm. 'This is such a lovely spot! Why not meet back here in a few days? It's surely better than an office? Breakfast Danish, bear claws, excellent coffee—'

'Skeletal remains,' Burns piped up with a measured blend of lifelessness and sarcasm as she eyed a thin couple two tables over clad in the barest of bathers, sipping something green I could almost certainly guarantee had kale in it.

'Awesome cloud break,' Esmerelda said, nodding towards the beach and biting into the croissant.

'Yes. It is also an exceptional location for ichthyology,' Bailly added.

'All good things,' I powered on, having no idea what cloud breaks or ichthyology were.

Searing was staring at my hand on his bicep. It was like putting your hand on a hot, hot surface. My skin stuck to it. It was not easy but I peeled it off.

Searing coughed, drank the rest of his chai latte and then nodded in agreement. 'Okay. Bailly, we'll meet you here again, say 7 am Sunday?'

'Yes. No need to call the coroner. 7 am Sunday,' Bailly said. She mentally calculated something. 'Yes. Sunday should suffice. I'm going to work now.' And she walked away without saying goodbye. Searing being Searing went after her with an offer to escort her to her car. It seemed like something a friend would do.

The second they were out of earshot, Burns turned on me.

'Listen, princess, you need to stay the hell away from him. You've derailed his career enough. I've not enjoyed being busted down to cold case with him on *your* behalf. And I don't like my partner keeping secrets from me. Especially when those secrets get us in the shit with the AFP.' She poked a finger at me for emphasis. 'I'll stick with him 'cause he's a good cop, a fucking good detective and generally a nice guy, and I think this will blow over, but if you think you're going to waltz back into town and drag him down again, I've got news for you and it's *not* good.'

'I've got news too, Burns,' Esmerelda growled. 'And it's not good for you either if you keep talking with your hands.'

Watching Burns and Esmerelda size each other up was scary. Burns might have carried a gun but Esmerelda had grit and was willing to fight dirty. It would be messy but my money was on Esmerelda.

'I gave Searing the USB,' I blurted.

'Well, that's not news,' Burns said, unimpressed. 'The whole fucking world knows that.' She waved down another waitress. 'My coffee?'

'Yes, ma'am,' the waitress responded, immediately redirecting herself to the barista.

'Another couple bear claws?' Esmerelda called hopefully after her.

'Searing said he didn't share that information with anyone!' I gaped at Burns. And to Esmerelda, 'More? Really?'

'What? I'm gonna need my strength.' And she eyed Burns. 'You know.'

'He didn't tell a soul,' Burns said, ignoring Esmerelda. 'The man's pure Boy Scout. Always has been. But it doesn't take a genius to figure out that USB came from your camp. It's obviously the work of your whacked-out, mobbed-up dead doctor hubby.' She paused to take her coffee from the terrified waitress. When the waitress was out of earshot, she started again. 'I know. And Searing *knows* I *know*. But he hasn't outright told me. So, I don't *know, know*.'

'So, you know?' I said slowly.

'Yeah, but he didn't tell me. So that shits me. Then you turn up at another crime scene. Now you're at this meet. It's like drama's attracted to you.'

I was crestfallen. Mainly because Burns was right: drama did tend to follow me around. But no one had ever said it to me directly before. Out loud. Then again, I was ludicrously rich, so that probably took care of a lot of it.

'Searing told me being moved to cold case was not related to protecting his,' I leaned into her and whispered, 'CI.'

'Sure,' Burns said, rolling her eyes so far back they had a quick dip in the ocean. 'Withholding the name of your CI from the feds is wonderful for your career trajectory.'

'They for sure know it's her?' Esmerelda chimed.

'What do you think?' sniped Burns.

'Don't get friggin' crabby with me, Burns. One day, I won't be on parole.'

'Look forward to it,' Burns said, taking a long sip of her bitter coffee. 'It'd be a fucking miracle, Esmerelda, but I *do* look forward to it.'

'Perhaps your career trajectory has been impacted by your language,' I suggested unhelpfully.

I'm almost certain Burns growled at me. This act was tempered by her drinking her coffee in large gulps. You could see it soothing her addicted nerve cells.

Was she right? Was I bad for Searing? Wait. I was an *Heiress*. He was a civil servant. It simply wasn't possible *he* was out of *my* league. Or was it? Searing was so startlingly attractive, he made Jason Momoa look homely. I reconsidered. No. I was too rich. It was not possible.

'You're thinkin' about that Aquaman dude, aren't cha?'

'No!' I retorted, rearranging the expression on my face.

Burns finished her coffee and stood. 'Stay away,' she rumbled.

'I have no intention of injuring Searing.' That was true. 'I have no illicit intentions towards him at all.' That was utterly untrue.

It was all I could do to keep my hands off him. The attraction was palpable. Visceral. He was gorgeous, beyond delectable. The truth was I did not know *how* to stay away from him.

I tried. But my brain kept going back to him. Hearing that he was a trustworthy, reliable Boy Scout who had stalled his career to protect me did *not* help. I wanted him more than ever.

Another truth was this: I was accustomed to getting what I wanted.

'If you care about him, leave him alone.' And with that, Burns stalked off.

'You gonna stay away from him?' Esmerelda asked me.

'Not a chance in hell,' I said and ate his bear claw.

Searing didn't make it back to the table, so he didn't miss the bear claw. He was ambushed by Burns, who herded him into a car Esmerelda assured me was police-issue. Burns was so annoyed with me she didn't investigate my connection to Bailly. She assumed I had been there to see Searing. I decided not to peer into that particular gift horse's mouth.

I was in a sugar coma by the time we pulled into Mother's garage. For the next nine hours I slept (on a mattress that cost almost as much as the Lexus).

I woke feeling some light guilt about possibly ruining Searing's career and having eaten my body weight in baked goods for breakfast, so I did an impromptu night session with my flexible and highly motivated trainer, Robyn. She added some intense kicking and punching to the mix. Nothing alleviated guilt like physical violence against inanimate objects.

I woke early at 10.15 am to a furious Patricia. She was so angry she'd forgotten breakfast. A cup of tea—not a *pot*, but a *cup*—with a *string* in it and four barely browned crumpets did not count as breakfast. By the time Esmerelda had hunted me down there would be nothing on the plate but jam, crumbs and a suspicious ring of damp melted butter.

'I thought Esmerelda was taking care of the whole Dylan Moss harassment thing?'

'Obviously not,' Patricia said, placing the plate and mug on the bedside table. She *was* distracted. If Patricia didn't lure me out of bed by placing my breakfast tray out of reach, I might never get up.

'Where is she?' I glanced around.

'Beats me,' Patricia said, fluffing my pillows while I was still using them. Perhaps this was a new strategy. If I didn't get out of bed soon, I would become a part of it. I slipped out of the other side when she started pulling the sheets up.

Then the hallway started ringing.

Patricia and I both cocked our heads in the direction of the bedroom door.

'I thought you removed all the phones down here?' she said.

'I did.' When I said I, I meant someone else did because I told them to.

The hallway rang again.

'Is that …?'

'Yeah, the hallway is ringing. I think it's coming from the hall table.'

I pulled my robe up over my shoulders and tiptoed to the door. The hall table was a four-legged Italian Rococo topped with a D-shaped golden veined marble top. Alarmingly, the small, delicately carved wooden drawers had been attacked by Mother during one of her craft phases. Drawer number one featured a translucent grid of pink hearts on a pale aqua background, the middle drawer was pinstriped pink and gold, and the final drawer featured pink gerberas on a background of impossibly green baby's breath. The table was always topped with an exquisite fresh floral arrangement and today was no exception. A large square, glossy-green ceramic pot sat atop. A massive spray of pink roses rang out like an oversized bridal centrepiece. Come to think of it, it lacked the emblematic elegance of a Tom Trainer, florist to the stars (Mother being one of the stars), composition.

The ceramic pot vibrated.

Patricia and I stalked the table, circling it like urban jaguars.

'Is it …?' I asked.

'Yeah. The flowers are ringing.'

'That's not a usual occurrence. Is it?'

Technology moved so quickly and fads were so odd that ringing flower arrangements *could* be a new phase I had simply missed. Grown adults had chased imaginary Pokémon through people's weddings. How were ringing flowers different?

Patricia shook her head and gave me a derisive stare. I was going to take that as a negative.

I put my hand in the pot and felt around. Sitting above the floral foam was a ringing phone. In retrospect, I should not have answered it. It could have been a bomb. It could have been sprayed with a virus with no known vaccine. It could have been a telemarketer selling insurance. Or the taxation department.

It was worse.

'Hello?' I said naively into the handset.

'Indie!' Dylan Moss smiled enthusiastically at me through the phone. 'You got my roses! I've booked us a table for lunch at La Cotta. The risotto is incredible. You've had it, I'm sure. It's five minutes from you. I'll pick you up at twelve. I remember you like to eat early. See you then.'

I blinked, stunned.

'Telemarketers?' Patricia asked me. 'Solar panels?'

I shook my head.

She inhaled sharply. 'The ATO?'

I shook my head again and placed the phone back on the florist's foam inside the arrangement in horrified silence.

I watched Patricia's gears crank over. Finally, her eyes narrowed and she said through gritted teeth, 'That sneaky little SOB!'

'How good is the risotto at La Cotta?' I asked, searching for a silver lining.

She peered quizzically at me. 'Are you kidding? I wouldn't know. We only get food from places without stoves. Or tastebuds. If I did know, and I don't, I would say it was amazing. As well it should be at fifty bucks a pop. But not amazing enough to eat while sitting next to a snake.'

She was right. Dylan was a snake. However, Patricia was clearly at the end of her tether, Esmerelda had not followed through on her promise and Dylan was exceptionally persistent. I had no idea why he had such a sudden, overwhelming interest in me, but I needed to put an end to it. I did not want to be responsible for Mother's staff losing their minds from harassment. And I couldn't take another day of tea in a cup with a *tea bag* or jam and butter crumpets *in* bed. I had standards.

It would take Franny at least two hours to do hair and make-up. I knew from harried experience I could get the bare minimum done in an hour.

'Have Esmerelda call Franny,' I said to Patricia, heading back into my bedroom.

'I don't know where Esmerelda is,' Patricia said, standing hands on hips.

'Then *you* call Franny.'

I ate half a crumpet and drank a third of the tea before I made it to the shower. I was a hungry waker. If my eyes were open for business, so was my stomach. By the time I got out of the shower, Franny was waiting. She gave me the Sicilian eye and told me she had only packed brushes, not magic wands. There was no time for full hair and make-up, so we went with my non-negotiable bare-minimum make-up, which was black liquid and pencil eyeliner, and lengthening black mascara. There was no time to properly iron or curl my too-thick wavy locks, so they were smoothed instead. The result was Italian peasant woman crossed with green-eyed racoon.

Not wanting to encourage Dylan, I chose a non-sexy, light and flouncy full-length floral Nicolas Ghesquière skirt and a high-necked, sleeveless black jersey top. Any other colour top was out of the question at an Italian restaurant. It was a certainty that pasta sauce in some form or colour would attach itself to my clothing. Although spilt sauce on one's front would likely repel an OCD neat stickler like Dylan, I was not prepared to be mortified in the process. I was sure I could find a cleaner, neater way to move him along.

Against every instinct, I put on a pair of almost flat, open-toed, slip-on silver leather Burberry sandals. Dylan liked tall woman. I was, in the regular world, relatively tall. However, in the world of superstars and models, and my six-foot-plus parents, I was short. It didn't take Freud to work out where my love of towering heels came from.

I exhaled, gazing down at my sad, flat little feet. No one would see me. Midday lunches were almost unheard of. I glanced back at an even sadder sight; a plain white teacup with a square, red teabag tag now firmly stuck to the side. Sacrifices had to be made.

I strode up the garden path, past the pool, outdoor showers, lounges, gazebo, the croquet lawn, the tennis and basketball courts, vegetable and herb gardens, through the grove of fruit trees and the lawn to the main house. I made record time in my never-before-worn flats.

I was still late. Patricia had already endured ten minutes of Dylan. Most people were beguiled by Dylan. Not Patricia. She stood at the front door, her arm firmly locked across the doorway like a metal carnival ride safety bar. Dylan was chatting away, exuding charm; Patricia was having none of it. I admired her dedication and loyalty. So many years after Mother's anti-Dylan decree, it was still steadily enforced.

The talking stopped as I slid into the airy marble foyer. Patricia's mouth fell open and she stepped away from the door, dropping her arm from the safety belt position. When Dylan went to step into the newly opened void, she neatly swung the door closed.

Swoosh. Clap. Closed.

She rushed over to me. 'What are you doing?' she hissed.

'I'm getting rid of Dylan Moss once and for all. You can give *me* Esmerelda's waffles.'

'What are you wearing? What have you done to your hair? You look like, like …' She was wide-eyed, running an open palm up and down the outline of my outfit.

'I didn't have time to have my hair and make-up done properly,' I spluttered back, feeling defensive. 'I know I'm a little shabby. I thought that might help deter him.'

'Are you insane? Styled like that, you're the freaking spitting image of your mother!' she sizzled. 'The bouncy hair, the radiant natural skin, the floaty skirt? You look like a siren goddess! Get back in there and put some more make-up on, young lady! And a few less clothes while you're at it! Something short and dreadful.'

There was no way in the many universes that I resembled my mother. She was blonde. I was not. She was blue-eyed. I was not. She was impossibly tall and thin. *I* was *not*.

Never one to miss an opportunity, Dylan discovered the fatal flaw in Patricia's closed-door plan. She had not locked the door. While she was catching her breath from her tirade, he snuck up behind her.

'Indie! Wow! You look … so different. I like it,' he said, putting out a hand to stroke my floaty skirt.

I tried to assess Dylan for signs of lying. His shock was genuine and he was telling the truth about my appearance being different, but I had trouble with the 'like it' part.

I noticed for the first time that Dylan Moss was not a tall man. He was taller than Patricia, but with my flats on he was the same height as me. I glanced down surreptitiously. The heels on his shoes were much higher than mine, which meant … Dylan Moss was shorter than me! He was Richard's height, maybe smaller.

I had no issues with Dylan *not* being tall—I had no height type per se. Searing was exuberantly tall, yes, but Richard's incredibly hot brother James Smith only had an inch on me, and his status as delicious demigod was undeniable. What was shocking was that I had never *noticed* Dylan's stature. In my mind he was towering. A giant. A pinnacle. In real life, in real time, he was … less so.

Patricia shook her head and nervously flicked her thumb into her curled fingers. 'This is a bad idea. Cat's gonna skin me.'

I put a reassuring hand on top of her worried hand. 'It will be fine. I am fine.'

'See?' Dylan beamed. 'She's absolutely fine. We're five minutes away. Patty, why don't you take the afternoon off?'

I thought Patricia might do Dylan harm. She looked like a lioness sizing up an impudent gazelle for imminent eradication.

I politely shoved Dylan across the foyer and out the door.

Dylan did all the right things. He opened the car door, the restaurant door and pulled my seat out at the table. He drove a nice car, made excellent wine and dining suggestions and was dressed immaculately. He was an attractive man by any standard, came from a perfectly acceptable family, seemed to have a successful career and was undoubtably clever. He appeared flawless. On paper. And in my memory. Except for the part where he cheated with Tiffany Goldstein.

Even then, teenage boys and girls make mistakes. Their frontal cortexes are not fully formed. That's why they are not allowed to vote, drive, operate heavy machinery or run corporations, kingdoms or countries. Even if I couldn't absolve Dylan *the adult*, remaining furious with Dylan *the kid* seemed increasingly unfair. I felt forced to forgive youth. However ...

Dylan's car was the most ostentatious form of Rolls-Royce, the Phantom. I knew via the grapevine his usual vehicle was a Lamborghini of some description. After my father's death behind the wheel of his Ferrari, my dislike of sports cars was well documented. The Phantom, then, was the vehicle he had *deliberately* chosen to replace the triggering Lamborghini. The one he thought would *most* impress me. I had Esmerelda's words ringing in my ears: a Phantom *was* the car old men drove. Old men with drivers. Okay, so she said that about Bentleys, but a Rolls-Royce Phantom seemed much worse in the old man stakes than a Bentley Mulsanne. And …

His work cutting deals to promote and protect artists I'd never heard of seemed unnecessarily protracted, sharkish and mean. His aftershave was too strong, his shirt too far unbuttoned, his black Zegna pants too tight.

He moved from suggesting the wine to outright choosing the wine. He annoyed the La Cotta waitstaff by having our seats rearranged and our table moved to the 'best harbourside view'. He talked throughout the critical explanation of the day's specials.

And he answered his phone. Twice.

I had also completely forgotten about his passion for gossip. And himself. In the last hour I had heard the latest rumours about three American celebrities, four prominent families, two from Melbourne and two from Perth, a royal and an elderly medical tycoon. Dylan loved the sound of his own voice.

On the upside, he certainly knew his menus. The risotto alone was enough to make up for a dismal breakfast. I was considering the correctness of ordering two desserts after I had already eaten entrée, main and two sides, when he started a new topic of conversation, in the same gossipy vein, about a Sydney family. The Holly family.

'You know, there's always been a scandal around the Hollys,' he said, ignoring his gnocchi. I had spent the last few minutes wondering if he was going to eat the last two pieces. How misleading would it be to eat food off the plate of a man you had no intentions towards going forward?

'Of course, you know that before Dame Elizabeth was Lady Elizabeth Holly, she was *Miss* Elizabeth Hanson. Of the dairy cow Hansons. Everyone knows her father, Dashiell Hanson, was a shocking tart,' he said, smirking, forking the second last piece of pasta.

I nodded as I watched the gnocchi disappear into his mouth. I was going to need to buy a few pallets of this pasta and have it shipped to Mother's and stored in a deep freeze system of some sort. I was going to need to buy a deep freeze system of some sort.

'You know, they say the only person who had more mistresses than Earl Alexander Holly was his father-in-law, Dashiell Hanson!' He then paused momentarily to chew and swallow his pasta.

Was Dylan's gossiping *always* this bad?

'So, who knows how many little Hollys and Hansons are running around out there!' He winked. 'Old Lizzie is exceptionally generous, though, and such a lovely lady. My clients adore her. Mind you, half of them had art, design or acting school scholarships funded by her. Con scholarships too. Some people say it's a guilty conscience because old man Hanson was such a devil,' he said, grinning mischievously, sipping his wine.

God, yes, wine! There was wine! I put my hand out to my glass and recalled in dismay that it was empty. I glanced about desperately trying to catch a waiter. I physically hailed one like a taxi.

'Wine?' I asked the waiter, trying to suppress the desperation in my voice.

'Have I told you about my clients? The business?' he asked in a self-deprecating tone that belied the fact that he had, several times, told me about both things in great detail. He was an up-and-coming public-relations-public-affairs-publicist to *many* hot, new, up-and-coming stars.

'Yes,' I said, taking a sip that bordered on a gulp of crisp wine from my newly filled glass. Hello, sauvignon blanc, my old friend.

'You're awfully quiet, Indie,' Dylan said, leaning over the table to squeeze my hand. 'Trouble in paradise?'

'Paradise?' I queried.

He laughed. 'Just a euphemism. Paradise. You know, life in the Hasluck-Royce-Jones lane.'

This was one of the things that made me, as an Heiress, furious. The assumption that life was always 'paradise'. In the last year I had lost my home, my husband and aside from the contents of my safe and my safety deposit boxes, all my worldly possessions, *including* my shoes. I had also lost my pride, any hope of social comeback this decade and an inordinate amount of sanity. I had been accused of, and investigated for, a double homicide and discovered the life I had shared with my husband was a myth. All this while enduring Esmerelda, my family and the fluctuating price of platinum. Last week, I had tripped over a non-existent, has-to-be-a-millionaire corpse dressed as a homeless man while trying to have a casual caipiroska with a borrowed Monet. I was being blackmailed by my grandmother and a Dame who used to be a Lady. I was also telling some fairly serious untruths to a high-ranking coroner's court employee, withholding information from the federal police, who may or may not be following and/or bugging me, and bending other laws by breaking into a hotel, impersonating a maid and eavesdropping. I was unsure if eavesdropping or impersonating a maid was illegal, but it seemed unsavoury. Regardless, paradise was *not* the correct term.

This was especially grating when *I knew* that *he knew* that my life was a PR disaster. He'd said so.

'I'm going to need a cherry biscotti and the vanilla mascarpone panna cotta,' I said to the waiter who was now re-filling Dylan's wine glass. 'Two,' I said, reconsidering. 'Two biscotti.'

I turned to Dylan. 'What's it to be, Dylan? Am I the *flambéed-husband-clueless-bungling heiress*? Or am I living in a best-life paradise?'

Dylan beamed at the waiter, then at me. 'I love that you have such a strong appetite. My performance clients don't eat anything. They're so worried about staying thin. It's wonderful you're still not worried about that.'

The waiter gave Dylan a hostile, derisive look then rearranged his face and smiled before walking away. The smile was good enough to land him one of Dame Elizabeth's acting scholarships.

The moment the waiter was out of earshot, Dylan leaned back across the table and patted my hand. 'Don't worry about the gossip, Indie. I've got it under control. Everyone knows that the deeper the family's pockets are, the shorter society's memory is about scandal. Besides, long scandals are for mediocre families. You're a Hasluck-Royce, for goodness sake! Your mother is Cat Jones! Just two million dollars in the right hands, four at the most, and I can have you back on every list before the end of summer.'

Ahh. So *that* was what he was up to.

'Of course, I would do it for free for *you*, Indie. If I could afford to. I have business partners, unfortunately.'

I suddenly realised that I didn't like Dylan Moss. Esmerelda was right: he was a douche.

A series of crashes emanated from the restaurant entrance, followed by what sounded like quacking and the fluttering of feathers, then much oohing and ahhing. I could not see what had taken place from our 'best harbourside view' table, but I could think of only one person capable of making that kind of ruckus without raised voices coming immediately after.

While Dylan took his third phone call, I rose, motioning towards the bathrooms. Dylan gave me his trademark grin and a sexy nod-wink combination. He was a *very* good-looking guy with zero morals who did absolutely nothing for me.

This made me *very* happy. I had depth! Who knew?

Dylan's personality, pretence and presence were such enormous turn-offs that no level of handsomeness could overcome them. I was suddenly relieved of a long-held ghost, healed of a long-open wound. I was no longer afraid of Dylan Moss. He held no power over me. It was extremely liberating.

He had fallen from grace in the world of delectable man treats. He was no oven-warm blondie. He had no hot caramel fudge. He wasn't even a dull, seemingly healthy Bran

Muffin. Dylan Moss was a strawberry jelly whip, made up of only two ingredients: ground-up cow bones and chilled evaporated milk. Very little substance, able to mould into almost any shape, and high in sugar and artificial colours and flavours. Just the thought of it made my teeth hurt. No wonder Mother didn't like him.

I didn't even bother with the pretence of walking towards the bathroom. Instead, I headed directly towards the commotion at the entrance.

There were several tables filled with nondescript patrons, several with tourists, and one with two Gucci-clad SILC graduates and their Prada-clad husbands. The SILC table fell silent as I approached and as I walked away, I heard one of the men say, 'You'd never get away with setting me on fire, dearest; you're not rich enough!'

A female voice squeaked in objection. 'I am so!'

So, yes, I was still high society roadkill, and yes, it might take more than a season to blow over, but, as Dylan had correctly pointed out, I was rich. Very rich. If I was going to spend $4 million on something to make me feel better, it would be shoes.

Esmerelda was leaning on the reception desk, waiting patiently. She had a bowl of fresh pumpkin and pesto crème ravioli in her left hand and a fork in her right. The only sign of a commotion was a bus boy disappearing into the kitchen with an orange mop and a sloshing bucket. And a large blue, black and white duck feather wedged firmly in Esmerelda's hair.

I didn't ask about the duck. You just don't need to know everything.

'How did you know I was here?' I asked her.

'It's the most pretentious, overpriced restaurant within two Ks of the house,' she said, spearing two or three ravioli at a time onto her fork.

'How did you get that?' I enquired, pointing at the dish.

She smiled at me as if I were a tad simple. 'Dude.'

'Dylan Moss is paying for that ravioli, isn't he?'

'Totally,' she said, forking in the last piece. That ravioli was worth every cent of whatever exorbitant price Dylan was going to have to pay for it.

'Shall we?' I said, heading for the glass doors.

A passing server collected Esmerelda's bowl. 'I've never seen anything like that before,' he said to Esmerelda, wide-eyed.

'You should totally get out more then,' she said, scooping a handful of gold Baci chocolates from a gold-edged glass dish on the reception counter.

'What did you do?' I asked, resisting the urge to pick the duck feather out of her hair.

'Nothing,' she said, shrugging innocently.

I didn't believe her for a second.

CHAPTER 15

WHITEBOARDS AND SNAPPLE

I was hoping that running away from Dylan mid-date at La Cotta was a signal sufficiently insulting and blunt to disabuse him of any notion of my having *any* interest in him personally or professionally. This was an optimistic view. Dylan was not a quitter. Moreover, I had a sinking feeling his ego was much bigger than his pride. Landing a Hasluck-Royce would be an enormous ego boost. Fixing a *broken* Hasluck-Royce would be a next-level personal *and* professional coup.

However, I refused to admit to Patricia that I may have failed to eradicate Dylan. I had food services to maintain. To safeguard my breakfast trays, I took extra precautions, instructing Patricia to hire a security firm to place a guard at the front gate. The guard was to refuse entry to everyone without an appointment except Searing, check all flower deliveries for hidden phones and answer directly to Patricia.

While delivering a real breakfast the next morning Patricia had questions. 'What about online shopping deliveries?' she probed. 'Can I tell him to let those in? Who checks those?'

After seeing Searing at the beach and receiving a stern warning from Burns to stay away, I had doubled down in the undergarment stakes, almost cleaning Guia La Bruna out of C-cups and flattering French knickers. I didn't want some burly gorilla named Bruce rifling through my new lingerie.

'Online package deliveries are fine. Esmerelda will check them.'

Wait, there was something wrong with that sentence.

'Except the Guia La Bruna packages.'

'Who's Guy La Brew-nah?' Esmerelda asked, waltzing in, no doubt having smelt the sweet scent of both tea and coffee.

'He makes Egyptian skincare, same recipe as the pharaohs used,' I said with the same amount of truth as the 'nothing' I had received to my question about the duck ruckus the day before.

I slid out of bed, robed, slippered and made my way to the table. I really needed to start formalising these breakfast arrangements and move the whole circus out of my bedroom and into the pool house dining room.

Esmerelda's phone pinged and she slipped it out of her back pocket. She managed to key the phone and pour herself a cup of English breakfast tea at the same time. I feared for the safety of the china cup in that juggling act. It was worth more than the phone.

'Awesome,' she said, setting herself at the table and attempting to add my French toast to her juggling mix. 'Rachael

White says she's tracked that batch of dental implants. It came into Australia via a wholesaler.'

'Great!' I said, waiting for Patricia to pour my tea. 'Can she contact the wholesaler and see which surgeons they sold them to?'

She examined the screen. 'The wholesaler went broke a few years ago.' She read on, 'Oh, and he's also dead.'

'Great,' I said dourly, pouring my own tea.

'She's lookin' for "a list of practices that purchased from the wholesaler",' she read, still eating.

'Is there a list?' I asked hopefully.

'She doesn't know if there's a list.'

Breakfast yoyo. I would have put my head in my hands or smacked my head on the table in frustration if the French toast were not disappearing so rapidly. I'd need both my head *and* my hands to compete.

'So, there is no way of knowing who those implants went too,' I huffed. I was going to need more maple syrup.

'Like, you're so touchy in the morning. There's *always* a list of buyers. I worked in retail, remember? There'll be one and she'll totally find it.'

How could I forget Esmerelda's 'retail experience' at the Bankstown Boutique? There was another suburb I had never driven to. I felt some justification since it apparently was populated by illegal sweatshops and counterfeiters and bordered by suburbs where cold case murders occurred.

'Has the new security guard arrived?' I asked, changing the subject before I received emotional whiplash.

'Yep.'

'And?'

'And what? He's a dude. He's from a high-priced-low-idea security company. And he's standing like a tool at the front gate. It's totally embarrassing. People will think we can't take care of ourselves.'

I gestured around the room in amazement. 'What part of my life or lifestyle says to you that I can look after myself? The maid? The assistant? The borrowed artwork.' I pointed to the Monet and the Vermeer on the wall. 'Or was living with my mother the big tip?'

'That's it. You're gettin' up at ten at the latest from now on. When you wake up after eleven, it's like a grizzly coming out of hibernation. Hungry and nasty. We should put *you* at the front gate. You could tear that dude a new one.'

I was about to argue with her but felt this action might support her claim. Instead, I ate my French toast, swam a few laps, lay in the shaded sunlight and read for an hour, took a long shower and bought a pair of vintage black and silver crystal Sergio Rossi heels online.

Previously I would have been too cautious to wear a pair of vintage anything, but in a post-Dylan Moss world, I would have them treated with a heavy-duty disinfectant then reheeled and re-soled. I was a freshly minted rebel with a black AMEX and a penchant for pretty, sparkly things. Second-hand status would no longer stand between me and happiness.

Esmerelda and I passed the evening in the tiny pool house theatre, alternating between Nancy Meyers kitchen movies and *Point Break*. I went to bed when *Point Break* went on for the third time. I fell asleep and dreamt of Searing, my new lingerie and sparkly shoes. This dream was rudely interrupted by subconscious machinations about the life and death of Max, the man in the lilies. Even in sleep my brain rudely continued to grind information, searching for solutions.

*

I was woken at 7.30 am by Patricia. She slapped a white plate with an unevenly toasted piece of chillingly square bread smeared with butter (God, I *hoped* it was butter) and Vegemite down on my bedside table. Next came a *thunk* and a *slosh* and the stinging odour of instant coffee invaded my nasal cavities. In a random mug! Were there words written on it?

Maybe if I rolled over and pretended, this breakfast would magically turn into poached eggs and smoked salmon on sourdough covered in hollandaise sauce. I rolled over, then back. Damn! Instant coffee and Vegemite. It was like a budget lock-in.

'What did he do?' I exhaled, sliding out of bed.

'The guard out at the front gate doesn't answer the inside bloody phone, does he? No. That Dylan creature keeps calling. If I don't answer, he leaves messages and the system won't let me delete them without playing them. I'm sick of the sound of his smarmy voice!'

Patricia plunked herself down in the shell chair and put her head in her hands. She gazed up at me with a deadly serious expression.

'I did something stupid. It's bad, Indigo, it's very, very bad. I was desperate. I didn't know what else to do.'

Had Mother's maid ordered a hit on Dylan Moss, PR guru to none of the stars you have ever heard of? I forgot all about my slippers and robe and crossed the room to her.

'What did you do?' I asked, terrified.

'It was late. He'd just left a two-minute sonnet. And not one of the good ones either.'

'What did you do?'

'I … I gave him Esmerelda's mobile number. Told him to go harass her instead of me.'

'Ooh!' I gasped and I shrank back. This was bad. Esmerelda had some serious privacy issues. She was ferocious about it. *I* didn't even have Esmerelda's mobile number. Then again, I didn't have a phone. And I couldn't seem to shake Esmerelda.

We were so engrossed in our discussion about ways to break this news *to* Esmerelda, we didn't notice Esmerelda enter.

'Like, what are you two like?' she said, snacking on the Vegemite toast. 'Just block his frigging numbers.'

I eyed Patricia. 'You didn't block his number?'

She blinked heavily a few times. 'Would you've thought to block his number?'

That didn't seem like a fair comparison. Thinking of techy things was not really my specialty.

'Sure,' I lied. 'I would have thought of it.'

'Really?' Patricia countered disbelievingly. 'Do you know *how* to block a number?'

'I think Esmerelda is waiting for an apology,' I said, blatantly trying to derail her by pointing at Esmerelda. Patricia rolled her eyes.

'Don't stress. I've blocked his mobile number, his home number, his office number and some other random number he uses on all the personal, business and private home

and mobile phone lines,' she paused for effect and
Patricia, 'including mine.'

Patricia immediately got to her feet and walked out the
door.

'Where are you going?' I shouted after her.

'To make waffles!' she gaily shouted back. 'Lots and lots
of waffles!'

Esmerelda fist-pumped the air before resuming her cool
demeanour and polishing off the final uneven triangle of
Vegemite toast.

'What?' she said to me. 'Like you were gonna eat it.'

'Oh,' came a final shout from Patricia outside, 'another
letter came for you.'

I scanned the room until I landed on it propped up against
the window. A typed envelope with a golfing Santa stamp,
addressed to Indigo Jones-Bombberg.

I had a long jasmine-scented shower and waited for a *real*
breakfast to arrive. I was not opening that envelope on an
empty stomach.

'There is something medically wrong with you,' I said to
Esmerelda when I caught her mid-giant waffle in the pool
house dining room. 'You just should not be able to do that.'

'It's totally not that hard to program a phone to block a
number,' she said, dipping an end into a puddle of maple
syrup before using it as a scoop for her whipped cream.

I didn't have the emotional energy to get into a protracted
discussion with Esmerelda about metabolic rates *and* open
another mystery envelope.

This was the third envelope. If letters were like dates, this
was a significant step in the relationship. Opening this letter

would be like committing to the search for Max Weller. The *real* Max Weller, whoever he was. Was I ready for that type of commitment?

In an eerie, worrying sign, while I was mentally pondering this question, my body raced ahead of me. I came to having already opened the latest envelope and eaten three waffles.

There were two cards in the envelope and their content cemented my relationship with Max. I was not only going to find out who he was, but, I decided, I was also going to find his killer. Tough talk for a woman who could not boil an egg or finish a crossword. Or start a crossword. The cards read:

> The dead body you found had:
> • vertebra degeneration
> • arthritic changes in both hands
> • historical thickening of skin on hands, knees and feet

I had no real idea what any of that meant beyond the obvious. Nor did I know what anything on the next card meant, except the last line:

> The dead body you found had:
> • faint prepatellar bursitis scarring
> • a mastoidectomy
> • severe whipping scars on back, likely from childhood & adolescence

Whoever Max was, he'd had an abhorrent childhood. Somehow, he had survived and grown into a man who had managed to amass a great fortune. A rich man, yes, but also a kind man, a generous man, a man people seemed to like. Then he had found love with Dame Elizabeth. And *then* he had been smashed over the head and murdered, left out in the open dressed as a homeless person, perhaps so that he would once again be overlooked and discarded.

The idea that Max would be uncared for in both the *first* and *last* moments of his life was unacceptable and repugnant.

'What day is it today?' I asked Esmerelda, pushing my plate away.

'Sunday,' she said, without looking up from her riveting handset.

'What time is it?' I pressed.

At this, she set down her phone and raised a suspicious eyebrow at me. 'Eight twenty-five. Why?'

I needed to speak to Bailly. I needed to know if the things written on the cards were true. I needed to know what the other things written on the cards *meant*. I needed a whiteboard to keep up with all these clues.

I was certain the clues were accurate and authentic and that they were *not* coming from Bailly. For better or worse, I trusted her. They weren't coming from Rope or Winters either. I'd been oblivious about these new clues, so they certainly weren't coming from me or the house or the car being bugged. Plus, Searing had swept the place. That left me ... nowhere.

If I asked Bailly what these new clues meant, she might become suspicious I was a phoney relative. She might cut me off. But ... what if *I* could work out what the new clues meant? Then I could feed the information back to Bailly.

This might give me more credibility as Max Weller's niece, and Bailly might be able to give me some more insight into Max's life. Insights that might help me find out who he was, and who had killed him.

Surely there were lots of doctors around who knew what a *prepatellar bursitis* was? Maybe I didn't even need a doctor. Maybe I just needed a search engine.

While I had little faith I could actually solve these mysteries, I had nothing else to do, and about a billion dollars to do it with.

I turned to Esmerelda. 'Could you go to Officeworks and get a whiteboard, a cork board thing and some of those coloured pins? Oh, no, wait, just get whiteboards and a load of magnets. And whiteboard markers.'

She stared at me in disbelief. 'Officeworks? Seriously? You know that word has like, the words office *and* work in it?'

'Thank you for that, yes, I am aware.'

I handed her the cards. As she read them, her face became set and her posture changed from frolicking seal pup to great white shark on the hunt. She stiffly handed the cards back to me and stalked out of the room.

By midday, Esmerelda and I had turned the pool house's largest room, the open-kitchen-informal-dining-informal-lounge area into a mashup of a police detective squad room and a film director's office.

The walls were lined with a series of whiteboards, set up much like movie or television storyboard panels. Each whiteboard panel had a set of clues on it, things we knew about Max Weller/UP Rose Bay 0909 Winters in the order we had discovered them. We were about halfway around the room and had somewhat deciphered the latest set of clues.

It turned out that *vertebra degeneration* was when your spine slowly started to fall apart and didn't work as well as it used to. Usual cause? Ageing. *Arthritic changes* were something about cartilage and bones and cushions. Usual cause? Normal wear and tear. These sounded like things that just happened as you aged. We had written *Got old* under both of those.

Historical thickening of skin on hands, knees and feet was a bit of a weird rabbit hole. Skin thickening was caused by any number of things, from various unpronounceable skin diseases to OCD rubbing. Although how you could compulsively rub your hands, feet *and* knees was a mystery to me. Thickening also ranged in severity. We had no idea which end of the spectrum Max fell into. Or how long ago *Historical* was. We put *Old rubbing* and then a question mark under that one.

Prepatellar bursitis was also known as housemaid's knee. It came from repeatedly kneeling for extended periods. The card said *scarring*. I guessed that meant the injury was old. Perhaps he used to have a job where he knelt a lot? Like a gardener or a plumber. Perhaps it was related to the knee rubbing? We wrote, *Used to kneel a lot? At work?* under that.

A *mastoidectomy* was a type of ear surgery. People often had it to fix damage caused by severe, untreated middle ear infections from childhood. It sounded painful. I felt sick as I wrote *Untreated childhood ear infections*.

The final point about scars from severe childhood beatings did not require further explanation.

The morning was not all misery. Patricia was so thrilled to be rid of Dylan Moss that she had immediately filled Mother's walk-in pantry and protein fridge with all manner of illicit sugar-filled processed foods and beverages for Esmerelda's benefit. On her last visit down to the pool house, she had brought ice-cold Peach Snapple and Grape Fanta (apparently these were Esmerelda's favourites), along with a vast array of cavity and artery plaque forming snacks.

Esmerelda was currently sitting on the marble kitchen bench, munching on a giant red bagful of something called Samboy Atomic Tomato Sauce chips which she was washing down with a perfectly chilled Peach Snapple. Esmerelda had, much to everyone's surprise, rejected the Grape Fanta. Apparently too much time with Mother had taken all the fun out of the multitudes of artificial colours and flavours found therein.

Patricia was so bubbly with joy she took no offence to the rejection and promised to give the Grape Fanta to the security guard. That seemed logical: iced tea for the blocker of phones, grape soft drink for the blocker of doors, diabetes all round.

Since I was seen to be the cause of the Dylan Moss problem, I received no special treatment or treats, which was fine. The fridge in the pool house was well stocked with crispy sauvignon blanc and the remainders of the La Cotta risotto I'd had delivered the night before.

Patricia left, promising Esmerelda a spotlessly clean room and bathroom, new sheets, all clothes washed, ironed and hung, and a tidy underwear drawer.

Once we had filled as many whiteboards as we could with what we knew, we sat and stared at them. For hours.

'Like, we might totally need Bailly,' Esmerelda said, emptying the crumbs out of the final bag of chips into her mouth then fishing around for the last red snake in the lolly packet.

'No, we do not,' I said, sipping on a sparkling water, eyeing the boards. I had switched from wine at about 2 pm, when the whiteboards began to collide. 'We can do this.'

Esmerelda shook her head, stood up and walked to the first board. 'Rich dude with fancy shave and nails somehow ends up dressed like a homeless dude in your nanna's yard.'

'Check,' I said, surreptitiously stealing several yellow jelly snakes from Esmerelda's lolly packet.

'Dude is like, totally Max.' She eyeballed me.

He almost certainly was. However, I didn't want to be the one to tell Dame Elizabeth that the man she had fallen for, a man who had apparently fallen for her too, was dead. Murdered.

In a freakish coincidence, Esmeralda's phone rang. She slipped it out of her pocket and looked at the screen. It was Dame Elizabeth. Esmerelda shook her head and tried to hand the phone to me. This was bad. Esmerelda hated me touching her beloved phone. I pushed the phone back to her.

'You're the assistant! Answering phones is quite literally your job!'

'Nuh-uh. What if I'm like in the bathroom?'

'But you're *not* in the bathroom!'

'But, like, I *could be* in the bathroom.'

'If you don't answer that call, I can guarantee that both Dame Elizabeth *and* my grandmother will appear here, in person, within forty-eight hours. It is a mathematical certainty.'

We both stared at the ringing handset. Surely bad news over the phone was far better than in person? Esmerelda gingerly touched the phone's screen, but she was too late. We stood staring as the missed call screen morphed into the dreaded 'ping' of voicemail.

Dame Elizabeth sounded shaken. Max had missed the ballet last night. She had repeatedly called his mobile phone and received no answer. Could we possibly locate a photograph of the man in the lilies (presumably so she could check it was not Max). The tone in her voice said she suspected it *might* be him.

Thirty seconds later, Esmerelda's phone pinged with a photo text message from Dame Elizabeth. It was a candid photograph of her with Max. They were sitting together in the back row of a theatre, mid-conversation. They wore unquestionably joyful expressions, seemingly unaware they were being included in a wider photo of the group in front of them. I wondered where Dame Elizabeth had acquired the photograph.

Max Weller was clearly visible. He *was* the man in the lilies, UP Rose Bay 0909 Winters.

'Is it?' Esmerelda said to me, motioning to the photo.

I nodded.

'Bugger,' she said, tucking the phone back in her pocket.

And then the screaming began.

CHAPTER 16

I'VE GOT YOUR REDBACK

The thing about wearing high heels day in, day out is that you become accustomed to them. I ran on instinct and nothing else (apart from my black satin Manolos), neck and neck with Esmerelda up the garden path, past the blur of outdoor facilities, through the back door of the main house and up the stairs, following Patricia's screams, my black and white, graphic etched, somewhat sequined, silk lurex Armani jacket and pants making a perfectly good substitute for a running tracksuit.

I dashed down the wide hallway to the left of the back-stairs and collided with Patricia who was running hysterically full tilt down the hallway. She bounced off me and landed on her bottom. She scrambled wildly to her feet, grabbing at door handles and side tables, trying to leverage herself to her feet. She was in such a state that she couldn't get herself off the ground and began crawling on her hands and knees in a desperate attempt to escape.

Esmerelda must have been full of adrenaline; she picked Patricia up by her armpits and set her on a chair. But Patricia would not stay. She immediately attempted to get to her feet again and flee.

'It's coming!' she screamed over and over, trying to get out of the hallway. 'From your room!'

That could only be Esmerelda's room. I had never been a child in this particular home.

Esmerelda strode up the hallway, head peering forward. She looked around for a weapon, quickly extracting the pipe section of a yellow Dyson vacuum cleaner that had been left in the hallway. She peered at the last door on the left, pipe in hand. 'Like, the door's closed.'

Patricia was white. 'It doesn't matter! It might get *under* the door! *They* might get under the door.'

Now I was frightened. Was Patricia being attacked or haunted? I looked her over. Her clothes were not torn. That was an unimaginable relief.

'Did someone try to rob you?' I asked her, concerned. 'Is something missing? Are they still here?'

'No! Yes! No! Yes!'

Well, that was super helpful.

'There's—in there. In there!' she said, pointing down the hall.

'Yes, Patricia, okay. There's something in there. What is it?'

Esmerelda was closing in on the bedroom door, holding the metal tubing like a cricketer or a baseball player ready to bat. She adjusted her grip on the pipe.

Patricia breathed deeply, and stepped backwards onto the staircase, gripping the timber handrail, squatting to take shelter behind the glass plate balustrade. 'Snakes! There's snakes! In Esmerelda's underwear drawer!'

Was that a metaphor?

'Seriously?' Esmerelda and I echoed.

'Like, you know most snakes aren't even poisonous,' Esmerelda said in a quasi-calm voice, not, I noted, stepping closer to, or opening, the door.

'Actually, snakes are never poisonous,' I pointed out to her.

'What?'

'Snakes. They're never poisonous. Poison only comes from things you touch or ingest. For example, you might *touch* a poisonous frog or *eat* a poisonous blow fish. They are poisonous. A snake is *venomous*. It bites. It has venom. Like a scorpion or a spider.'

I had to stop using David Attenborough documentaries as white noise when I couldn't sleep.

'Huh,' Esmerelda said.

Patricia gawked from Esmerelda to me. 'Are you two for real?' Then her jaw dropped and she thumped herself on the head. 'Spiders! There were also spiders in there! In the bed. I found spiders in the bed.'

'Honestly?' I asked. 'Spiders in her bed?'

Esmerelda said something imaginative. While snakes in her underwear did not frighten her, spiders in her bed, it seemed, were a different matter. Or was it the combination? I was happy to admit that the idea of either, in either, was enough to put more than a little wrinkle in my day.

'I thought the spider was just a one-off. Maybe the window was left open. But the snakes in the drawer ...'

Snake*s*? A vacuum cleaner pipe was really not enough to combat snakes *and* spiders. Although an assembled, functioning vacuum might be quite helpful.

*

It was dark by the time the Wildlife Rescue people had cleared the bedroom and en suite of snakes and spiders. And checked and cleared the hallway. And all the other rooms on the second floor. And the ground floor. And the pool house. Why take chances?

They had found thirteen redback spiders, thirteen white-tailed spiders, thirteen funnel webs, a tarantula, three tiger snakes, three dugites, a cobra and two rattlesnakes. While it was possible that *a* snake *might* have slithered in of its own accord, perhaps even a snake *and* a spider (it was Australia after all), it was *not* possible that nine snakes and three dozen spiders would have spontaneously called a wildlife convention in Esmerelda's bedroom. Especially since two of those snakes were native North Americans and one was an Asian import. Patricia, in her rapture at being devoid of Dylan Moss, had, as promised, gone on a cleaning spree in Esmeralda's living quarters. She had cleaned the bathroom vanity, floor, mirror and bath, vacuumed and dusted the bedroom, taken an abundance of jeans and T-shirts to the wash (I had not told her that several spiders had been found in the washing machine filter) and changed the sheets.

Patricia had been prepared to tolerate the native redback spiders she had found in the bed as an aberration when, as promised, she began tidying Esmerelda's underwear drawer. It was understandable that she became hysterical when a cobra and two rattlesnakes sprang out at her from said drawer. The dugites were in the bathroom drawers and the tiger snakes in the shower.

I sedated Patricia with several emergency Valium. She stared at me across Mother's Karri wood bench, slightly stoned, holding a mug of tea.

Esmerelda was completely in denial, emphatically stating that the snakes and spiders performing a choral concert in her quarters were an accident. A quirk. She refused to believe any theory except her own: a local snake and spider collector had left the lid off their terrarium. Or the terrarium had broken. Or several terrariums.

I didn't know what to think. It was obviously intentional, but who was it intended for? Supermodel celebrities get all kinds of crazy stalkers. Mother had once come home to find her bathtub full of rose petals. Another time, she'd had a three-metre ice sculpture of a cat encased in a love heart delivered to her front door. Maybe snakes were the new roses?

That was probably optimistic.

I sent Esmerelda out to pick up more food from La Cotta. I was hoping a good meal and a solid night's sleep might wake her up.

I fired the sub-par security company Patricia had hired to fend off Dylan Moss. After a few calls, I managed to hire a small flotilla of bodyguards from the security company that took care of the many high-profile, high-risk celebrities who floated in and out of Sydney. I had two bodyguards at the house on continuous eight-hour shifts until further notice. If they could keep Charlie Sheen, Alec Baldwin and Justin Bieber in their heydays out of trouble, surely they could keep an Heiress, a personal shopper and a maid safe?

I was just settling in opposite Patricia with a Bordeaux merlot, waiting for my gnocchi, when an impossibly large man poked his highly paid head into the room, eyes sweeping from floor to ceiling. He came in a set. As dark and huge as he was, his partner was lean and blond. They were both armed.

'Police,' the big one said, making eye contact with me.

My head, which felt like it was just barely hanging onto my neck, stood to attention. 'Did *you* call them?' I asked him.

'No, ma'am.'

'Searing,' lilted a somewhat stoned Patricia.

Damn. One too many Valium for her.

'Well,' Searing said, walking into the rapidly darkening kitchen, 'it seems I'm destined never to be invited *by you* to anywhere *you are*. I'm beginning to feel a little offended.'

He was in off-duty dress. A black wool-knit top with long sleeves and a scoop neck that showed off his clavicle *and* his nape, over perfectly fitting leather-belted dark blue jeans and soft leather ankle boots.

'Patricia?' I asked.

'Yep.'

I should have blocked the outgoing calls on the house phone too. It was too soon for Searing. I was still coming to terms with the fact that my attraction to him may not have been as fleeting as I had hoped. Not even close. My run-in with Burns seemed to have galvanised my desire to take my Searing action figure out of its box to play with it. At the same time, I was not emotionally fit enough to make a commitment to him.

Plus, there was the Mediterranean Men's Club fiasco.

And the not-so-down-low Max investigation that he knew too much about.

And now, the house of snakes. And spiders. The house of snakes and spiders.

'She called. Something about a cobra and a redback?' he said, crossing the kitchen to Patricia, who had put her head on the bench and was almost asleep.

He knelt down to her. 'Patricia? Are you okay?'

She tilted her head to him, eyes only one quarter open and smiled. 'A cobra and *two* rattlesnakes. In Esmerelda's *underwear* drawer.'

Searing stared up at me. 'Is she serious?'

I took a large sip from my merlot. 'Sadly, yes. We seem to have run into a spot of bad luck with an ... infestation. Just in one section of the house.'

He stood and narrowed his eyes at me. 'Did you give her something? She's in pretty bad shape.'

He had no idea. She was positively healthy compared to her mental state a few hours earlier.

'I hope she's not driving home like that.'

I looked at Patricia. She was dimly smiling, fast asleep.

'She can't drive. Esmerelda side-swiped her car a little ... well, perhaps quite a lot, last week. It's going to take some time to fix. Patricia *might* need a new car,' I said quietly, checking again to make sure she was asleep, filling my wine glass and tiptoeing towards the back door. 'There's a suite here she often uses. Either way, she won't be driving.'

'Stretch side-swiped a car?' Searing asked, following me towards the oversized sliding glass doors that led to the outside porch.

'Yes.'

Wait. Was that a question? Was he implying that *I* side-swiped Patricia's car?

'Yes!' I hissed emphatically, quietly opening the door. 'Esmerelda said the brakes were faulty. Sticky. It wasn't me.'

He stepped over the threshold and out onto the wide wooden deck, scratching his head. 'So the brakes in Patricia's car failed while Esmerelda was driving it? Were you coming or going?'

I stared at him in amazement. 'Why?'

'Just curious. Humour me.'

'We were coming home after a spa night.'

Mainly true. I'd had a manicure at the Holly Park Hotel and Esmerelda had had a haircut.

'The car was parked on the street or in a garage?'

'Garage. Look, she's just accident-prone,' I explained defensively, sipping. 'Dylan said she almost got run over by a string of luggage trollies at the airport the other day. How is that even possible? Insufferable gadgets. It's impossible to push *one* of those things, let alone *fifty*. I tried. Once.'

'Dylan? Let's circle back to "Dylan",' he said, following me across the deck. 'So, in the past week or so, Esmerelda has had *three* near-death experiences?'

'No!' I retorted, stalking down the path along the lawn, past the fruit trees and vegetable garden. The night had turned cold and I needed a long, hot shower and to change into something with less sequins and more jersey.

'But she was almost hit by a train of luggage trollies at the airport?'

'Yes.' I looked at Searing's outfit. That seemed comfortable. I might like to get into that.

'And then the brakes failed in a car she was driving, which had been parked in a garage.'

'Well, I don't know if I would be so dramatic to say the brakes failed but, I ... I suppose so.' This conversation seemed to be taking a peculiar direction.

'And then a bunch of lethal snakes and spiders were found in her bedroom?'

'Her suite, yes.'

'Huh,' he said, strolling after me past the courts. 'Trollies, brakes and venom.' Of course, *he* knew snakes and spiders were venomous and not poisonous. 'That's a lot of bad luck for one parolee. Bad luck that seems to be getting progressively worse.'

I sipped my merlot in silence as I continued my journey towards the pool house. Was he right? Was that a pattern? An escalating pattern?

'Where're you taking me?' Searing asked as we passed the cabanas.

'*I* am not taking *you* anywhere. *I* am going home. I mean to the pool house. I desperately need to have a hot shower. I need to get into something like you. I mean, something hot. God!' I started again, this time slowly. 'I need to have a *hot* shower and *get into* some warm clothes.'

We were passing the pool and would be at the door too quickly.

'I should wait outside for you,' he said, slowing down.

'Why?' I asked, turning back to him.

'Do you think it's safe for me to come in there?'

No.

'I mean, why would you wait? Is there some policing reason you're here? That is, are you here officially or are you ...'

He scratched his head. Even he didn't seem to know in what capacity he found himself at my door.

'I don't exactly run through doors anymore. Not a lot of call-out action in cold case. Technically, I'm not on the clock. I guess when Patricia called saying someone had put a cobra in the ninja surfer's sock drawer, I just dropped everything and came,' he said, crinkling his golden eyes. 'I'm not a hundred per cent sure which crimes have been committed here, but something's going on.'

'There was a cobra *and* two rattlesnakes in the dresser drawer. And three tiger snakes in the shower and three dugites in the bathroom vanity,' I clarified.

'And how many spiders exactly?'

I mentally tried to count them. And by mentally, I mean I used my fingers. When I ran out of fingers, Searing interrupted me.

'Okay, I'm going to revise my statement. That much deadly wildlife sounds like intent to cause serious harm. Plus, the car brakes and the runaway trollies? I'm going to call Burns and have her find Esmerelda. Where is Stretch?'

'Picking up dinner at La Cotta.'

'Great gnocchi,' he said, shooting off a text.

'Esmerelda is not going to appreciate a police escort,' I said.

'Burns is a pretty good shadow. She'll never know.'

I seriously doubted that.

Searing insisted on standing guard in front of the pool house.

I was too tired to argue with him. I walked through the door and down the hall, immediately banking left into my bedroom. I undid the hooks on my heavily embroidered jacket and slipped it off my shoulders. It dropped solidly onto the floor. Quality clothing always makes just the right sound when it hits the floor. I undid the invisible zipper in the back of my black sequin pants and the pants slid down my legs, over my heels and onto the floor. I stepped out of them. There was a trail of etched silk Armani in my wake. I was left in a pair of lovely black heels. They featured a leather-bound, skin-coloured panel which ran from the back of my ankles to the top of my foot. I sat on the bed to untie the leather bows that held the panels together. I was exhausted. As lovely as my black lace lingerie was, I just wanted to get out of it.

'I should have stayed outside,' Searing said, looking terrified in the bedroom doorway. 'You left the front door open. And your bedroom door. I just came in to close them. I'll just close them.'

I stopped undoing my heels, looked up at him and said, 'Did you close the front door?'

'Yes.'

'Close the door.'

'Okay.' He stepped backwards and began to pull the bedroom door in.

I shook my head. 'No. Close it the *other* way.'

He gazed at me and swallowed, stepping into the room. 'This way?'

'Yes.'

He carefully closed the bedroom door and walked with painstaking deliberateness towards me.

I maintained constant eye contact, fearing a break would see him scuttle. Or, worse yet, see me lose *my* nerve. I had Searing alone in a dark room, not on duty. There was no one home but a completely knocked out Patricia and two giant bodyguards who would stop anyone but Esmerelda from entering the property. La Cotta was a busy restaurant and we had a big order. She would be a while.

Searing finally reached me. I thought he would kiss me. But I was wrong. He knelt down in front of the bed. Because he was so tall, he was still almost eye level. He silently put both of his palms on the outside of my thighs and gently stroked my naked legs, all the way down to the ankles. Then again, hip to ankle. Then again, but this time, the inside of my thighs all the way to the inside of my ankles.

He put his palms down on the bed and hoisted himself over me, but without actually touching me. He nuzzled my neck, kissing under my ear, the front of my throat, the back of my neck, my clavicle, my shoulder. Bells rang in my head, and a moan usually reserved for new shoes escaped me when he slid his hands, with just the right pressure, up and around from the small of my back to my stomach, my ribs, up, up …

Wait … were those *actual* bells?

I cocked my head. They *were* bells. His phone was ringing. But his ringtone was bells tolling.

'Don't even think about it,' I growled as his hands, so close to their rightful destination, moved away. I was only just beginning to get some serious returns from my Guia La Bruna investments. 'No! No!' I yelped as he attempted to back away from me.

I put my lips on his mouth before he had a chance to use it to answer his phone. Against my better or worse impulses, I found myself following the same pattern he had. Slowly, softly grazing his lips. A small open-mouthed kiss. Tiny tension-filled kisses, floating in and out between us. I could *feel* that he had completely lost control of at least one part of his body, two if you counted all the delicious, delectable groaning coming from him, but he continued to fight me, fight the desire, fight the electricity, continued to try to restrain himself. He'd deliver a passionate kiss, then try to back away, only to be drawn in for one last taste seconds later. He made a valiant effort, but he lost.

We were splayed on top of the gold silk sheets, me still respectfully in my bra, panties and heels, him still a Boy Scout, fully dressed except for his belt and boots. There had been writhing. A *lot* of writhing. My skin felt raw from grazing. He was attempting once again to let go of my thighs, which he was holding onto with his pianist hands, when the phone stopped ringing and the door started knocking.

Damn. How much clearer could instructions be? One of everything and don't let anyone except Esmerelda into the compound.

'Hey, Searing!' I heard Burns's voice call. 'You'd better get out here, mate. We've got a situation.'

There was no way *her* situation was more important than *my* situation.

CHAPTER 17

GRAPE FANTA

The voice of his partner at the front door was enough to shock Searing to his feet. Once he was up, he tried to get himself in order. He hopped from one foot to the other and put his hands in his pockets attempting to reposition himself. He repeated a mantra: 'Don't look at her! Don't look at her! Think about tax law.'

I wanted to leave him with no uncertainty that this conversation was far from over. I slid off the bed, unhooked my bra, slipped it off and dropped it leisurely to the floor before turning to give him a suggestive wink while strutting into the en suite for a hot shower.

That was in my mind. In real life, I slid *off* the bed, landed with an ungodly *thud* on the floor, attempted unsuccessfully to hoist myself up, failed, finally righted myself, adjusted myself back *into* my half cup bra, pulled my underwear back into position and *then* walked gracefully into my bathroom for a hot shower.

Oh yes. He would remember *that* exit.

I took a long shower, dressed myself in a thick sapphire blue Joseph knit jersey and a pair of soft wide-legged black wool Chanel pants. Even I was not cruel enough to call Franny in the middle of the night to the arachnid house to do my hair and make-up for the benefit of Burns. Searing ... well, Searing had already seen some of my parts naked. I put on the bare basics: mascara, eyeliner and tinted moisturiser, brushed my still-damp hair back into a ponytail and hit the road. Well, the path up to the main house.

If I was hungry before, I was ravenous now. There were ten brown paper carry bags sitting along the Karri wood bench, along with five La Cotta pizza boxes. Esmerelda had not opened a single container or box, not unpacked a single bag. I could smell the Italian aroma, but the kitchen was oddly deserted. This was bad.

I followed the sounds of quiet chatter and a low hush of commotion out to the front of the house. An ambulance was parked in the driveway, lights flashing in the darkness, but no sound. The enormous security guard sat in the back being checked out by a paramedic, chatting to Searing and Burns. There were two new bodyguards standing by the gate looking extremely serious.

Where was the massive guy's smaller counterpart? Mr Blond-and-lean?

Esmerelda sauntered out of the front door with a Peach Snapple in her hand. 'Snapple?' she asked me.

'No. I have a feeling I'm going to need something harder after you tell me what's going on.'

'Blond dude like had a heart attack or something.'

I blanched. What were the chances of that happening? Surely these guys were super fit? At $500 an hour, I hoped these guards had been checked for congenital heart disease, fitness levels and deep-seated chromosomal disorders inherited from their great-grandmother's second cousin.

'Where is he?'

'Like, totally gone.'

'He's dead!'

'Dude, no. They took him to the hospital.'

'What are they doing with the other guy?' I asked her.

'Dunno.'

As helpful as ever.

The guy in the back of the ambulance pointed to a large plastic ziplock bag held by Burns, then to Esmerelda.

'What?' I demanded from Esmerelda. 'What is he saying? Why is he pointing?'

'Dude, what could he be saying? He's worked here five seconds.'

She had a point. What could we have possibly done? Well, that he would have known about, anyway.

I was hungry. 'Why is all the food from La Cotta still packed up?'

'I was waiting for you?' Esmerelda tried.

I gave her an 'as if' look.

'Burns got crabby. Said I had to wait for her okay to eat. Her okay! I mean, where are my civil rights to pasta? Like, I don't even think it's legal to stop a citizen from eating pizza. I've got Italian food in-tidal-ments.'

'How much of it did you eat before she caught you?' I asked her.

'Half the margarita pizza and a couple arancini.'

'In the car?'

'Yep.'

I understood. It had been a long day. I was hungry too. Burns might be able to stop me snacking on Searing, but she wasn't going to stop me from devouring pink Napolitana gnocchi smothered in freshly shaved parmesan.

'Take the food down to the pool house kitchen. I will be with you in a minute.'

Esmerelda turned heel and headed into the house as Burns sauntered over. Searing seemed to be finishing up with the big man in the ambulance. He put his hands back in his pockets when we made eye contact.

'What?' I griped to Burns before she had spoken. 'The man had a heart attack. That's not a crime.'

She held a clear ziplock bag up to me. It had an empty can of Grape Fanta in it. 'Yours?'

I narrowed my eyes at her.

'Didn't think so, princess. Grape Fanta is more the grungy personal shopper's speed, huh? Or is she your assistant this week?'

'Both,' I said, smiling sweetly.

Burns grinned, unamused. 'She wash it down with some Skittles and a bit of B&E?'

'Funny. What do you want?'

'Your bodyguard had a massive coronary.'

'Yes, Esmerelda told me. Terrible.'

'After he drank this.' And she rattled the bagged empty can at me.

Mother was right—that stuff will kill you.

'Apparently went down straight after he chugged it.' She moved the bag close to my face. 'See that,' she said, pointing to the can.

All I saw were too many artificial colours on the ingredients list.

'The top of the can? That's a needle mark. Someone tampered with it.'

I peered closely at the top of the can. Burns was right; there was a tiny hole.

Patricia had only bought those for Esmerelda this morning. How was this possible?

'Anyone else in your house drink Grape Fanta?' she asked. 'No.'

I looked to Searing. He was now taking notes from the female paramedic.

'Poison soft drink. Snakes and spiders. Faulty brakes. Renegade luggage trollies,' Burns said, eyeing me. 'I'd say she was either *very* unlucky or …'

Poison … venom … poison …

For the second time that day, I took off in a dead run in a pair of stilettos. This time, in and out of the main house and down the garden path into the pool house. I burst through the door and bolted up the hallway, past the bedrooms, past the main bathroom, past the formal lounge and dining rooms and into the open kitchen.

Every single La Cotta bag was unpacked and every container and pizza box sat open on the kitchen island. Esmerelda was sitting close by on a pale grey Cattelan bar stool, arms on the armrests, feet on the buttery leather of the stool next to her. She had a giant white Vera Wang bowl filled with a kaleidoscope of Italian food hanging casually from one hand and a silver Vera Wang fork in the other, two ravioli speared on its prongs. She was staring at the white-boards plastered all over the walls.

I whipped the fork and bowl away from her. 'How much of that have you eaten?'

'Hu-du-ho,' she mumbled, mouth full.

Burns was so close behind she just about ran into the back of me. I whipped around to her. 'How long? How long after he drank the soft drink? How long did the poison take?'

'Pretty quick,' Burns said, her eyes taking in the open boxes and containers everywhere. 'Minutes. He was down in minutes.'

Esmerelda had eaten the pizza and arancini long before. And she had been in the pool house chowing down for at least five minutes.

It was plausible that someone had managed to slip through Patricia's paltry security man this morning to meddle with the Grape Fanta cans and place the snakes and arachnids. In fairness, he had only been there to keep an overly enthu-siastic ex-teen boyfriend at bay. But how could they, who-ever *they* were, slip past *three* Sheen-level bodyguards and two detectives to meddle with our risotto? Plus, Esmerelda seemed perfectly healthy and I was still *very* hungry.

I exhaled deeply and handed Esmerelda back her dish and fork. I turned to Burns. 'It's fine. She's fine.'

'Are you sure?' Burns probed, unconvinced.

I nodded. 'It's impossible. She ate half a pizza on the way home. She would have,' I held my hands to my throat, then realising my mistake clutched them over my heart instead, 'you know, by now.'

'Figures,' Burns said, shaking her head.

'Like what the hell?' Esmerelda wanted to know, her eyes bouncing between Burns and I.

It seemed almost certainly true that someone was trying to kill Esmerelda.

'Do you know of anyone who would want to off her?' Burns asked me.

I would perhaps have put it more subtly than that.

I was sure there were many people who Esmerelda drove crazy. Who may, at times, want to *figuratively* kill her. I did not know them, but I felt certain they were out there. But *actually* murder her?

'No,' I said.

'Like, again, what the hell?' Esmerelda demanded, poking her fork in the air.

I explained to Esmerelda about the needle hole in the Grape Fanta and the guard's almost immediate heart attack. The car brakes. The trolleys. She soon made the connection and relented on her theory that a local herpetologist had had a mishap with a few snake terrariums. She had a new theory.

'Do you know anyone who wants to off you?' Burns asked her.

'Dude, like totally! It's that crazy Heinsmann!' Esmerelda insisted, stabbing her fork, this time loaded with spaghetti, enthusiastically at Burns. 'He won't let me go! He keeps harassing me. I say "no, no, no" but, he totally won't listen. Maybe it's like one of those, "if I can't have you no one can" deals.'

'Jealous ex-lover,' Burns said, taking out her notebook. 'An oldie but a goodie.'

'No way, man.'

'No?'

'I wouldn't let that freak touch me.'

'But it's a "he wants you but you don't want him" deal?'

'Yep. Totally.'

So clearly explained.

I exhaled deeply and pulled several matching bowls out of the cupboard. 'Laurie Heinsmann is the editor-in-chief of *Pazzia Australia*. He has Esmerelda in a very tightly bound editorial contract which she no longer wishes to participate in. It's pure business. There's no romantic involvement.' I stopped and peered at Esmerelda. 'Is there?'

'I'm not gonna condone that with a response,' she said sourly.

I shrugged. With Esmerelda, it never paid to assume.

'You think the editor of *Pazzia Australia* tampered with your brakes, set snakes loose in your room and poisoned your Fanta?' Burns asked, still standing hands on hips near the doorway.

'I think it is about as likely as an Heiress building multiple explosive devices to try to kill her husband,' I said, smiling sarcastically at Burns and loading one of the bowls with honey, pine nut and pumpkin risotto.

'Stranger things have happened,' Burns shot back.

I stuck a fork in the mountain of risotto and handed it to Burns. She wasn't fast enough to avoid having it foisted upon her. She stood awkwardly with the bowl and her pen in one hand and her notebook in the other, not eating.

'So *how* has this Heinsmann been harassing you?'

'Manolo Blahnik shoes. Chanel cleansers and masks, and make-up stuff. Dior handbags. Gucci sneakers.' Esmerelda shook her head in disgust. 'Tiffany sunnies. He won't stop.'

Burns's jaw dropped. She plopped into the lacey provincial armchair in the corner by the doorway, a bold choice for a woman holding a biro and a pumpkin risotto (it was rattan and Canadian oak, upholstered in a pale linen). She squeezed her eyes and attempted to concentrate.

'Are you *sure* he's not,' Burns eyed Esmerelda, 'romantically interested in you?'

Esmerelda shook her head.

'Esmerelda probably has one too many X chromosomes for Laurie Heinsmann,' I said, ladling gnocchi and ravioli into my bowl.

'What does that mean?' Esmerelda growled defensively at me.

'It means you're a female,' I explained, ignoring the bark.

'Oh yeah, dude's totally into dudes,' she said, emptying her bowl of its last scrap of spaghetti.

'Okay,' Burns said, setting her bowl on the low table beside her. 'Is this Heinsmann trying to bribe you into doing something illegal? Something you don't want to do?'

'Yeah!' Esmerelda yelped. 'Like totally he is.'

'No,' I said, shaking my head. 'He is not.'

Esmerelda whipped her head around to me. 'But I totally don't wanna.'

'Yes, but what he is asking you to do is *not* illegal. In fact, you signed a contract saying you would do it. It is a simple business contract, not a mafia blood oath to hijack semitrailers filled with electrical goods from the docks.'

They both stared at me. 'What?' I said. 'I watch movies.'

Burns shook her head and tried, very professionally, to bring the conversation back on track. 'So, what's the contract about? The business deal? Do you owe him money?'

'No,' Esmerelda admitted. 'He wants to pay me to do it. But I don't wanna do it. It's gross and embarrassing.'

Burns sat very still for a moment. 'We *are* talking about *Pazzia* the fashion magazine, right? It's not some new, weird pornographic *Pazzia* with one of the letters changed or something, is it?'

'No,' I said. 'It's the original *Pazzia*, but plenty of models *have* been asked to take their clothes off on cover shoots before. True, most of them were pregnant—'

'You're pregnant?' Burns blurted to Esmerelda.

'No!' Esmerelda shot back.

'He wants you to get naked?'

'Nuh-uh.'

'What then?' Burns asked. 'What does he want you to do that's so shocking?'

'He wants her to do a cover shoot. Heinsmann wants to put Esmerelda on the cover of *Pazzia*.'

Burns looked to Esmerelda for confirmation. Esmerelda gave her a red-faced nod. At this, Burns burst out in laughter. I had never heard Burns laugh before and I suddenly understood, at least in part, why Searing was so loyal to her. Her laughter was sincere, unreserved and throaty. Her whole body participated in the laughter which slowed only when she had run out of breath, tears appearing in her eyes.

Esmerelda looked like she was going to choke that last chuckle out of Burns.

I decided not to tell Burns that Esmerelda had *already* appeared on one *Pazzia* cover. I didn't want her to choke on her risotto. And I didn't want Esmerelda to strangle me before I had eaten my gnocchi.

'What the hell …?' Searing said in wonderment as he walked into the scene: admissions of felonious cover model contracts, Italian food everywhere, Burns laughing hysterically, Esmeralda halfway across the room, hands out ready to choke her, and me, trying to lean in strategically to see if Burns was armed. But it seemed Searing had already processed and bypassed all of it. He was standing in the middle of the room, back to me and the kitchen, mesmerised by the whiteboards.

'What is this?' he said, pointing to the back wall.

'Oh, uh,' I said, not sure I wanted to share this information with Searing, and certain I did not want to share it with Burns.

In my haste to get to the pool house kitchen to see if Esmerelda had been poisoned, I had briefly blanked that day's Max whiteboard project.

Burns got herself together, stood and walked into the room proper for the first time. She paused beside her partner. Searing nodded at the centre board and nudged Burns. 'I see it,' she said slowly.

After a small eternity, Burns motioned towards Esmerelda, then said quietly to a cross-armed Searing, 'You think someone's trying to—'

'Oh yeah. These two have any leads?'

Burns shook her head.

'What?' objected Esmerelda. 'Heinsmann's totally a lead!'

'Fine,' Burns relented. 'One ridiculously generous high fashion magazine editor to run down.'

Searing glanced down at Burns. 'What?'

'Tell you later,' she said in resigned tones.

Searing uncrossed his arms and pointed to the board with the latest clues. 'Where'd you get this information?'

'I would prefer not to say,' I said, hoping that would work.
Burns rolled her eyes. 'What's this then? A science project?'
'Yes,' I readily agreed.

'Nah,' Esmerelda said simultaneously before changing her mind. 'It's like yeah, kind of a science project, but mainly like, uh …'

'An outline. For a movie. We're writing a movie.' I smiled. Plausible. Unlikely, but plausible.

'Sure,' Burns said flatly, reading our heading, 'The *Great-Uncle Max* project.'

Damn that woman. She always knew enough to get you into trouble but never enough to get you out of it.

Searing sucked on his bottom left lip. 'How unprofessional would it be to ask them?'

Burns shrugged. 'Mate, your belt is missing a couple loops. We passed professional a while back. Besides, nothing wrong with a bit of *hypothetical* questioning,' she hedged. 'Plus, I know nothing about nothing.'

Searing glanced down. She was right. He had managed to get his belt back on, just not correctly. He had missed the second and fourth loops. 'Agreed. Hypothetically,' he said, turning to me, 'we might have a cold case with some of the same injuries.'

'UP Greenacre 0101 West?' I immediately asked.

Searing raised an eyebrow but did not ask how I knew his cold case number by heart. 'Yep. The guy who went from being a sixty something Caucasian, to a forty something south-east Asian. Thanks to Jem Bailly. Hypothetically, that is.'

'*Maybe*, hypothetically,' Burns added.

What on earth could a middle-aged Asian cold case have to do with Max, the recently deceased elderly white millionaire?

'Which injuries?' I asked, stepping towards the pair. 'Manicure, pedicure? Expensive shaving habits?'

'Fancy hair stuff?' Esmerelda added, seating herself at the kitchen island, conveniently close to the food and *behind* the police detective duo.

'Vintage scented hair oil,' I clarified. 'Bleached hair? Dental implants?'

'Ah, no, no and no,' Burns said. 'Although,' she paused and peered up at Searing, 'UP Greenacre 0101 West, he had a plate with teeth on it, right? A denture plate?'

Searing's eyes widened. 'That's right, he did! He was missing most of his top teeth and some from the bottom too.' Searing turned to me in wonder. 'He wore dentures.'

'Your cold case was hit over the back of the head? And had a dental plate?' I asked.

'The star thingy?' Esmerelda asked.

'No, no, that's not it,' Searing said, walking towards the middle board, arm out, hand waving. 'Jem thinks UP Greenacre 0101 West died from a coronary after massive blood loss from what she says looks like an industrial accident.'

'Ew,' squirmed Esmerelda.

'Hypothetically,' Burns quickly put in.

'No, no, he had these,' Searing said, tapping two boards sitting side by side. 'Hypothetically.'

- Vertebra degeneration
  Got old.
- Arthritic changes in both hands
  Got old.
- Historical thickening of skin on hands, knees and feet
  Old rubbing?

- Faint prepatellar bursitis scaring. 'Housemaid's knee'
  Used to kneel a lot? At work?
- A mastoidectomy
  Untreated childhood ear infections
- Severe whipping scars on back from childhood &
  adolescence.

'Well, he had some of them, and others were similar.'

I felt sick all over again. 'Which ones?' I asked, stepping back. Burns took over as I removed Esmerelda's feet from the Cattelan's leather arm and sat down next to her.

'Theoretically, he had vertebra degeneration and arthritic changes.'

Esmerelda furrowed her brow. 'Forty's old but it's not *that* old. How'd he get 'em?'

'Jem thinks it might be from performing a lot of manual labour from quite a young age. He also had thickening of the skin, mainly on the hands.'

Cogs cricked and turned in my overwrought brain. 'Was the skin thickening from manual labour too?' I asked.

Burns and Searing nodded.

'What about the ear surgery? For the untreated childhood ear infections?' I asked the pair.

'Is that the mastoidectomy?' Searing asked me.

'Yes,' I said.

'No. No ear surgery,' Burns responded. 'But he had damage to his ears from untreated childhood ear infections, plus he had other injuries that indicated he wasn't cared for as a child in the way you'd expect to see in Australia.'

'You think your UP was an immigrant?'

'Or a refugee. It's certainly a possibility,' Searing said.

'What about the scars?' Esmerelda asked, now in crocodile mode.

'Our UP had scarring too. Some likely from childhood beatings, like your guy, but he also had other scars, probably from fighting.'

I had no idea if Max had scars from fights. I didn't see any scarring on his face. And there was nothing in the notes.

Burns nudged Searing and pointed to one of the earlier whiteboards. 'Our guy was five foot five. That's a relatively short stature too.'

Esmerelda turned back to the bench and served herself some more pasta. 'Maybe they worked in Willy Wonka's chocolate factory together when they were kids. Only Willy Wonka was a real dirtbag.'

'More likely poor nutrition,' I said to myself. Burns nodded in agreement.

I was eight centimetres shorter than my mother, twelve shorter than my father. As a teenager, I had done a *lot* of research into how and why people do and do not grow.

It was odd that no one in the hotel, nor any of the Hollys, nor Dame Elizabeth herself, had mentioned Max having an accent. Then again, Max could have arrived in Australia at any age. If he was a *child* migrant, would he still have had an accent as an adult? People do lose accents. Especially if they work at it.

Even taking generational differences into consideration, imagining what the Australia of sixty or seventy years ago was like for a child, it seemed unlikely that Max had grown up as an average Australian child.

I suddenly felt as if I had been doing a lot of giving to Searing and Burns, but not getting much in return.

'Apart from possibly growing up somewhere else, what does Dr Bailly, theoretically, think happened to your UP to give him those injuries?' I asked with as much confidence and nonchalance as possible.

'Guy had a hard life. Started working young. *Really* young. Hard manual labour. His body was worn,' Burns said matter-of-factly. 'Hypothetically.'

To the outside world, Max seemed to be in excellent form. When he ate, he ate well, he swam quite regularly, and certainly he didn't scrimp on personal grooming, entertainment or accommodation. He was sounding more and more like a successful immigration story. Boy flees country of origin where life was horrid and unjust, lands in Australia, the land of opportunity, works hard, breaks no laws (his fingerprints were not in the system) and is extremely successful.

With his new wealth, he fixes the scars from his childhood: he has dental implants to replace decayed teeth and ear surgery to correct hearing loss from ear infections. Maybe even a nip and a tuck. A lot of money can buy a lot of aesthetic pleasantries.

He immerses himself in culture: art, jewellery, opera, ballet.

He finds love. He finds death.

'So,' Burns said, pointing expectantly to our whiteboards, 'who is this guy? This character in your *movie*. Great-Uncle Max. Where'd he come from? What'd he do?'

I served myself one of the last pieces of margarita. Even cold, it was still good. Made in an Italian pizza oven by a handsome twenty-five-year-old pizzaioli freshly imported from Naples. It was almost as good as having it at Lake Como.

I shrugged my shoulders at the detectives. 'I don't know. Great-Uncle Max is a work of fiction. If I knew who he was, I would tell you.'

Much of that statement was absolutely true.

It was indeed the multi-million-dollar question. Who was Max Weller? Because he certainly was not Max Weller.

'What'd you know about all of this?' Burns asked Searing.

'Theoretically? A little bit.' He looked to me for approval. I shook my head and let out an exasperated sigh.

'Good deal then,' Burns said in irritation to Searing. Then to me, 'Well, great *not* having this conversation with you. Super helpful. Let's *not* do it again. And since I'm *not* here anyway, I'll *not* grab dinner on the way out.' She walked to the bench, opened a pizza box and picked up a slice of the prosciutto, parmesan and rocket pizza. She made a sound similar to the one I made when unwrapping a new Dior handbag. She recovered herself and gave me a most unpleasant expectant stare.

'Last chance. Whaddaya know, princess?'

'Indigo?' Searing appealed.

Okay, so I possibly owed Burns reparations for her demotion to cold case. And I felt a little bad about placing Searing in another situation where he had to keep things from his partner. If push came to shove and he had to choose between us, I doubted I would come out on top.

'I don't know who Max was,' I said truthfully. 'Or where he came from, but I think it is pretty safe to say Max was successful. Very financially successful. And since it's almost impossible he was *born* into wealth, I'm going to surmise he worked extremely hard from a young age and was a self-made success story.'

'Or he was a crook,' Esmerelda said, wiping her hands on her jeans.

'No fingerprints in the system. For his character,' I clarified. '*Not* a crook.'

'Maybe he just never got caught,' she countered.

Searing had begun staring at Esmerelda. He walked slowly towards her. You could almost hear his brain working. '*Maybe they worked in the same chocolate factory as kids. Only Willy Wonka was a real dirtbag,*' he said, paraphrasing her. '*He was a crook.*'

We all turned and stared at him. He was now standing next to Esmerelda, tapping his fingers on the marble island bench and muttering, 'Yes, yes, he was.'

'Dude!' Esmerelda barked. He was standing too close, in her personal space. And he was blocking her ability to reach the deep-fried, ricotta-filled cannoli.

'Burns, we've got to go,' he said, coming out of his trance. 'I think I've got a ... we have to go.'

Then Burns did something I had never seen her do before. She smiled. It was a little disconcerting. She glanced from me to Esmerelda to Searing and then back to Esmerelda. 'Do you need police protection, Esmerelda? Do you feel you're in danger?'

'Dude,' Esmerelda said drolly. 'I'd rather *be* dead than get police protection.'

'Duly noted,' Burns said.

As he was walking out the door, Searing asked if I intended to keep the bodyguards as private security.

'Are you kidding? Someone put rattlesnakes in Esmerelda's underwear drawer and tampered with Patricia's brakes. Consider them a permanent fixture.'

Our answers seemed to make the detectives happy. Ten seconds later, they were gone, and so was the prosciutto pizza. And half of the cannoli.

CHAPTER 18

TUNNEL OF LOVE

As predicted, Grandmother and Dame Elizabeth arrived like uninvited clockwork at 9 am the next morning. But I was ready for them. I had awoken at 7 am, swum a few laps on *purpose*, showered, and had had Franny come for pared-back hair and make-up. By the time Dame Elizabeth's polite knock came, I was drinking tea in a pair of pale beige Gabriela Hearst wool and silk pants, a sleeveless Valentino roll neck in caramel wool and a pair of simple calf skin Jimmy Choo stilettoes. Esmerelda was even on hand to open the door and show them into my room. I could not risk them entering any other part of the pool house—I didn't want them seeing the open kitchen/murder room.

Grandmother seemed almost disappointed to see me dressed and ready to talk. Dame Elizabeth was delighted. 'How lovely you look this morning, dear,' she said, kissing me on both cheeks before delivering a warm hug.

She seated herself across from me, leaving plenty of room for Grandmother to slide into the seat beside her, next to the window. Esmerelda attempted to take up her perch on the windowsill, but Grandmother was having none of it. She did not like being looked down on. Grandmother insisted Esmerelda sit beside me, opposite her.

'I am sorry we were not able to speak with you yesterday,' I began in earnest to Dame Elizabeth. 'We had some unforeseen events here.'

'Yes, Carlo told me,' Dame Elizabeth said empathetically. 'I am *so* sorry. How horrible. Not that he divulged specifics, very discreet. You did well, Indigo. Carlo is one of the best.'

'Who's Carlo?' I asked, dumbfounded.

'Heavy one at eight,' Esmerelda said helpfully.

I squinted at her.

Dame Elizabeth turned earnestly to Grandmother. 'Chris and Cate, Kylie and Keith, they all swear by him.'

'Don't forget Shane,' Patricia added, bustling in to remove the breakfast setting and laying out a fresh morning tea. She was smiling from ear to ear. 'Carlo *and* Shane.'

'Heavy *two* at eight,' Esmerelda said.

'Carlo and Shane are the new security guards?' I guessed. 'They started their shifts at 8 am?'

'God help us,' Grandmother said, shaking her head. 'You really must put that brain to better use, Indigo. Speaking of which, please report.'

This unsubtle segue took most of the room by surprise. Patricia quickly excused herself, putting an abrupt end to the conversation she was having with Dame Elizabeth about Carlo. And Shane. It also put an end to my enjoyment of some fine miniature Florentines. And Esmerelda, well, Esmerelda was rarely taken by surprise.

'Wait, wait, wait,' Esmerelda said. 'There's some other stuff first. Like, have you gotten me out of that contract with Heinsmann yet? He's killing me. And he's totally *actually* trying to kill me.'

It took me a second to recalibrate. 'I don't think Heinsmann is trying to kill you.'

Although I had spent much of the night considering the possibilities, in truth, I had no idea who was trying to harm Esmerelda or why. Was it related to our investigation into Max? Was it related to her previous life, the one that had landed her in Silverwater Women's Correctional Centre? Could it *actually* be related to her *Pazzia* cover? Or was it something completely different? Esmerelda could be a little prickly. Perhaps she had simply rubbed someone mentally unstable up the wrong way.

'It is all going quite well,' Dame Elizabeth said confidently. 'I should have an answer within the week.'

'Are you quite finished?' Grandmother said to Esmerelda.

'Yeah, just checking,' Esmerelda said, leaning back in her chair.

'Max did not arrive to escort Elizabeth to the ballet on Saturday. Nor did he arrive at the ballet as a latecomer. Elizabeth, am I correct?'

Grandmother could always be relied upon to be a verbal freight train.

Dame Elizabeth peered deeply into her teacup and exhaled. 'Yes.'

'Have you heard from him at all since he broke his dinner date with you the night before a body *coincidentally* arrived in my oriental lilies?'

'No.'

Freight train with a side of Tin Man. Well, Tin Woman.

Poor Dame Elizabeth. She was about to have her heart ripped out, and she knew it. At least I was prepared. I leaned across the table and took her hands in mine. 'I am so sorry, Aunt Lizzy. Max Weller, your Max, *is* the man in the lilies.'

'The photo?' she asked heavily. 'From the theatre. It was him?'

'We were fairly certain by then, but yes, it did confirm it.'

'Max is gone?'

'Yes. He's gone.'

Esmerelda and Grandmother were both deeply uncomfortable with the display of vulnerability and raw emotion. This was not their wheelhouse.

'So, like, how did your dude, your Max,' Esmerelda said, pointing to Dame Elizabeth, 'end up in like your backyard?' she asked pointing to Grandmother. 'There's a crazy high fence around most of your place, like all kinds of gate security.' Esmerelda pointed back to Dame Elizabeth. 'No front gate security at your place, but, like yours,' she pointed back to Grandmother, 'is heavy-duty. Dude was pushing eighty. He's not scaling fences.'

'Did Max know about the false hedge-gate between your properties in the back garden?' I asked.

'Oh no,' Dame Elizabeth said.

'How do *you* know about the gate?' Grandmother demanded.

Dame Elizabeth answered on my behalf. 'When I found Indigo in your garden, she had already been detained by the police for *hours*. Standing next to ... standing in the sun. She looked exhausted. I forgot it was a secret, I just acted. I unlatched the boxwood hedge, opened the gate, went through and removed her to your drawing room.'

Grandmother tried to work up some anger at Dame Elizabeth, but just could not manage it.

'Does anyone else know about the gate, Dame—Aunt Lizzy?' I asked gently. 'Gilly? Bettina? Was it there when Astor and Gregory were growing up?'

'Oh no,' she said, shaking her head. 'It's just a little short cut Florence and I put in a few years ago. The children had been gone for decades by then. We are not as young as we used to be and,' she paused and glanced at Grandmother, 'it's just *faster* if you just want to pop over. The walk to my door, to the front of my estate, and then the rigmarole of Florence's security and gates and whatnot, then the walk from the front of her estate to her front door, even getting through her home, my home ... they are not small structures. It is *not* a short journey. For the most part, we end up sitting in the garden anyway. And your grandmother is so busy, so often away. Time is precious.'

The two older women regarded each other cautiously, meaningfully. I sensed something was brewing. After a minute or so of non-verbal back and forth, Grandmother arched her left eyebrow and crossed her arms. This was a sign.

'Expect a visit from Loraine today. I want her cleared by your security immediately. No delays, no questions asked,' Grandmother said. 'She will have two NDAs. You will sign one each and return them to her immediately.'

Wow. This was going to be good.

'Absolutely,' I said.

'Like, totally no way,' Esmerelda piped up, crossing her arms.

I turned to Esmerelda. 'You have already signed an NDA for me. You *will* sign this one or you can put the repairs for Patricia's car on your own Visa.'

'Hey!' she objected. 'That accident wasn't even my fault! Searing said so.'

'Oh,' I said sympathetically, patting her hand, 'I know. I would just like to hear *you* explain it to an insurance agent. Remember how much fun those insurance meetings were? You have all the proper documentation, right?'

'You're meaner than before,' Esmerelda said. 'And sneakier.'

'She is, isn't she,' Grandmother said proudly.

'The NDA?' I pressed.

'Yeah, okay. Spill it, Nanna.'

Grandmother narrowed her eyes and appeared snakelike for long enough to make Esmerelda lean incrementally back in her chair.

'Indigo,' Grandmother began, 'you were quite young when your grandfather died, so you probably don't recall that he and Alexander were, at various stages, quite close.'

She was right. I had only faint memories of Earl Alexander Holly.

'For some absurd reason, the two of them had a secret underground tunnel constructed to join our two properties. It runs from my orchid palace to Elizabeth's garden shed.'

'Pardon?' I asked, astonished.

'There's a hidden door behind the second row of Vandas on the left-hand side of the orchid palace. It opens onto a stone staircase that leads to an underground tunnel.'

'I knew there was something sus about that orchid palace floor!' Esmerelda said victoriously.

I'd had no idea. You had to hand it to Esmerelda, when it came to deceitfulness and fraud, her extra-sensory perceptions were genius level. She was a duplicity savant.

'The tunnel runs underneath the two gardens. It's quite wide and tall enough to walk through. We have used it on occasion to have particularly *private* conversations,' Dame Elizabeth added.

'I must have that tunnel paved,' Grandmother chided. 'I have *never* liked that pebbled flooring. Tiny pebbles everywhere. Disastrous on one's shoes, messy, slippery. Most unpleasant.'

I turned to Dame Elizabeth as she spoke.

'Alexander thought it ever so clever to have his entry built into the garden shed. The rack where the metal rakes and forks hang is actually a false door. It too opens onto a stone staircase that leads to the tunnel. He always said no one worth listening to would be caught dead entering a garden shed.'

It seemed someone who *had* ended up dead may well have entered that garden shed. I'd been over it so many times in my mind. I thought Max must have known about the secret hedge-gate and used that, but what if it was actually the secret tunnel? Either way, I was now convinced Max had begun the evening at Dame Elizabeth's, had used one of the secret entrances to get into Grandmother's and had been murdered.

'Or was it worthwhile?' Dame Elizabeth mused as I tuned back in. 'No one worth*while* would be caught—' She stopped short, hearing her words.

'Alexander was an awful snob,' Grandmother broke in. 'Trying to make everyone call him Earl Holly. Really!'

The women shared a derisive shake of the head.

'Are you sure Max didn't visit you the evening you were supposed to have dinner together?' I pressed.

'No,' Dame Elizabeth said. 'He called to say he had an urgent family matter to attend to in WA. That was it.'

Esmerelda eyed Dame Elizabeth. 'Like, was he coming to you?'

'Yes.'

'In a car?' Esmerelda probed.

'No, Max didn't drive. But he was very modern. Ubers.'

'If you don't mind me asking, where were you going for dinner?'

Dame Elizabeth turned a slight shade of pink. 'We were dining at my home.'

'You cooked and he didn't rock?' Esmerelda let out a puff of disapproval.

I was certain that was not quite how it happened. I pushed. 'What a shame. I hope the food didn't go to waste. I know you love fresh, local produce. Did your chef cook you a meal for one instead?'

'No, Chef had already cooked by then. Dinner was all prepared. The soup was lobster bisque, Max's favourite.'

'How long before dinner did he call?' I asked.

'Not long,' she hedged.

'Specifically,' I asked.

'A minute or two before he was due to arrive,' she said sadly.

'Had that ever happened before?' I asked softly.

'No, never. Max was always punctual. He was a gentle-man.' A tear dropped into her tea. 'He had never done anything like that before.'

Bingo. I was betting Max was already at Dame Elizabeth's when he called to cancel.

But that still didn't answer our original question: who was Max Weller *really*? If he had family in WA, why hadn't they reported him missing? Honestly, how often do disappearing millionaires fly under the radar? I inhaled deeply and attempted to anchor myself for this portion of the conversation.

'Esmerelda and I have been unable to find anyone named Max Weller who fits the description of Max Weller,' I said apologetically.

'Max was very private,' she quickly responded. 'I am sure you will find his family. In time. If you persist.'

'No one named Max Weller has been reported missing,' I added. If they had, I felt sure Bailly would have notified me.

'Where did you look?' Grandmother wanted to know.

Esmerelda fielded this question. 'Facebook, Instagram, Twitter, LinkedIn, the minor socials, driver's licences from all over the country, fingerprints, lost and found.'

'Company directors?' Grandmother asked me.

'He's not listed,' I responded.

'What about other executive positions? CEO, CFO, COO, CMO?'

'We checked all those positions on the top 100 ASX companies,' I said regretfully.

'Boards?'

I had not thought of that.

'Nup,' Esmerelda said, gnawing on a Florentine. 'Totally checked 'em.'

She was good.

Grandmother eyed Dame Elizabeth. 'Was he,' she whispered, 'poor?'

Dame Elizabeth delivered a withering stare. 'No. But had he been, it would not have mattered. I would still have—'

She stopped short. We all knew what she was going to say—she would still have loved him.

'He was totally one of you,' Esmerelda chewed. 'He dropped a lotta cash on a lotta rich people shit. I mean, stuff.'

The older women looked at me.

'She's right. He spent a substantial amount at the Holly Park Sydney. Did you know he was staying there?'

'He mentioned it early on. I assumed it was just a coincidence. Max never asked me to his room. He was a—'

'—gentleman,' Esmerelda filled in.

Dame Elizabeth nodded.

'So, you were hiding your relationship from your family,' Grandmother bluntly assessed.

'I was keeping the relationship *private* until I was ready,' she corrected. 'My family can be overly protective.' Dame Elizabeth suddenly welled up. 'He was a wonderful man. You would have liked him, Florence.'

'I'm sure I would have,' Grandmother said firmly, *almost* experiencing an emotion.

'He wasn't in no regular room either. He was in the Forrest Suite,' Esmerelda put in, bulldozing through the moment.

Dame Elizabeth's watery eyes widened in surprise. 'The Forrest Suite? Are you sure?'

'Uh-huh.'

'What does that mean?' Grandmother asked.

'Like, you could like buy a place with what he paid for two months in that suite.'

Grandmother was startled. 'You have a suite that costs five million dollars a month?'

Esmerelda spat up her tea. 'Like, you guys live in a crazy world. It's seventeen kay a night, half a mill a month. That's already totally insane. Where does a house cost *ten mill*?'

'A house?' Grandmother rebuffed. 'I meant an apartment.'

We were getting side-tracked. I turned to Dame Elizabeth. 'Max was an excellent guest. The staff at the Holly Park were all *very* fond of him. He was kind and polite.'

'And a hella tipper.'

This seemed to bring Dame Elizabeth some solace.

'Perhaps you're right. Maybe we were just looking in the wrong place for Max's identity. His family.' I poured Dame Elizabeth a fresh cup of Lady Grey. 'Is there anything else you can tell us? His family background? A profession?'

She shook her head. 'No. We didn't discuss our pasts much. It was quite lovely. We lived in the day, immersed in the arts, culture, each—'

'God help us,' Grandmother sighed.

I ignored the Tin Woman and her missing heart and leaned forward to encourage Dame Elizabeth instead. 'Did he tell you anything about his life? His family?'

Her hand shook ever so slightly as she picked up her tea. 'Not really. Of course, I told him, *very* briefly, about Astor and Gregory and the girls. He told me, likewise, very briefly about his two girls.'

I was leaning halfway across the table. 'Daughters?'

She nodded. 'Two daughters.'

'Did he tell you their names?'

'Yes,' she said, her forehead wrinkling as she tried to recall the names. 'Tara? No. Marnie? No. Carley? Yes! Carley was the eldest, I think, and Ellie the younger.'

'Grandchildren?' I asked.

'None were mentioned.'

Esmerelda already had her phone out and was no doubt searching Google and the social media platforms for Carley and Ellie Weller.

'Are his daughters married?'

'I didn't ask,' she said. Her teacup clunked heavily into its saucer. This received a sideways glance from Grandmother. Ladies do *not* clunk their saucers. I was on borrowed time.

'He was from Western Australia. He had two daughters. He was well versed in fine arts, the arts in general. And ...' I struggled to recall more information. 'He wore a black prayer bracelet that may or may not have been made from black pearls.'

'Yes.' She paused. 'Yes, perhaps they were pearls after all. Yes, I think they were. Did they find his bracelet,' she paused again, 'with him? What about his phone?'

I shook my head. I had not seen any jewellery on the body. Dr Bailly had not mentioned a phone or any jewellery.

'Oh,' she said, quietly drifting off. 'Of course not.' She looked at me with watery eyes. 'Why was he dressed in rags? Where were his clothes?'

'I don't know.'

'Was he ... did someone hurt him ... on purpose?'

'It does seem—'

'At the beginning of this meeting, I asked for a report,' Grandmother snapped tersely, cutting me off. 'I still have *not* received one.'

I gazed across the table at Dame Elizabeth. She was now staring fixedly out the window. She was not in good shape. I couldn't tell her any more. Not about his childhood: the strong likelihood he had been involved in hard labour from a young age, that he had been uncared for, whipped, beaten. Nor about his death: that he'd been smacked so hard across the back of the head with a flat, heavy object that his skull had fractured like a star.

Esmerelda glanced up from her phone. 'Nothing.'

'I don't have time to sit around and listen to your excruciatingly slow tale. I have a meeting to attend. You will send a *written* report with all the *other* pertinent information about Max Weller,' Grandmother said, pursing her lips and rolling her eyes unsubtly towards a silent Dame Elizabeth, 'back with Loraine.' She gathered their handbags and pulled out Dame Elizabeth's chair, forcing her to stand.

'A *written* report?' Esmerelda said, on her feet. 'Like, what more's to know? Dude's a ghost millionaire. Had a shit childhood, worked crazy hard, made a crapload of cash and wasn't afraid to spend his coin.'

If looks could kill, Esmerelda would be dead and Grandmother … well, Grandmother would have excellent lawyers. Subtext and nuance were *not* Esmerelda's fortes. Dame Elizabeth, however, hadn't heard. She had already slipped into shock.

'What?' Esmerelda asked rhetorically, clapping Dame Elizabeth on the shoulder. 'Max sounds ace. You did totally good, Lizzy.'

'Thank you, dear,' Dame Elizabeth managed. 'He was ace.'

CHAPTER 19

UNWANTED SERVICES

Between the harrowing snake and Searing dramas of the day before, the morning's brutal Max update, and the possible risk to Esmerelda's life, I felt entitled to the rest of the day off inside the guarded gates of Mother's estate.

The gods of spring had smiled on us and the thermometer nudged thirty degrees. Patricia, high on trading Dylan for Carlo and Shane, served me an overindulgent albeit fruit-based lunch in the poolside cabana which I washed down with some perfectly chilled sauvignon blanc. This was accompanied by shocking volumes, even by my standard, of online and videoconferencing shopping, with a side of good old-fashioned magazine flipping and sunbaking.

I was nearing a complete shoe coma when a shadow passed over the cabana. A shadow that felt illogically warm and smelt faintly of Amouage.

It could not be.

The property was locked up tighter than a Buccellati exhibition at a Bvlgari store.

I used a *Marie Claire* to shade the glare off the water and removed my sunglasses to focus. Be still my beating everything, it *was* him, James Smith, my dead husband's too charming, too gorgeous brother.

'How on earth did you get in here?' I stuttered, grappling for a sarong to cover myself. A season in the islands had rendered me browner than usual, and Patricia's mainly gourmet breakfasts, curvier than usual. My white and gold baroque print swimsuit cinched my waist, while the corset-like top rendered me positively buxom. The plunging V neckline didn't help either. I was clearly *not* expecting company. The water had destroyed Franny's hair taming and I felt certain my black-rimmed eyes were smudged. I was a *damp* Italian peasant woman.

'I heard you had a bit of trouble,' he said, seating himself on the sun lounge next to me. 'Something about snakes? Or was it spiders? Thought I'd best check in on you. You're family, after all.'

'Aren't you supposed to be on the other side of the world driving a train?' I said, putting the magazine down and my sunglasses back on.

'Ah, I never said train driving was a *current* profession,' he said in his lilting Irish accent. An accent, I had noticed, that ranged from potato farmer to landed gentry, depending on his need. Today, it was global tech company executive who called the tax-friendly city of Dublin home. It was sexy, though to be fair, all his accents were pretty sexy.

His dress likewise changed. He moved from the poly-cotton car crash I had first met him in, to something like today: black Galliano pinstripe pants paired with a grey, loose-neck, short-sleeve Missoni knit. His shoes were Prada.

'How on earth could you have possibly found out about that?' I asked, giving up on the sarong and crossing my arms across my chest instead. 'The snakes and the spiders?'

'Now, don't forget the poisoned Fanta, the tampered car brakes and the runaway luggage trolleys,' he said, passing the sarong.

So much for discreet security. I snatched the sarong and pulled it across my chest.

'*Carlo*,' I fumed. 'Or was it Shane? Perhaps one of the others? Maybe the pizza delivery person?'

He smiled. 'Ah, the price of fame. I guess there's just no secrets among celebrities.'

'I am not a celebrity,' I returned, getting to my feet, knocking over my stack of glossy fashion magazines and golden fruit platter.

He gazed around the opulent grounds of the estate: the pool, the cabana, the courts, the main house, the pool house. 'This is a *type* of celebrity.'

That was somewhat true. Few were the subject of more unsympathetic gossip than the rich. Except maybe rich women. Or rich women with political ambitions. Or maybe it just felt that way. Not that I had any political ambitions. My greatest ambition was to be unknown to the masses and left alone. Setting fire to my husband had pretty much knocked that out of the realm of possibility.

James Smith had a delightful habit of not answering questions. I tried again, this time staring down at him. 'How did you get in here?'

'The head of your security company is a friend,' he said with his most charming smile.

'Your friend is fired. They are all fired,' I said, storming off to the pool house. 'So much for Cate and Keith and confidentiality.'

'Maybe not quite yet. You do seem to have some troubles. And my friend, she's a she, not a he,' James said, strolling after me.

As much as I loved a company with a female leader, I also enjoyed working up a fury at James Smith. It helped to keep the lust at bay.

I stormed into the pool house, almost colliding with Patricia as she was exiting my room, her arms full of slightly used sheets and towels. 'Not Carlo!' she pleaded. The woman had the ears of a fox. A nosy fox. 'He's so helpful. He carried the dry-cleaning in this morning. And the fruit delivery.'

'And he's gorgeous?' I shot back.

'It wouldn't be right to judge a professional by their physical appearance,' she said, trying hard to sound sincere.

I shook my head and kept going into my room. The new bed linens were a nude silk. With James in the vicinity, I found that somehow unnerving. I locked myself in the bathroom and took an exorbitantly long shower, hoping that by the time I was done, James would have evaporated.

I emerged in a robe, my wet hair wrapped in a towel. James had *not* evaporated. He was sitting at the table by the window, reading my *Vanity Fair*.

'So your mum's gone to Bora Bora with Jed,' he said, looking up from the magazine.

'How on earth could you know—' I stopped myself. It was obvious that James Smith was not even remotely close to the man he sometimes pretended to be, the humble son of a train driver from County Clare. The question (for another day) was, who *was* he?

'Nice guy, Jed,' he continued. 'I like a fireman. Don't worry, I checked, he's a good 'un.'

I stormed into my wardrobe and, to my surprise, found there was a lock on the inside of the door. I clicked it into place then carefully selected the unsexiest underwear I could find, which was difficult because since meeting Searing, I had bought nothing but exquisite lingerie. To counteract this, I picked mismatched colours and fabrics: tan satin and black lace.

I dressed in an impeccably fitted knee-length, silk-cotton cyan dress with kimono sleeves, an embroidered stand-up collar and an invisible zip running all the way down the back, nape to bottom. Very sensible. My dress was accompanied by four-inch Jimmy Choo strappy sandals. Their turquoise leather was buffed to a mirrored shine. Not so sensible, but completely essential.

I exited the closet with as much dignity as possible. Halfway across the room, I realised he was drinking one of Esmerelda's Snapples, albeit from a cut crystal glass filled with ice. My heart stopped and my hand sprang up in front of me.

'No! Don't! That's Esmerelda's—'

'Don't worry, I checked the lid and the seal. Hard to puncture glass,' he said, clicking the side of the bottle with perfectly manicured nails.

As my heart started again my gaze settled on a cream envelope propped up at the edge of the table, below the windowsill. Hand-typed on the front of the envelope was *Indigo Jones-Bombberg*. It had a golfing Santa stamp.

'Esmerelda!' I yelled, my eyes glued to the envelope. 'Esmerelda!'

'Is that an immediate threat?' James asked forcefully.

'Esmerelda!'

James stood, his chair falling back. In seconds, he'd swooped me up, thrown me over his shoulder and was headed for the door.

'What on ... stop that, you neanderthal!'

'Evacuate first, ask questions later,' he said.

'You listen to me,' I growled, blood rushing to my upside-down head as I pointed my finger at him. 'Whatever is or is not in that envelope is none of your bloody business. I am not in danger. If I thought it was going to blow up or sprout fangs, I have legs. I am perfectly capable of walking myself out of a room.'

He put me down. But only once we were past the front door.

'Dude,' Esmerelda said, appearing from nowhere, 'like, there's just way too much macho action around here. It's embarrassing.'

Carlo and Shane were several seconds behind Esmerelda. Whatever I was paying her, I was getting a good deal.

'I wouldn't, lads,' James said to the tardy security men. 'The lady's perfectly fine and has the bull by the gonads.'

'Huh,' Esmerelda said as she strolled inside and saw the envelope. 'No offence but, uh, have you got a knife or something to open it with?'

'Do you think it's unsafe?' I whispered.

'Nah, but like sketchy shit has been going down and I'd rather not put my finger in there.'

Fair point.

'If I could be of service, madam,' James said from the doorway, flicking out a shiny silver dagger and offering it, hilt first, into the room.

'Dude's like friggin' Macbeth,' Esmerelda said.

James raised an eyebrow.

'Yeah, I totally know classy stuff.'

'Well, close the door and come in then,' I said, taking the dagger and trying to sound like I was doing him an enormous favour.

Our unlikely trio sat around the table. I slit the envelope open and carefully shook out the contents. It was another typed card.

The dead body you found, get autopsy results for:
- toxicology
- DNA
- trace
- chemical

'What the frig?' Esmerelda lamented. 'Usually *they* tell *us* stuff. Now *they're* telling *us* to *get* stuff?'

I grimaced unintentionally. She was right. This was *not* how a CI worked.

James pointed to the card without touching it. 'Is this related to the snake, soda, brakes stuff?'

I had given it some thought. The luggage trolly incident happened mere hours after Max's body was discovered and most likely before Dame Elizabeth had charged me with finding his identity. And although I could have been caught in the crossfire, the actions did all seem to be specifically directed at Esmerelda.

'No.'

'You sure?'

'Dude.'

'Right, sorry. It's about the homeless John Doe you found then?'

So, James Smith's eyes and ears were limited. He knew only that the body was an unknown person, a colloquial John Doe.

'Doe's name is Max,' Esmerelda reprimanded.

His brow wrinkled. 'You IDed him?'

'Yes. No. It's complicated.'

'Okay,' he said, his eyes moving sharply from me to Esmerelda. 'Why?'

'Did you know that like old unknown dudes get locked in a deep freeze forever and ever?' Esmerelda said, wrinkling her nose.

'Don't go there,' I said to him. 'It's quicksand.'

'I see it,' he said. And to Esmerelda: 'You wanted to ID him so you could bury him?'

'Like, totally no, not my jam. But, like, stuff grows on you.'

'Someone else wants to bury him?' he guessed. 'And they're ... paying you to ID him so *they* can bury him?'

'Old Lizzy's not paying me!' Esmerelda cried, indignant.

'*I'm* paying you,' I reminded her.

'Yeah, but you pay me anyway. And that's kinda our deal now. We find shit.'

'It is *not* our deal,' I corrected her, vigorously shaking my head. 'Dame Elizabeth is swinging huge influence to get you out of *that* contract in exchange for your services.'

'And what are you getting in exchange for your services, Heiress?' James enquired with a penetrating stare. He pointed to the card. 'It's addressed to *you*.' I desperately wanted to wriggle around in my chair and adjust myself.

'Nothing,' I managed.

He turned his blue eyes on Esmerelda. 'It must be something.'

'Dude, no. Nothing. What could you pay her? Look around.'

God bless Esmerelda. She was a champion liar when she put her heart into it.

James's eyes probed my face and hands, his mouth opened a fraction. 'From the goodness of your heart?'

'Yes.'

While this had been completely untrue in the beginning, Max had, as Esmerelda said, grown on us. I was shocked to find, upon reflection, that I couldn't let go of Max now even if I wanted to.

Damn.

James leaned back, either satisfied I was telling the truth or prepared to let the lie go. 'So, your man, your woman, Dame Elizabeth, wants you two to ID him so she can bury him?'

We both nodded silently.

He opened his palms. 'And that's it?'

'Oh, and like his name isn't his name. He's not real, but he's real. And I think we might wanna catch his killer,' Esmerelda said. She turned to me. 'Right?'

James's head shifted slightly to the left, his eyebrows raised as he side-eyed me. 'You want to ID a homeless John Doe who was living under a pseudonym *and* find the person who killed him?'

Elbows on table, I rolled my eyes and planted my head in my hands. 'Yes, that's exactly what we're doing.'

'Feck me, Heiress,' James said. I raised my head to see a broad grin blooming across his face. 'I'm in,' he beamed. 'Totally in.'

'We do not need your help,' I said. 'You are *not* in.'

'Like, we might need him, we just don't want him,' Esmerelda corrected me.

She was probably right. We could use all the help we could get, but I would be accepting no help from James Smith.

Someone I did want help from was Jem Bailly. I needed to contact her to get the autopsy results, and the results from toxicology, DNA, trace and chemical (whatever they were).

'James,' I said as politely as possible. 'Would you mind very much just popping up to the house and asking Patricia for a cup of milk.'

'Milk?'

'Yes. Milk, sugar, anything. I just need a moment to confer with my ... my Esmerelda.'

'Sure, look it.'

I had no idea what that meant.

'Sure, listen.'

Still no idea.

'I'll, uh, I'll fetch something. Give you ladies a moment to "confer".'

As the door closed behind him, Esmerelda pulled out her phone and began dialling. We connected with Bailly's office phone within ten seconds but received her terse tidy voice-mail. We dialled the FMCCC. We were told, 'Dr Bailly's on leave'. Bailly didn't seem the type to take impromptu leave.

I made sure the pool house door was locked and the bed-room door and windows and even the bathroom and closet doors were closed.

'Do you have her mobile number?' I asked. 'Home?'

'Dude.'

Of course.

'Dial please.'

Esmerelda pulled up a number, dialled it, and put Bailly on speaker between us.

'Hello,' Bailly said after two rings.

'Bailly, this is Indigo-Daisy-Violet-Amber. Indigo.'

This got me a mocking eyeroll from Esmerelda.

'Hello, Indigo-Daisy-Violet-Amber. How did you get my mobile phone number?' she asked bluntly.

'A friend gave it to me,' I said ambiguously. Esmerelda grinned proudly. 'I need to ask you a question about my Great-Uncle Max. And I have some more information, from a distant relative. It might be helpful. Can I meet you in your office later?'

'No.'

'No?'

'No, you cannot meet me in my office. I cannot meet with you again.'

Feck! We had been found out. She knew we were frauds. She was cutting us off. Turning us in. A wave of panic and embarrassment washed over me. My old friend fuzz crept up my throat.

'Dude, don't even,' Esmerelda warned me in a loud whisper.

I inhaled and exhaled deeply, getting the faint under control. Time to face the music. I didn't think I would enjoy the experience.

'Dr Bailly, I am so sorry if my actions have in any way caused you problems. I apologise unreservedly.'

'Your actions have not caused me problems. My actions have caused me problems. Tests are expensive. UP Rose Bay 0909 Winters was not a priority. I ordered all the tests. I was not supposed to.'

Maybe it was all the fruit, or the fact that I had risen at 7 am and consumed less than a bottle of wine with lunch, but my mind moved more rapidly than usual.

'You *cannot* meet with me because *you* cannot meet with *me*.'

Crickets.

Emphasis was not a good communication strategy with Bailly.

'You were fired?' I hedged. 'For ordering too many tests?'

'Suspended without pay,' she said matter-of-factly. 'By the deputy state coroner, Mr Kevin Pasty. He's not a forensic pathologist. He's not even a doctor. He's a lawyer.'

An expression of disgust crossed Esmerelda's face and her body tensed.

'Mr Pasty limited the scope of the autopsy. He will not assess all the results. His preliminary report will find UP Rose Bay 0909 Winters was an unknown homeless man. You should have gone with Dr Eric Blackstone.'

'Which tests did you order, Bailly?'

More silence.

'Can I guess? More autopsy tests.' I was winging it now. 'Toxicology. DNA. Trace. Chemical.' I had no idea what any of it meant.

'Yes,' she said. 'I ordered all of those tests.'

'You did the right thing. My Great-Uncle Max was much loved. I will keep looking for more information to help you definitively identify him. Then we can claim him officially. We are trying to track his ...' I stopped.

Bailly didn't know we had the batch number for Max's dental implants. It might not be helpful to tell her we had this inside information until we had something more definitive. Something more legal. Like the name and address of his next of kin, his daughters.

I finished my sentence, '... his more current acquaintances.'

'That would be helpful, yes,' Bailly said. I could hear the roll of the ocean in the background. She was near the beach. She was probably at home or walking or at the bakery.

'And the test results? Max's test result? It would really help me if you could share any new information.'

There was another extended pause. 'Have you found any additional, historical information about your great-uncle?' she prodded.

'Yes?'

I scrutinised Esmerelda. She shrugged, ever helpful.

'Great-Uncle Max lived with a distant relative in his youth,' I lied rapidly. 'This relative was unkind, physically abusive. Max was not cared for properly, medically.'

'Yes,' Bailly agreed. 'That does fit with some of my findings. Is that all the information you have?'

I held my hands out for help. Esmerelda began mimicking digging in the ground, mopping the floor, banging nails with an imaginary hammer.

Criminal charades.

'Work?' I guessed.

She wiped fake sweat from her brow.

'He did *physical* work.'

Esmerelda doubled her digging efforts, adding in what looked like a wrenching action and picking up heavy things.

'Laborious work?' I elaborated.

'That is also consistent with my findings, Indigo-Daisy-Violet-Amber.'

I mimicked wiping sweat from *my* brow.

'Now can you tell me about the test results?'

'No.'

I mimicked trying to strangle myself. Not helpful.

'Can you tell me why you cannot tell me?' I tried, taking my hands from my throat.

'Yes.'

Okay. Progress.

'Why is it,' I said, choosing my words carefully, 'that you cannot tell me about Great-Uncle Max's test results?'

'I was put on leave before the results came in from the various departments. Toxicology department. The DNA lab. The trace lab. The chemical analysis department. I don't have access to the results.'

'So, the results are back, you just don't have access to them?' I clarified.

'Correct.'

'I'm sorry to hear that,' I said sympathetically. 'That must be very frustrating for you.'

It was frustrating the hell out of me.

'Correct. It's very frustrating. Scientists often have tunnel vision. They perform tests only in their area, in isolation.

They don't look at the results of the other scientists' tests. Scientists don't always put two and two together. Unless you tell them to compare their results along with other test results from other areas, or directly ask them a question, "Is result A from test A related to result B from test B?" they might not tell you. They might not notice. They might not find things. All of UP Rose Bay 0909 Winters's results must be put together in one place.'

'Is putting the test results together something you do, Bailly?'

'Yes.'

Now we were getting somewhere.

'But you're not there, so the test results won't get put together?'

'Correct.'

I pushed my luck. 'Could you perhaps contact a colleague and get the results from them?'

'No.'

'No, you cannot contact them? Or no they would not give you the results? Or no they would not have the results?'

'All three. Each scientist will only have access to their own results. Only three people in the facility will have access to all the results. Me, the state coroner and the deputy state coroner, Mr Pasty.'

How important was it to get those test results, really? I didn't *have* to do what the card from the envelope with the golfing Santa stamp told me to do. There could be other ways. We had the batch number from the dental implants. That might yet be helpful.

'I see,' I said in resignation. I expected the conversation to end there, but it did not.

'I do not think Mr Pasty is correct. I do not think UP Rose Bay 0909 Winters was homeless or his death accidental. I do not think Mr Pasty will try to put A and B together.'

I think we had established that.

Several long moments passed. Again. This time, it was so long I wondered if she was gone. 'Hello?'

'Mr Pasty has two Chinese Cresteds. One is called Boris, the other Horace,' she said before spelling out the names. 'All lowercase. Born May 8th. A Wednesday. I was born on Friday the 13th. In October.'

I was baffled. 'Chinese what?'

'Cresteds. Dogs. Chinese Crested dogs. Mr Pasty doesn't follow security protocols. He uses the same passcodes for everything. He should change his passcodes weekly. He doesn't.'

Wait.

Was Bailly giving me her boss's passcode?

Esmerelda opened an app on her phone and started taking notes. 'Like, ask her,' she said, nudging me, 'if there's like a pass card to go with the passcode.'

'Mr Pasty is particularly fond of young ladies with fair hair, brown eyes and full-sized mammary glands. His favourites have small skeletal structures. He attempts to find these types of women when he drinks at a bar called Anna's Inn. He often drinks too much. Mr Pasty's wife is a brunette with a larger skeletal structure. She does not drink at the bar with him.'

'Totally a yes on the pass card,' Esmerelda put in.

'His office is on the third floor of the FM triple C. Second door on the right. He never locks it with the key. Due to budget cuts, there are only security guards from 8 am to 5 pm, Monday to Friday. At all other times, security is done via cameras. The cameras are monitored offsite.'

Was she suggesting we somehow acquire the deputy state coroner's pass card, guess his doggy-themed passcode and break into the FMCCC?

'Mr Pasty's passcode and pass card will open the facility's doors and turn off the alarms, but not the cameras. They will also give you access to his desktop computer and its contents. This computer will have all the results and my autopsy findings.'

That was a yes.

This was crazy and I was about to tell her so. Instead, I found myself asking where the bodies were stored. My mind kept circling back to that small thing that had prickled at me that day in the lilies. I had thought it was the familiar scent of the California Poppy Oil, but that might not have been it. It might have been something else about Max, something familiar … I couldn't ask Bailly about it because if I was wrong, it would out me as a big fat fibber. I needed to see Max myself, in person.

'You don't wish to see the bodies. This is common,' she responded, completely misunderstanding me. 'You needn't worry. They're well contained in refrigerated drawers on the ground floor. Just walk straight past them.'

How convenient.

CHAPTER 20

DRIVEN

A brusque knock at the front door of the pool house ended the somewhat cryptic and certainly criminally conspiratorial conversation with Bailly. It was Loraine with the NDAs. I was surprised to see Loraine tugging at her usually perfect hair—it was flyaway and lopsided. And then I saw it: walking behind her, speaking in professional yet honeyed tones, was James. If James could make Loraine and her hurricane-proof hair lose control, what hope did the rest of us have?

Esmerelda and I signed the NDAs and Loraine, carefully avoiding James, departed. That left *us* with James.

I wondered if I was being unfair, wanting James out of my life. He was right, we were family, of a sort. I tried to assess whether I was imagining the mutual attraction. Just because many, *many* women were attracted to him didn't mean he was attracted to all those women in return. He would have been exceptionally busy otherwise. And quite sore, I imagine.

There was also no way I could break into the FMCCC to hack the deputy state coroner's computer. Even if he was a cheating cheapskate. It was simply too dangerous. Which brought me back to James. I had a reasonable suspicion that James was an expert at successfully gaining access to places not meant to be breached. Maybe he knew something about disabling cameras too … no, it was definitely too dangerous. Or was it?

Before I could even contemplate breaking into a highly secure government facility, and thus possibly getting caught, I would need to seriously assess how much political sway I could muster in a crisis.

The prime minister still detested Grandmother, but the state premier Jason Tripp had been a superfan of Mother's for years. I doubted her public dating of fireman Jed had altered that. Jason was a true politician, resilient when it came to rejection, and patient, like a big cat.

Then there was Dame Elizabeth. Everyone loved her.

No, it was still too risky. Too dangerous. There had to be another way.

I came to sitting at the kitchen island with a glass of wine in my hand, Esmerelda and James standing by the fridge, sharing a bag of Lolly Gobble Bliss Bombs, staring at me.

'Is she often like this?' James was asking.

'Yeah, it's like her thinking thing,' Esmerelda said, dipping her hand back into the yellow foil bag.

'She's fascinating,' he said earnestly.

'Oh yeah, dude, she's totally the Heiress on Fire.'

He nodded and ate a few pieces of nutty caramel popcorn from his hand.

'How long have I been in here for?' I wanted to know.

They exchanged glances. 'Oh, like not long at all.'

I looked down at the island. The bottle of wine was half empty and there was a puddle of condensation around its base.

'Do I often do this?'

'Eh,' Esmerelda said, wrinkling her nose and waving her hand in mid-air.

'I don't process verbally, do I?' I asked.

Esmerelda gave me a dumbfounded expression. 'Huh?'

'Does she talk out loud when she's thinking,' James translated.

'Nah,' Esmerelda said. 'Like your lips move but totally nothing comes out.'

Thank God.

'So, you need someone to break into the coroner's office with you?' James asked, helping himself to a small bottle of sparkling water from the fridge.

My head turned towards Esmerelda like a predator eyeing an annoying animal lower on the food chain. 'You said I *didn't* talk out loud!'

'Oh, like you totally don't,' she said, reassuring me, hands up defensively. 'Not a word. Like your hands and mouth move, but no words.'

'*You* told him?'

Esmerelda raked her eyes over James. 'Well, he's like obviously not a cop. And see, I'm still on parole. I can't break into a state government facility. Once I'm off parole, I'll totally break into government shit with you, but like, until then, you might want the young Irish Brad Pitt over here to do you a solid. He's clearly shady. No offence, dude. Like in a good way. Respect a professional.'

'None taken,' he said, raising his eyebrows and unscrewing the cap from his—*my*—bottle of blood orange mineral water.

'And we're running out of clues,' Esmerelda continued, pointing to the whiteboards. 'Like I said, we might not want him, but we totally might need him.'

My issue was that I *did* want him. My greatest fear was that I would end up needing him too. Wanting was bad; wanting *and* needing would be a catastrophe.

'We still have clues!' I said, stalking up to a board. 'The implants!'

'Oh yeah,' Esmerelda said, pulling out her phone. 'While you were doing your thinking thing, Rachael White got back to us. She found out where the batch went. It was a small batch, custom. They all went to the same guy. Dr Lucas Carr. He's a period-dontist?' she read, a look of confusion crossing her face. 'Why would an old dude need a period doctor? And how would that help with his teeth? And isn't that a gyno?'

'He wouldn't. It wouldn't. And it is peri-*o*-dontist,' I clarified. 'A periodontist is a special kind of dentist. Completely unrelated to gynaecology.'

'That's still fully hinky,' she returned.

James nodded in agreement with Esmerelda. 'Very suspect.'

'Thank you, James,' I said with as much sarcasm as I could muster, and then to Esmerelda, 'It's not hinky. It's a lead. A good lead. See! We don't need James.'

'Oh sure, no offence taken, Heiress,' James announced, arms wide. 'I travel halfway round the world, fifteen hours straight, dead concerned, to make sure you're safe and sound, offer you a wee hand, and I'm kicked to the kerb! Oh no, why would I be offended?'

I must have drunk too much wine while in my brain-musing coma. I felt bad. *About James Smith.* The *enigma.* The *chameleon.* The human equivalent of a Barbie doll: race car driver, astronaut, tennis pro, Marine Corps sergeant, computer programmer, yoga teacher, seal trainer. Just strip and redress for a new persona. He could be anything.

Actually … that might be quite helpful. Also on the redeeming side, no matter which skin he appeared in, the personality he presented, to me at least, stayed the same.

'Are you really upset?'

He took stock of himself, performing an internal emotional assessment. 'I was winding you up, but I might actually be a *little* offended. Huh.' He seemed surprised. 'Regardless, Ma and Pa would be most upset if you were hurt. Or arrested.'

Despite thinking Richard's parents were dead for the entirety of our marriage (or perhaps because of it), I had developed a strange bond with them. And with an Irish bond came black-belt level guilt.

I rolled my eyes and huffed loudly.

'What about the periodontist?' I said, trying to get back on track.

'Yeah, so, like the custom batch went to the … the fake tooth dentist dude.'

'It's a bit unusual for a homeless man to have dental implants, isn't it?' James asked. 'They're pricey.'

'Yeah, totally.'

This was good news. The batch *could* have been comprised of hundreds of implants, thousands even. However, Max had had twenty-four implants, so the entire custom batch could well have just been for him.

'Where is Dr Carr's surgery located?' I asked. 'We could take a drive.'

'Like, that's a long drive,' Esmerelda said. 'He worked at Darwin Dental, in like, Darwin. And also,' she said, referring to her phone again and reading, 'he had "rooms in Broome".'

That made sense. Broome was in Western Australia.

'Darwin as in the Northern Territory Darwin?' James enquired. 'Isn't that where the crocodiles live?'

'They don't let them wander around the town, James,' I said with much more bravado than I felt. That said they did seem to let an awful lot of them wander into the Hermès factory, where they morphed into a rainbow of $30,000 Birkin bags. 'But Darwin is a little too far to drive. How long is it by plane?' We could arrive before sundown or leave first thing tomorrow morning. The chances were much greater that we would catch Lucas Carr at the larger surgery.

Esmerelda plugged the question into her phone. 'Four and a half hours.'

Maybe not by sundown then. Wait ...

'Did you say *worked*? As in, he does not work there anymore?'

'Totally.'

James squinted at Esmerelda. I sipped my wine and decided to let someone else have a dip in the quicksand.

'So, he doesn't work there anymore?'

'No. Well, like kinda, but nah.'

Much clearer. I thought about it. Max was in his seventies or eighties. He might have had implants thirty years ago. Or ten years ago. I was going to go with thirty.

James persevered. 'Esmerelda, is Dr Carr retired?'

'Totally.' She nodded.

'Great. Good for him. Did he retire in the Northern Territory?'

'Like when he like retired? Or like now?' she asked, leaning on the island. 'Because I don't know where he's *been*. I just know where he is now.'

'Why would you say he kind of works there still?' James asked before I had a chance to tell him it didn't matter. We were on the cusp of finding out if the man was in Guatemala or Fiji or Bondi.

'Oh, because the dude's retired, but like he still does the occasional client. Like the old ones, the special ones, they said. He's still the boss, but not like, in the place.'

'So, he's still in the Northern Territory?'

She tsked in annoyance. 'Ah, *no*.'

James glanced at me for support. Amateur.

'Where does Dr Carr live now?' I asked.

'Palm Beach.'

'You have his home address?'

'Yep.'

'Okay, let's go,' James said, suddenly on top of the conversation. He patted his pants, checking for keys.

I was so close to asking him how he knew where Palm Beach was when I realised Palm Beach was to Sydney what Malibu was to LA. And while *Baywatch* was only *set* in Malibu, a local beach soap opera with a revolving cast of ever younger and more beautiful actors was actually filmed at Palm Beach. It was also where the Sydney elite had enormous beach compounds, successful professionals like Dr Carr retired and where humblebragging local homeowners, for reasons unknown to me, all wore white shirts with navy blue stripes, drove Range Rovers and were obsessed with sourdough.

I doubted James knew about Palm Beach because of the bread.

If we could convince Max's periodontist to give us his real name, a large slice of this mystery would slot into place and this whole mess would be a lot less complicated.

How much cooperation could we expect from a retired dental worker from the Top End where, truth be told, crocodiles did roam? And what kinds of lies would we have to tell him to get it?

It was not the worst idea to let James drive. It was unlikely that someone would have tampered with *his* brakes, and it saved Esmerelda and I from our usual skirmish over who drove what where.

James didn't drive a Ferrari, or a Maserati, or a Porsche, or even a Mercedes. He drove a Volvo. Safety was clearly top-of-mind for him. The car was examined Bali-style at the gates: square mirrors mounted on selfie sticks were poked under the chassis, the boot was opened, the engine examined. Nothing except James's black leather carry-on. It was probably the most exciting thing Shane and Carlo had done all day, apart from the dry-cleaning and the fruit. They nodded terse goodbyes as James, Esmerelda and I drove off the property.

We made good time to Palm Beach in the Volvo. I telepathically asked Esmerelda to add Volvo to the list of cars

I might like, because despite having a deep-seated and unreasonable bias against them, I liked being driven in this car. It was a shame all Volvos did not come with a James Smith driver. I could guarantee a dramatic increase in sales.

I peered into the back seat to see if she had caught my unspoken request. Esmerelda, however, was asleep. It was the first time I had ever seen her sleep. This was an impressive feat given we had been virtually joined at the hip for months. There were moments where I'd felt sure she simply didn't need sleep, like a vampire. But there she was, head wedged between the beige headrest and the door panel, her breath on the glass, mortal after all.

She must have been severely sleep deprived to pass out in the back of a Volvo driven by 'shady' James Smith, heading for Palm Beach (where a large percentage of the stripe-clad inhabitants were most certainly lawyers. Or judges. Or senior public servants). That alone should have alerted her to a disturbance in the Force and set her into Doberman mode.

It dawned on me, for perhaps the first time, that Esmerelda could be in danger. Real danger. Danger real enough that she was not sleeping.

I resolved to contact Searing once we were back in the city and tell him I'd had a change of heart. That I wanted him to find whoever was trying to hurt Esmerelda. There was no way I was up to the task. I was struggling just to find Max's real name. Hunting down someone who was methodically orchestrating supervillain type 'accidents' against the super-sensory Esmerelda felt much harder. And scarier.

'You really are beautiful when you think,' James said to me.

I turned to face him.

'You worried about your man? Your woman?'

'Not really,' I lied. I was in no mood to be vulnerable with James Smith, nor to explain my plan to elicit Searing's help. Or to explain who Searing was. I didn't think I would ever be in that particular mood.

'I see,' he said, smiling. 'You might have to work on your feigning skills.'

I was insulted. I had become quite a good liar in recent times. It was, however, not an attribute I was about to defend.

Dr Lucas Carr, retired periodontist, lived in a modest cottage two streets back from the beach. His small front garden was surrounded by a green picket fence with a hip-high gate opening onto a painted concrete path that led to a small veranda. The path was flanked on both sides by neatly mowed grass sprinkled with fallen yellow and pink frangi-panis from his neighbour's trees.

I stared out of the window at the front door. I had been so busy debating the idea of breaking into the FMCCC that I had not thought about how I would perform the task of lying to a retired medical professional to extract confidential patient information. I had absolutely zero ideas.

'What on earth am I going to say to this man?' I asked myself and, since he was in the car, James.

'Just tell him the truth. You can practise on me if you like, since I'm not clear on all the details. Specifically, like.'

What the heck? It might help me get it straight in my head if I went through it all again.

So … Visited Grandmother. Borrowed a tiny paint-ing. Found a body. Dame Elizabeth's aversion to eternal freezers for homeless. Esmerelda's *Pazzia* contract. Favours for favours. Dame Elizabeth's missing boyfriend. The mystery typed letters via post. Dr Bailly. The Hollys. The things we knew about Max: people liked him, he was rich and well-kept but that had not always been the case, and he was, as far as we could tell, *not* Max Weller. He bleached his salt and pepper hair white, probably in an attempt to disguise himself. He had a quarter of a million dollars' worth of dental implants. Neither his name, nor his fingerprints, nor his DNA were in any database. He had two (presumably) adult daughters.

The questions: what was his real name? Where was his family? Why did he lie to Dame Elizabeth? Who killed him? Why?

I skimmed over the blackmail and the parts that involved Dylan and Searing by name.

James scratched his thick dark blond hair and his aeroplane stubble. 'You know quite a lot about Max already. I think you're pretty close.'

That was a surprise. I felt like I had a whole lot of nothing.

I got out of the car with a renewed sense of hope. James opened his door and followed me. While I appreciated the support, I didn't want to overwhelm this poor retired periodontist. I'm not sure how I would react if 007 and Miss Fisher randomly arrived at my front door.

James stood watch by the Volvo, guarding the sleeping Esmerelda.

I guessed Lucas Carr had moved to Palm Beach to retire by the ocean. Although one can retire *by* the ocean in Darwin, one can only *look* at the beach. Crocodiles. These highly curious creatures hamper almost all water sports and water-based recreational activities. Which was a shame because the weather in Darwin was toasty year-round. It was a cruel taunt.

I approached the door armed with Dame Elizabeth's photo from the play and a plan that was no plan at all: the truth.

Lucas Carr's front doorbell made the sound of an old-school ice cream truck. Lucas was clearly a sophisticate. A man in his early seventies, dressed in open sandals with plastic buckles, pleated khaki shorts and a collared cotton T-shirt that was probably once redder, opened the door. According to Google Images, this was Lucas.

'Lucas Carr?' I asked him.

'Yes,' he said, cleaning his thick spectacles on his fading shirt.

'I ...' It was all I could get out. 'I ...'

Lucas leaned forward, as if I was just speaking quietly, thinking if he leaned in hard enough, he might pick up a full sentence.

I rummaged through my Givenchy tote until I came out with a printed A4 version of the photo Dame Elizabeth had texted me. It was slightly grainy. 'Max,' I said stupidly.

He opened the security screen and somewhat hesitantly took the photo. He studied the faces and said, 'Yes?'

'This is Max,' I said, pointing at the photo.

'Yes.'

That was all I had. At least we agreed this was Max.

'Do you know Maxwell?' he asked, trying to help.

'Yes,' I said, instantly coming out with what had become my standard, a half-truth.

'Actually, my, uh, Aunt Holly. She has been dating Max, Maxwell.'

'Is that so,' he said, giving me a small smile, like I was a simple but kind-hearted five-year-old. 'That's nice.'

'You see, she would like to know more about him.'

'Ah,' he said, taking a step back. 'I see.'

'No, no,' I said, reaching out to reassure him. 'Nothing intrusive. Nothing negative. You were his periodontist?'

'Ye—' he said before stopping himself. 'Did Maxwell give you that information?'

'Yes,' I said, trying hard to be semi-truthful. Bailly found the implants *in* Max, so in a way Max had *told* her, and then she had told me. If you ignored the fact that the mystery informant had given me the batch number, and Rachael had used her Sydney Plastic's connections to track the batch to Lucas Carr, you *could* say Max had *given* me that information.

'Maxwell's a very private man,' he said firmly.

No kidding.

'Oh yes,' I agreed, 'she's aware of that. Aunt Holly is also extremely private.'

'I think you need to address your questions to Maxwell,' he said, stepping back again, starting to close the screen door.

That's going to be a problem, Lucas.

'You see Aunt Holly is *very* fond of Maxwell,' I said quickly, resisting the urge to wedge my foot in the door. 'They've been spending a *lot* of time together. Plays, opera, galleries. You know how these arts lovers are. Great supporters of local productions.'

He, apparently, did *not* know.

'Here? In Sydney? Not in the Northern Territory?'

'Yes,' I said with truth and enthusiasm. I pointed to the photo in his hand. 'See. There they are at an STC play in Walsh Bay.'

He examined the photo again, tilting it, bringing it closer to his face. 'Maxwell looks … different.'

'Love does give a person a certain glow,' I said, smiling.

'That's not it,' Lucas said. 'His hair, it's different. And his beard, it's gone. That man has had a beard forever!'

'Ah,' I said, bubbling with excitement at this new information and delivering him my best smile. 'Perhaps he shaved it off because he didn't want to be labelled a hipster? Are there many of those in Darwin?'

Lucas eyed me. 'No.'

Okay then, moving on.

'My aunt would very much like to send Ellie and Carley a gift. A nice-to-meet-you gift.'

'Ellie?' he said, brows knitting together. 'Carley?' He thought for a moment, then nodded in understanding. 'You mean Lizzie, that is, Elizabeth, and Tahnee?'

'Yes,' I said in mock embarrassment, 'sorry, Lizzie and Tahnee. My aunt's hearing isn't what it used to be.'

He bobbled his head and his jowls jiggled a little. 'I know how she feels.'

'She's unsure of their preferences. Perhaps a nice crocodile Birkin bag for Lizzy? A piece of jewellery for Tahnee?'

His jaw dropped. His blue eyes squinted, the eyelids above them almost obscuring them altogether. His whole body withdrew from me. I had made a misstep.

'No?' I squeaked.

'Who are you?' he asked, waving the photo at me.

'Me? Just a niece trying to help out an aunt who is very much in love.' Finally, I had told a whole truth. Almost.

'And you came to Maxwell's retired periodontist to do that? Seems like a bit of a strange choice.'

He had me there. What kind of a creepy person would stalk another person's periodontist for personal information if there were any other choices available? The crazy kind, that's who. The kind of person who might like to keep your teeth in a velvet drawstring bag under their pillow after you broke up with them.

'You were the only one of Maxwell's healthcare professionals who was local,' I tried.

Crickets.

'He's very private,' I said, parroting back his initial comment. 'I don't suppose you could give me his home address in Darwin?'

'No.'

He pulled the screen door shut and locked it. He then closed the main door. It too clicked as he locked it.

'Or his surname?' I asked the closed doors.

Wait. Max. Maxwell. Max/well. Max Weller. God, it was so obvious!

James was sitting on the hood of the Volvo, enjoying the beginning of a spectacular sunset.

'Max!' I said to him. 'Maxwell. Max-well. Max Well-er! Get it?'

'Oh, you got that, did you?' He smiled.

'You knew?' I was outraged.

'Knew? No. Suspected, aye.'

'How?' I demanded.

'I guess *creative* people think like other *creative* people,' James said.

By *creative*, did he mean shady?

I pointed to the back seat of the car where Esmerelda, perhaps woken by the shrill sound of my screeching, opened her eyes and stretched.

'She's a *creative* person,' I wailed. 'Why didn't *she* see it?'

He shrugged, noncommittal.

'See what?' Esmerelda asked, climbing out.

'Did you know the name Max is short for Maxwell?' I immediately asked.

'For real?' she responded. 'Huh.'

I was going to take that as a no.

'Maxwell? Like Max Weller?' she instantly surmised. 'So, his totally fake last name Weller is actually his totally real first name, Maxwell. Smart. Creative.' She eyeballed me. 'You totally should have thought of that.'

It was clear I simply was not cut out to be *creative*. I had the wrong neural pathways for it. I wondered if my current programming, that of overly curious heiress, coupled with some assistances from a creative, would be enough to track down Maxwell and his killer.

I might need more than one creative to make it happen.

And wine. I was definitely going to need wine.

And new shoes. Just for the moral support.

CHAPTER 21

A BATHROOM WITH
A VIEW

The sun continued to set as we all piled back into the Volvo. Esmerelda was hungry, I needed a drink, and if James had just come off a fifteen-hour flight, he must have been tired too, even if he didn't appear to be. It seemed a little redundant to drive all the way back to the city when I had a house in Palm Beach.

I had not been there since Richard's death. Although the house was technically mine, and had been since I'd turned eighteen, it was Richard's pet project. He was always fitting it with ever more sophisticated gadgets I neither cared about nor knew how to use. I realised with some dread the basement may well have been full of mind-blowingly overpriced model trains. I blocked that thought. I just didn't have the mental space to deal with it.

On the upside, the beach house had a well-stocked cellar, four en suited bedrooms overlooking the Pacific, and lots of exposed open space to discourage room-to-room fraternisation. If that didn't keep me away from James, I could lock myself in the garage. Or the cool room.

The other lovely thing about the Palm Beach house was its proximity to an endless array of local restaurants, cafés and eateries. The obsession of the striped locals with food and beverages was a real pay-off for the FIFOs* and Sydiots**.

Both FIFOs and Sydiots annoyed the locals because of the congestion produced by their migratory patterns. That is, we came en masse, causing long queues that restricted access to *their* bakeries and baristas.

I directed James to the beach house, then gave him the six-digit security code, which he punched into the panel beside the gate. The twisty driveway disappeared from sight into a valley overgrown with palms and green vegetation. We wound our way down through the greenery to a timber panelled six-car garage. The first two garage doors opened automatically when the front gates were keyed. We drove straight in.

Bailly was right. You really should use different codes for different devices, and those codes should be changed regularly. My codes were all the same and I never changed them. I was a security nightmare.

By the time we parked, disembarked and punched the code to the front door, Esmerelda had already ordered food deliveries from a dozen local eateries. She was disappointed

---

* FIFO: those who Flew In to holiday once or twice a year at their $20 million homes only to Fly Out again a few weeks later.
** Sydiots: idiots from Sydney, who owned $10 million homes and visited on long weekends and during school holidays, and were never seen in between.

to learn that none sold Snapple, and was once again forced to settle for No-Sugar Vanilla Coke.

'Holy shit,' she said, walking in.

'Nice,' James said, holding the carry-on he had retrieved from the Volvo's boot. 'Shower?'

I directed him to the bedroom at the far end of the house. I tried to block out last summer's memory of him in a towel. I was unsuccessful.

'Like, why don't you just live *here*?' Esmerelda wanted to know as James disappeared down the hallway.

'Here?'

'Yeah, here,' she said, spreading her arms out, pointing in turn to the high-tech kitchen, the sapphire ocean view, the azure infinity pool sunk into the cliff (the side that faced the ocean was clear acrylic, giving underwater swimmers ocean views), the various decks, the lovely window seats and the nap-perfect lounges. All of which were currently ablaze with colour thanks to the never-ending sunset.

'But it's so far from the city.'

'Like, you never even go *out* in the city.'

'*That* is not the point. The point is I *could* go out. To the best spas and salons. To the opera. To museums. To plays. I could go shopping at Dior or Chanel or Jimmy Choo. There are galas, beaches, yachts, opening parties, birthday parties all on my doorstep in the city.'

'Beaches?'

Okay, so she had me there; both places had beaches aplenty.

'All the *things*,' I argued.

'But, like, you totally order everything online. Or shop by videoconference. You don't go to parties or galas. And,' she pointed to her far left, to the calm, protected bays and harbours, with their gently curving stretches of white sandy beaches and their many jetties and bobbing yachts, 'there are like a shedload of yacht type things right there!'

She was right. I went almost nowhere. I attended nothing. I never shopped in-store. I wanted to cry.

The fact was, I *used to* go to all those events. I *did* shop at all those stores. I just didn't *anymore*, not since I became the Heiress on Fire. Widow. Murder suspect. Heiress to yet *another* fortune. I was a high-end oddity, a billionaire social shut-in. Those *never* ended well.

I huffed out my frustration. 'The point is, by living in the city, after I … once I … when I … when I am *ready* to go out, in public, to all of those places, they will be right at my fingertips.'

But when would that be? It occurred to me that my billionaire social shut-in status was self-imposed. I had not been arrested. I was not in jail. I was innocent. Yes, I was going to be a fiery punchline for several years to come, but was I making it worse by hiding? Was I injecting myself with the venom of shame and isolation and expecting my critics to be poisoned? Figuratively speaking.

Perhaps I *should* buy four million dollars' worth of shoes and wear them to every high-flying social, fashion, art and cultural event I could wedge my size-nine foot into. I had the vomiting-when-mortified thing completely under control, and the eradication of the fainting-when-humiliated reflex was progressing well. Perhaps I could stage a comeback.

Did I *want* to stage a comeback?

I had never been overly social but I did miss shopping. And the kind of treatments that could only be found in the most dedicated, cutting-edge luxury spas, the kind that had their own indoor lagoons filled with oxygen-infused waters.

I pulled myself from my reverie. 'Besides,' I said, 'if I lived here, you would have to live here too. Miles from everything. How would you cope?'

'Dude,' Esmerelda said, pointing to the surf-perfect ocean to her right and the flat, beautiful, sandy bays to her left. 'I'd totally find a way to cope.'

'Perfect,' I said abruptly. '*You* live here.'

A buzz from the intercom and a video feed showing a delivery person on an electric bike with a black zip-up canvas hotbox mercifully ended the conversation and sent Esmerelda scuttling for the door. I would take firm bets that she could beat Usain Bolt up that driveway if there was takeaway involved. A call for help from James seconds later saw me dragging myself up the hallway, which felt about the same length as the driveway, and into the guest room. I was reasonably sure my Brazilian Palm Beach housekeeper was still on the payroll and had assumed she would have kept the house in fresh linens and towels. But I could have been wrong.

James sat on the bed, fully dressed, minus his shoes, his shirt untucked. The carry-on was open on a low-legged turquoise velvet tufted lounge near the bay window.

'No towels?' I asked.

I walked through the room, past the bed and into the adjoining bathroom. There was a white lacquered cupboard against the wall behind the door. It usually held towels, robes and linen type things. The cupboard was just to the left of a massive floor to ceiling window which took up the entire wall and featured one-way privacy glass and, at the press of a button for those who did not enjoy daylight, instant tint.

The back wall of the room was a sapphire green tiled walk-in shower, the right-hand side held an oversized double oak vanity, and dead centre in front of the window was a carved oval bath that always reminded me of a white chocolate Easter egg laid flat on its back and sliced in half. The room was finished with a generous smattering of lush green palms, which were very much alive. So, there *was* a maid.

James had moved quickly, a razor and toothbrush already wet on the vanity.

I waved my hand over the front of the cupboard. Nothing. I searched for a lock or a key or a panel of some sort. Nothing. I said, 'Open,' and, 'Open door.' What was wrong with a handle? A perfectly nice invention. Why reinvent the wheel? Especially when the original wheel was so user-friendly.

An impeccably manicured yet very masculine hand came over the top of my shoulder and pressed a spot in the dead centre of the top left panel. It sprang open. *Click.* Pear coloured bath sheets, mats, towels, robes and shimmery sheets for miles.

He stood behind me, unmoving. I found myself wedged between the shiny white doors (one open, one closed), the fluffy towels inside and James Smith. God, he smelt so good! Why did he have to smell so good?

I tried to focus on the panoramic view through the window—the last moments of the pink and orange sunset, a full moon already rising over the endless ocean. It was ludicrously romantic and most unhelpful. All thoughts of Searing and brother-in-law damnation melted away with the daylight. I could feel my body stand to attention. Parts of me went hard, parts of me went soft. All my parts should have behaved like ladies and stayed in neutral.

'Are you attracted to me?' he asked.

What did he just say?

'Uh, me, to you? Uh, no, of course not. That would be ...'

'Bad?' he said. I imagined an eyebrow strategically arched.

'Yes, very, very bad. Obviously. Bad.'

'And if you kissed me?' he asked simply.

'No, no. That wouldn't be good, not good.'

'Bad.'

'Yes. Bad.'

I was frozen. I couldn't move. Not because he had pinned me down—he wasn't technically touching me—but because I didn't want to leave. I wanted to be close to him. Really close. *Too* close.

My resilience was ebbing away with every second we stood together. My eyes were transfixed on the deserted beach and the never-ending colours of the sky and water.

'I won't lay a single finger on you if you don't want me to,' he said with a throat crackle. 'Do you want me to?'

I wished I could say something simple, like 'My head said no, but my heart said yes', but that was not it. My head was screaming 'No!' My heart was MIA. And my body? My body unfortunately said, 'Yes!' and my mouth, being the head of the body committee, was the spokesperson.

'Yes.'

'Will you promise to say something, to stop me if I do anything you don't like?'

It was difficult to imagine that happening, but I appreciated his detail-oriented proposal.

'Yes,' I agreed.

He gently lifted my hair from the back of my neck and put it to one side. He leaned into me and kissed the side of my neck. Once, twice. His lips felt even better than they looked. And they looked incredible. Full, pink, with a perfect bow. He kept going. Lower on the nape this time, three, four, five times. I started to melt and put my hand on the shiny white surface in front of me to steady myself.

Zip. He unzipped the back of my dress just enough to slip it to one side and kiss my shoulder. *Zip.* He unzipped it further, just enough to kiss the other shoulder. It was quite possibly one of the most erotic things I had ever experienced while technically fully dressed. I was too afraid to turn and face him. And not being able to see him heightened the pleasure to an unbearable level. The only way I was getting out of this bathroom was at a flat run or by tidal wave.

Zip. The zip came down to my waist. He gently slid the sleeves down my shoulders, running his hands up and down my arms. The fabric draped around my waist and the kissing started again. It became more and more urgent. Deeper. Open mouthed, scattered with small, gentle bites. I put both of my hands up for support, hanging onto a shelf with my left hand, while my right hand was pressed flat against the shiny, hard door.

Deep sounds came from my core. I tried desperately to stuff them back down or at least quiet them. I had limited success.

I felt him take a knee as he pushed in, splaying his hands across my back, moving his attention to the back of my ribs and the small of my back. Then he lifted his hands off me. For several excruciating seconds, I stopped breathing. Was he leaving? He didn't leave. He slipped his hands up under my dress, and onto my outer thighs, gradually moving higher and higher, slowing only when his splayed hands reached the perimeter of my underwear, where he stopped on my bare hips, his index finger grasping my front hip, his thumb resting gently on the edge of my bottom.

There was moaning, and not just mine. Believe it or not, moaning with an Irish accent is distinctly sexier than moaning in any other accent.

This had to stop. If that zip came down any more or those hands went any further, I was going to be standing in nothing except some very scant mismatched Italian lingerie and my Choos. And quite possibly not even those.

I inhaled deeply and gathered my strength to pull away. But it was too late. He slid his hands off my body, stood, albeit slowly, and re-dressed me: hips, waist, ribs, arms, shoulders, gently pulling the silky fabric of my dress, smidgen by excruciating smidgen, up, up, up, until it sat on my shoulders again. And then he zipped the zip all the way back up, right to the top.

'It was all me,' he said, laying one last inconceivably, incredibly delicious kiss to the side of my neck. 'I take the blame.'

If I had died then, I would have had no regrets. No woman who was consensually kissed and caressed like that would. Guilt, yes. Terrible, *terrible* guilt, but absolutely no regrets.

To my astonishment, I spoke. 'This should never happen again,' I said calmly. What I was thinking was, *This should absolutely happen again.* Happily, my brain seemed to have regained control of the body committee.

I heard him take off his clothes, turn the shower on and step in. Exactly a millisecond later, Esmerelda yelled down the hall. 'Food's up!'

I glued my eyes to the ground and fumbled my way out. If I peeked even slightly towards that shower, I could be lost for good.

As I stumbled down the hall, I suddenly realised all the places he had kissed, nipped and caressed me were unseen, or at least hidden. He had been careful with my hair, skin and clothes so I was not mussed, marked or blemished in any way. On the outside, I appeared perfect. Under my dress, I was shattered. I might never walk or sleep straight again. And I hadn't even kissed him.

How could something feel so incredibly wonderful *and* so guiltily dreadful? This is exactly why one marries a Bran Muffin. These types of predicaments simply don't come up.

I marched straight to my bedroom at the opposite end of the house. I stood under the hot water for a long time, attempting to calm myself and make sense of what had just happened. I achieved neither.

It was well and truly dark by the time I walked into the kitchen. I was dressed in last season's loungewear (found in my bedroom drawers), thankfully a rather floating fit, no make-up except slightly topped up residual mascara and eyeliner, and nothing in my hair but conditioner and a plain black elastic holding it in a simple, swishing ponytail.

Esmerelda's idea of dinner service was laying the take-away containers out on the breakfast bar with a fork stuck in those she had already opened. No china, no silverware, no napkins.

I served myself a tempura soft-shelled crab bao with a side of perfectly sticky plum pork belly and a scoop of downy coconut rice. I added a fine coleslaw to the bowl and told myself the raw vegetables made the ensemble healthy. I'd had a big day.

Esmerelda was stretched out on a sun lounge overlooking the pool. James sat next to her in a deckchair, managing to make a white cotton T-shirt and loose cotton Bali pants look designer, his dark blond hair damp.

'So, like, what happened?' Esmerelda said when I sat in the chair next to her.

'Nothing. Nothing at all happened,' I said quickly.

'You didn't get anything out of him?' she said, disappointed.

'What? No. What would I get?' I answered, alarmed.

'You totally got no goods from the dude?'

How could she be so blatant? He was sitting *right* there. And how did she know? Sure, she had a nose for crime, chicanery and law enforcement personnel like a truffle hound, but this?

'No,' I said firmly as I tried to telepathically signal her to stop.

'I'm surprised to hear you say that, Indie,' James said, preparing to bite into his own bao. 'You were at Lucas Carr's front door for some time. Did he not leave you with *anything* memorable?'

Indie? Wait. Front door? Thank you, God, she was asking about the dentist!

In the midst of all the debate about whether or not we should drive back to the city, giving James directions and Esmerelda's rapid-fire phone ordering, I had not had a chance to pass on the information about Max.

I mentally tried to scheme my way out of my previous answers.

'He didn't give me new information,' I said, 'but he did clarify some of the things we knew. Or thought we knew.'

Esmerelda squinted and poked her spoon at me. 'Huh?'

'For example, Dame Elizabeth thought Max's daughters' names were Carley and Ellie. She was a little bit off. Lucas said *Carley* is *Tahnee*. And *Ellie* is *Lizzy*, short for *Elizabeth*.'

'Oh yeah, okay. I get it. So, like, we totally thought his name was Max, but really it was Maxwell. Clarity.'

'Exactly,' I said, breathing an internal sigh of relief.

'What else?' she said, forking noodles. The woman never used chopsticks. Maybe it was a form of cultural rebellion.

'Dame Elizabeth said Max was from Western Australia. The rest of the Hollys and the staff at the Holly Park Hotel said he was from South Australia. Lucas made it seem like Maxwell was from the Northern Territory. Darwin.'

'Do you like think he was straight with you?' she asked.

'Yes. Absolutely.'

'What else?'

'Nothing else. I must have said something wrong and he clammed up.'

'That's quite a lot,' James said, standing up and heading back into the house. 'Sounds like you're much better at this than you give yourself credit for.'

'No, I'm not,' I protested.

Esmerelda went to work on her phone. James came back with two glasses of cold, almost clear white wine and a small bottle of No-Sugar Vanilla Coke with a metal straw.

I lay back on my lounge, watching the fairy lights secreted along the walls, in the floors and ceiling, in the pool, along the cliff and in the palms and greenery glitter like white diamonds.

'Got 'em,' Esmerelda said seven minutes later. '"Darwin darlings Elizabeth and Tahnee Harraway, daughters of Northern Territory pearl baron Maxwell Harraway, whose estimated net worth is $2.5 billion, sparkled at blah, blah, blah." No other kids. No photos of him. Says he's a widower and a full-on public recluse.'

I guess that prayer bracelet *was* made of black pearls.

Before I was aware, James had clinked his glass to mine. I almost dropped it in surprise.

'You did it,' he said.

Did I? Did we? We did! We'd found Max! The man in the lilies, UP Rose Bay 0909 Winters, was Maxwell Harraway, pearl baron.

I knew Maxwell Harraway. Well, I knew *of* him. He'd made his first fortune fifty or sixty years ago as an old-school pearl diver in Broome. He'd famously started out using no scuba gear, just an extraordinary lung capacity, an iron will and a supernatural understanding of the ocean. Harraway then opened a small pearl jewellery store in Darwin called Phoenix Pearls. He used the store's profits to open a small gold mine and then a pink diamond mine, eventually creating Harraway Industries. The world's most spectacular pearls and pink diamonds were sold at dozens of Phoenix Pearls stores globally. *I* shopped there.

Esmerelda was correct. Harraway was a serious recluse. He was fastidiously private, hated the media, rarely attended public functions and was never photographed. As a result, you almost never heard about him.

'Do his—' I asked.

'Both daughters live in Darwin,' Esmerelda pre-empted me.
'Is—'

'Harraway Industries is based there too.'

'Please call—'

'Already emailed Loraine and asked for your nanna's plane at nine tomorrow.'

'Seven,' I said, contradicting her.

I was being completely unfair and petty. She was right, 9 am was much better than 7 am, but I hated it when she read my mind. It made me uncomfortable to think our brains had become so similarly aligned.

'Awesome,' she said. 'I booked it for seven anyway.'

Kill me now.

'Congratulations, Heiress,' James said, giving me a stout wink. 'You're quite the detective.'

Kill me twice.

Franny agreed to be picked up en route to do my hair and make-up during the four-and-a-half-hour flight to Darwin. Among the last season's clothes I found in my room was a gorgeous low-backed wide-legged floral Dior jumpsuit and a white Hermès jacket with a palm leaf motif, lined in white satin. There was even a pair of new-in-box cork Prada wedges.

James insisted Esmerelda sleep in the room next to his so he could keep an eye on her. This was a genius strategy as it also meant Esmerelda would be a buffer, sleeping between my room and James's (although our rooms were at opposite ends of the house, I felt an extra layer of deterrence couldn't hurt). Esmerelda, however, objected, proposing to sleep in the glass conservatory under a blanket of stars.

I won her over by promising on the soul of Coco Chanel that I would be ready to go, no complaints, at 5.30 am if she slept in the allocated room. So, I had Esmerelda as a buffer and a leisurely eight hours to sleep. Theoretically. My mind kept clicking over information, rudely delaying valuable REM hours.

*

I had never slept in the same house as Esmerelda. Astonishingly, she was a morning person.

By the time I woke and stumbled, robed and bleary-eyed, into the kitchen to boil my very own kettle, to make my very own tea, Esmerelda had already swum (location unspecified), showered, eaten, collected the mail and was on her second cup of coffee.

James likewise had been in the pool, showered (thank God I had slept through that), toasted some leftover naan bread from the night before and was making a jug of French press coffee.

I would not need to make my own tea after all.

The sun was in the process of waking over the bay and the ocean. Burgeoning streaks of pink and red ricocheted across the endless surface of the sleepy turquoise water. It was spectacular. At least there was *one* advantage to being up at 5 am.

Esmerelda was not particular when it came to stealing breakfast, happily snagging a piece of James's crispy naan and abandoning the cup of instant coffee she had made herself (the odour coming from the cup on the sink was impossible to mistake) for the Brazilian blend from James's freshly pressed pot. She was simultaneously attacking the sticky-taped sealed edges of a red and white Australia Post box with a steak knife. She slit the edges and opened the box. Inside was a black matelassé nappa leather Mui Mui handbag, the kind with handles, a detachable strap and a push-lock clasp. She pulled it out of the box, unclasped the lock, parted the handles and pulled a purse in the same fabric from inside. Both the handbag and the purse smelt, well, odd.

She put the purse on the breakfast bar and shook the handbag upside down to make sure there was nothing else in it.

I glanced at the discarded box. It was addressed to Esmerelda. Great. Now even she got more mail at my beach house than I did.

'Like how did Heinsmann even find me here?' she asked.

There was something strange about the way Esmerelda handled the handbag. It was all wrong. Only a canvas bag with no hardware could have been that lightweight. Matelassé nappa leather with metal hardware was much heavier.

'It's been less than twelve hours!' she complained. 'Rich people gossip is off the hook.'

The purse looked like it had seen a full day's shopping with someone who liked to use cash and kept receipts. It was full to bursting, but the surface was unblemished.

I stared at the bulging purse and the feathery light handbag.

'Mui Mui don't make full purses,' I mumbled, cogs gradually moving in my waking brain. 'Only coin purses ... and ... that handbag is too light. It can't be leather. It smells almost as bad as your coffee. Are those clips painted plastic?'

In a microsecond, James swivelled from the toaster to the counter and scanned the items.

'Where'd you get those?' he asked flatly.

'Delivery dude.'

'When?' he pressed.

'Like two seconds ago, when you were in the shower.'

'Delivery people don't come at 5 am,' I said slowly.

'Huh,' she said. 'Not even for rich people?'

'No,' I deadpanned, pouring myself some of James's coffee.

'It's hard to tell what's normal for you people,' she defended.

James took a soda spoon from the drawer and inserted the long, thin handle under the closed flap of the paunchy purse. It made a crunching sound, like it was full of bath crystals. He snatched the purse and ran.

I watched in horror as he sprinted out to the back deck and pitched the overstuffed Mui Mui purse high over the edge of the infinity pool. It sailed through the air, far over the incline, to the beach, landing on a soft patch of white sand a metre from the water's edge. It was a black speck with a minuscule gold logo sparkling on a deserted beach.

I suspected a significant amount of James's childhood had been spent playing sports that involved throwing balls long distances.

'Jesus!' I gasped, having followed him outside. 'What is it with you and overreactions?'

'Dude,' Esmerelda said, strolling outside with the handbag. 'This is a knock-off.' She wrinkled her nose. 'I'm totally insulted. You can't bribe a person with a counterfeit.'

She *was* the resident counterfeit designer goods expert.

James took the handbag from her and ran his hands across the lining, then the iconic stitched exterior.

'Best to be safe,' he said and pitched the handbag over the edge too, this time in the opposite direction. It was lighter and much more aerodynamic than the purse. The wind caught the open bag like a sail and blew it at least 100 metres down the beach.

We stood and watched, three sets of eyes peering through the dawn light, moving from the purse to the handbag and back again. They sat listlessly on the beach for a full minute.

'Drama queen,' I said to James, turning to walk back into the house.

And then the little black Mui Mui purse exploded with such ferocity, I was jolted forward into a piece of outdoor furniture and the hairs on my arms singed. I put my hand to my heart.

'Jesus!' I stammered, turning around, wide-eyed. 'God!'

What was it about spending time with James that brought out the blasphemy in me?

'Huh,' Esmerelda said, staring at the charred black hole the size of a minibus in the beach. 'They totally don't make 'em like they used to.'

No kidding.

Esmerelda's eyebrows were almost completely gone— singed straight off. Sometimes it just didn't pay to face a fight head on. Or eyebrows on.

Sand does not burn. But it does, as it turns out, melt. A significant section of the beach had, quite shockingly, *melted*. It was like a scene from *Frozen*. But in reverse, and with red hot glass instead of freezing cold ice.

I turned to James. 'What on earth was that?'

'PETN,' he said, turning back to the house.

Well, that was much clearer.

Esmerelda and I trailed after him. 'Like, what now?'

'Pentaerythritol tetranitrate. PETN,' he said, gulping his coffee and putting on his jacket. 'It's a crystal explosive. Very powerful. Can be detonated by a variety of things, including small electric shocks, like the kind delivered by mobiles.'

'I knew I heard it ticking!' Esmerelda exclaimed, wide-eyed, pointing to the post box.

'You could not have heard it ticking,' I said. 'It wasn't built by Wile E. Coyote. And mobile phones do *not* tick.'

'Like, I could *feel* a phone in there, dude. It was counting down.'

'If she can be at one with the Force, perhaps she can be at one with a phone,' James said wryly, lifting his carry-on to his shoulder, heading for the front door. 'I'm going to do a quick walk around the grounds. If we get separated, I'll meet you at the airport.'

'Separated? You're leaving?' I should have been happy. I had spent hours yesterday willing him to leave.

'Not immediately, no, but I need to have a look around. I won't be far and you won't be alone for long. I've a feeling the cavalry will arrive *very* shortly. You can't get too many mass detonations in this neighbourhood.'

Before I could object, he was gone. No lingering stares. No mention of the necking, pecking and generally mind-bending canoodling from the night before. Nothing.

I hurried to my room and dressed, trying to push the flaming images out of my mind. *It was not a fire*, I told myself in a mantra-like loop. *Breathe.*

It was a PETN detonation. Substantially different to the penthouse incident.

Breathe. Breathe.

I was dressed and buckling my wedges before it dawned on me that James had invited himself to the airport and therefore on the Northern Territory expedition, and I had failed to object.

Damn.

He was right about one thing, though: the locals dialled 000 the moment the faux purse hit the beach. And the cavalry *did* arrive.

CHAPTER 22

MUI MUI, IS THAT YOU?

I emerged to find Esmerelda sitting at the window seat, window wide open, drinking coffee and playing on her phone. 'Like, they're outside,' she said, pointing with her non-phone hand.

'The police?'

'Yup.'

I wanted to deal with the police quickly and get out. To this end, I decided to lie. *That could have been anyone's exploding fake Mui Mui purse, officer.*

It was Palm Beach.

Over a dozen uniformed police swarmed the beach. Two plain-clothed detectives stood on my deck, observing them.

'Ms Hasluck-Royce-Jones-Bombberg,' Searing said, turning to face me. 'I've officially run out of ways to say we must stop meeting like this.'

'Told you,' Burns said, drinking from a takeaway coffee cup. 'She's a catastrophe magnet.'

How on earth did they get here from the city so quickly? Even with sirens blazing it would take forty minutes. The explosion could not have occurred more than five minutes ago! How could they possibly know I was involved?

'You cannot prove that purse came from here!' I gasped.

'Ah,' Burns said, taking a final sip and shaking the now-empty paper cup. 'A purse, was it? That makes sense. Betcha that's the matching Moo Moo handbag.'

On top of the reclaimed wood table, in a large clear plastic evidence bag, sat the battered faux Mui Mui handbag. It may have been half a beach away from the exploding purse but it had not escaped unscathed. Or unnoticed.

I tried again.

'What are you two doing here? How did you even get here? An exploding purse in Palm Beach cannot be related to your cold case! Are you back in homicide? No one died, did they. Did they?!'

'So many questions,' Burns said, rolling her eyes. 'No, not back in homicide. No, no one died. Drove here in an unmarked Holden.' She turned to him. 'Your turn.'

'Well,' Searing said, 'I'm happy to report UP Greenacre 0101 West is an unknown person no more.'

'Really?' I said, thrown off, staring from one detective to the other. 'You solved it? Already?'

Just how good were Searing and Burns as detectives?

'Not quite solved, but we IDed our UP. His name was Terence Lopez,' Searing said. 'Forty-two, husband, father of one, solid employee, owner of a quiet two-bedroom apartment in Balmain. Born in the Philippines.'

The Philippines? That was a long way from Balmain and Greenacre.

'Known to his friends as Smooth,' added Burns.

'The injuries. How did he receive those injuries?' I immediately wanted to know.

Although Esmerelda and I had done a deep-dive into the life and times of Maxwell Harraway last night, we had thus far found nothing about his childhood or youth. He was not just an enigma when it came to his current life, but his past too.

Searing pulled up a chair at the outdoor table and Burns sat too. This all but forced me to sit with them.

I dusted my seat down. I didn't have time to get changed again if there was charred Mui Mui on my cushion. 'The injuries?'

'He had a crap childhood,' Burns said.

'No kidding,' I shot back. 'Specifically. What happened to him?'

Searing exhaled and rubbed his eyes. 'He was trafficked.'

'What?'

'Trafficked.'

'As in human trafficked, trafficked?'

The pair nodded. 'Also known as modern slavery,' Searing, ever PC, added.

'No!' I exclaimed. 'Here? In Australia? No.'

They nodded. I felt distinctly ill. I was not equipped to swim in this end of the pool.

'How?' It was all I could get out.

'Most of Australia's trafficked people come from Asia. Thailand, Korea, the Philippines, Malaysia. Mr Lopez was from Manila originally. He was trafficked as a kid, forced into slave labour to pay off a jacked-up, unlawful and completely illegitimate "family debt".'

'Why didn't he run away?' I asked.

'He did. Many times. But he was only successful when he was sixteen. He probably became too strong. Too fast. The results of his unsuccessful attempts were ...'

The scarring.

Poor Terence Lopez. This end of the pool was a cesspool.

Wait. Max Harraway, pearl baron billionaire, was a trafficked child? A slave?

I shook my head—it wasn't possible. 'Could that have happened to a child seventy or eighty years ago, from the UK or Europe?'

Burns scratched the back of her neck. 'I don't think so. I mean, maybe? It's not exactly our area of expertise.'

I scrutinised Searing.

'From what we can gather, it's mainly those four Asian countries people are trafficked into Australia from. But as Burns said, it's not, well, hasn't been our area until now.'

'How did Mr Lopez get those injuries, the ones he shared with Max?'

'I'm gonna go inside and fill up my coffee cup,' Burns said. 'Have a chat to my old mate Esmerelda.'

Searing gave her a tight smile of thanks and she walked away. Esmerelda could fend for herself.

'The injuries we saw, the vertebra degeneration, the arthritis, the thickened skin, the knees,' he listed them on his fingers as he spoke. 'Jem said they were from the work. The forced labour. Cleaning, scrubbing floors, washing dishes. Labouring illegally on farms, in factories and kitchens, on building sites.'

A horrible thought occurred to me. 'Was he …?' I blanched.

He shook his head. 'No. Nothing sexual. Your guy was clear of that too. I checked.'

My brain clicked and clacked as I tried to process this information. I was relieved, and *completely* outraged.

'You spoke to Bailly?'

'Briefly,' he said. 'She was pretty peeved.'

'They suspended her. Will she lose her job? I hear people are fond of those.'

'Ha! A little heiress humour.' Searing smiled. 'Hard to tell. Kevin Pasty is … well, he's not one of the better deputy state coroners. Not too popular either, but he still is a deputy state coroner.'

I had a few ideas around the Bailly situation. I felt confident I could help dig her out of any hole I had helped put her in.

'Do you have any coffee?' he asked.

'Yes, sure, in the kitchen,' I said, standing.

We found Burns and Esmerelda fighting over the use of the French press. Sadly, Esmerelda was attempting to treat the ground coffee in the same manner as instant coffee. Burns was no better, insisting the press did not need to be, well, pressed. Searing took over and decent coffee was had all round. How was he single in Sydney?

The coffee kicked in as the sun travelled to a respectable height in the morning sky. My brain started functioning. Esmerelda, bless her, had had the forethought to order this morning's pastries last night. I noticed she had not disclosed this information to James Smith. She made him eat toasted Indian leftovers.

We stood around the breakfast bar, drinking coffee, eating croissants and watching the sun.

'How *did* you get here so quickly?' I asked again.

'In the neighbourhood,' Searing said in a noncommittal tone.

'You were in Palm Beach, tracking down a suspect in your cold case? An adult who had been a trafficked child, who worked as a—something, and lived miles away in the inner west?'

'He was an asphalt salesman,' Burns helped. 'Yep, we were.'

'Dude,' Esmerelda said, finishing her apple and custard twist, 'like that's totally not possible.'

'Oh yes, it is,' Burns piped. 'Once we had an autopsy that wasn't completely fucked, we found Lopez in missing persons pretty quick. His wife listed him missing on October 31. Halloween.'

'Body was found in Greenacre on New Year's Day,' Searing added, extracting an A4 manila folder out of his leather case and handing it to Burns.

'So,' Burns said, opening the folder, 'we dig into Mr Lopez's background. Read his file. Find that he was trafficked as a kid. Poor bloody bastard. And who does Mr Lopez claim he was trafficked by? None other than our old friend—' She slapped two photographs down on the white marble.

'Stollywood?' Esmerelda frowned, pointing to the first photo.

Searing's jaw jumped ever so slightly and Burns's eyes twinkled, but they remained silent.

'Jeff?' I said in confusion, pointing to the second photo.

The first photo had obviously been blown up from a group shot. Parts of other people had been cut out. It featured a balding man with a hooked nose, yellow teeth, a sunken chin and eyelids that might swallow his eyes at any moment. I recognised him immediately.

Jeff was a man I *also* recognised. This man had darker hair and more of it, white capped teeth, a smaller nose and a chin implant. Altogether better looking. Different, but not so different, if you looked closely. If you knew what you were looking for. If you were, for example, the wife of a reconstructive plastic surgeon. Or if you'd seen a certain USB.

'*Jeff,*' I said, tapping the second photo, trying to convey a meaningful expression to Esmerelda.

'Like, Stollywood,' Esmerelda said, tapping the first photo.

'This is fun,' Burns said. 'Stollywood's real name is Ivan Stolonosky.'

'Do you know this man?' I asked Esmerelda. 'Stolonosky?'

'Yeah.' She nodded, then, looking around at the detectives, said, 'Maybe.'

'From the USB?' I asked her.

'Nah, that's Stollywood. He used to be the big boss at,' she eyed me and spoke slowly, 'the *Bankstown Boutique.* Like forever ago. We called him Stollywood because,' she leaned close and spoke in low tones, 'he was a big fan of *designer stuff* from Hollywood. Clothes, shoes, *handbags.*' Her eyes were wide in encouragement, her head bobbing as she spoke. 'He liked to make *hoe marshers* of them.'

'Homages?' I deciphered.

Esmerelda nodded.

'Repros. Knock-offs,' Burns added.

'Whatever,' Esmerelda said, moving the rectangular cardboard box of pastries out of Burns's reach. She then checked her phone, which had not beeped or vibrated. 'The car's waiting.'

Burns grinned at Searing like a cat who had finally managed to work out how to open a carton of cream.

'Stollywood was your old boss when you were a rookie crook, wasn't he, Esmerelda? He was the big boss at the Bankstown Boutique.'

Burns knew what the Bankstown Boutique was!

'No comment,' Esmerelda said, crossing her arms, getting her crocodile on.

Burns thumped her hand on the island so hard, the marble nearly cracked. 'I knew it!'

Searing grinned. 'Lucky guess.'

'Lucky? Bullshit! You're buying coffee for the rest of the week.'

'Deal.'

I ignored their bonding session, turning away and, leaning into Esmerelda, I quietly asked, 'You don't recognise him from the USB? The Mediterranean Men's Club USB?'

'Dude, no,' she whispered back. 'I never looked at the USB. Just passed it on to Inspector No-Gadgets here.' She pointed her thumb at Searing. '*Theoretically.*'

'Unfortunately, I suspect Stolonosky doesn't know that,' Searing said.

His hearing was excellent.

I put my hands on the photo of Stolonosky or Stollywood or whatever his name was, and then on the photo of the Mediterranean Men's Club 'Jeff', and moved the pictures together until they were edge to edge.

'This man, Stolonosky. He's the *before* photo of this man, Jeff. *Jeff.*' I waited for recognition to sink in, but it never happened.

'Jeff,' I ploughed on, 'is one of the Mediterranean Men's Club people from the USB.'

Realisation dawned on Esmerelda's face. 'Fuck. Off.'

I shook my head. 'It *is* him. This,' I tapped the before photo, '*is* Mediterranean Men's Club Jeff.'

'Fuck off,' she said again. 'Totally can't be. Stollywood didn't get no plastic surgery makeover—he's like, dead. Car crash.'

Searing made a 'not so much' sign with his hand. 'Let's just say he re-branded on the down-low. The AFP and INTERPOL long suspected Stolonosky was into human trafficking.'

'Counterfeiting high-end knock-offs was just his side hustle,' Burns added.

Searing continued. 'People were terrified of him. No one would talk. The feds couldn't make anything stick. Until they found themselves a witness. Someone who could ID him *and* was prepared to talk.'

'Terence Lopez,' I said slowly, gears grinding. 'Mr Smooth.'

Burns made a clicking sound with her cheek and her tongue. 'You got it. See, when Terence Lopez escaped his captors in Far North Queensland, he ran as far as he could, to Tasmania. There, Mr Lopez told his story to the AFP but said he couldn't ID the guy. He was a kid and he was terrified. Anyways, he applied for refugee status, got processed, granted a visa and lived pretty happily. All things considered, anyway,' Burns continued. 'Put himself through school. Got a job. Met a girl. Had a baby. Regular guy. Until one day, he gets a big promotion from his asphalt company. Out of state.'

'He had to move to Sydney for the job,' I guessed.

The detectives nodded.

I guess all those new freeways didn't asphalt themselves.

'One day, Lopez's supermarket shopping and *boom*, who does he see in the cereal aisle between the Fruit Loops and the Frosted Flakes?'

'Stolonosky,' I answered.

'Yup. Small world.'

'Small underworld,' Esmerelda put in.

'Lopez'd had twenty years to think about this guy. He got braver, or more outraged. Either way, he went to the AFP. Said he'd seen Stolonosky and could positively ID him as his trafficker. A week later, Lopez disappeared.'

'Not long after that, Stolonosky conveniently died in a car accident,' Burns said. 'In the Philippines.'

'Jeff is the brand-new, re-branded Stolonosky,' I concluded. I stared at Searing, then at Burns in complete amazement.

There was something circular and very strange about this whole thing.

'What are the chances of you two being moved from homicide to cold case because of the *not real* but *definitely real* Mediterranean Men's Club, only to be given a cold case where your victim was killed by Stolonosky, whose trafficking and counterfeiting crimes involve the AFP and who had, by way of a major Mediterranean Men's Club cosmetic surgery makeover, re-branded himself as Jeff?'

I could not believe I was able to say that sentence. Or that I had come up with such a ludicrous conspiracy theory involving the federal police and international crime syndicates.

Or that this was now my life on a Tuesday morning.

'Pretty bloody slim, I would reckon,' Burns answered, pouring the last of the French press into her Versace coffee cup.

The whole thing was making my head hurt.

'So, someone gives you the cold case, hoping you will make a connection with the Mediterranean Men's Club?' I puzzled.

'Possibly,' Searing said, tempering Burns's enthusiasm. 'But without Bailly doing the second autopsy, we'd never have IDed Terence Lopez. We could've chased our tails forever.'

'Like, what makes you so sure Stollywood offed Lopez? Maybe they called him Smooth 'cause he was up to shit,' Esmerelda said, the seared bald patch above her eyes, where her eyebrows *used* to be, rising. 'That could totally happen.'

Burns squinted, assessing Esmerelda's face, but said nothing.

'Lopez was clean,' Searing said. 'We asked everyone from his boss to his wife to his old landlord in Hobart. He was a regular guy. A geology nerd. They called him Smooth because he sold asphalt.'

'Besides,' Burns said to Esmerelda, 'Bailly says Lopez died after coming off second best in a fist fight with an industrial sewing machine. The kind you might use to make knock-off designer shoes and purses and,' she shook the plastic evidence bag, 'handbags.'

Cogs whipped around in my head.

He used to be the big boss at the Bankstown Boutique.

Greenacre. *Dude, it's like next door to Bankstown.*

I was shaking, and not just because I'd had too much coffee. I grabbed Searing by the arm.

'What did you mean when you said, "Unfortunately, I suspect Stolonosky doesn't know that"? What did you mean by that?'

Searing and Burns slid their eyes to Esmerelda.

'What?' she demanded. 'I didn't open the USB! I told you. Besides, why would Stollywood care about me? I only saw the guy a couple times. We didn't hang out. I was totally small fry. Not that I was there,' she added hastily. ''Cause I totally wasn't. But if I was, he'd like never even have noticed me.'

'It's hard to believe you could *ever* go unnoticed,' Burns said sincerely.

We all assessed Esmerelda. She was five foot ten of striking Asian–Australian potential-supermodel who sounded like a surf hippy, dressed like a teen skater and had a mind like an ACME steel trap. Unless she was feeling threatened, then she was more like a designer crocodile or a furiously beautiful assassin. Not a particularly forgettable combination. Even without eyebrows.

'Esmerelda's new role with *you* may not have gone unnoticed by Stolonosky either,' Searing said solemnly to me.

'People in the underground know Esmerelda works for me?'

Burns tilted her head. 'Princess, people at *People* know she works for you. There're photos of the two of you hanging out on a tropical island together. I can google them right now.'

Oh. I had forgotten about those. They'd felt inconsequential. Deep in *People* magazine, a few throwaway pictures taken at a distance. Besides, I looked quite good. They shot me in the water and captioned it *Heiress on Phi Phi*. It was a step up from *Heiress on Fire*. Esmerelda had not been named, but she *was* hard to miss.

'Are you serious? This Stolonosky-Jeff character saw us together in *People* magazine, remembered that Esmerelda worked for him years ago at the Bankstown Boutique, and now, what?'

'Your surgeon hubby getting flambéed was big news. A few select people, serious criminals, knew he was a cutter for the Mutants. It's likely that other, even more serious, serious criminals knew he was a cutter for the Mediterranean Men's Club. Probably because he was *their* surgeon and they were *in* the club. You were *married* to Bombberg. Esmerelda now works for you. It's not a long reach.'

Cogs whirred. Gears creaked.

Unfortunately, I suspect Stolonosky doesn't know that.

'Stolonosky thinks Esmerelda has seen Richard's USB? That she recognised his before face and can now tell the police about his new face?'

'Or something like it,' Searing said soberly.

'How would he even know about the USB?' I demanded.

'There are a few ways,' Burns said through a tight jaw.

Searing shook non-existent crumbs from his tie. 'The USB is under lock and key at the AFP.'

'I thought you said they said it wasn't authentic?'

'Yeah,' Burns said, 'funny how that works.'

'Yes,' he agreed, 'something of a contradiction. A file of no importance being top secret. Anyway, very few people at the AFP have seen it, all of them extremely senior. And as I said to you before, they suspect it came from you, although they've been unable to confirm that.'

Burns shot me an unfriendly look.

He continued. 'The USB's existence is a secret.'

'So how does Stolonosky know about the USB?' I asked again.

Burns pursed her lips.

'Dude. 'Cause some of the biggest criminals,' Esmerelda explained, somewhat condescendingly, draining her coffee, '*are* cops. Someone in the AFP told Stollywood about the USB. For a price.'

'Or,' Searing challenged, 'it's all just suspicion on Stolonosky's behalf. Let's assume Richard did Stolonosky's reconstructive surgeries. Stolonosky *suspects* Richard kept before and after photos, maybe for medical reasons, maybe as insurance. Stolonosky *suspects* Richard left his little photo album to you, Indigo. Stolonosky *suspects* you might have shared the album with Esmerelda.'

'Like that's a lot of *suspects* and totally not a lot of *evidences*.'

'For all Stolonosky knows, Esmerelda is the only person alive who can positively ID him from *personal criminal* experience as Stollywood and who *also* knows about his new identity as Jeff. He might have no clue the USB is with the AFP.' Searing turned to Esmerelda. 'That makes you a real threat to him.'

'And a real asset to us,' Burns chewed.

Uh-oh. *Asset.* It sounded good. But it wasn't.

'Do you two,' I pointed at the detectives, 'think that Stolonosky has been trying to kill Esmerelda?'

'We do now,' Burns said, eyeing the faux Mui Mui handbag and snagging the last croissant.

'You think Stollywood put a rattlesnake in my knicker drawer? A tiger snake in my shower? That he rigged Patricia's brakes, poisoned my Fanta, pushed those airport trollies?'

Esmerelda rattled the plastic evidence bag. 'You think he tried to blow me up with a fake purse?'

'It was just a theory before, but I'm certain now,' Searing said contritely. 'Sorry.'

'This blows!' Esmerelda growled, hands on hips. 'If you hadn't just put those photos in front of me, I'd never have known! Dude! My day started so good too.'

'What?' I shrieked at her. 'You almost got blown up an hour ago! We all did!'

'Yeah, but like, *before* that, it was awesome.'

Searing inspected me, then Esmerelda, then me again. 'Who's "we all"?'

There was no way I was going to answer that question. It wasn't even 7 am and I had already escaped an assassination attempt (even if I wasn't the intended victim), uncovered a deeply disturbing clue about Max's childhood, formulated a conspiracy theory about an undead international fugitive and federal law enforcement and found out my personal shopper/assistant was the target of an insane people trafficker who was one of my dead husband's patients and who, it seemed, enjoyed a bit of high-end counterfeiting as a hobby.

And I could have been inadvertently instrumental in putting Esmerelda in the man's crosshairs just by employing her! I was *not* going to have a conversation about James Smith with Detective David Searing. I did the only thing I could: I answered a question with a question.

'That still doesn't explain what you two are doing here.'

'Yes, it does,' they said.

'Yeah, like it does. They totally came out here to save me. Right?'

'Oh, uh, sort of. Yes.' Searing nodded. 'In a way.'

'We were staking out one of Stolonosky's known associates, a lowlife called Borrag. We followed Borrag to a house down the road in Avalon. He picked up a package and delivered it here.'

'You were *here*, at my house, and you just sat back and watched as a known criminal dropped a catastrophic explosive device at my front door?'

Silence.

Our tax dollars hard at work.

'To be fair,' Searing said, putting his hands up in defence, 'we only just managed to catch Borrag getting buzzed in. He drives like a maniac. We had no idea you lived here, Indigo. You can't even see the front door from the street.'

Palm Beach. Palms everywhere.

'Oh,' Burns said under her breath. 'It's *Indigo* now, is it?'

'We didn't know what was in the package,' he continued.

It was time to go. I began pacing the open kitchen, hunting for items to pack in my handbag.

'Dude,' Esmerelda said, following my lead, not that she had anything to pack, but she checked her phone and re-did the laces in her sneakers. 'I totally could have been blown up!'

'Again, that was obviously a mistake. But as I said, we didn't know who lived in the house, we had no hard evidence Esmerelda worked at the Bankstown Boutique, or that she could formally ID Stolonosky. Or that Stolonosky was trying to kill her. Although,' he paused, 'Burns suspected.'

Burns smiled victoriously.

'I totally never got busted doing that Bankstown Boutique gig,' Esmerelda said, smirking proudly. She immediately spread her arms out and began backtracking. "Cause I totally never did work there. And like, for the record, I never saw the dude, never did meet Stollywood or Stolonosky or whatever his name was. No idea what he looks like. Nope.'

'A back-pedalling parolee,' Burns stated deadpan. 'Shocker.'

'You were only here when the explosion went off because you were looking for Stolonosky?' I asked.

'Yes. Which makes sense,' he replied, 'because Stolonosky, or one of his cronies or associates, has been following Esmerelda. By following Stolonosky, we found Esmerelda. So, it follows that if we shadow Esmerelda, Stolonosky will eventually appear.'

'You want to use Esmerelda as bait?' I asked, wide-eyed.

'Yep,' Burns said.

'No,' Searing countered.

I eyeballed him. 'Really?'

'Okay,' he relented, 'maybe a little bit.'

There was no way on earth that was happening.

'How many properties are there between this one and the spot on the beach where the explosion occurred?' I asked calmly.

The detectives exchanged uneasy glances.

'A couple,' Burns said.

'Four.'

Boy, Searing really *was* a Boy Scout.

I hefted my last season Chanel tote over my shoulder. 'We have a meeting to attend. You may, as my guests, use the outside areas in your investigation. Nowhere inside. Unless you have a warrant. Or want to make coffee. Or have a cold drink.'

I wasn't a *savage*.

I thought I saw steam shoot from Burns's nose and ears.

'We,' I took Esmerelda by the shoulder and made for the front door, 'are leaving.'

'Being rich *rocks*,' Esmerelda exclaimed triumphantly.

'*You're* not rich,' Burns spat.

'Totally close enough,' Esmerelda counted.

'There are three properties between this one and the site of the explosion,' I said sweetly. 'Not to mention the properties on the other side of the explosion. The Mui Mui purse could have come from any one of them. You only saw this Borrag character enter the gates, not the house. And you just said you have no idea what was in his package. Plus,' I added, 'the Mediterranean Men's Club isn't even a real thing, *officially*.'

'Indigo,' Searing warned. 'Stolonosky is dangerous and determined. You need protection. You need to cooperate. Both of you.'

'Our official response at this time is no comment.'

'Indigo, this is a bad idea,' he said, approaching me.

'Any other questions?' I asked, continuing without waiting for an answer. 'Please call Earl Stevenson or Nigel Barker. Or both. You still have my lawyers' numbers, right?'

'But—'

I made the universal hand symbol for telephone as I opened the front door.

'Call my people, Detective.'

CHAPTER 23

COME FLY WITH ME

Shane and Carlo were, as promised, waiting for us in the Lexus. I could see why Patricia was so reluctant to let them go. It was like driving with several *Avengers* cast members. Not at all unpleasant. Against Avenger advice, I rearranged the seating, moving Carlo and Shane into the back. I was on edge. As trustworthy as the Avengers seemed, I needed a known quantity at the wheel, even if that meant letting Esmerelda drive.

Carlo and Shane were at the beginning of their shift and were unopposed to some quick interstate travel (and the accompanying overtime). But would two security people provide enough protection while in transit, and in Darwin? No. We needed at least three. I was about to order more when I remembered we already had a third: James Smith.

Two people also seemed suddenly insufficient to guard Mother's moderately sized Vaucluse estate from a ruthless human trafficker. I had Esmerelda call and double the security there. I'd grown fond of Esmerelda and was not about to let some underworld zombie take her. Not to mention the risk I might get taken with her.

Searing and Burns would no doubt double down on their efforts to find Jeff 'Stollywood' Stolonosky and, much to my dismay, they would shortly be sticking to us like tape under a swimsuit model's breasts or find another set of detectives to fulfil the same purpose.

The late departure from Palm Beach sank us deep into morning traffic. It took over two hours to get to the airport. We could have flown almost halfway across the country in that time. On the upside, it served as a segue, allowing my mind to move from the Esmerelda's-being-targeted-by-a-killer-because-of-the-Mediterranean-Men's-Club space back into the who-killed-Maxwell-Harraway? space. I would not let a man like Jeff push a man like Max aside.

How was a pearl baron a trafficked child? Or was he simply a child who had laboured excessively hard? Perhaps for his family? This was rare, but not unheard of seventy or eighty years ago. Commonplace a hundred years before that. Perhaps his parents had a factory, or a farm, or a really weird cleaning business?

The revelation about the tunnel connecting Grandmother's and Dame Elizabeth's properties, along with Dame Elizabeth's claim that punctual Max cancelled dinner minutes before he was due, had convinced me that Max did *arrive* but was lured away before he made it to her front door. I also suspected that those shallow but identical and precisely spaced stab wounds in Max's thigh came from a metal rake or some other tool one might find inside a garden shed.

But there were still so many questions. Why did Max lie to Dame Elizabeth about who he was? He was an extremely successful, well-liked, self-made man. I would have to check when we had more privacy, and when Esmerelda was not operating a car on the freeway, but I suspected the Harraways had more money than the Hollys. Was he ashamed to share his past? Were unpleasant childhoods even a topic of conversation between couples dating in their seventies or eighties? What did he think would happen when she found out who he really was? And why hadn't Maxwell Harraway's daughters reported him missing? Where did they think he was?

And the biggest question: at what point should I tell Dame Elizabeth that Max Weller was really Maxwell Harraway?

True to his word, James was waiting by Grandmother's Dassault Falcon 900, ready to escort us, uninvited, to Darwin to meet Maxwell Harraway's daughters, Tahnee and Lizzy.

Before James, Shane, Carlo, Esmerelda and I trooped on board, Grandmother's rather surprised flight crew were frisked by James, Shane, Carlo and *Esmerelda*. The cabin was then searched by Shane, Carlo and Esmerelda. The jet's engine was then checked by James and Esmerelda. And the breakfast and lunch supplies were checked by Shane, Carlo and Esmerelda. All except the latter were given a clean bill of health. The food supplies were found lacking by Esmerelda because of their high fruit and vegetable content.

This brought a whole new meaning to pre-flight checks.

Despite having been on board multiple times before, Grandmother's jet never failed to impress Esmerelda. Her fascination with it was, well, fascinating. It was just an overgrown limousine, except it had a kitchen, a bathroom and a bedroom, and maybe a few more seats and lounges. As far as mogul air transportation was concerned, the Falcon was *very* tame. The nutmeg leather recliner seats, silver satin metalwork and high gloss rosewood were standard. Esmerelda had informed me, on more than one occasion, that this was the same aircraft Taylor Swift owned. I was fairly certain that was a compliment.

We buckled in and were in the air just before 11 am.

Esmerelda and I sat in the midsection of the plane, on opposite sides of the aisle, facing the front. James, left with the choice of sitting in a section separate from us, either in front or behind, or sitting with his back to the pilot, elected to ride backwards opposite me. Carlo and Shane were seated at the very front of the plane, probably eating Esmerelda's rejected fruit salad.

Twenty-five minutes into the flight, James informed me he had formulated a foolproof jail-proof plan to break into the FMCCC to retrieve Dr Bailly's test results. However, the plan involved rendering Kevin Pasty unconscious. This was problematic for me. As sub-par as the deputy state coroner was, I was sure he would still recall being made unconscious. My already iffy commitment to the whole break-and-enter-of-a-government-facility was ready to topple.

'It's the only way, unless you know a buxom, doe-eyed, natural blonde who hangs out at your man's local,' James said, unbuckling his seatbelt, 'who'd be happy to relieve him of his swipe card for a few hours. And who's available on short notice.'

Esmerelda and I exchanged glances. Frighteningly enough, we knew just such a young lady—Josephine. White-blonde Bambi-eyed Josephine and her feisty and equally gorgeous brunette counterpart Halle, who commanded $10,000 an hour *each* as Magic Model escorts, had been inadvertently instrumental in solving Richard's murder. In a moment of whimsy, I had made a real estate purchase that, along with the arrest of their bosses, enabled the genetically blessed entrepreneurial pair to take over the Magic Model operation.

Josephine, who sent me updates far more often than was necessary (the necessity being that she *never* send updates) had informed me they'd moved the business into a highly liberal, highly financially beneficial profit-share situation with their exclusive employees. They had also hired a gun accountant from Deloitte to set up generous superannuation accounts for each and every escort, waitress and barmaid, even the cleaners, and to host free monthly financial investment classes. A podcast was no doubt imminent.

'Esmerelda? Josephine, please.'

'On it.'

'This isn't how I imagined heiress business on a private jet got done,' James said, getting to his feet and stretching.

Me either. I generally spent my flights planning my purchases or unpacking my purchases. Or sleeping.

'Have you a plan to meet with the daughters?' he asked.

'Yes. We're meeting to discuss a commission piece of jewellery,' I said, unclipping my belt.

Esmerelda nodded in confirmation. 'A black Tahitian pearl prayer bracelet.' Her eyes wandered to the front of the plane.

'They'll meet in person over a pearl bracelet?' he quizzed.

'Dude, they'd meet *her* about a plastic squirt ring.' Her eyes roamed forward. Again.

'What?' I bit in exasperation. 'What are you looking at?'

'Like, fruit salad?' She pouted in exasperation. 'Seriously? And beetroot salad? That can't be right.'

'Just go up and ask if they have anything else. And if that fails, you could try eating the fruit.'

She shot me a steely gaze, undid her buckle and stalked up the aisle to the galley.

'Esmerelda is determined to make the very least of her God-given beauty,' I said by way of explanation.

'Fair enough,' he said, immediately taking her vacated seat. 'We don't all want to move along the path of least resistance.'

I was about to say I did when I realised I wasn't.

I desperately wanted to make pointless conversation with him. In my previous life, that had been one of my top five skills, but I was not fast enough and a silence fell between us. Silence between two people who are insanely and inappropriately attracted to each other is très awkward.

I forced myself to make eye contact with him.

'About last night. I'll understand if you've troubles with me,' he said evenly.

Troubles? He should get a medal for being able to use his fingertips and lips like that. He should teach classes. On YouTube. *Everyone* should have access to that knowledge. Peace would reign. The attraction itself, however, *was* troubling.

'I try to walk away from you,' he said, staring at the floor, ruffling his hair in unconscious emphasis. He turned his eyes to me. 'But I keep slipping. I can't seem to get a handle on it.'

If he was telling the truth, that was one of the most romantic things, said to me by one of the most delicious men, ever. If he was lying … it was still hot. Not enchanting, but still.

I had no idea what to say. He was five foot ten of flawlessly crafted (and dressed), mysterious, stylishly tousled, sandy blond, blue-eyed Celtic delight. He was also the brother of my dead husband. Even if, for argument's sake, I *was* on solid moral ground, did I want a relationship? Did he? I had the distinct impression that James Smith's lifestyle was more gypsy than girlfriend. And what about Searing? He was much more grounded, but if he couldn't commit to a pet, a relationship was surely a long way off. And again, did *I* want a serious relationship? I'd already had several of those. None had worked out well for me.

No one was more surprised than me to realise I wanted to have my triple-layered sponge cake with clotted cream and sticky raspberry jam and eat it too. I didn't want to be tied down to a one-man, Bran Muffin-type relationship. I wanted a no-ties, crème pat-filled, toffee-coated croquembouche tower. Hadn't I racked up some mouth-watering, freewheeling relationship karma? Isn't an Heiress, on occasion, entitled to some cream without committing to the entire dairy? Perhaps there was nothing wrong with a little slip, from time to time?

This was, of course, all in theory. In reality, I was frozen, unable to speak, let alone act.

Esmerelda saved me from having to commit to or articulate these thoughts by strolling down the aisle wielding a $300 cheeseboard. 'She's thinking again, huh?' she said to him. 'Like, did she say anything this time?'

James squinted at me, then turned to Esmerelda. 'Yes. Something about not buying a dairy.'

Esmerelda stood pointedly next to him, waiting for him to renounce his hold on her seat. I saved everyone a large amount of trouble by standing and excusing myself.

I needed to see Franny. My skin was the unique pallor of something-large-recently-exploded-quite-close-to-me. Franny was rapidly becoming the world's premier mayhem makeover queen.

I emerged several hours later from the makeshift salon in the back of the plane, a new woman. I had no idea how people got along without a personal stylist.

The Northern Territory may be hot, wild and infested with many things designed to kill or maim you, but even with *my* limited experience I knew it was also imbued with a sense of peace, space and majesty. While downtown Darwin is more country town than grand capital city, the gorgeousness of the surrounding national parks like Kakadu and Litchfield propelled it into a class of its own. Besides, there were things trying to kill and maim us back in Sydney.

We moved like a ridiculous circus car parade along the dust-covered roads, through Darwin's four stop lights to the first and, to the best of my knowledge, flagship Phoenix Pearls store. I had it on good authority that we were in possession of every bulletproof Range Rover limousine in the city. Both of them.

Carlo drove the first car with Esmerelda and I floating around in the back. Shane covered our rear, as it were, with Franny, who was keen to shop the famed store, and Grandmother's long-time steward, Steve. Much conversation regarding the best products for frequent flyer skin was no doubt being had. James and Grandmother's pilot, Emily, stayed to babysit the plane.

I slipped gracefully out of the car upon arrival and was immediately blasted by a fierce wave of dry heat. Only in Darwin was spring thirty-four degrees. Esmerelda's lanky form lolloped out of the car, drawing much attention and completely torpedoing our mission to blend in.

The Phoenix Pearls store front was exactly what one would expect from an ultra-exclusive, high-end jewellery retailer: luxurious, elegant and highly secure. The gold-rimmed, perfectly lit front windows, three on each side of the double door entry, housed jewellery with six figure price tags behind bulletproof glass.

We walked through the doors into a beautifully lit square vestibule. The floor literally glowed with cool, pale azure lights and the vents pumped in blissfully chilled air. The glass walls on our left and right afforded us a new angle on the jewels in the shop front display cases. I felt the pressure seal as the front doors closed behind us, and then release again as the second set of doors unlocked, allowing us into the store proper. I nodded politely to the security guard as a new wave of freshened air washed over me.

'Like, wow,' Esmerelda said.

It was impressive.

Phoenix Pearls was a kaleidoscope of pearls and diamonds, running from strands of blindingly flawless pearls the size of golden grapes to enormous bright pink diamond studs. The rich and diverse shades of gold, cream, pink, silver and white ran not just from the gems in the display cases, but also through the sumptuous décor and the classical architecture. Literally *everything* in Phoenix Pearls sparkled and shone. Max had reinvented Aladdin's cave. Even I had never seen anything quite like it.

Six upright display cases were built into the back wall, a mirror image of the six display cases you could see from the street, complete with matching vestibule doors in the centre. I imagined the interior vestibule doors led to the offices, workshop and gem vault.

There were two freestanding gold and cream glass-topped and fronted display counters to the left and to the right. A perfectly pressed and presented salesperson stood behind each one. Two female security guards stood silently at either end of the store. They were armed.

There would be bulletproof glass screens secreted under the floor in front of the display cases and hidden in the ceiling above. In the event of a robbery, they would swiftly emerge, connecting in the middle, imprisoning jewellery and salespeople alike in glass fortresses. I'd bet a pearl necklace there was a big red press-in-case-of-emergency button on the back of all four counters to lock down the store. The vestibule we had just entered through would no doubt lockdown too, as would the vestibule leading to the offices. I'd left our security detail outside; it was not getting much safer than this.

And there, in the corner of the room, *outside* the hidden boundary of the secret security screen, was a simple but beautifully crafted wood and cane occasional chair with a small worn gold velvet cushion. It was inconspicuous and empty. From its position, it had a view of the entire store. I imagined that was where Max sat, quietly surveying his dazzling empire. It said something about him that he had chosen not to be locked in in an emergency.

I now understood why the retired tooth man Lucas Carr thought buying Max's daughter Tahnee a piece of jewellery was such a bizarre decision. You did not present a gold-medal winner at the Chelsea Flower Show with a bunch of dripping cellophane-clad Woolworths roses.

By the time I reached the centre of the room, the doors of the internal vestibule had opened. A long, lean First Australian woman in her mid-thirties with impossibly smooth light brown skin briskly stepped out. Her dark hair was pulled back into a slick ponytail and she sported a blunt fringe that perfectly suited her alert, carefully rimmed eyes. She wore a white silk camisole tucked into a perfectly pleated black silk skirt that fell below her knees. I recognised her close-toed, black with white edging, elastic clasp Manolo Blahnik pumps. They were elegant and classic. I had an identical pair.

Although she did not have Max's fairer features, she carried some very distinctive markers that made her identifiable as his daughter. She had the same swimmer physique, the same cheekbones and, when she extended her hand to mine, it was Max's hand I was shaking. The long, elegant fingers and oblong nail beds were unmistakable.

'Tahnee Harraway?' I asked.

'Yes, Indigo-Daisy … uh, Amber, ah … Mrs Hasluck-Royce—'

'Indigo. Indigo is fine.'

She put her hand to her chest. 'Tahnee.'

'Thank you for seeing us on such short notice, Tahnee.' I smiled.

'Us?' she said, glancing at the blank space behind me.

I turned around. Esmerelda had not made it a metre past the front vestibule. She was staring around the store, slack-jawed. Franny and Steve had also entered but *they* were politely perusing. Carlo, who I had specifically asked to stay outside with his SWAT counterpart Shane, was standing next to Esmerelda, making a brave attempt not to look impressed.

'Friends with absolutely no benefits,' I assured her.

'Is that the same as relatives with no benefits?' she replied, checking her certainly 24-carat gold watch.

'Almost identical I would expect. Except mine can be fired. Probably.'

She nodded in understanding. 'You wanted to commission a black pearl prayer bracelet for your mother?'

'Yes, she's currently a Buddhist and I thought it might be a bit nicer than the one she picked up at the Ubud markets.'

'Yes,' she said with a smile. 'I think we can comfortably top that.'

'I saw your father, Maxwell, wearing a black pearl prayer bracelet last week,' I said, diving right in. 'It was quite beautiful, and I thought Mother might like one just like it.'

'You saw my father wearing—' She stopped and said quizzically, 'You saw my father? Last week?'

'Oh, yes.'

'Here? In the Northern Territory? But I thought you'd only just flown in.'

'Yes, I did. We just touched down. I didn't see him here.'

'You saw him in Sydney? You *do* live in Sydney?'

'For the most part, yes.'

'Like, don't you also have houses in New York and Italy?' Esmerelda asked, finally joining the conversation. 'Your stuff in here is like totally wild, man,' she said to Tahnee. 'Like, you know. Wow.'

'Esmerelda, my PA,' I said tightly.

Tahnee assessed Esmerelda the fine jewellery aficionado up and down: sleeveless T-shirt, worn skinny blue jeans, Converse sneakers.

'Sure,' Tahnee said slowly. 'Okay. Thank you.' Tahnee unglued her eyes from Esmerelda and refocused. 'You saw my father in Sydney, or overseas somewhere?'

She seemed perplexed. Not surprising since Maxwell Harraway was a notorious recluse.

'Honestly, I just cannot remember where I saw him. Has he been in Sydney recently? Or in Europe? The US? Asia?'

'No. Father does not enjoy travelling out of the Territory.'

'For real?' Esmerelda asked. 'Like he's mega-rich and he just stays, like, here?'

No insult to the Northern Territory intended, I'm sure.

'Yes,' Tahnee said, clearly stretching the limits of her politeness. 'He feels a deep connection to the ocean and the land here. To the art. The people.'

Before Esmerelda could comment, I began piloting Tahnee towards the back of the store. 'I understand. I feel connected here too.'

Okay so it probably was not the deep, abiding spiritual and artistic connection that Max felt, but there was certainly something awe inspiring about the natural beauty of the Territory.

'I would love to meet your father again,' I said, skimming over the trivial question of where I saw him last. 'He is *such* an impressive man.'

'Yes. He is. He's also very private,' Tahnee said in a practised apology. 'My sister and I deal with our clients for the most part.'

'Oh, I wouldn't be any bother,' I said, flashing my best Heiress smile. 'Perhaps just a quick handshake? I'll lock Esmerelda in a cupboard.'

'I'm afraid that's just not possible,' Tahnee said shortly.

'Oh, Nee, don't be so mysterious,' said a young woman, clapping Tahnee on the back. The woman was dressed in a pair of knee-length cut-off denim shorts, worn tan sandals and a faded T-shirt. She was tropical Esmerelda.

'Lizzy,' she said, introducing herself, offering her hand with a smile. That smile. It was the smile Max shared with Dame Elizabeth in the accidental snap from the theatre.

Lizzy's smile. Tahnee's hands. I was almost positively sure these sisters were Max's children. But almost positively sure is not *sure* sure. *Sure* sure is DNA sure. Court-of-law proof sure. Our goal here was not just fact-finding, it was DNA hunting. Wait. What were the chances of Maxwell Harraway naming his youngest daughter Elizabeth, and then, in his twilight years, falling in love with a woman named Elizabeth? Elizabeth was not a dramatically rare name, true, but it was an odd coincidence.

'Dad's on a three-month retreat up bush. Won't be back for weeks. Nee and I'll fix you up. Custom black Tahitian pearl prayer bracelet, was it?'

'Yes,' I said, trying to stay on target. 'For my mother.'

Esmerelda's fascination with the jewels in the room faded as her attention locked onto the sisters. To the untrained eye, it was an almost imperceptible shift.

'Your mum's Cat Jones, right?' Lizzy quizzed me.

'Yes, that's right. I'm afraid you have me at a disadvantage. I have no idea who your mother is, although I'm sure she's delightful.'

'Our mother *was* delightful. She passed almost ten years ago. Breast cancer,' Tahnee answered promptly.

Mental palm face. Esmerelda said Max was widowed.

'I'm so sorry,' I said sincerely.

'You're so bloody mysterious, Nee!' cried Lizzy, nudging her stalwart sister. 'Mum's name was Wula, she was a Yawuru woman and she knew more about the waters around Broome than anyone else, including Dad. He would have drowned penniless without her. She liked Pop Tarts and Hazelnut Rolls, and always won at Yahtzee. She was a total legend.'

The lines around Tahnee's mouth tightened. '*And* she appreciated privacy. As does our father.' She raised her perfect brows at me. 'Your grandmother isn't exactly known for *her* socialising skills.'

Ooh, snap.

'True,' I readily agreed. 'Grandmother does *not* play well with others.'

This got a throaty laugh from Lizzy.

'Like, what's up bush? And like what if he totally gets eaten by a crocodile or bit by a snake? What happens to him then? Do they have phones up bush or what?'

'She doesn't get out of the city a lot,' I said to the sisters. 'Does your father "go bush" often?'

'A bit,' Lizzy said simply. She gave Esmerelda a wink. 'No, mate, no mobile phones up bush. There's a chopper if someone gets bit. That's about it.'

'No phones?' Esmerelda was horrified. 'No internet? No Netflix?' A thought occurred to her. 'No ocean?'

'Nope. Just quiet bush and the Katherine River in Nitmiluk.'

'Dude,' Esmerelda said gravely, shaking her head. 'That's totally harsh.'

Lizzy smiled. 'That's totally the idea.'

Tahnee rolled her eyes in exasperation. 'Let's take this to my office. I have some black Tahitians you can choose from. Lisa,' she said to a woman behind the jewellery counter in the back-left corner, 'the door please.'

Lisa the sales assistant nodded and touched something at the back of the counter. The double doors buzzed and Tahnee took the last few steps towards them and pushed. We all shuffled along behind her like ducklings. I was too afraid of all the security to break the line.

After passing through the vestibule, we entered a wide hallway with floor to ceiling glass on both sides. We passed two offices on our left and a jewellery workshop on the right. In the workshop, two men and two women in white aprons sat on high stools, intently focused on their workbenches. One was studying a large pearl under an oversized magnifying glass, another had what appeared to be a crème brulée torch in her hands, the last two were sorting through black velvet trays of diamonds and pearls with oversized tweezers.

The offices were just as opulent as the store. Polished wood floors covered with soft silk rugs, antique furniture accessorised with small precious objects. Everything was perfectly placed, artful, delicate, wonderful.

I understood why Max had taken up residence in the Forrest Suite at the Holly Park Hotel. It was a good fit. It did, however, seem contrary for that same man to, on multiple occasions if Lizzy was to be believed, 'go bush' with no comforts. Then again, Max was obviously a complicated guy. Plus, affluent first-world Buddhists are somewhat renowned for their annual attendance at sparse meditative retreats.

We were led into Tahnee's luxurious office, third on the left. A refined yet still rustic Acacia timber desk sat at the head of the room. It was fronted by an eclectic collection of single armchairs; a creamy silk-covered wingback, a caramel leather slipper, a mahogany bergère in a simple lime cotton. A peach and pearl coloured hand-woven silk rug sat under two side tables fashioned from what had probably been the stern of an old pearl diving boat. A small array of spectacular shells and ancient sea trinkets sat on the tables. And photographs.

The first three photos were black and white. A barely post-teen boy, presumably Max, on the beach. Then the same young man and a few older men aboard a rickety boat. The same man, definitely Max, at least ten years later, smiling, holding a giant oyster shell, and standing next to him, an exceptionally beautiful First Australian woman holding a pearl the size of a small apricot.

The first coloured photo was of a middle-aged Max with a trim beard. This time he had his arm around the woman and two young children stood in front of them. Max with his wife and daughters.

There was also a recent photo of Max. He was bearded with rather dashing salt and pepper hair, cut in a precisely executed, almost military, short back and sides style. He wore a black pearl prayer bracelet on his right wrist and a diving watch on his left. He sat with a heavy, faraway expression on his face. Tahnee and Lizzy sat on either side of him, trying to force relaxed smiles. The photograph had been taken in this office, the Harraway family resting on the front of Tahnee's desk.

Then, behind all the others, a small square photo in a simple silver frame. It was a teenage Max, resting on a farm fence, cows and chickens in the background, his arm around a teenage girl, their smiles sparkling, their eyes aware. I didn't mean to pick it up, but I found myself grasping the silver frame, stroking the glass surface.

'Dad's only living relative,' Lizzy volunteered. 'His cousin, Elizabeth. I was named after her. She died young, in childbirth.'

'Yes, thank you for the history lesson, Lizzy,' Tahnee said, crossing the room and removing the photograph from my hands.

'I'm sorry,' I mumbled, embarrassed. 'I didn't mean to … it's just such a beautiful photograph.'

I mean, I had come with the specific goal of poking very deliberately into their family history, but still, I had intended to be more subtle about it. I suspected those few photos, plus the one Dame Elizabeth had given me, were the only photographs in existence of Maxwell Harraway.

Tahnee ignored my apology. She carefully put the photograph back in its place and scanned the room. 'Where did they put those Tahitian blacks?' she asked herself. She peered through her glass wall into the hallway, searching for a staff member. No luck. She pointedly assessed each of the wayward women in her office. 'Please, take a seat. I'll be back in a minute.'

Lizzy, apparently accustomed to ignoring her older sister, wandered to the window on the other side of the office the moment Tahnee left the room. It looked out onto a private garden that seemed to form a green central square at the heart of the Phoenix Pearls facility. The garden was alive with colour; fluffy white baby's breath, carefully trimmed spherical bushes of pink and purple Geraldton wax, furry kangaroo paws in deep red and emerald green, all begging to be patted.

'I didn't mean to pry,' I outright lied to Lizzy. 'I'm sorry to hear your father had no family at such a young age.' That last part was true. 'Did his parents pass in the war?'

'Yeah,' she said, focused on the garden.

'He was orphaned?' I pressed.

She nodded.

'That must have been difficult for him. Did he live with his aunt and uncle? The parents of his cousin, Elizabeth?'

'I think so. Until Elizabeth died. Then he was on his own,' Lizzy said, tracing her finger along the glass. 'Dad doesn't like talking about the past. He's a live-in-the-day type of guy. That's probably why he's so into Buddhism.'

'Has he always been Buddhist?' I asked.

'No, just since Mum died.'

Esmerelda, who had been prowling the office, plopped herself down on the slipper armchair (which had no arms) and began peppering Lizzy with questions, none of which related to Max's youth or family.

I had prodded inappropriately, but necessarily, enough into their family's painful past. Esmerelda was the perfect distraction. I now needed to discreetly borrow something small from the Harraway sisters. And I needed to not get caught.

'So, like, you can't swim in the ocean at all?' Esmerelda asked.

'I'm afraid not,' Lizzy said, turning to her. 'The crocs have the run of the waters around here.'

'Huh,' Esmerelda said. 'Do, like, people do it anyway?'

'Swim?' Lizzy asked, settling into the middle armchair, the Bergère, turning to face Esmerelda and the picturesque green square, conveniently showing me her back.

'Yeah. Swim.'

'Oh yes,' Lizzy replied. 'Quite often.'

'Totally okay to swim then?'

'No, not at all. Those people generally get eaten. And then those poor crocs get hunted down and made into cowboy boots and Birkin bags.'

'You're not into Birkin bags?' Esmerelda asked, puzzled. Evidently, in her mind, all the female offspring of wealthy parents required a crocodile Birkin bag.

'God, no!' Lizzy cried. 'My goal is to be completely vegan and animal product free within two years.'

'Two years, huh? Like, how's that goin'?'

'I'm almost completely vegetarian. I have a weakness for chilli crabs. I've tossed my animal product jackets and belts, but I'm having trouble giving up my leather sandals. Shoes are a weakness.'

Amen to that.

'Huh,' Esmerelda said, looking down at herself. She had no belt and was currently sporting a pair of canvas sneakers. I assumed she ate meat, but I had never seen her do it. I only ever saw her eat pastries, pasta and pizza. And food that came from stay-fresh foil packets. For all I knew, Esmerelda was a non-leather using vegetarian.

I surreptitiously made my way around Tahnee's desk. And there, sitting on the floor behind the desk was her very much cow leather, albeit snakeskin-effect, blue and black Chloé handbag. No Birkin. The handbag was overflowing with items, which happily meant it was wide open. Poking out of the top was a black leather purse, a purple Oroton make-up case, and a wooden hairbrush.

The make-up case was also open and full of shiny black cosmetic palettes stamped with the iconic interlocking Cs enclosed in a white circle. Sitting conveniently at the top of the pile was a shiny black lipstick case with a gold stripe. My money was on red.

Just as I was devising a way to procure the lipstick by stealth, the front edge of my shoe caught in a wrinkle in the silk rug. I was suddenly hurtling to the ground. How was this even possible? I had worn wedges! Not a stiletto in sight! As I fell, a frightening thought occurred to me. Perhaps this wasn't just another unfortunate clumsy heiress occurrence. Perhaps misfortune *was* my fortune. Maybe Esmerelda was right about birthdays. Maybe I'd been born under a falling star.

I put my hands out to catch myself, perhaps veering my left hand ever so slightly towards Tahnee's Chloé handbag and the Chanel lipstick sitting so tantalisingly close to the surface. I closed my hand around what I hoped was the lipstick, and because I had used my hands to steal instead of steady, I clipped the edge of the desk with my head. *Thunk.*

The karma of the thief is harsh and swift. Well, it was for me anyway. The pain was instant and searing. My head felt as if it had been split in half. All I could think was what an awful mess my blood was going to make on that gorgeous rug. And that I'd really wanted to buy the pink diamond earrings I had seen in one of the front windows.

CHAPTER 24

COMMITTED

I woke up in yet another bed. Just when I thought those days were behind me. At least I was familiar with this one. It was the queen bed in the rear section of Grandmother's jet. I hauled myself up into a sitting position. The window was filled with white cloud. We were in the air, en route, I assumed, to Sydney.

'Dude,' Esmerelda said. 'Like you were *totally* committed back there.'

'I should be committed?' I asked, certain I had mis-heard her.

'Nah, you're too rich to be crazy,' she assured me. 'You *were* committed.'

'What happened?'

'You were awesome. You totally created an amazing distraction. I got everything!' She beamed.

When Esmerelda said she 'got everything' from a multi-million-dollar jewellery store, I became concerned.

'Could you be a little more specific?' I pressed, sitting back into the tufted white silk headboard.

She hauled her phone out of her pocket and opened her photo app. She had taken photographs of all the photographs, from the most recent colour shot of forlorn Max with his daughters to the oldest black and white snap of smiling teen Max with his cousin Elizabeth.

'Wonderful work, Esmerelda,' I said with as much enthusiasm as I could muster. 'Really. Wonderful.'

The photographs were great, fantastic even; they were certainly proof enough for me that Maxwell Harraway was Dame Elizabeth's Max Weller. But what I really needed was irrefutable scientific proof. DNA proof. I needed Maxwell Harraway's DNA so I could have it matched to UP Rose Bay 0909 Winters's DNA, and I also needed DNA from Max's daughters to prove they were UP Rose Bay 0909 Winters's children, giving them legal rights, and access to his remains.

Alas, I had once again managed to trip over myself. On the upside, instead of passing out, I had been knocked out. I think I preferred the fainting. It was less painful. I put a hand to my head. It was bandaged. I had come away empty-handed. The only thing I had acquired was a scar.

Wait. I *had* grabbed something when I landed on Tahnee's handbag.

I raised my right hand to my face and opened my closed fist. It was empty.

I gazed up at Esmerelda. 'Did I get it? The lipstick?'

'Dude. You totally snagged a tampon. Maybe leave the borrowing to me.'

'Oh, God.'

'But, like I said, you totally rocked at being an awesome distraction.' She lifted my Chanel tote onto the bed. Then she held both her hands out in front of her, fists closed.

'Really?' I asked her.

'What? You're too fancy to pick a hand? Like, I don't think you can say that after you've nicked someone's sanitation products.'

'It's sanitary … never mind.' I tapped the left hand.

'Boom,' she said dramatically and produced Tahnee's Chanel lipstick.

'The lipstick!' I yelped, sliding to the edge of the bed.

'And it's totally been used.'

What a place I was in my privileged young life that stealing a used lipstick from a fellow heiress was the highlight of my week. Possibly my month.

'You wonderful woman!' I beamed. We had DNA. I felt things begin to mentally slide into place. There was still one hand left. The bonus round. 'Lizzy?' I asked, tapping her right hand.

'Nope,' she said. Then, like a magician flourishing a stolen watch to a bewildered audience, she dropped a strand of black and white pearls so mesmerising in their beauty, I was almost speechless. If Coco Chanel had been a mermaid, this was the strand of pearls she would have worn when emerging from her giant clamshell. Each pearl was almost the size of a grape, the blacks were a purple so dark, they were almost actually black, and the whites were so luminescent, they glowed even under the poor lighting in the plane. I ran my hand over them. I could feel the tiny bumps that screamed natural product of the sea. Even with my limited knowledge of pearls, I knew that made them a hundred times more valuable and extremely rare.

I blinked, at a loss for words.

'Huh!' she said excitedly, jiggling the strand so the pearls clicked and clacked against each other.

'Please tell me ...' I swallowed hard. What could she tell me that would make stealing a priceless strand of pearls okay?

'While they were like checking your vitals on the stretcher,' she said, grinning happily, 'I had a quick look through Tahnee's desk drawers—'

I cut her off, jumping to my feet. 'I *specifically* said something small and discreet! Just something with DNA. A napkin. A pen. A hair tie. This is a priceless strand of pearls!'

I immediately felt sick. And dizzy. I didn't know if it was because I had a self-inflicted head injury or because I had a self-inflicted Esmerelda.

Mental note come back to the part where I was on a stretcher.

'Yeah, but like, they've got a shit ton of pearls,' she defended. 'Seriously, how many pearls and diamonds and stuff can one rich chick need? And it's not like we're not gonna give 'em back. We totally will.'

'But Esmerelda,' I said, clutching the strand for emphasis, 'these are not run-of-the-mill pearls! A strand like this must be ridiculously rare!'

'Well, yeah, that seems about right,' she said, removing two envelopes from my tote bag. ''Cause they were a birthday present from Max to Tahnee. Lizzy gave her handmade soap. Lizzy told me they've got one of those homemade gift only deals going.' She rolled her eyes. 'Rich people.'

She foisted an envelope with *Tahnee* inked on the front at me. 'See?'

Wait. Lizzy and Max gave homemade birthday gifts and cards to Tahnee?

I examined the envelope. It was a heavy stock embossed with a gold leaf silkscreen print. Of course. Maxwell Harraway did nothing by halves. It had been slit at the top. That meant it had been sealed shut. Envelopes like that did not use self-adhesive glue, they used old-fashioned dextrin adhesives. The kind you had to use moisture to seal. The kind some people, older people, out of habit, sometimes still sealed by licking.

We had Max's DNA.

I lurched forward to hug Esmerelda but my concussed head did not appreciate the gesture. Everything swam and I fell backwards onto the bed. I opened my eyes as widely as possible to revive myself. 'We have Max's DNA,' I squeaked, dumbfounded.

'Plus, Max wrote in the card that he made the necklace himself.'

That's a homemade gift I could get onboard with. Not like sad pressed flowers, unusable candles or knitted tea cosies.

Esmerelda took an orange and purple lump out of my messenger bag and attempted to hand it to me.

'What *is* that?' I asked, leaning away. It smelt like mandarins. And ginger. And bark. Well, the way I imagined bark smelt.

'The soap Lizzy made for Tahnee.'

Add lopsided soap to the list of unwanted homemade gifts.

Wait.

'You thought Lizzy's DNA might be *in* the handmade soap she gave to her sister?'

'Uh-huh.'

'And that Max's DNA might be *on* the necklace *he* made?'

'Yep.'

I had to admit, that made sense. But I still really needed to be *extremely* specific when charging Esmerelda with future tasks.

I held the heavy strand in my hands. If Max had made it for his daughter, and I had no doubt he had, the chances of it holding his DNA were excellent. Plus, we had the envelope *and* the lipstick. *And* Lizzy's homemade soap and birthday card. It was truly a treasure trove.

On the off chance we pulled off this Top End Heiress heist, Grandmother's ever efficient PA Loraine had retained the services of a private DNA lab. They were ready and waiting for samples to process. Now all I needed to do was acquire UP Rose Bay 0909 Winters's DNA results from the FMCCC for comparison.

'What happened to Mother's prayer bracelet?' I asked.

'Oh, I totally bought the crap out of that thing for you.'

Just as all fine jewellery should be purchased.

'Tahnee and Lizzy?'

'Just happy you weren't gonna sue.'

I put my hand to my head. The bandage was small, but I could feel the lump underneath. 'Stitches?' I asked hesitantly.

'Nah,' Esmerelda said. 'Tiny bump.'

I had the distinct impression she was lying.

'It's totally weird that his cousin's name was Elizabeth and his daughter's name is Lizzy and Dame Lizzy is like, both those names, right?'

'Yes, it is. I think we might need to get a few more DNA samples. Holly DNA samples.'

Esmerelda went to play cards and I went to sleep. I emerged from the back of the plane in time for a late afternoon/early evening (depending on your time zone) tea service and found James Smith deep in thought on his laptop. Watching him work did not reduce my attraction. Being intelligent *and* gorgeous seemed like double-dipping. James had already been dipped way too many times.

I was standing opposite him for several moments before he glanced up. His eyes moved immediately to the bandage.

'Three stitches, eh? You're CIA-level committed,' he grinned, closing his laptop.

Stitches? I knew it! Esmerelda was a big fibber. I was officially the most inelegant heiress in the world. I silently prayed I had been stitched up by a decent plastic surgeon.

'Yes,' I responded as cavalierly as possible. 'I think I might try my hand at the SWAT team if this whole heiress thing doesn't work out.'

'Careful,' he said. 'Carlo and Shane might try to hire *you* for protection.'

'I'm not sure they could afford me.'

This got me a short chuckle.

There was a brief silence as Server Steve put a pot of tea down on the rosewood table between us, along with some finger sandwiches. If James wasn't going to bring up the happenings at the beach house and the subsequent conversation, neither was I.

'Do you still think we can safely get into the deputy coroner's office?' I asked once Steve had returned to kitchen. Presumably to continue swapping make-up tips with Franny or playing cards with Esmerelda. Or both.

He raised an eyebrow at me. 'Sure. How's tonight work for you?'

It was short notice but might be good to get all my thieving activities out of the way in one day, before my brain woke up and realised what I was up to.

'Okay.'

'Okay?'

'Okay.' I sipped my tea.

'You're serious, aren't you?'

I nodded, not sure I understood. He had made an offer. I had accepted. We had settled on a date and an approximate time. As loosely acquainted as I was with deal-making, this seemed like a contract. The fact that the whole scheme was bananas was surely apparent to us both from the start. Had I missed something?

Wait. I mentally backtracked. It might be best to give Dame Elizabeth an update this evening while simultaneously acquiring some of *her* DNA to give to the private lab Loraine had found. I was not prepared to float the idea that Dame Elizabeth may have been dating her long-lost cousin until I had DNA evidence, one way or the other. As much as I thought the teen girl in the black and white photo could absolutely have been Dame Elizabeth, it was old and grainy. Comparing it to the single shot of a young Dame Elizabeth that Esmerelda had managed to find online, at her wedding more than half a century earlier, had helped, but I wanted to be certain.

Surely Dame Elizabeth would have recalled having a cousin named Max? And then there was the whole 'Elizabeth died young' issue. But if I had learned anything from my dearly departed husband, it was that when someone *said* a family member was dead, it did not necessarily mean they *were* dead.

'Could we make it tomorrow night?' I asked him. 'Am I correct in saying it has to be at night? Otherwise tomorrow lunch would be fine.'

'Oh, well, sure. I'll see if I can swing a lunchtime break-in,' he said in his velvety Irish accent, sipping his tea.

'Is that safe?'

'No.'

Oh. Sarcasm. It was hard to tell with the accent. And looking at him was in and of itself quite distracting. 'I see. You're making fun of me,' I said, sitting back on my chair.

'I didn't think you'd go through with it,' he said, the smoked salmon, dill and brie rye finger sandwich stopping midway to his mouth. 'You're an heiress. Surely you have people to do these things for you?'

'I'm an Heiress, not a mafia boss. I have no *people* for these *types* of things. Mainly because heiresses generally do not require these types of *things* to be done. There's not a lot of precedent. Most of my kind don't trip over dead bodies, or set people or cathedrals on fire. They don't get dropped from windows. They do not faint, fight or fall over.'

I was managing to work up a real anger now. Mainly because I *was* angry. I didn't ask to be involved in this Max mess, but I was up to my neck in it. Past my neck—up to my hat line.

'My relationship with Max is more advanced than my relationship with most men I've dated,' I inexplicably confessed. 'I need to find out who killed him and I need information from inside the FMCCC to do that. And I need it now.'

Once I put the pieces together, I could provide the completed puzzle to Max's family, and to Dame Elizabeth. They could do with it whatever they wished. My obligation to all, including the mysterious one I felt to Max, would be fulfilled.

He finished chewing and swallowed. 'You're certain?'

'Oh. My. God!' I yelped in exasperation.

'Right then. Okay, tomorrow night. I'll collect you at four. Esmerelda's organised your man Josephine to make friends with the deputy coroner down at his local. We'll grab the swipe card from her at five and stake the place out 'til it gets dark. Then we'll go in. Together. You and me.'

'Is it safe?' I asked him.

'Oh, sure,' he said, eating the remainder of the sandwich. 'Sure.'

The sun was setting across the tarmac as the Falcon rolled into Sydney airport. A courier from the private DNA lab met the plane and collected the samples we had 'borrowed' from the Harraways: homemade soap, birthday cards, priceless pearl necklace. Shane and Carlo clocked off and one of the new bodyguards, who also resembled a Marvel character, escorted the courier and the samples back to the lab.

Esmeralda had scheduled an early dinner with Dame Elizabeth, who was understandably anxious for news. It was also understandable that she was not in the mood to dine in public. Her chef was preparing something simple for us at her home. Grandmother was somewhere in Europe and would not be back for another day (hence the availability of her short-trip Falcon).

There was *some* good news. Searing and Burns had Stolonosky pinned down at a house in the western suburbs. His associate, the man who had delivered the exploding Mui Mui, had been followed from my Palm Beach house and was arrested before he even hit the border of Avalon Beach. He rolled on Stolonosky, giving up his location while still in the back seat of the police cruiser. This meant we could get rid of the crazy bodyguard parade. However, we had already dispatched one to follow Tahnee's necklace, and the other two were on hand to drive us from the airport. I decided to wait until morning to cancel their services. This also gave James a get-out-of-jail free card. We no longer needed a babysitter.

'Grand, then,' he said upon hearing the news. 'I'll be off. See you at four tomorrow.'

It was dark by the time we reached Dame Elizabeth's. The maid answered the door and showed us into the informal dining room. I was surprised to find Grandmother seated at the Spanish walnut dining table next to Dame Elizabeth, who sat at the head of the table. The lights were low in the room and the two women were deep in conversation.

'Indigo!' Dame Elizabeth beamed, standing to greet me. The happy pitch of her voice was betrayed by her frail frame and red eyes. Even under the pale light, her grief was palpable.

Grandmother tapped a manicured nail on the table. 'This better be good. I should be disassembling someone's life's work right now, not sitting here. *Sitting.*'

I made a mental note to send Grandmother to a meditation retreat should I ever want to kill her. Spending any amount of time with her own emotions would surely be the end of her. On the upside, it was good to know the Tin Woman had a heart, even if it was probably made of iron ore.

'Lovely to see you too, Grandmother.'

Esmerelda wanted to check on Dame Elizabeth's progress in getting her *Pazzia* contract pulled but seemed conflicted by her obviously vulnerable state. Esmerelda's unsure eyes darted from one woman to the other. She eventually took a restrained seat at the opposite end of the table.

Dame Elizabeth was having none of it. 'Esmerelda,' she said, smiling. 'Come sit by me.' And she patted the padded walnut seat next to her. 'I have good news for you. Mr Heinsmann has been convinced to void your contract. The documents are with the lawyers now.'

'Really?' Esmerelda exclaimed. 'Like, okay! Awesome!' And she lolloped down to the end of the table and sat herself next to the Dame.

Dame Elizabeth put her hand on Esmerelda's hand. 'I did want to let you know the reason Mr Heinsmann was so keen to have you repeat your cover.'

'He hates me,' Esmerelda said bluntly.

'No, you moronic girl,' Grandmother snapped. 'He's had the best numbers in a decade with you on the cover. That's why.'

'Really?' I said, hoping, once again, I sounded less shocked than I was.

'Yes,' Grandmother snorted. 'With those numbers, they'd put your personal shopper there on every cover in that entire stable if they could.'

'A decade?' I echoed, seating myself opposite Grandmother.

Esmerelda held her hands out in question. 'Like, what the?'

'You sold more copies of *Pazzia Australia* than any celebrity or supermodel has in the past ten years. You've made the publisher a lot of money,' I explained.

'And,' Dame Elizabeth added, 'provided a much needed boost to the Australian fashion industry. My dear girl,' she said, squeezing Esmerelda's hands, 'we need young Australian women like you!'

'God help me,' uttered Grandmother.

'I would consider it a personal favour if you would reconsider the cover,' Dame Elizabeth said. 'You could just about name your terms. You could wear an unknown designer. You could wear,' she scanned Esmerelda's ensemble, 'that.'

'Uh,' Esmerelda looked to me for help. 'Like, I don't think so.'

'Leave it with us,' I interjected. 'We will reconsider the offer under these new terms.'

Esmerelda shot me a death stare. I gave her a tiny but reassuring shake of the head. We would let Dame Elizabeth down gently another time.

'Wonderful!' Dame Elizabeth clapped.

'So glad I could postpone the takeover of a billion-dollar company to witness that,' Grandmother griped. 'Are we going to be fed at some point, Elizabeth?'

Right on cue, the maid delivered the first course—green pea soup. Esmerelda stared down at the table. There was a lot of cutlery. It was going to be five courses, six including the cheese. Dame Elizabeth always ended with a cheese course.

'Just move from the outside in,' I said and demonstrated by picking up the outermost utensil, the soup spoon, collecting the pea soup in it front to back. Esmerelda's jaw slackened as she tried to concentrate on the foreign movements.

'If you would be so kind, Indigo,' Grandmother said, making the hurry up sign with her right index finger.

I turned to Dame Elizabeth. 'We found Max's family.'

Dame Elizabeth's cheeks began to shudder and she pursed her lips to hold back the emotion.

'They think he's on a three-month retreat in a national park. Max Weller was *not* Max Weller,' I said to her, offering as sympathetic a face as possible.

'Like, totally not even close,' Esmerelda said, poking at her soup with a dessert spoon.

'He was Maxwell Harraway,' I said, soup spoon hovering.

Thoughtful expressions crossed the faces of both women. Grandmother got there first. 'Maxwell Harraway, the pearl baron?'

'Phoenix Pearls, Maxwell Harraway?' Dame Elizabeth added.

'Yup,' Esmerelda said, poking her tongue in trepidation into a spoonful of soup. 'Same dude.'

'That's not possible,' Grandmother said. 'Maxwell Harraway is a recluse. The man never steps foot outside the Northern Territory. I've tried to get him on a number of boards, but he's like a hermit crab.'

'Are you sure?' Dame Elizabeth asked me.

'Quite sure, yes. Esmerelda, would you mind showing Dame Elizabeth the most recent photograph of Maxwell and his daughters?'

As Esmerelda retrieved her phone, I continued to explain. 'You were very close with the names of his daughters. Carley is Tahnee and Ellie is Lizzy. Elizabeth.'

I let that information hang in the air for a moment.

Dame Elizabeth held Esmerelda's phone in her hands and examined the photograph.

'Is that Max?' I asked gently. 'Your Max?'

She nodded, stroking the screen where Max's face sat. 'His hair was longer, and whiter, and he was clean shaven, but yes, it's definitely Max. Are those his girls?'

'Yes.' I pointed to the screen. 'That is Tahnee. And that is Elizabeth.'

It finally dawned on her. 'Elizabeth? What a small world.'

'Dude. You have *no* idea.' Esmerelda slurped enthusiastically. 'This weird green soup is not totally disgusting,' she added.

'Maxwell Harraway,' Grandmother said, still shaking her head in disbelief.

Dame Elizabeth's eyes moved from the picture on the phone to me. 'Why wouldn't he tell me who he really was? Why would he lie?'

'He's not in financial trouble,' Grandmother put in. 'Harraway Industries turned a healthy profit last quarter. Hermit habits aside, Harraway has a solid reputation, professionally and personally. No mistresses. Very clever wife, who he built the business with, also reclusive, died several years ago. Cancer. There's nothing for him to hide.'

Grandmother liked to keep abreast of her fellow billionaires. However, I suspected her assessment of things Maxwell Harraway had to hide was somewhat lacking.

'Why would anyone hurt him?' Dame Elizabeth asked, staring once again at the photograph.

I wanted to answer both of her questions and, with a little help from some unorthodox friends, I was confident I could.

I gingerly put my hand under the hand Dame Elizabeth was using to hold the phone and supported it. I swished the screen gently, going backwards in time: Max with his wife and young children, Max on the pearling boat, Max on the beach, Max on the farm with his cousin, Elizabeth.

Dame Elizabeth stared at the final photograph.

'That,' I said, pointing to the teenage boy in the photograph, 'is Max. And that,' I pointed to the teenage girl, 'is his cousin, Elizabeth.'

Grandmother narrowed her eyes, finally catching on. 'Another Elizabeth?'

'I know, right?' Esmerelda put in, pushing the soup dish away. Apparently not totally disgusting was still not good enough to finish. 'Like Lizzy, Max's daughter, is named after the cousin Elizabeth.'

Dame Elizabeth's hand shook slightly. 'He named his daughter after … his cousin?'

'Yes. They must have been close,' I nudged.

'She's like totally dead but,' Esmerelda added.

'Dead?' Dame Elizabeth queried, looking up at Esmerelda.

'Yes,' I said. 'According to Max's children, his cousin Elizabeth died in childbirth at a young age. She was his only real family. Max was an orphan.'

A tear slid down Dame Elizabeth's well-preserved cheek.

Grandmother leaned in over the phone, scrutinising the black and white photograph.

'What?' I asked her. 'Do you recognise the location? The people? Max? Elizabeth?'

'No,' she said shortly, but her eyes were glued to the screen.

'They must have been close,' Dame Elizabeth said, pulling back from the phone. 'For him to have named his second daughter after her.'

She motioned for the soup to be taken away. A small tomato salad replaced it.

'Why not the first child?' Grandmother wanted to know. 'That *is* the tradition.'

'First kid was—'

'Tahnee,' Dame Elizabeth mused, cutting Esmerelda off. Unintentionally, I am sure.

'Yep. It's Kaurna for "breaking wave",' Esmerelda said, poking a tomato with her main course fork.

Dame Elizabeth swallowed hard. 'Is it?'

'What on earth is Kaurna? It sounds Danish, but Harraway's wife wasn't Danish,' Grandmother said, swishing the picture on the phone back to the family photo. 'She was First Australian. See.'

'Yeah, totally,' Esmerelda agreed. 'Like, the wife's name was Wula, water. Kaurna's a First Australian language.'

'So, the first child is named after the mother and the second after the cousin. Honestly, it could have been Danish, the man was so secretive.'

Grandmother was right: almost nothing was known about Max's family. His parents or grandparents or great-grandparents *could* have been Danish. He was a recluse's recluse.

'Did you tell his daughters about me? About their father?' Dame Elizabeth asked.

'No,' I said hesitantly. 'They think he's on a meditation retreat. They're not expecting him back for several weeks. I wanted to be completely sure Max Weller *was* Maxwell Harraway before I ...'

I was not quite sure what I was going to do when I had DNA confirmation. Perhaps notification of next of kin was a job for the authorities? Perhaps not. As for telling his children about his relationship with Dame Elizabeth, that was a thousand per cent not my job.

'Yes,' Dame Elizabeth said stoically. 'I think you've done the right thing, Indigo. Wait. Be sure.'

The untouched salad course was removed. Meanwhile, I was onto my second glass of sauvignon blanc, as was Grandmother. Esmerelda had burned through three iced teas. Dame Elizabeth had not drunk anything. I poured her a small glass of merlot from the decanter that had been waiting patiently for the roast chicken.

'This is a lot to take, I know. Perhaps you should have a little wine? Or would you prefer water, or a tea? Or something stronger?'

'Scotch,' Grandmother said immediately to the maid, who proceeded to pour two—one for Grandmother, one for Dame Elizabeth.

Dame Elizabeth put the crystal tumbler to her lips but couldn't bring herself to drink. She put the glass back down on the table and blinked several times, deep in thought.

'You're right, Indigo. This is a lot of information for me to process. I am going to need some time. My apologies but I think we have to postpone. Perhaps we could reconvene tomorrow evening? Please, finish the meal without me.'

She stood to leave and we all stood with her, even Esmerelda.

'Don't you have a standing family dinner on Wednesdays, Elizabeth?' Grandmother asked.

Dame Elizabeth exhaled, leaning on the back of her chair for support. 'Yes, of course. I've rather lost track of the days. Perhaps after dinner then? Nine?'

'Absolutely,' I readily agreed. 'We'll be here.'

'You won't proceed without me?'

'No,' I fibbed.

'I've missed my window to move. No point in going to London now,' Grandmother said, making an exorbitant fuss about pulling out her own chair. 'I might as well stay in Sydney for the remainder of the week.'

Dame Elizabeth stepped away from the table, far more upright than I would have been in her shoes. 'You may tag along if you wish, Florence, since you seem to be at a loose end not pulling something apart. Or buying something. Or selling something.'

'A lady needs a hobby,' Grandmother retorted.

I had the impression Grandmother would have liked to see Dame Elizabeth out of the room but delaying business to stay in town had probably already stretched her Tin Woman heart to maximum capacity. Dame Elizabeth left alone. Her maid moved to remove the chicken and her Scotch tumbler, but I put myself between her and the table.

'Could you possibly ask the chef for a vegetarian main alternative?' I said, tipping my head towards Esmerelda. 'For my assistant.'

The maid looked uncertain.

'Vegetarian?' Grandmother barked. 'For a main?'

'Oh, yeah. What I really feel like after weird green goop and a heap of tomatoes is like, more green stuff.'

I smiled at the maid, which completely threw her and she backed out of the room like a gazelle leaving a lion convention. I pulled a plastic ziplock bag out of my tote and, turning the bag inside out, used it like a glove to pick up Dame Elizabeth's scotch tumbler. I poured the remaining scotch into Grandmother's tumbler then sealed the top. Dame Elizabeth might not have drunk from it, but she did put it to her lips. I prayed that was enough.

'What on earth are you doing?' Grandmother demanded.

'I need her DNA,' I said simply, slipping the bagged glass into my tote. 'To test against Maxwell's DNA.'

'You have Maxwell Harraway's DNA?' she asked, on the verge of sounding impressed.

'Totally,' Esmerelda responded.

'Because of an old photo and a coincidental name? Do you have any other reason to think that Elizabeth and Maxwell Harraway are actually cousins?' she said to me, her voice becoming lower with each word.

'I just need to rule it out,' I said with more calm than I felt. This was not how conversations with Grandmother usually went. I was being positively confrontational.

I quickly began to scour the room. Although asking the chef to prepare a vegetarian main would cause some delays, and some silent cursing, it would not keep Dame Elizabeth's staff away all night.

'I totally love birthdays,' Esmerelda said from the other end of the room. She stood next to a side table covered in birthday cards. There were no envelopes this time. Surely just *writing* in a card caused a few hand or finger skin cells to rub off? I hoped so.

Esmerelda started on one end of the row of cards and I on the other. Esmerelda claimed Gregory and Bettina's in moments and, after dizzyingly long seconds, I found cards from Gilly and Astor. The cards were halfway into another ziplock bag when the maid suddenly entered the room with a vegetarian quiche. The chef must have kept a few in the freezer for just such nuisance guests. I shoved the cards into the plastic bag as I spun away from her. 'Oh my, what lovely … walls. Wallpaper. Yes, wallpaper. Very … papery,' I said, patting the silver stencilled birds on the lavender wallpaper.

Esmerelda attempted to rush the maid, but Grandmother was too quick.

'Ridiculous millennials,' Grandmother sniped at Esmerelda, scanning the quiche in the maid's right hand. 'Is it vegan? She now says she requires *vegan*.'

The maid was too terrified of Grandmother to respond; she simply turned heel and left.

The moment the maid was out of earshot, Grandmother rounded on me. 'Elizabeth had better come out of this smelling of roses,' she warned. 'If that's *not* going to be the case, you can stop right now and forget everything you have found. Max could still be a nameless homeless man.'

'She will,' I responded without hesitation. 'Absolutely. Roses.'

There was no certainty of that, but it was rather liberating to oppose Grandmother's will with such conviction.

'Are you lying to me, Indigo?'

'No,' I lied.

CHAPTER 25

BATMAN IN CHANEL

For the first time since Richard had passed, I slept soundly. This seemed strange since I had not yet clicked the last few coloured squares into place in my Max Rubik's cube. That said, I had put a rush on last night's final DNA samples and if the lab wanted their bonus, I would have all the results by dinner.

I collected the breakfast tray Patricia had left in my bedroom: French toast with Canadian maple syrup and Devonshire clotted cream with a soy latte. The quality of the tray and the relative silence with which it was delivered indicated Dylan Moss must have found another Heiress to harass. Or represent. Or was plotting new ways to penetrate our security. Perhaps I would keep the Avengers detail for a few more days. The things an Heiress had to do for a quality breakfast tray.

I was so close to the end. We had *actually* discovered Max's identity. It was astonishing, and fabulous. Such a significant win really should be celebrated. Plus, I had nothing to do until 4 pm.

'How about a spa day?' I asked Esmerelda. 'My treat.'

I was feeling brave. Perhaps I could just dip my toe into the public arena at a very private spa. My fear of gossip was losing the battle against my fear of mottled, bumpy skin, fine lines and unwanted body hair.

'Are people gonna touch me?' Esmerelda asked suspiciously.

'Only if you want them to. You could have a day-long back massage or you could have every laser treatment known to spakind. Lasers don't touch you.'

Esmerelda was semi-hackles up, unsure.

'You can decide on the drive over,' I said.

Thirty minutes later, we were greeted by Alexis Felix, the eternally effervescent owner of the Alexis Felix Spa, who declared her establishment a Team Indigo Zone. I had no idea what that meant, but Alexis seemed genuinely thrilled to see me and at this stage, that was enough. Her staff conspiratorially glowered at any clients who stared or whispered, and often forgot to refill their beverages.

In no time, I was sipping Champagne in an aquamedic pool filled with oxygenated water while being tenderised by needlepoint massage jets. This was followed by an aromatherapy steam, a five-headed hydrotherapy Vichy shower, a full body exfoliation with salt, ylang ylang, lime and mandarin, a frangipani and coconut body wrap, another Vichy shower and a full body massage. A quick light therapy laser facial, hair removal laser, a hydro-microdermabrasion session, a vitamin A peel, some microneedling, and a Sisley Black Rose Cream mask and I was done. Almost. A spray tan, manicure and pedicure also seemed in order. Plus hair and make-up. I was a hardcore spa athlete, a beauty black-belt, back in the ring.

Esmerelda spent the day floating on her back in the 'totally Roman bath' (the aquamedic pool), gazing at 'the stars' (tiny LED lights secreted in the concave night sky ceiling) and buying things on her phone. Which, it seemed, *was* water resistant. An underground sanctuary where no one could see her in a bathing suit appealed. She was eventually coerced, with much protest, into a treatment room. She emerged several hours later looking insanely incredible. People with genetic gifts like Esmerelda really had an unfair advantage when it came to spas. They went from a nine out of ten to a seventy-four out of ten. They should be charged *much* more. Having seen her in a bathing suit and post-treatment, I could only imagine what she looked like styled with *Pazzia*-standard hair, make-up and wardrobe. I understood how she had sold so many copies.

When James drove through Mother's front gates at 4 pm, I was prepared. I was dressed entirely in black from Karl's 2011 Grand Palais burglar collection: oversized black crêpe pants rolled up at the ankle, a fitted three-button wool jacket with a plunging neckline and oversized black flower ruffle collar, a sheer sleeveless rolled neck top and heavy leather ankle boots with flashlights secreted in the soles. And sheer gloves. I followed the collection's hairstyle too: slicked down with a strong left part, secured in a bun at the back of the neck.

'Are you wearing Chanel to a break-in?' he asked.

'*You're* wearing Valentino,' I shot back. And he was. Black Valentino jeans, turtleneck and boots.

'Fair call,' he said.

Esmerelda disappeared in the Lexus, heading to the deputy coroner's favourite bar, Anna's Inn. Mr Pasty was about to have an unbelievably fortuitous evening chatting with the exceptionally gorgeous and exceptionally blonde Josephine. It was astonishing to be the beneficiary of personal favours from an escort agency. I would have to send flowers and a large muffin basket along with the $10,000 per hour payment.

We rode in silence to the cross-city tunnel. Once inside, James promptly reached into the back seat and pulled two Happy Meals from a heated container.

'How could you possibly have known?' I gasped. Having a Happy Meal habit was one of my dirtier little secrets. It would be bumped down the list after tonight, but still, it was up there.

'A little bird told me,' he said playfully.

'A little bird called Patricia?'

'Ah now, if I told you, the bird might get hurt.'

He was right. And hurting the bird might endanger my breakfast trays.

The call of the pickle-laden cheeseburger was too much for me. I stacked it with crispy French fries and bit in, trying hard not to make moaning sounds as I ate. It was possible I had made moaning sounds when he kissed me all over, and I didn't want him to feel in competition with a cheeseburger. It would be an uphill battle, even for him.

He ate his burger in five bites and his fries one at a time, which I found inexplicably erotic. It didn't help that he smelt amazing, Amouage yes, but also a body wash I could not put my finger on. And his hair was still damp from a wash and trim.

He cleared his throat to speak on several occasions, but nothing followed. As much as I tried to erase his words, hands and lips, I couldn't. I exhaled heavily and tried to articulate myself but failed. We were doomed. Like nervous teenagers, we exchanged nothing but sighs and curbed glances.

I realised with some surprise that the Volvo we were in this evening had a slightly different interior to the last one.

'Is this a different car?'

'Of course. It'll be different again in a few hours. Just in case.'

'Will there be a just in case?'

'No.'

Such romantic banter.

We slid into the car park of a thoroughly suburban bar and pulled up next to the Lexus with Esmerelda in the driver's seat. Esmerelda powered down her window and handed James a soft drink can. He took the can and buzzed his window up. Not a single word was exchanged. Creative professionals.

An hour later, the Volvo was parked at the rear entrance to the FMCCC. James unscrewed the top of the can, revealing a hollow silver interior containing Mr Pasty's ID pass card.

'Are you sure the cameras are off?' I asked.

'Aye. I had a good chat to a lad in the firm. From six to six-thirty, they'll see the footage from last night. Still, best be safe,' he said, handing me a pair of oversized, no-brand sunglasses, black gloves and a black cap.

The low bun worked perfectly with the cap. Just as well; it would have been awful to ruin such wonderful hair. I swapped my glasses for the no-name brand but discarded the gloves. I had my own.

At the back of the facility was a massive roller door with a thick-looking human-sized door to the left. The smaller door had a camera above it and a swipe keypad beside it.

My hands were sweating under my gloves and my lower stomach was in complete turmoil. We got out of the car and stood together on the concrete ramp. 'You're sure?' he asked.

For Max, I thought, fortifying myself. For Dame Elizabeth.

'Of course,' I said, feeling stroke-level terrified.

He slid the card along the keypad reader and punched in the code: *0805*. Pasty's dogs' birthday. The light went from red to green and the door clicked open. My heart ricocheted around in my chest like a pinball.

He slid through the door first. He reached back and his splayed, leather-gloved left hand landed hard on my belly, stopping me from entering. He surveyed the blackened surrounds then nodded. He pivoted to me and, moving his hand to my waist, guided me through the door into the darkened room.

In a single hammering heartbeat, I was through, he was through and the door clicked closed behind us. I felt for the wall, using it to navigate my way to face him behind me in the murkiness.

'Is this it?' I asked.

'Aye,' he lilted, 'we're in it now.'

I put my hands out and onto his shoulders, my eyes adjusting enough to find his outline. My entire system was flooded with adrenaline, I was my own little drug lab. My body seemed weightless as I felt my way down his chest. His pullover was thin enough to feel every muscle underneath and soft enough to invite more touching. I moved my hands up his body to his neck and face. My brain was so busy coping with the shock of the break-in it didn't have the chance to object as I guided his face towards mine. It was so dark I needed to put two fingers on his lips to make sure I was in the right spot. I was.

'Absolutely the last time,' I murmured into the shadows.

His head nodded in my hands and I kissed him. It was everything I imagined it would be. His intensity lifted me off my feet. He slipped his gloves off and his bare hands held my face and stroked my neck. He used just the right amount of pressure. There was a soft yearning, a provocative tenderness and then a hungry explosion, all in a hypnotic rhythm. It was mesmerising. Quite possibly the back door of the forensic medicine and coroner's court complex was not the most appropriate place for it, but this was my fourth break-in, albeit the first into a state facility. Other insurmountable undertakings felt imminently more doable.

He pulled away from me. 'I lied,' he gasped. 'I lied about coming here. At first because I didn't think you'd go through with it. It was so crazy. You're ... *you*. Then I wondered if you *would* go through with it. Then I was worried you'd go through with it. In the end, I did it. For you. But you came. You're here! But you don't need to be here. We don't need to be here. It's already done.'

'I *do* need to be here,' I said. My eyes had adjusted and I could see the outline of his face. I stepped back, attempting to make meaningful eye contact and to get some distance.

'It's unfortunate you chose to lie to me.' I paused. 'What *specifically* did you lie to me about?'

'Mr Pasty's account was hacked four hours ago and all the folders relating to UP Rose Bay 0909 Winters were downloaded. I had the DNA results sent to the lab you hired for comparison. I didn't think you'd go through with it. I didn't think you'd come tonight. You're either crazy, Heiress, or you've balls of steel.'

'Esmerelda says I'm too rich to be crazy,' I inexplicably informed him.

'Balls of steel 'tis then.'

As somewhat complimentary as that was, I did *not* enjoy being lied to. And although it was information I would have *liked* earlier, it would not have altered my plans. I really needed to see Max up close and in person one more time. As much as Tahnee and Lizzy resembled Max, they were both missing one unique physical quality I was now almost certain Max possessed. It was something I couldn't ask Bailly about without potentially endangering Dame Elizabeth. I needed to get into the FMCCC to see for myself.

So, it seemed we'd traded omissions.

'I need to see the body,' I said simply. Then I stomped my right foot twice. The heel of my Chanel boot lit up and a white flashlight with a blue ring shone out from the toe. I stomped the other foot and identical lights flashed on. My boots were lighthouses, shining through the inky FMCCC sea.

'Feck off!' he exclaimed. 'You're Batman in Chanel.'

I had been called worse.

I stalked forward into the gloom of the cavernous garage structure. I assumed vehicles drove up the concrete ramp, through the garage door and into the giant car bay. And I didn't think they were delivering UberEats. I imagined ambulances and coronial vehicles coming in and hearses coming out. A rush of satisfaction ran through me knowing that Max would soon be coming out rather than being trapped here for an icy eternity. Or at least until the FMCCC had a meltdown-level power failure.

At the end of the garage was a double door. The kind with a foot-wide metal panel running horizontally along the centre with large mesh-and-glass windows above. The kind that swung in and out. The kind you get in hospitals. There was a human-sized metal stretcher parked beside the door. I carefully pushed it aside and leaned in on the door. Locked.

James scanned the double doors. There was no keypad. No card slot. We were in trouble. He ran his gloved hand along the wall to the left of the doors. He was three metres away before I heard a *click* and the heavy doors opened. A blast of cold air greeted me. Before walking through, I squinted backwards: there was a large green plastic button set into a metal circle. The door wasn't locked, just push-button automated, to save you from holding it open while pushing a stretcher through.

The chilled room was filled with metal drawers housing the dearly departed. They lined the walls, left and right. The fact that it was scarcely lit by rows of faint green downlights didn't help with the terror factor.

'You go right,' I whispered with absolutely false bravado.

He nodded and began methodically reading the labels on the right drawers. The drawers were stacked four high and I had to crane my neck to see the names printed on the top ones. We searched unsuccessfully for what seemed like an icy eternity. We were rapidly closing in on a white dead-end wall at the end of the room.

'We're burning time,' James warned. 'We've only five minutes left of tape.'

Perhaps less time should have been dedicated to making out. Not definitely, just perhaps.

I read the last set of drawers. No UP Rose Bay 0909 Winters. No Max. James was a fraction ahead of me. He'd begun examining the white wall.

As I approached, I realised the dead-end wall had a set of cleverly camouflaged doors set into it. A keypad and a card swipe sat beside the doors. There was a small glass window set high in the right door. I stood on my tippy-toes, cupped my hands and (almost) pressed my face to the glass. It was a small chamber, resembling a private crypt. It had twelve drawers, three wide, four high. *UP ROSE BAY 0909 WINTERS* was printed in bold capitals on the top middle drawer. Max was dead ahead.

James took the card out and swiped it through the reader. It flashed green. I pushed against the doors. Nothing. He swiped the card again. Green. He entered Mr Pasty's code. Angry red. A flush of fear went through me. The code wasn't working.

'Three minutes,' James said calmly.

Okay, I had worked out Richard's passcodes, I was sure I could work out Pasty's. Except I knew Richard and I had never even met Pasty. The only person I knew who worked here was Bailly.

'Two minutes, thirty seconds.' Not even a waver in his voice. He kept punching numbers. Red. Red.

Dr Bailly. Interesting woman. She risked her job by doing the extra tests. She risked jail by telling us about Pasty's dogs' birthdays. All so Max would get justice. Some people take social equality *very* seriously.

'Two minutes.'

Birthdays. Bettina's. April Fools'. Terence Lopez went missing on Halloween. October 31. Bailly was born on Friday the 13th. October 13.

I pushed James aside and punched in *1310*. Green light!

I knew I wouldn't be able to see into the top drawer without a ladder, and there were no ladders. So the moment the doors hissed open, I bolted in and began pulling out the drawers below Max's. I would have to use them as steps. I prayed they were empty. And if not, well, for forgiveness.

I heaved drawer one open and stepped up. It was mercifully empty.

James pulled drawer two, also empty, and I stepped again.

I pulled drawer three and found myself face to bone with … a mermaid skeleton?

'Jesus, Mary and Joseph,' James murmured in slow astonishment. He crossed himself and then shook his head, like someone trying to void their ears of salt water after an ocean swim.

I unglued my eyes from the skeleton mermaid long enough to look down and put my second foot on the second drawer. I hiked my right foot up to the third drawer, and history cruelly repeated itself as I slipped and toppled onto the skeleton. I felt a long scream escape my lungs as her bones crunched beneath the weight of my body. I grappled with her ribcage and bendy spine, trying to hoist myself over her, but the cold metal was slippery, and not perfectly horizontal. My foot went with gravity and slid down the tray and I found myself bent over, face to fin with her flared spiny tail. I may have stopped breathing. Bones or no, she still smelt fresh, like clean water, and there was a mesmerising sense of calm about her. Not enough to calm me, though. In my panic, I tried to stand up and smashed my head into the tray above. Max's tray. James was suddenly beside me, putting my hands onto Max's tray, and guiding my right foot back down to the second tray.

'One minute thirty.'

I closed my eyes and hauled myself up to Max.

I would have liked some time to say goodbye; unfortunately, I had a more pressing business. 'Hi, Max,' I said. 'I just need to have a quick peek at your ears.'

I brushed his long white hair off his face and tucked it behind his ears. I could now clearly see the pin-sized holes located just in front of both ears, on the very edge of his face. The medical term for the tiny holes was *preauricular sinus*. According to my somewhat limited research, the hereditary holes were the evolutionary remnants of fish gills. Preauricular sinuses. Bethany-Lyn Kilmer had been right, even if she was a horrid person with no sense of kindness.

The odds of Max sharing such a rare genetic anomaly with Gilly and Astor were astronomical. Unless, of course, they were related.

Cousin Max.

'One minute. We need to be gone.'

I climbed back down the drawers, pausing for a split second to glimpse the skeleton again, before dropping to the floor. The sudden stomp of my feet switched the flashlights in my Chanel boots off and we were plunged into darkness. We slid the drawers back in by feel and thundered through the doors into the army green dimness of the steel-lined room.

'Fifty seconds.'

Although my personal training regime is consistently adhered to twice a week, the only cardio involved is kick-boxing, which is more of a frustration release mechanism than anything else. Running was not in my wheelhouse, though I could see now why some people were so attached to it.

'Forty seconds,' he said as we reached the second set of double doors, both of us searching for a green plastic button. There was none. We were back to the keypad and the card swipe.

'Bloody hell,' he growled. 'I should've seen that.'

I would have taken some responsibility for distracting him had it been the first set of doors, but the second set was on him.

He slid the card out of his pocket and through the reader, punching in Pasty's code. 'Thirty.'

We bolted the short distance to the next door, which, on this side at least, opened with a good old-fashioned door handle. We hurtled through it and out into the night.

'Fifteen seconds,' he said, already in the car.

I threw myself into the passenger's seat of the Volvo as it reversed out of the driveway, heaving the moving car's door shut with both hands. *Ding, ding, ding.* The Swedish car objected to something unbuckled. I could hear James counting down. 'Ten, nine, eight.' We crossed dozens of empty, white-lined car park spaces as we headed for the exit.

'Five,' he said. I was violently jolted as we ran over the concrete hump separating the public and private car parks. 'Three.' *Ding, ding, ding.* The Swede continued to complain. I jammed my seatbelt buckle into the clip as we skidded in a dramatic turn onto the main road. I reached over and fastened James's belt too. The car stopped screaming.

'One.'

I sat in silence, trying to digest what I'd just seen and done, attempting to lower my stroke-inducing heart rate.

'Well,' he said, navigating the Volvo back to Anna's Inn, 'that's one way to pass an evening.'

'Quite.'

'Burgers and a break-in. Might we consider that a first date?' he asked.

Traditionally, one is asked out on a date *before* indulging in break and enter. Suitors do not enquire afterwards if the felony counted as a date.

'No.'

'May I ask you on a date?'

'No,' I said, my hands shaking so hard I could not get a grip on my McDonald's cup.

'You sure?'

'Yes,' I said, spilling sugar-free cola as I abandoned the lid and straw, and gulped directly from the side.

'Okay,' he said with a wink.

Had my body not been awash with adrenaline, I might have been able to formulate a comeback. On the upside, the adrenaline was the only thing stopping me from passing out.

I was still attempting to get my breathing under control when we caught a set of red lights across from Anna's Inn.

Between deep breaths, I scanned the car park for the Lexus. James turned to me while waiting for the colour to change. 'Did you … uh, see a mermaid skeleton in there?'

'I absolutely did not.'

'Right then,' he said as the lights turned green. 'Me either. But, uh, do you think whatever it was, was real?'

'Definitely not.' I shook my head vehemently. 'Probably just someone getting ready for Halloween.'

He put his foot on the accelerator. 'Aye. Practical jokers.'

CHAPTER 26

FAMILY

Mr Pasty's FMCCC pass card was returned to him without incident. By all accounts, the deputy coroner was having an excellent evening. One he no doubt reminisced about with Mrs Pasty when she found an envelope in her letterbox a week later with a dozen glossy photographs recording the event for posterity.

I arrived at Mother's at exactly 7.38 pm. The private lab had hand-delivered the DNA results from the Holly and Harraway families to Patricia at 7.30 pm. The results from Dr Bailly's *many* tests on UP ROSE BAY 0909 WINTERS (including DNA) that James had 'acquired' had been with the lab most of the afternoon and their analysis arrived at 7.30 pm too. The information was most helpful.

After reading for forty-five minutes, then googling for fifteen, I was forced to ask James for one final itty-bitty favour. Low risk, low skill. Probably. He kindly obliged and agreed to meet me at Dame Elizabeth's just after 9 pm. Esmerelda was home by 8.20 pm (this helped with the googling). Twenty minutes later, she won a sixty-second argument over who would drive to Dame Elizabeth's. This turned a pleasant six-minute drive into a harrowing four-minute drive. We arrived early at 8.45 pm instead of the requested 9 pm, quite by design.

We always seemed to catch the Holly family in the middle of dessert. Tonight, it was apple and rhubarb crumble with warm custard. Someone in the house must have been feeling nostalgic.

The maid showed us into the castle-sized formal dining room. Pale wood floors, parquet of course, high ceilings, hand-carved gold cornices, silk-lined walls peeping through dozens of giant gold-framed paintings, a tapestry style rug and ancient chandeliers that threw such low yellow light, there were shadows in every crevasse. Very Fontainebleau. Climate control must have been a nightmare.

Dame Elizabeth sat at the head of the table with Astor and Bettina to her right, Gregory and Gilly to her left. The other fifteen seats were unoccupied.

'So sorry to disturb you, Dame Elizabeth,' I lied apologetically, overtaking the poor maid, and somewhat pushing my way into the room.

'Quite alright, dear,' she said, ever the consummate Dame. 'Perhaps you and Esmerelda could wait in the drawing room?'

'Esmerelda?' squeaked Gregory who had already turned to scan Esmerelda and her outfit. 'You actually know her by *name*, Mother?'

Bettina narrowed her eyes at Esmerelda. 'Don't I know you?' Shock was a wonderful thing. Regaining one's memory after shock faded? Not so much.

'Nope,' Esmerelda said, sweeping her hair across her eyebrow-less face and attempting to fade into the shadows.

'I have news,' I said to Dame Elizabeth meaningfully. 'About Max.'

'Max!' Gregory barked, immediately on his feet. 'That old gold-digger again! You listen to me, Indigo Hasluck-Royce-Whatever, that crazy old marauder is out of the picture, and I won't let you or your meddling control freak grandmother try to drag him back in.'

Dame Elizabeth whipped (well, as fast as a Dame in her seventies whipped) towards Gregory. 'Pardon?' she asked, pausing deliberately for effect. '"Out of the picture"? What do you know about Max? *How* do you know about Max?'

'Oh, do be realistic, Mother,' Gregory said, throwing his napkin onto the table. 'We *all* know about Max.'

Gilly smirked. Bettina looked like she was mentally trying to place the name Max. Astor just shook his head at his brother.

'Shut up, Astor,' Gregory barked, even though Astor had not spoken. 'Max is nothing but a moth-eaten, money-hungry old loon. The second I gave him a serve, he backed off. We haven't seen him since. Good riddance.'

Dame Elizabeth appeared to have stopped breathing. 'When might that have been?'

Gregory began to colour. 'A few weeks ago,' he said vaguely.

Dame Elizabeth blanched, then, gathering herself, asked hopefully, 'At the hotel?'

'Of course at the hotel,' Gregory growled, regaining some of his steam. 'Right in the middle of the foyer.'

'Uh, like, I definitely don't think so,' Esmerelda put in from the side of the room. 'We totally checked. No way you could get away with having a brawl in that joint without like everyone knowing. The place is a *total* gossip machine.'

Gregory swallowed, but kept on. 'Put your pet back in your purse, Indigo—'

Oh, if only I could.

'—and go back to your conniving grandmother's garage or your mummy's gazebo or wherever the hell you live now.'

The insult was so weak, I could hear Esmerelda snickering behind me. It didn't warrant a single hackle. But it did provide me with an excellent opening.

'You might be right about Grandmother, Gregory. It's probably not ideal, your mother living next door to someone so calculating. Especially when she's so crazy for tech. And security. And tech security.'

Gregory's face looked less indignant.

'You should see her set-up. She's got it all: motion sensors, heat detectors, microphones, cameras … *so* many cameras. And she *is* quite nosy, so her cameras don't just cover *her* property. They cover the yards of the neighbouring properties too.'

That was a complete lie. Grandmother's cameras didn't reach over the fence into Dame Elizabeth's garden. But I was betting Gregory didn't know that.

'Guess what Grandmother's cameras caught *you* doing in this very yard,' I asked, pointing sternly at Gregory and then somewhat vaguely towards the front of the house, 'the night before a dead body turned up in her garden? They caught you having a not-so-friendly *chat* with Max.'

What was left of Gregory's indignant face melted and guilty sweat prickled his skin.

'Gregory,' Dame Elizabeth choked. 'What did you do?'

Gregory baulked and, to draw attention away from himself, went on the attack. 'Would you mind buggering off, Indigo? This is a *family* dinner.'

Dame Elizabeth eyed her son. 'Indigo is here at my invitation.' She repeated her question to Gregory. 'What did you do?'

'What did *I* do?' he raged at his mother, indignant at being thwarted. 'What did *I* do? What the hell did *you* do?'

'Don't speak to Mother like that,' Astor growled.

'Ask her!' Gregory yelled again, pointing at his mother. 'Ask her what she did!'

'It's okay,' I said calmly, kindly, to Dame Elizabeth. 'You did nothing wrong. You were very young.'

'Oh my God!' Gilly said, staring at me with upwardly rolled eyes. 'Would you shut the fuck up, Indigo?!'

Poor Bettina was completely lost, eyes darting from her beloved grandmother to her ineffectual, indulged father. 'What did you do, Daddy?'

'Would you like to tell them?' I asked Dame Elizabeth respectfully. 'Or I can, if it's too much.'

'I'll tell you what happened,' Gregory interrupted. 'Our mother was a teenage whore!'

At that, Astor sprang to his feet, reached over the table and slapped Gregory plum across the face. Not lightly either. Full palm. *Whack.* Gregory then attempted to jump across the table to attack Astor, but he was too unfit to make the leap.

'She slept with the farmhand!' Gregory yelped, attempting to claw back face. His mouth narrowed into a mean sneer. 'Your father, Astor, was a *farmhand*!'

Astor stood frozen. I was not the only person to have trouble breathing this evening, and the night was still young. Astor's eyes moved to his mother.

A wistful expression crossed Dame Elizabeth's face, followed by a soft smile. 'Actually, Gregory, Astor's father was much more than a farmhand.'

'Oh my God!' Gilly said, grabbing fistfuls of her own hair.

'Yeah, "oh my God" is right,' Gregory said. 'The crazy bastard told me he was Astor's father and *your* grandfather, Gilly! That's not even possible! The only way that would be possible would be … would be if Max was Astor's father,' and at this, Gregory sank into his chair and broke into tears, 'and *my* father!'

'Oh my God, Dad, shut up!' Gilly screamed, jumping to her feet. 'Get out, Indigo!' she yelled, pointing to the door. 'Just get the fuck out!'

Esmerelda nudged me. 'Like, I'd have told you to bugger off way more by now.'

I nodded in agreement.

'You cheated on Father!' Gregory exclaimed, ignoring me and Gilly in his tirade, thumping his fist on the table, making the spork in his crumble jump. 'For years!'

It was Dame Elizabeth's turn to be amazed. 'Pardon?'

Esmerelda's eyes narrowed as she tried to process all this information.

'Yes!' Gregory yelled theatrically. 'I came to visit *my mother* and found *that man* in the front garden. Coming to dinner. With. His. *Mistress!*'

Dame Elizabeth put a hand to her chest.

'Dad!' Gilly begged her father. 'Shut up!'

'Why?' Gregory demanded. 'I've done nothing wrong! The man is a scoundrel. And a liar! When I told him to hit the road, to leave you alone, he said he would. He didn't even fight me. He pulled out his phone, called you and cancelled dinner. Boom. Made up some bullshit excuse about a family emergency. But he didn't leave, fucker. No, no, he wanted to *talk*. He started babbling about being Astor's father and Gilly's grandfather.' Gregory turned to his mother. 'He went on about the two of you being teenagers in love. How you got pregnant. How your family bought him off with a hundred pounds and married you off to Father. How you passed Astor off as Dad's. How could you?'

Dame Elizabeth cupped her right hand in her left, straightened her spine and interjected. 'Your father knew. He had dozens of mistresses.' She paused and took a fortifying sip of wine. 'I only had one love. I was unfaithful to no one. And your father received a lot more than a hundred pounds, Gregory. I believe the price on my tainted head was £25,000.'

'Bullshit!' Gregory yelled. Everyone's cutlery jumped as both fists hit the table. 'He said he was Gilly's *grandfather*! That could only be possible if he were *my* father too.'

'Do not despair, Gregory,' Dame Elizabeth said calmly, '*you* are most certainly your father's son. I didn't see my love from the day I told my parents I was pregnant with Astor until—' She stopped.

'When did you know Max was your teen sweetheart?' I prompted her. 'From the start?'

'Oh no,' she said, turning to me.

'When?'

'Not until last night, when you showed me the photograph of us together at one of the farms.' She smiled sadly. 'Gordon. His name was Gordon Taylor.'

Gordon Taylor. Maxwell Harraway. Max Weller. UP ROSE BAY 0909 WINTERS.

Max.

'Oh, he was going to tell you!' raged Gregory. 'That night, but—'

'Stop! Out!' Gilly interrupted, jumping from her seat and heading straight towards me. 'Get out, Indigo!'

The interruption startled Gregory and when his eyes moved to Gilly his brain switched gears. 'Max, he had the holes, the gills, exactly like you, Giuliana.'

'Oh, *Giuliana*!' Esmerelda exclaimed with her usual majestic timing. 'It's like short for Gilly. 'Cause she's got them gill things. I *totally* get it now.'

'Gilly is short for Giuliana!' Gilly spat. '*Not* for gills!'

'Children can be so cruel,' I said.

Gilly gripped my arm and tried to manoeuvre me towards the door, but she was immediately blocked by Grandmother, who emerged from the doorway shadows like the eavesdropping Ghost of Christmas Past.

'I am quite sure you do not mean to have your hands on my granddaughter,' she said icily. 'She and I are both here at your grandmother's invitation. At her insistence, actually.'

'I totally am too,' added Esmerelda, stepping towards Gilly in her quiet-but-terrifying way.

Gilly let go of my arm. She pinched her mouth tight and stalked back to her seat.

Bettina was still seated, blinking rapidly, trying to catch up.

Astor put his hand to his face and unconsciously played with his hair before tucking it away. I could see the tiny holes in front of his ears.

Preauricular sinuses. Hereditary.

'You hit Max,' I said to Gregory, stepping towards the table, steering the conversation back on course.

'Damn right I did!' he said without regret. 'Man stands in front of your childhood home and tells you that he's your brother's father! That he's the grandfather of *your* child! That your daughter is—'

'What?' I wanted to know. 'That your daughter is *what*?'

Gregory looked across the table to his brother. 'He thought Gilly was Astor's daughter. Because of the sinus gill things. He said he had them, Astor had them, and Gilly had them. But if Max isn't my father, those gills could only be possible if Giuliana is …'

Dame Elizabeth's jaw dropped. Astor's snapped closed.

Giuliana screamed across the table at her ill-fated non-biologically outed father. 'Dad! For God's sake, shut the fuck up!'

'Weren't you worried you'd killed him when you hit him over the head with the shovel?'

There was trace in the head wound: bulb fertiliser, high-end soil, fragments from various plants, including tulips, and a variety of elements commonly found in the material they coat garden tools with. Heavy, flat garden tools, like shovels. Similar trace was found in the thigh wounds.

'No!' Gregory barked. 'He was still breathing. I didn't plan to hit him over the head with a shovel, it was just there, and when he started talking about Astor and Giuliana, and showed me *his* gills, I … I don't know. I lost it.'

I nodded. It was somewhat understandable. It was a lot of information for someone like Gregory Holly to take. For anyone, really.

'It's *you*, Astor. I should have smacked *you* over the head with a shovel,' Gregory sneered at his brother. 'You slept with Sue-Anne, didn't you? You're gay, for Chrissake! What the fuck?'

Astor leaned across the table, patted Gilly and said, 'I am sorry, my darling.' And to Gregory, 'We slept together once, but I *did* love her. Which is more than I can say for you. You cheated on her at your own wedding! And I've told you a hundred times, I'm not gay. I'm queer.'

'Pfft, queer! That's not even a real—'

Gilly stomped her foot and cut Gregory off. 'Shut up! Both of you! Shut up! Shut up! *Shut up!*'

Gregory's eyes filled with tears and he began shaking with rage. He was losing his grip. It was now or never. Esmerelda nudged me. 'Go Maple some shit.'

Marple. But I appreciated the support.

'Why did you take him into the gardening shed?' I asked.

'What?' Gregory asked, peeling his eyes off his brother.

'The gardening shed. Why did you take Max in there?'

'Privacy, I guess.'

'Why did you undress him?'

Grandmother stopped mid-step, frozen halfway across the room. For the first time ever, she did not seem sure-footed.

Dame Elizabeth's eyes seeped long rows of quiet tears and Bettina's face went from shock to mortification.

Gregory clenched and moved his eyes back to Astor. 'I wanted to humiliate him,' he growled unthinkingly. 'The way he had …'

'Humiliated you?'

Gregory's anger began to dissolve into regret, his head bobbing in agreement. Dame Elizabeth, ever forgiving and regal, gathered herself and stood from her chair. She embraced her younger son.

'I was just so shocked,' he stammered.

'Yes. What an awful surprise,' she said, patting him. 'A terrible blow. I can't imagine why Max, that is, Gordon, chose to reveal such an ancient and enormous secret in such an insensitive, peculiar way.'

'Tell him I'm sorry. *Really* sorry. But when he said you two had, you know … and that Astor was his son and Gilly was his *granddaughter* … I just … Tell him I'm sorry. Honestly.'

Gregory Holly thought Maxwell Harraway was still alive. Oh, dear.

He began sobbing into his mother's shoulder. 'I should've hit Astor with the shovel! I *wish* I'd hit Astor with the shovel.'

'You weren't worried that the dead homeless man found in my garden the next day was Max?' Grandmother asked in astonishment.

Gregory looked up at her, red-eyed. 'No. I came back to check on him once I'd calmed down. He was crazy, but he was, you know, *old.*'

Such compassion. Who would have guessed?

'When?' I asked.

His eyes moved to me. 'On the way to the health retreat the next morning. But he was gone. His clothes were gone from where I'd left them in front of the garden shed. He must have come to, walked out of the shed, found his clothes, re-dressed and run off into the night.' He turned to his mother and gave her a childlike half smile. 'I scared him off, I'm afraid.'

Bettina's brain finally processed something. 'A farmhand? Seriously?'

Dame Elizabeth surveyed the room: her sons, her grand-daughters, her tyrant neighbour and friend, her neighbour's Heiress on Fire granddaughter, and Esmerelda, Australia's fashion antihero.

'I may need to borrow some of your NDAs,' she said to Grandmother.

'I brought a dozen with me,' Grandmother responded, flapping a heretofore unseen sheaf of papers.

'Is it true?' Bettina asked, oblivious. 'Did you really have an affair with a farmhand? Is Uncle Astor,' she whispered, 'illegitimate?'

I knew from the DNA results that this was true. Astor was the biological son of Maxwell Harraway and Dame Elizabeth Holly. Gregory and Astor were half-brothers. Lizzy and Tahnee Harraway were Astor's half-sisters.

Max, to my great relief, was *not* Dame Elizabeth's cousin. Max *was*, however, Gilly's biological grandfather. This explained the movement of the genetically linked gills from Max to Astor and from Max to Gilly. Astor was Gilly's bio-logical father, making the Harraway sisters Gilly's aunts. At least one of the rumours about the Hollys was true—they had serious problems when it came to fidelity.

During this evening's terrifying four-minute car ride to Dame Elizabeth's, I'd called Mother in Bora Bora and she had confirmed that she and Astor had, long ago, spent one very memorable night together. Hence the yearly Chanel basket. Astor's bisexuality was not even a secret. A quick look at his Instagram account confirmed Astor openly identified as queer. I guess I'd missed that.

'I have never thought of you as illegitimate,' Dame Elizabeth said to Astor. 'I loved your father. You were a gift.'

Esmerelda, who had not read the report, could hold it in no longer. 'But like, the dude from the farm, Gordon, or Max, whatever his name was, he was like, your *cousin*. That's not cool, man.'

This brought the room to an abrupt stop.

'Technically speaking,' Dame Elizabeth said to Esmerelda, 'Gordon was my brother.'

Grandmother immediately marched across the room and began forcefully distributing NDAs.

CHAPTER 27

A LONG TIME AGO

'You must remember, this was a long time ago. Things were different.'

How had the lab missed *that*? And how different could things have been to make having a baby with your brother okay? I snuck a peek at Astor; he looked normal—one head, two arms, an enormous property portfolio.

'Ho-lee shit,' I heard Esmerelda whisper. 'Rich people.'

'Gordon was one of many *sons* my father technically fostered. One of the many boys who passed through our dairies. My father didn't even know their names. Nor did my mother. My "brothers" were never allowed in the house. They slept in a shed, like cattle. In those days, it was common to move children, I suppose they were teenagers, but really, they were still children, from orphanages and state homes out to farms to work.'

'Hard labour,' I said involuntarily.

'Yes, it was. Extremely hard labour. The government placed them with families on farms as foster children. Only many of the foster children had no contact with their foster parents and worked instead as unpaid farmhands. Meanwhile, the government provided the foster parents with a stipend, supposedly to pay for the care of the children. It was one of the reasons my father's dairies were so very profitable. Not only did the boys work for free, but my father was paid for the privilege.'

And one of the reasons, I quickly realised, why Dame Elizabeth was such an enormous philanthropist. She gave out of guilt for an ill-gotten fortune. She was Australia's answer to the Nobel Prize. It also explained Max's bizarre range of injuries and why he never saw his 'aunt' or 'uncle' again.

'Supposedly, it was to give the boys work experience so they could get a job on a farm in later years. But it was a swindle. They were child slaves.'

I felt like I had been hit by a shovel. But not Esmerelda; she had a question.

'And like, the chicks?'

'Yes, girls too. They were sent into domestic service. Kitchens, laundries, cooking, cleaning, childcare.'

'No, no, no, no!' Gilly simmered, scrunching the tablecloth in her hands. 'That's just gossip! Rumours. Untrue slander.'

Dame Elizabeth held Gregory's hand and reached her other hand out to Gilly. There was no interest from Gilly. Dame Elizabeth sighed and continued.

'Gordon was such a special young man. He'd had an unfathomably difficult life, but he refused to give up. He always saw the beauty in things. The art. He was spiritually connected to the land. I had never met anyone like that before. I was barely seventeen and I thought, somehow, he was so exceptional that my parents might accept him. I was wrong. The day I told them I was pregnant, Gordon disappeared. A week later, I was married to Alexander and became Lady Elizabeth Holly.'

'Gordon moved south or west or north, or all three. He changed his name and started fresh,' I mused. 'He became Maxwell Harraway. And then, when he came looking for you a few months ago, he took on another assumed name, Max Weller, in case you or your family investigated Maxwell Harraway's past, found he had none and became suspicious.'

'Maxwell Harraway?' Gilly asked, her eyes darting from me to Gregory then to her grandmother. 'The pearl baron? Phoenix Pearls? Harraway Industries?'

'Yep. Same dude.'

'No, no, no, no,' Gilly repeated, letting go of the cloth and holding onto the table for support.

'Problem?' I asked Gilly, walking Perry Mason-style around the table.

'He wasn't Maxwell Harraway. No way. He was a gold-digger. A blackmailer. He knew our secret and was out to ruin the family.' She shot Astor a hard stare.

'What?' Astor asked.

'The Forrest Suite? For over eight weeks? Come on. He was blackmailing you.'

'No, he wasn't. He paid for the suite fortnightly, in cash, in advance.'

Gilly shook her head. 'No way. It was blackmail.' She glowered me. 'If you're going to play Nancy Drew, at least be useful. Tell him. It had to be blackmail. Who spends a million dollars on a hotel room?'

'Ah, like, super-mega-rich-diamond-gold-pearl-mine dudes.'

I had some ideas around that. The hotel bill, not the mining of pearls. There had been a Phoenix Pearls store in the Sydney CBD for decades. However, for the past few months it had been partially closed for renovations. They were, among other things, installing security upgrades. It would explain Max's easy access to large amounts of cash. That said, he probably had accounts with multiple banks and could easily have been making large, quiet cash withdrawals from an account he knew no one was keeping an eye on. He certainly had no shortage of funds.

'Phoenix Pearls,' Bettina said, coming up for air. Grandmother shoved an NDA under her nose and a pen into her hand.

'Daddy,' Gilly pleaded, plopping back down on the chair in defeat (and ignoring her sister). 'You said he was a lech. A user. After our trust funds. That he was exploiting Granny.'

'Yes, well, it certainly did seem that way. But if he *is* Maxwell Harraway, well, then that's obviously not the case. I was mistaken.' Gregory turned to me. 'Uh, how much is Maxwell Harraway worth?'

'Two and a half billion,' I said as casually as possible.

Gregory straightened up and smoothed down his shirt, as if Max might walk through the door and find him wanting. 'I will apologise in person,' he said gravely to his mother.

'Maxwell Harraway is dead, Gregory,' I said.

'Is he? That'd be a shame. Why do you say that?'

I shook my head. Gregory really needed to join Grandmother in Dorothy's entourage and ask the Wizard for a brain. The Tin Woman handed the Trust Fund Scarecrow an NDA and a pen. 'Sign.'

I pulled the chair next to Gilly's out and sat down next to her. 'I hear you're the head of organic food at the Holly Park Hotel,' I said, sliding the knives away from her place setting. 'Considering you obviously didn't like him, Max got a lot of complimentary meals during his stay.'

Everyone in the room was suddenly focused on Gilly. She was unfazed.

The results from Bailly's wide-ranging toxicology tests, which took samples from blood, tissue, hair, nails, skin and saliva, showed that Max was slowly, and quickly, being poisoned.

'Where *does* one find arsenic in the city, Gilly?' I asked her.

I'd only had forty-five minutes to read over 150 pages of reports and had just managed to glean the basics.

'Bunnings,' she said nonchalantly. 'Or eBay.'

Astor's hand moved to cover his shocked mouth.

'Oh, relax,' Gilly said, frowning at him. 'It wasn't enough to kill him. Just enough to make him sick so he'd go home and leave us alone. I was protecting my family. It's hardly a crime.'

I could feel Esmerelda formulating a rebuttal and I shot her a sharp stare and a small but blunt shake of the head.

'Prolonged exposure to arsenic can cause liver, lung and kidney damage. It also impacts the nervous system,' I said. Online science sites are wonderful things.

'Not with Max,' Gilly said, irritated. 'He hardly changed at all. Maybe a few less day trips, a few more trips to the toilet and a bit of dizziness, but, otherwise, nothing.'

'Max was stoic,' I said to her. 'He probably tried extremely hard to seem as healthy and normal as possible to you, his only granddaughter.'

It was Dame Elizabeth's turn to say, 'Oh my God.' I nodded my head in agreement as I slowly spoke.

'You didn't think arsenic was working. *That's* why you gave him something else. Tell me, Gilly, how did you get Max to eat nicotine? What food did you use to disguise the taste?'

'God you're stupid, Indigo,' Gilly said. 'Haven't you heard of vaping? Liquid nicotine comes in about a billion yummy extra-strength e-cigarette flavours. Everything from watermelon to fairy floss.'

She was right. Sugar, alcohol and shoes were my drugs of choice. I knew nothing about smoking or vaping or whatever it was now called.

'You were trying to give him cancer?' Bettina asked her sister.

'That's a bit of a long-term caper, Gilly,' Gregory said. 'He'd already be dead by the time he died of cancer. The man's ancient.'

Gilly exhaled and rolled her eyes in frustration. 'Not if you *drink it*, Dad.'

'Did he drink it?' I asked her.

'No. Drinking liquid nicotine can kill you. I didn't want to kill him.'

Well, thank goodness for that.

'Besides, flavoured liquid nicotine smells so artificial and he was so bloody healthy, he'd never have drunk it. And he was turning the free food away more and more. But Max loved pampering himself. He was forever in the bloody barber or the salon. So when he broke out in that rash, I mixed up a little cream for him.'

'The rash was from arsenic poisoning,' I told her.

'Is that what it was? Huh. Well, that worked out well. Yes, he'd come down with a rash. I told him the cream was some homeopathic mango and almond concoction. It was just a pot of La Mer Body Crème with mango-flavoured liquid nicotine mixed in. Guaranteed results.'

La Mer Body Crème was $400 a pot. Between that and the arsenic-laced lobster, it seemed like a disturbingly extravagant way to kill someone. It was murder most fancy.

'How long had he been using the cream?'

'Don't try to trap me, Indigo. He only used the cream once, that Saturday night,' Gilly shot her grandmother a hard stare, 'before his big date. You can't die from nicotine cream. It's like a nicotine patch.'

'Like, how much of that mango stuff did you put in?' Esmerelda asked, helping herself to an uneaten bowl of apple and rhubarb crumble. Grandmother snatched the bowl away and handed her a pen. Esmerelda signed another NDA, under protest, then immediately retrieved the crumble.

'Only a couple of bottles. That's barely a day's worth of smoking in France.'

'Yeah, but like, it's heaps worse if it gets on your skin,' Esmerelda said, spoon to mouth.

'Is it?' I asked Esmerelda.

'Well, like, probably.'

I had recently learned there were a raft of rapid and rather nasty repercussions from ingesting nicotine, the worst of which was death. It made sense that absorbing it through the skin would be bad too. Who knows how much poisoned cream Max had used? He might have slathered it on like sunscreen at the beach. He might have used the whole pot.

I looked at Gregory. 'That may have been why he spoke to you the way he did. Why he told you about his relationship with your mother. He might even have confused you with Astor. He had arsenic poisoning which, among other things, can cause confusion. Then he had been given a substantial dose of liquid nicotine. Nicotine poisoning can also cause confusion, as well as extreme excitability and hallucinations.'

'No way!' Gilly yelped.

Esmerelda swallowed the crumble. 'Like, totally yes way.'

'After you,' I pointed to Gregory, 'left Max in the shed, he probably came to dazed and confused. It was dark. He was cold. He stumbled around inside the gardening shed searching for something to wear and, finding nothing but old gardening clothes, put those on. Because of the dark and the poison—'

'Poison*s*,' Esmerelda corrected.

'—yes, *poisons* in his system, and the fact that you had just given him a severe head injury, he was no doubt extremely confused. He walked into a wall. The back wall, where the metal rakes are hung.'

'The false wall,' Dame Elizabeth said in realisation, 'that leads to the tunnel.'

Holly brows furrowed around the room. The secret tunnel really *was* a secret.

I nodded. 'I think so. This not only accounts for some shallow thigh wounds, but also for his appearance in Grand-mother's garden. He walked into the rakes on the wall, accidentally opening the secret door to the tunnel. I think if we check the tunnel, we'll find a trail of Max's blood. He made it through the tunnel, into Grandmother's orchid pal-ace, and then out into the garden, where he ...'

Where he lay down among the lilies and died.

Gregory began to pale. 'What are you saying? Are you saying that Maxwell Harraway is *really* dead?'

Oh, Scarecrow.

'Yes, Father, you moron, of course he's bloody dead!' Gilly spat across the table. 'No, I'm not signing that bloody thing!' she yelled at Grandmother. Astor patted his niece/ daughter's hand and signed.

'No, there would have been blood on the lawn,' Bettina put in. 'Even the idiot police would have spotted that.'

I'd had the same thought.

'It rained that night,' Dame Elizabeth said slowly. 'Quite heavily. I remember hoping Max's flight to Perth didn't have to take off in the rain.'

'Yep. Totally checked. It bucketed.'

'It would have washed the blood away,' I said.

'But his clothes!' Gregory demanded. 'His clothes were gone.'

'As was the shovel,' I put in. Bettina was right; Rope wasn't so inept that he would have failed to find a bloody shovel *and* a bloody rake. Not to mention the fact that someone had closed the secret door on Dame Elizabeth's side and Grandmother's side, *and* cleaned up the blood that was no doubt on the gravelled ground in the shed and the polished concrete of the orchid palace floor.

Bettina was the first to notice that the Hollys had two more guests for dinner. Standing in the shadows, a shovel in one hand, a metal rake in the other and a dark green plastic garden garbage bag tucked under her arm, was Claire the gardener. Deeper in the shadows behind her stood her escort, James Smith.

It's always the help who cleans up after the debauched family.

'What the hell are you doing in here?' Bettina demanded.

Claire's eyes darted around the room in a panic, landing on her mistress, Dame Elizabeth, who issued her a kind, reassuring smile. 'It's fine, Claire. Come in. Speak with Indigo.'

Poor Claire was frozen. I felt her pain. Paralysing mortification was an awful sensation. I stood and crossed the room to her, touching her gently on the arm. 'It's okay, Claire, really.' I bet my new Choos I knew the answer, but I asked anyway. 'Are his clothes in the garbage bag?'

She nodded, her shaking hands rattling the metal tools and the plastic bag.

'His phone, bracelet, watch?'

She nodded again.

'Here, sign this,' Grandmother said, poking an NDA at Claire. Claire, being the loyal employee she was, signed.

Before Grandmother could hand Claire's escort an NDA, he was gone.

'You kept the shovel and the rake too?' I asked. This was a pleasant surprise. Forensically speaking.

'Well, yes,' she finally managed. 'I didn't want Bettina to yell at me … for losing gardening tools … or for buying new ones. I was going to bring them back. I've cleaned them.'

I eyed Bettina. 'What?' she defended. 'Our tools are expensive.'

That was a gigantic understatement.

CHAPTER 28

MONEY WELL SPENT

Claire had come into work at 7 am that Sunday (beating Gregory Holly by hours) to check on the tulips. She quickly discovered a bloody shovel and a pile of clothes lying on the ground outside the garden shed, a bloody metal rake hanging on the back of the door inside the shed, and the secret doors in both the shed and the orchid palace wide open. Claire had no idea what had happened and although she had no love for Bettina, Gilly or Gregory (she liked Astor), she would have walked through fire to protect her beloved Dame Lizzy. So she said nothing, hosed down the ground in the shed, tunnel and orchid palace, closed the secret doors and smuggled the shovel, rake and clothes into her car boot. Incredibly, she then went back to work. Which is where I'd first found her, being berated by Bettina.

Gregory was charged with grievous bodily harm for his impassioned heat-of-the-moment work with the shovel. He pleaded guilty in exchange for a reduced sentence (three to six years). He now lives on a minimum-security prison farm, labouring without pay in the garden, kitchen and paddocks. He says it's a little bit like a health spa.

The police did not agree with Gilly's theory that feeding hotel guests small amounts of arsenic for weeks on end was not a crime. They felt that deliberately plying an elderly man with nicotine-laced lotion, even if it was $400 a pot and mango-flavoured, and even if it was just the one time, was also a crime. They charged her with homicide.

Dame Elizabeth hired Nigel 'Barking' Barker, guardian of the rich and guilty, to defend Gilly. Barker had the first-degree murder charge dismissed in exchange for pleading guilty to manslaughter. Gilly will serve her time at Silverwater. According to Esmerelda, it's not at all like a health spa.

Claire was charged as an accessory after the fact. Dame Elizabeth hired Barker to defend her too. Barker found a doctor who claimed Claire was colourblind and therefore had no idea the gardening tools or gravel had blood on them. Besides, why would she assist Gilly or Gregory to cover up a crime? She didn't even like them. No one did.

She was found not guilty. Dame Elizabeth gave her an enormous pre-Christmas bonus.

Photographs of the deputy state coroner Kevin Pasty having a torrid make-out session with a mystery blonde in a public bar were leaked by his wife and caused something of a sensation. That scandal paled in comparison to what came next, information indicating the very same deputy state coroner had hindered the full autopsy of one of the country's 'most beloved' (read: richest) men, pearl baron Maxwell Harraway.

Pasty was fired.

Bailly was promoted. She declined the promotion. Being a forensic pathologist was her greatest ambition. She did, however, accept my offer to send Mother's manager Eddy in to negotiate some benefits on her behalf *before* declining. Her budget was increased by two hundred and fifty per cent and she received a grant to complete her doctorate in her pet passion, marine forensic science.

A Symphysodon discus is a type of fish.

Esmerelda and I met Bailly for breakfast at The Cranky Baker. I asked her about the mermaid skeleton. She claimed it was an elaborate early Halloween trick perpetrated by a group of her UNSW medical students (it turned out Bailly was also a professor) who thought it amusing to tease her about her fondness for marine life. We all agreed that those students were *not* friends and Esmerelda encouraged Bailly to provide them with grades that were equally unamusing.

While Esmerelda and Bailly were at the counter ordering bear claws and raisin toast Esmerelda discovered she earned more than Bailly. I *really* needed to find out how much Esmerelda was paid. Regardless, I felt that a woman with an undergraduate degree, a medical degree and two, soon to be three, doctorates, should *not* be earning less than a personal shopper, so I offered her a job as a consultant. An Heiress never knows when she might need the help of a forensic pathologist. Or a marine forensic scientist. Especially an Heiress as accident-prone as me. She accepted on the condition she could run all the tests she wanted.

Perhaps Esmerelda was right. Perhaps I did need to learn how to spend my money better. I started by anonymously paying for Terence Lopez's funeral. And mortgage.

Grandmother collected all the NDAs, except Gilly's (and James's). She offered me the Monet as a reward for discovering Max's identity, and the Vermeer as a bonus for also unearthing his killers. I accepted. Perhaps I was an Heiress for Hire after all.

Mother remained in Bora Bora bliss with Jed.

Work finally began on the rebuild of my penthouse. Hopefully, it will be finished before Esmerelda finishes parole. Or Gregory starts parole. I adjusted the plans, dividing the ballroom into four uneven spaces: a smaller ballroom for balls; a small lab for Bailly; a lush office filled with Esmerelda appointed whiteboards, and computers, and my newly acquired art; and a panic suite in case of snakes. Or spiders. Or ex-boyfriends.

Searing and Burns lost human trafficker, counterfeiter and generally grotesque human Jeff 'Stollywood' Stolonosky. The house they'd had him 'trapped' in had a secret tunnel. Those seemed to be making a comeback.

On the upside, they solved an almost impossible cold case. Terence Lopez's family finally had closure and were able to bury a beloved husband and father. That was *two* men out of the FMCCC's deep freezer. I hoped this would inspire the AFP to officially open an enquiry into the Mediterranean Men's Club. Then again, Esmerelda and I were getting the hang of investigating. Perhaps between shopping, snacking and spa commitments, we could find the time to, very quietly, dig something up ourselves. Perhaps an Heiress does need a hobby.

I tried to avoid contact with Searing. It was clear we could not be in the same room without getting physical. While this was not a terrible thing, I thought I might try to limit these instances to the times we just *happened* to be in the same room together. To be fair, I assumed that was going to happen quite regularly.

James Smith vanished into the night at Dame Elizabeth's, which was no small relief since I had no idea what to do with him.

I was forced to rehire Carlo and Shane and the rest of the Avengers to protect Esmerelda from Jeff. This made Esmerelda furious but Patricia *very* happy.

Shale started dating Mayson.

Bettina Holly started dating Dylan Moss. He was helping her with the PR disaster that comes from having your sister *and* father in jail. I had her ex-boyfriend, the no-fly concierge, fired. Then I felt bad and had him re-hired.

I bought Bettina a replacement phone.

I sent Dr Lucas Carr, discreet periodontist, a fruit basket for his loyalty to Max. And a gold Rolex for his unintentional but helpful name slip.

According to the news, a freak lightning storm turned sand into glass at Palm Beach. This *was* freakish since no storms were recorded. Palm Beach children abandoned their au pairs and set about collecting the glass. Their 'lightning glass' art exhibition opens next week. It's sold out.

Josephine refused payment for her time with Pasty, instead asking me to come real estate shopping with her and Halle. It hardly seemed like a fair exchange so I booked the Diamond Goat Health Spa out for a full week for them. They opted to take their Magic Model staff along for a well-earned vacation. I received many thankyou notes from both male and female spa staff.

I had the mystery informant cards checked for DNA. The lab found a tiny spec under one of the golfing Santa stamps. Bailly ran it through the state justice DNA database and got a hit: my CI was Detective Winters. After he broke his arm, Winters had had some concerns about Rope's ability to find Max's identity and he wanted Dame Elizabeth to be able to bury the poor homeless man found in her neighbour's garden. He felt he owed her that much.

As luck would have it, both of his daughters were recipients of Holly Family scholarships, one a music scholarship for high school, the other an acting scholarship for NIDA.

He had assumed I would pass the notes on to Dame Elizabeth and she would hire a hot-shot private investigator. He was wrong.

Winters typed one-handed.

It occurred to me yesterday that I could just have asked Mayson the barber if Max had gills. He would probably have noticed, right?

Tahnee and Lizzy met Astor and Dame Elizabeth. They immediately bonded and started a foundation to provide assistance for children in foster homes and state care. They plan to fund everything from nursery furnishings and free gourmet school lunches (vegan options included) to after-school sports, tutors and psychotherapy. And full school and university scholarships. The combined Holly-Harraway fortune is a philanthropical force to be reckoned with.

Astor visits Gilly and Gregory in jail. Sometimes Lizzy goes too. Tahnee refuses to leave the Territory.

Astor is Scandinavian for 'thunder god'.

Esmerelda did the *Pazzia Australia* cover. The sight of Dame Elizabeth in tears at Max's funeral was too much for her, and it was the only thing she could think of to cheer the Dame up. She was paid an obscene amount of money and wore a white, deconstructed, upcycled tuxedo by Kit Willow with a neon blue wig (to 'protect her rep').

Esmerelda is the Banksy of the modelling world.

Franny was the stylist.

It did cheer Dame Elizabeth up.

Esmerelda's eyebrows grew back. Eventually.

Bailly's autopsy revealed that Max had collecting duct carcinoma, a rare and aggressive form of kidney cancer. Max was fit and relatively symptom-free, so the cancer was in its late stages by the time it was discovered. Watching his beloved wife waste away while undergoing violent cancer treatment had broken him, and he refused to put his daughters through the same ordeal. Tahnee and Lizzy knew about the cancer and had said their goodbyes before he went bush. They did not expect him to come home.

At some point Max must have decided to do something quite different with his last weeks and months. He flew to Byron, wooed Dame Elizabeth (again) and spent his remaining days living life to the full with the woman he had loved long ago and getting to know the child he had lost, but long loved.

And at only a million dollars, it was a steal.

EPILOGUE

Don't touch that red button.

Because that button activates the security system and it'll lock the store down.

By bringing all the security screens down.

I have no idea how much noise that would make.

We are here because Lizzy and Tahnee made me promise to attend the store's re-opening.

Re-opening. When a store shuts down and then—just eat the canapés.

No, they're not popping pearls, it's salmon roe.

No, not from rowing salmon—they're fish eggs.

Well, don't eat those ones then!

Yes, those three people are staring.

No, I don't care.

Okay, fine, I do care.

Yes, those are real pearls in the swag bags.

That bag they gave you.

Yes, they're free.

No, you don't get two.

Fine, take two.

Did you return that pearl neckla—Esmerelda! Is that Jeff coming into the store? *Stollywood Jeff.* It *is*!

Yes, he's definitely had more work done. The nose. He's in the vestibule, quick, press the red button!

Because he'll be locked in there! Now, now!

You were right, it *was* loud.

Well, of course he looks mad, he's stuck! Quick, call Searing.

Fine, call Burns then.

Did we just catch a murderer? A wanted international criminal? One of the Mediterranean Men's Club criminals?

Why would I give *you* a raise? He wasn't trying to kill *me*.

No, you cannot drive home.

I can absolutely drive in these shoes!

ACKNOWLEDGEMENTS

Nicola Robinson, commissioning editor at HarperCollins Harlequin Books Australia. Thank you for your faith and support in the adventures of Indigo and Esmerelda, and your belief in making a difference. You are wonderous, both professionally and personally. Thank. You. X.

Annabel Blay, you are truly magical when it comes to orchestrating editing: from choosing perfect editors to your compassionate, heartfelt communications. You make this a better book. Thank you. X.

Libby Turner, editor. It was such a pleasure working with you. Just the right amount of yin and yang. Your love of the characters and crime shone through. And anyone who uses the words 'ridiculously talented' is obviously very bright.

A big thank you too to proofreader Annabel Adair. You made my life so easy. It was a pleasure. Honestly. Wonderful.

And to Kasthury who assisted in difficult circumstances to give me insights and clarity that have made this a kinder, better and more understanding book. Thank you.

Tracey Spicer, journalist, advocate and a believer that rising tides lift all boats. Many thanks not only for taking the time to read *Heiress on Fire*, but also for your encouragement during the process. For your kindness and kind words, I'm grateful.

To Hannah Hunter, the best sidekick a single working mum could possibly have asked for. Those months with your help were bliss. Birmingham, Ivy, Jack and Ziggy are lucky to have you. Thank you. And CONGRATS on baby! X

Dr Kendall Bailey, forensic pathologist at the NSW Health Pathology's Forensic Medicine service, your compassion for the living and the dead is extraordinary. Speaking and emailing with you gave me an insight into forensic pathology and autopsies I could never have achieved from a book. Thank you.

A big thank you to my bake-off partner-in-crime and unpaid focus group participant, Wendy. You are an all-round amazing soul and have been a beloved friend for many a year. Not that we're old. Because we're totally not.

Federal Agent Tina Westra of the AFP, I learned so much about the AFP from you. Your recall, understanding of laws, procedure and fine print, and eye for detail were so helpful. You are a complete legend. And I do literally mean that. I am beyond grateful for your time and expertise.

Federal Agent Jodie Hurley of the AFP (and sometimes policing partner of Tina Westra), you were so interesting to speak with. Your skills in analysing people and reading rooms is atomic level. Your frank unpretentiousness made me laugh. Thank you not just for the logistics, but for the stories.

Many thanks to Todd Harland, formerly of the Intelligence Division at AUSTRAC, and law enforcement, counter terrorism and intelligence expert. Todd was a veritable font of information about local and international organised crime and money laundering. And very free with his time. I could have chatted to him for hours. Oh, wait, I did.

Former AFP Federal Agent Mike Wilson, many thanks for your time and patience in answering my questions, especially those around joint projects between state and federal police, and the logistics of CIs.

Former AFP Chris Payne, many thanks for your time and patience during interviews about AFP history and background.

A huge thank you to the wonderful Julie Hope, assistant director media at the AFP, for sourcing some incredibly experienced female and male AFP detectives for me to interview. And then approving the interviews! I owe you coffee, Julie. You'll get to meet some AFP characters in book three!

Any mistakes regarding policing procedure and forensics are my own and are not the responsibility of the source. I stuck to real life as much as possible, except when it did not suit me. Such as planes from LA arriving in Sydney at 3 pm. No, I know they don't (when they're running), but it worked so much better for me.

Please note that the naming of the FMCCC forensic pathologist character Dr *Bailly* was actually a complete coincidence. Now I just need a Harry and a Lailah …

To my walking partner Lou. Thanks for the chats. Life saving, life affirming and life improving.

To Ms Shona, who put together my website and then instead of accepting a free lunch, made me a free lunch, well, that story pretty much sums you up. Lucky to count you as a friend. Oh, and first reader and feedback giver. I could go on …

To Steph and Brenda, it's been a tough year and you're both still powering on. You're wonders and I'm so grateful for you.

To my girlfriends, you know who you are. I could not do it without you. I big love you.

To my extended family, aunts, uncles and cousins, thank you for being my family. And pre-ordering my books! And telling people in Kmart to read my books.

Love to my mum and dad. I am so grateful for the positive support given over many years.

Thank you as always to my HP and my Ancestors who do so much of the heavy lifting.

To the readers, bookstore owners, buyers and book club members, thank you. Without you my hours, days, weeks and years of work are for naught. Like a tree falling in the forest with no one around. So, thanks for supporting me, buying my books, encouraging others to buy my books and most of all, for reading my books.

A shout out to those incredibly upbeat Bookstagrammers, social media and website reviewers and supporters who have enjoyed my books and encouraged others to enjoy them too. Writing carefully constructed, encouraging reviews is not as easy as it looks. It's often unpaid, thankless work done by everyday people who just want to make a positive contribution. I wanted to say I appreciate it. You really make an affirmative difference in the world of writing, books and in the lives of many authors. Thank you.

Please look me up on Instagram or Facebook @MissMcCourt @KellieMcCourt or visit my website kelliemccourt.com.au. I'd love to hear from you (and crash your book club and author events!). See you in the next Indigo and Esmerelda Murder Mystery adventure!

Kellie x

talk about it

Let's talk about books.

Join the conversation:

 facebook.com/harlequinaustralia

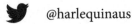 @harlequinaus

 @harlequinaus

harpercollins.com.au/hq

If you love reading and want to know about our
authors and titles, then let's talk about it.